NAMED A BEST BOOK OF THE YEAR BY
GLOBE AND MAIL · QUILL & QUIRE · 49TH SHELF

"*Songs for the End of the World* was always
going to be a great novel, no matter when it was
published. Appearing now, however, it also serves
as a pool of warm light in the darkness."

—*TORONTO STAR*

"A work of fiction that reads like the real world
playing out on the page. . . . Prescient."

—*GLOBE AND MAIL*

"A world apart from many of the dystopian stories
that preceded it. . . . Immersive and hopeful,
[Nawaz's] book is a reminder that we are not
alone, even in the most troubling of times."

—*MAISONNEUVE*

"A loving, vivid, tenderly felt
novel . . . I couldn't put it down."

—**SEAN MICHAELS,**
SCOTIABANK GILLER PRIZE–WINNING AUTHOR
OF *US CONDUCTORS* **AND** *THE WAGERS*

"Nawaz explores the importance of human connection and meditates on how we carry grief in unexpected times. She examines how we are bound to our loved ones and communities, raising questions about the world we are creating through our individual and collective actions. . . . The book feels like a symbol of hope."

—Maisonneuve

"This isn't merely a novel about a plague; this is a novel about family and parenthood, about loss and regret, about momentary connection and lingering solitude. . . . Nawaz, who spent seven years on the book, captures the personal and societal movements through a pandemic with an almost shocking accuracy. . . . That we can now relate so directly is not just a matter of timing but of Nawaz's skill, research and foresight. . . . Given the strengths of the book, and Nawaz's gifts as a writer, *Songs for the End of the World* was always going to be a great novel, no matter when it was published. Appearing now, however, it also serves as a pool of warm light in the darkness."

—Toronto Star

SONGS

for the

END

of the

WORLD

BOOKS BY SALEEMA NAWAZ

Songs for the End of the World (2020)
Bone and Bread (2013)
Mother Superior (2008)

SONGS

FOR THE

END

OF THE

WORLD

SALEEMA NAWAZ

MᶜCLELLAND & STEWART

This paperback edition published 2021
Original paperback edition published 2020

McClelland & Stewart and colophon are registered trademarks of
Penguin Random House Canada Limited.

Library and Archives Canada Cataloguing in Publication
data is available upon request.

ISBN: 978-0-7710-7259-8
eBook ISBN: 978-0-7710-7258-1

Book design by Lisa Jager
Cover art: Alan Labisch / Unsplash;
(spine image) Vladimir Kim / Shutterstock Images

Printed in Canada

McClelland & Stewart,
a division of Penguin Random House Canada Limited,
a Penguin Random House Company

www.penguinrandomhouse.ca

1 2 3 4 5   25 24 23 22 21

Penguin
Random House
McCLELLAND & STEWART

for those who have and share hope

CONTENTS

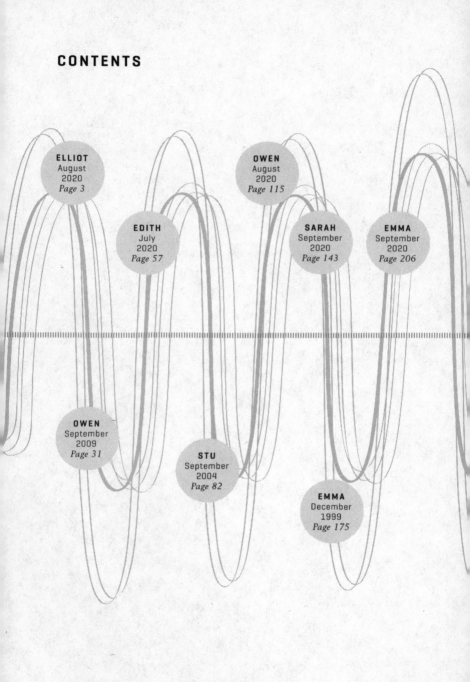

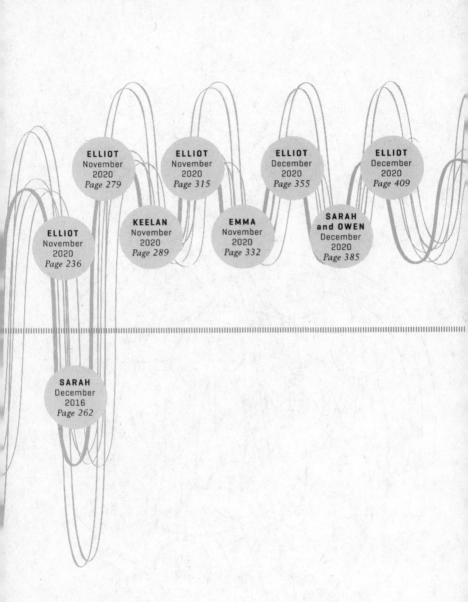

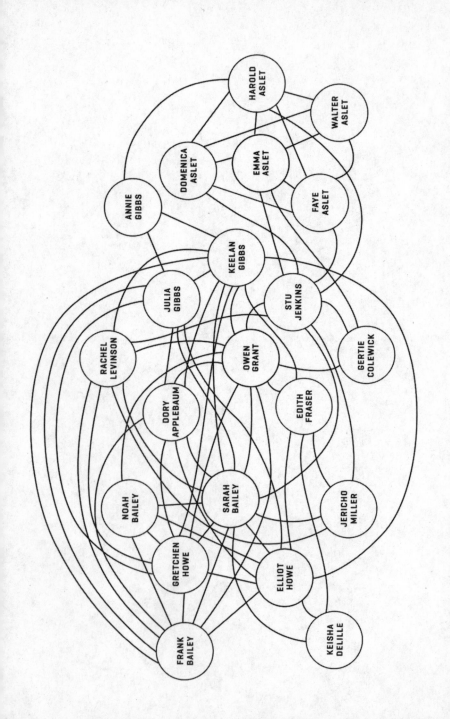

PUBLISHER'S NOTE

This novel was written and revised between 2013 and 2019. The fictional virus in this book—its transmission, symptoms, and treatment, as well as the containment strategies, media coverage, and overall global response to it, including ethical and legal considerations—was informed by the author's extensive research into computer modelling of infectious disease spread, the SARS, Ebola, and MERS-CoV outbreaks, and such historical pandemics as the Spanish Flu of 1918–1920. For more information, please see the Q&A with the author at the end of the book.

The end of the year is coming. A few miles offshore, *Buona Fortuna* drifts downwind on her sea anchor. The new year already seems tired.

And onshore, the lights of a hospital. Men with guns guard its perimeter.

The ocean is quiet but not silent. The boat itself is a friction against the water's flat expanse, a dissent against nature. Its mere presence creates resistance. The wind on its lines. The flap of a flag. Sails luffing.

The sun is going down. The woman reefs the mainsail and checks the tides. She surveys the cockpit to verify that a flashlight, binoculars, and a spare safety tether are close at hand. Her lips are working soundlessly, as though in recitation or prayer. Staring at the horizon, she waits for her vision to adjust to the failing light.

ELLIOT

—

AUGUST 2020

Calamity began, as usual, on an ordinary day. The city roiled with the amplified impatience of a million insomniacs, sleeping children breathed polluted air, low-level exploitation crept across neighbourhoods with insectile persistence, and a thousand everyday kindnesses failed to rise to the surface of consciousness. People were being born and people were dying, and joy and grief were handed out with a logic as blind as the human heart. But as far as Elliot was concerned, the first sign of the coming disaster was just a call buzzing in over the radio at four a.m. on a Thursday morning: a Molotov cocktail lobbed through the window of a restaurant on the Lower East Side. The fire department had already put out the blaze, but some uniforms needed to pass by to make a report.

Elliot and his partner Bryce dashed out of the convenience store, but by the time they reached their patrol car, Dispatch had assigned another unit a few streets closer.

"Damn it." Bryce fumbled with his seatbelt.

"Let's go anyways," said Elliot. It was the crawling middle of a dead night-shift, and none of the usual hotspots on their beat were turning up trouble. "I just want something to happen." He knew his partner shared his impatience for action on slow nights. Bryce steered them along Clinton Street to East Broadway and across to Seward Park, then, after a decent lap patrolling for the usual drug dealers, north on Orchard past all the tenement buildings and discount shops shuttered until morning.

At the restaurant, the wide front window had been smashed, and a fluttering cordon now established an extravagant perimeter that extended halfway into the street. Bryce stepped under the tape and held it up for Elliot. "Pretty sure the wife wanted to come here for date night," Bryce said. The tempered glass door was intact and lettered in goldenrod with the name *cipolla*. He pushed inside with a grin. "Guess that's off."

"Why cancel?" said Elliot. "Looks like you could finally afford it." Bryce punched him in the arm.

Elliot thought the restaurant seemed familiar, but so many of these hip eateries looked the same that he couldn't be sure. Though this one was finally unique now, with its soaked and blackened chaos inside, tipped chairs everywhere.

The owner had already turned up, pulling at his hair and weeping openly. "I knew it. I knew if our name got out it would be the end of everything." The man was shouting and coughing in the acrid air. "Why do they want to destroy us?" Witnessing his despair up close took some of the enjoyment out of their casual stop.

"Shouldn't have pissed off the wrong people," said Bryce under his breath, toeing a bit of charred wallpaper. He nodded to their colleagues before ducking towards the exit.

"What do you figure?" said Elliot, following him out. He paused on the curb, grateful for a deep breath of the cool night air.

"Mafia, obviously," said Bryce. His dad had been a cop, and his grandfather before him. He was full of New York City lore from the old days, when the streets were still a hard place and the police were merely foot soldiers in an unwinnable war. "Or insurance fraud, I guess." He tossed Elliot the car keys. "Poor schmuck. He really was crying like a little girl, wasn't he?"

"What, you never cry?" said Elliot. But he had to agree the tears had seemed genuine.

The rest of their shift passed quietly, and at eight in the morning Elliot bid Bryce goodbye in the precinct garage after they parked the squad car. The first day off after working three weeks on nights was always a strange beast: half dream, half disappointment. It was important to switch gears, to massage your circadian rhythms, to keep your expectations low. Over the years, Elliot had developed a routine for the transition, but sometimes the drag of having to stick to a schedule was worse than how bad he knew he'd feel if he didn't. Last fall his sister, Sarah, had sent him a study that said people who worked the night shift had years taken off their lives, suffered depression, and were more likely to develop cancer.

"Get a desk job," she told him at reliable intervals. "Something permanent, on day shift."

"Forget it," he'd reply. "Desk is death." Standing still was not something he enjoyed.

Elliot drove to a diner for breakfast; then, wired from the previous night's coffee breaks, decided to swing by the kung fu gym instead of going straight home to bed. He was feeling a tad reckless and impatient to get back to the world. He had three days off before a stretch of day shifts, when he would be able to work out again, get together with his buddies, even try to go on a date if any reasonable prospects materialized.

Socialization was something new on Elliot's radar, prompted less by a desire to go out than by an urgent need to remedy the hollowed-out feeling he'd been walking around with since his wife left him. Only after his divorce did he realize that Dory had been the one organizing and maintaining their entire social life. Finding himself friendless at thirty-five had felt not only lonely but careless. He'd met Dory while following up on a break-in at the publishing company where she worked, and she'd drawn him into her eclectic network of literati, DUMBO mixed-media artists, and PR specialists, who had welcomed him readily enough at the time but who had doubtless congratulated her on her shift to a more suitable partner. But thanks to his kung fu classes, Elliot had stumbled into a complete social circle, which gave him no less joy than he remembered from his very first friendships in grade school.

He parked and climbed up to the second-floor studio, where he was surprised to find the door locked and a sign taped up that read CLOSED UNTIL FURTHER NOTICE. He peered inside, but all was dark. Odd that there was no explanation, nor any forewarning. In the four years he had been coming to the club, the gym had only been closed twice: once when the masters had gone to China, and another time when a water pipe had burst in the unit above. Elliot returned to his car and, leaning against the driver's-side door, took out his phone and scrolled through his contacts, enjoying the slow sidling-up of a comfortable sleepiness as the sun warmed his face. He texted his friend Jejo, then Lucas, then Cameron, and everyone else he knew from the gym. He finally received a response from Jejo's cousin, Mina, who was studying for her grey belt.

Jejo's dead. So are Cam and Lucas and the master. Teresa, Declan, Felix, and Paloma are in the hospital. It's that bad flu that's on the news. Sorry for telling you like this but I can't talk now and it's better that you know.

Elliot drove home on autopilot, imagining himself as a robot, as though he could will away his too-susceptible flesh, and counted back through the days that had passed since he'd last seen them all. It had been during an evening shift at the end of July, just before this last block of nights. He'd heard something at the precinct about a bad virus going around, but he hadn't paid much attention. How long it took to get sick, he had no idea. There was a layer of sweat between the steering wheel and his pale, clenched hands, which already felt like they belonged to somebody else.

At home, Elliot turned on his computer and looked up the latest news on the outbreak. The virus was being described as potentially more infectious and deadly than swine flu. New York health authorities working with the CDC had begun reconstructing the movements of the first people to contract the illness and had released the name of a restaurant linked to their exposure: cipolla. The same restaurant that had been firebombed and the last place, he was sure now, where he had seen Jejo and the others. Torched, Elliot guessed, for fear of contagion, or by some relative of the dead in a futile railing against God. At the bottom of the news piece was a hotline number: *If you suspect you have been exposed, please stay home and contact the Department of Health.*

His phone rang. It was his sister, but he silenced the call, unsure of how to articulate the staggering extent of his loss or the danger he himself now posed. His grief was choked out by an overwhelming sense of unreality, as though he were watching a montage of his own suffering: Elliot staring at a wall, Elliot burying his face in his hands, Elliot slapping himself for acting like a prisoner of cliché during one of life's most serious moments—though, staring at his terrible, thin-lipped grin in the bathroom mirror, it occurred to him that the moment belonged rightfully to death. As the morning wore on, he tried to find information about the memorials planned for his gym buddies and discovered some of the funerals had already happened. The virus had struck the group with such efficiency that there had been no one left to call him. He stopped himself from texting Mina again, dreading more news even as he sought it out. The surface of his skin felt electric with mortality.

Feeling dizzy, he moved from his desk to his bed, but lying down seemed like giving up. He got to his feet and paced the length of his apartment before settling back in the desk chair and rolling it over to the window that looked out onto the street. There was no sign of movement in the facing apartment buildings. He tried to reassure himself that most people were at work during the day.

Quarantine Day One

Elliot reported himself to the authorities later that morning in a series of phone calls that escalated through a chain of increasingly flustered functionaries. Eventually he was connected to someone at the Department of Health, to whom he managed to portray himself as something more than the average hypochondriac. The woman on the phone wasn't up-to-date on the latest media coverage, and the restaurant name he kept repeating meant nothing to her, but she believed that he thought he had been exposed.

"Okay, Elliot," she said, after he told her his name and address. He could hear her typing in the background. "What you're going to do is stay at home."

"How long?"

"Twenty-one days," she said. "Now, do you share a toilet with anyone? Are you married?"

"I'm divorced." Why did he still find it so hard just to answer *no*? "What's this about toilets?"

"You need to flush two or three times to reduce the risk of contamination for anyone else."

"I thought I wasn't supposed to see anyone."

"You're not. I'm just telling you." The rhythmic clack of typing stopped for a moment. "Most importantly, take your temperature twice a day. If it spikes or if it reaches one hundred and four, call Emergency and explain that you're on the quarantine list."

"Okay," he said, already beginning to feel warm.

"Someone will call you back tomorrow," she said. "In the meantime, make a list of everyone you've seen, everywhere you've gone since the exposure."

"I was supposed to go out tomorrow." Elliot swallowed against a mounting tightness in his throat. "See my sister and nephew." If he died, what would happen to Sarah and Noah?

"I know it's hard, but try not to worry too much." Her voice was saturated with resignation. She sounded like someone who was not used to delivering good news. "If you already have it, there's nothing you can do."

Elliot asked then about the logistics of eating. "Is it better to order in or go grocery shopping? Or am I not allowed?" What was the exact calculation of risk relative to the need to eat?

She quizzed him about the closest places to buy food and how crowded they tended to be. "Okay, try to make do for now. We'll put you on the delivery list."

A few hours later the doorbell rang while he was taking a nap. He jumped out of bed, heart racing, confused and hopeful until he saw the text message on his phone: *Your supplies are at the door.*

"Here," said the health care worker. She was masked and gloved and held out two plastic bags at arm's length.

"Would you like to come in?" he asked as he took them from her. He watched as she recoiled and took a step backwards before adding, "Just a joke."

There was a muffled laugh. "Good one." She was gone before Elliot could thank her. He noticed that she had pasted a quarantine notice on his door. He wondered how long it would be before his neighbours complained to the landlord.

He called into work after lunch, and his supervisor's brisk attitude was a comfort. "I'll talk to Bryce, but let's keep it quiet as long as you stay healthy. I'd rather not spread it around, so to speak."

"Just tell the guys I've got something sexier, like mono."

"Sexy, ha." The sergeant barked a laugh. "No wonder you're still single, Howe."

"Hey, it's the kissing disease, isn't it?"

Elliot felt the strong urge to go for a drive, to speed as far away as possible from his present circumstances, but instead he spent the rest of the afternoon watching basketball, football, and even a world bowling championship while eating his way through two days' worth of food, his tears flowing as freely as water from an open tap. When he stopped bothering to wipe his eyes, his cheeks dried with a salty film that made them feel papery and exposed.

He heated up a can of baked beans and called Sarah to cancel, bracing himself for her disappointment.

"We were really looking forward to seeing you. Noah especially. You're always the main attraction around here." There was a small, plaintive note in her voice that he always found moving. Growing up, his kid sister had been a whirlwind of a girl who shouted down bullies, raced Lasers at sailing camp, and liked to face any fear by tackling it head-on. But ever since Sarah had shown up on his and Dory's doorstep, wan and fragile and fresh off a plane from Bolivia, she hadn't coped well with last-minute changes or any implication that Elliot would fail to keep his promises. Eight years after her return, she remained solitary and tentative, leading a life confined by routine and running even minor decisions past him, like which movie to watch or whether she should get a haircut. A watercolour version of who she used to be. Things had been better, though, since she had Noah.

"Sorry," Elliot said, "I'm sick."

"You're never sick," she said, worried now. "Do you need anything?"

"No, it's not that bad." He couldn't seem to form the words to tell her the truth. "Just a sore throat, but I figured better safe than sorry, these days." His voice started to catch, but he turned it into a cough. "Have you heard about this virus?"

"It's practically all I can think about," said Sarah. In the background, Elliot could hear Noah tunelessly singing a song about brushing his teeth. "It reminds me of the stuff we used to talk about at Living Tree. You know, plagues, wars. End times." Living Tree was what she had left behind in Bolivia, a communal farm run by a quasi-religious group of the same name. Though Living Tree purported to believe in harmony and radical equality, the reality turned out to be closer to an ascetic sort of doomsday cult, run by leaders who didn't seem to have a problem with personal enrichment. Sarah had mostly looked after the children until she became disillusioned enough to return home. "Actually, I started a new rug last night."

Making rag rugs was her particular outlet for anxiety. They used to make them on the farm—apparently to sell to tourists, though Elliot suspected it was really to keep the unhappy young people distracted with some kind of busywork.

"Perfect. I have a tiny strip of bare floor between the red one and the blue one."

Sarah gave a little chuckle: a mere acknowledgement that laughter was called for. "You're sure you're okay?"

"I hope so," he said. To let Sarah know about his exposure would be to commit it to the record, to confess his own mortality in a way he feared would destabilize them both. "Can I talk to Noah?"

"Yeah, here he is. Can you keep him going for a while? I need to drain this pasta."

Elliot said hi to Noah and listened to his nephew's meandering monologue about the things that mattered to him—the funny joke that a boy named Deshawn had told at daycare and an account of the goings-on of some cartoon fox on television. And even as he struggled to follow along, it occurred to Elliot that if he had to leave the world, there was nothing he would miss more than this: Noah's lisped conversation, with Sarah's loving annotations piping up in the background.

Quarantine Day Three

As night fell on the third day of his enforced staycation, Elliot began to feel less like the lucky one who might be spared and more like the one left behind to suffer alone—until he almost believed that succumbing to the virus might be a relief. He scrolled through his phone looking for photos of his friends and wondered why he so rarely used his camera. And when he couldn't find their faces, he let himself cry for them in earnest: great, wracking sobs that left him gulping for air.

Jejo was the joker, the social glue in their little clique. Cameron was a father to three little girls and a top-flight investment consultant who made money management seem wholesome instead of sordid. Lucas had started at the club at the same time as Elliot and had made a joking mission of finding him a girlfriend. And then the master, who had brought them all together. His wife was dead, too. They had two grown children who lived in California. Elliot wondered how long it would be before the children announced the school was closing for good.

He stared at the walls until he had memorized each crack and flaw, every hole imperfectly plugged and plastered over. All the renters who had come before had left their marks. Elliot had never taken pains with his apartment, which meant that the only thing on the walls was a free calendar from the Chinese restaurant around the corner. All at once he understood the value of decorating. He dug out a folder of Noah's daycare drawings and taped up a few of them with little rolled buttons of duct tape pressed underneath the corners. A blue scribble. A brown scribble. A scribble with all the colours. He felt himself breathing easier.

Quarantine Day Five
It turned out there was a limit to the ceaseless enjoyment television could provide, and that limit was eight to ten hours daily for five days straight. Elliot could no longer tell if the glazed and empty feeling he had came from grief or from sitcoms, and he found himself yearning for a book. He only had a few—fewer than he probably would have had if his mother hadn't commented on it the first time his parents stopped by. On that occasion, he'd told her that Dory got all the books in the divorce and that he didn't need to read anymore now that he was an armed pawn of the military-industrial complex. What Elliot didn't mention was that he had a library card and he knew how to use it. But now he saw the value of having books on hand and ordered some novels online—though no matter which category he browsed, the site kept recommending a book called *How to Avoid the Plague*, a perversely ironic suggestion that he ignored, especially once he realized the ad was sponsored by Dory's publishing company.

He found himself spending more time online than he usually did, following the headlines and the sports recaps. He was sitting at his computer that night when an email arrived in his inbox.

Hi Elliot. Hope you're doing okay. JKG

The display name associated with the email address was the same as the signoff. JKG. Elliot's first thought was that it came from his friend

Jejo. Jejo Galang. Maybe he had a middle initial that Elliot didn't know about. But Jejo was dead. All of his friends were.

He also knew that JK was a shorthand for *just kidding*, though it was hard to see how that might apply. It could be a message from someone on the force, if his supervisor had let the news leak. Or it was possible that Johnny, an elderly neighbour on the first floor, had seen the quarantine notice. At any rate, Elliot was glad his predicament seemed to be eliciting sympathy rather than fear. He wasn't sure he trusted himself to react the same way.

Quarantine Day Six

Then Elliot ordered a treadmill. He set it up in front of the window and jogged on it while watching the city, imagining the feel of the breeze on his skin. Ever since he could remember, he had wanted to run, to jump, to move, to not stay still. It had been aggravating for his parents—both academic, sedentary types—to have to deal with his restlessness when he was a child. Gretchen detested anything to do with sports, and though Frank was less opposed, he was bewildered by the passion roused by team loyalty.

Out on the street, there was not yet any outward sign that things had changed. The sidewalks were swarming with teens and joggers and well-dressed women carrying small dogs or briefcases, clopping their way to lunch. Elliot turned up the speed on the treadmill and continued watching the street scene as though the sight alone was proof of the blessed persistence of the commonplace. New York was the first spot where he felt he could linger longer than the time it would take to settle in. The churning pace, the relentless to and fro through the city's hubs, the very buildings rising to pen him in. It was a place that never stopped moving, which was why he knew he would stay.

———

Quarantine Day Seven

A week into his quarantine, Sarah called in the evening with an unusual urgency in her voice.

"I think your ex is on the news," she said.

"Dory?" Elliot's ex-wife was Sarah's boss, but he'd made it known that she was never to be mentioned unless strictly necessary, which it almost never was.

"No, not Dory. Keisha Delille," said Sarah. "Remember her? She's one of the experts telling us how we're all going to die."

"You're paraphrasing, right?"

"Barely." His sister sounded a bit breathless. "Worst of all, I believe her. She still sounds like a genius." Keisha had been a great favourite of hers until the breakup, after which point Sarah had toed the party line.

"What's she really saying?" Elliot switched on his television and flipped through the channels until he saw Keisha's face above a caption that read *Keisha Delille, Associate Director of Infection Control, Methodist Morningside Hospital*.

"From what we understand so far, this virus may be twice as contagious as the average seasonal flu and significantly more deadly. Today, researchers confirmed it as a novel coronavirus." Her voice was softer than he remembered.

"Can you believe she ever went out with me?" he said. The first time he'd made Keisha smile was still one of his best memories from college. He hadn't thought he had a shot with the statuesque black girl with the waist-length box braids, but for some reason she'd found him funny. Keisha had garnered attention at Lansdowne as the middle blocker on the volleyball team and for having the highest GPA in her pre-med program. She was the first person he'd met who'd actually grown up in New York City. Apparently, she had come back.

"People never really leave us," said Sarah. "Don't you find?"

He thought of his friends and his memories of them, thick as ghosts. "Are you talking about social media?" But he knew she wasn't. Sarah had once run into a high school acquaintance on a Jerusalem side street, and for a while this experience had convinced her that everything was connected and that the world was a place that would always take care of her. Though presumably she had given up that idea around the time she realized Living Tree had co-opted her free will as well as four years of her life.

"Well, sure," said his sister. "But what I meant was that our lives have a way of getting bound up with those of the people we've known. Like heavenly bodies caught in one another's orbit. Even once you go your separate ways, it's hard to get fully disentangled."

"I believe in moving on," said Elliot. "Going forward. Not looking back." But that was what had led to his mistake with Dory. Marriage had been the obvious next step in their relationship, and taking it was nothing more than getting on with things. He now understood what a terrible attitude that was to adopt towards your own life.

"Easier said than done." Sarah's voice dropped. "Remember Jericho? I found myself thinking about him again the other day. Wondering if he's okay now."

Elliot blinked. She hadn't mentioned that name since she was at college. It was after the business with Jericho that his sister had lost some of the single-minded certainty she'd been born with, first joining the Women's Kindness Alliance, then Meditation for Marxists, then the Interfaith Collective, before finally moving to Bolivia with her new Living Tree friends, in pursuit of community, or maybe seeking answers to questions that Elliot could only guess at. "People leave," he said. "We're just bad at letting them go."

"Keisha Delille," mused Sarah before hanging up. "I wonder if she still hates you."

———

The way things had gone with Keisha was not all that different from how things went with the women who followed, except for Dory. Elliot met women, dated them, and liked them well enough—sometimes he even liked them a lot—but before long he always concluded that there was someone else out there who would like them more, or do better by them somehow. And once he realized he wasn't the right man for them, he never saw the point of carrying on. In his experience, breakups just got harder the longer you put them off.

Sarah's take was that he was just afraid of commitment. The night he'd finally signed the divorce papers from Dory, his sister had insisted on hiring a babysitter and taking Elliot out to get drunk. After the bar closed, they went back to his apartment to finish off whatever liquor he had, and while downing horrific shots of Cointreau and Amaretto from his now-ex-wife's cocktail trolley, he listened to Sarah expound with hazardous new liberty on the real seeds of his divorce. Since Dory had left him for another woman—someone he had actually known since childhood; the daughter of one of their parents' colleagues at the university—Elliot didn't think fault-finding was strictly necessary, but when Sarah had a theory she was not to be derailed from sharing it.

"See, Dory never really needed you," she explained. "Not like the other women who've fallen in love with you. That's why you felt okay promising to never let her down."

"No, I like people counting on me," he slurred. "I'm a cop, remember? That's what I do, I help people." He overturned his glass on the table, and it made a closed, hollow sound.

Sarah had smirked. "But never the same person twice."

It was possible she was right.

Quarantine Day Ten

As the days passed, what had started out as panic and dread and a singular sense of his own mortality had turned into embarrassment at having to acknowledge his probable survival. But even allowing his thoughts to tend that way seemed like tempting fate. So Elliot continued to avoid reaching out to the families of his friends, or anyone else he knew, instead living like a ghost who had not yet passed over to the other side. He almost smiled thinking of how shocked Bryce would be by all the crying he'd been doing.

"Are you still coming for dinner tomorrow?" Sarah asked. Elliot could hear reggae music playing in the background, and the dull clack of dishes in the sink. "I'm making lentils and okra."

"I thought you loved me."

"Fine. I'll make brisket. I asked Daddy for the recipe last week."

"Dad's disappointment dinner?" Frank always served his one specialty whenever he and Gretchen tried to sway their children from decisions not to their liking. They'd dined on brisket when Elliot had signed up for the police academy, when Sarah had come home with packets of Living Tree literature, and again when she'd dropped out of graduate school to work on the farm. "It's actually pretty tempting without the side dish of crushing remorse."

"We'll skip that part. I'll substitute some sisterly love."

"I wish I could," he said, trying to keep his voice casual, "but I had to switch some shifts around."

"Darn it," said his sister. There was the sucking sound of water draining. "Noah says we haven't seen you in two weeks. But I told him it couldn't be that long."

Sarah was so busy, or at any rate harried enough by her own life, that Elliot had hoped she wouldn't notice just how often he'd been putting off his visits. The last thing he wanted was for her to look at a calendar. "Let me talk to him."

They put on the video chat, and Noah and Elliot chatted for ten minutes in the fond, distracted way common to small children and the people who love them. When they hung up, his apartment fairly echoed with emptiness.

Talking to his nephew always made Elliot wonder if having a child with Dory would have changed anything—if it would have changed him into the kind of person she could have kept on loving, after all. Becoming an uncle had made him realize there were parts of himself that had been lying dormant since his own childhood: silliness being foremost, but also an optimism that was innocent rather than willful—felt rather than contended.

And Noah, in the everyday modern miracle of how he arrived on the planet, sometimes led Elliot to think of his sperm donations in college, after his breakup with Keisha in sophomore year. It was the quickest money he'd ever made—enough for a nice used car. Elliot hadn't thought much about it before Sarah revealed she'd gotten pregnant via donor sperm. He'd never told Dory about his donations, which had been for research purposes only. Yet sometimes the thought that he might have helped bring some strange and funny child into the world struck him as a good thing, even though his parents viewed his donations as a thoughtless mistake, one they were generous enough never to mention.

Another email came that day.

Hi again. Sorry for writing out of nowhere, but I wasn't sure how else to reach you. I meant to say I'd love the chance to sit down and talk some time. JKG

Elliot started typing *Who is this?* But he deleted it. If it was a hoax or a spammer, better not to respond. And if it was a ghost, well, surely it would write again. He'd watched enough horror movies to know: ghosts always came back.

Quarantine Day Fourteen

Elliot saw Keisha on the nightly news again. Though he had begun his quarantine with only the vaguest sense of an illness circulating the city, it was no longer possible to avoid knowing about the mystery virus that had already infected over two thousand New York City residents in the span of a month. It had a name now: ARAMIS. Acute Respiratory and Muscular Inflammatory Syndrome.

Keisha was standing on the same hospital steps where she'd been interviewed before. She was holding something out for the cameras as the anchor set up the clip in voiceover: "The authorities are taking the unprecedented step of releasing a photo of someone who may be infectious." There was a particular intonation Elliot had noticed the news anchors using when reporting on the virus. Concerned, but not quite crossing over into panic.

"We're having trouble locating a person of interest from the first infection site," Keisha was saying. The photo was a dark, blown-up snapshot, flapping slightly in the wind. A trio of pretty girls in black dresses, with two of the faces blurred and a large yellow arrow superimposed above the group, pointing to an Asian girl with tousled hair and flashbulb eyes, red as a rabbit's. It looked like it had been taken inside cipolla, the restaurant that was now well-known as ground zero for the spread of the disease in New York City. "Her name might be Nicky or Naomi, and she was working as a server on the evening of Friday, July 31. Unfortunately, the restaurant's records were all destroyed in a recent fire."

The news cut to an enhanced version of the photo with the caption *Have you seen this woman? Call the Department of Health.*

The feed cut back to Keisha. "It's important from a research point of view to reconstruct the spread of the disease in order to understand it." Then she appealed directly to the camera. "And the sooner we can track down and monitor everyone who has been exposed, the better the chance we have of containing this." She was every bit as serious and no-nonsense as Elliot remembered her. He considered calling the Department of Health again to see if he could request to speak to her directly, but there was no point; he was already in quarantine and had sent in a detailed list of his prior movements.

Even when they were dating, Keisha had been a force of nature, practically dripping with verve and purpose and action. He wondered if she had somehow sucked up all the ambition around her, so that people like him came to drift in her slipstream. Like small boats caught in the wake of an ocean liner, bobbing on the water, unable to motor away under their own power. Maybe it was the same with him and Sarah. Their parents had enough drive and ambition for all four of them.

Quarantine Day Seventeen

As Elliot jogged on his treadmill, he could see that the world outside had changed while he'd been indoors, ticking days off on a calendar. The foot traffic had slowed. The runners wore masks. The ladies no longer lunched. The teens did not laugh their way down the street in a lolling clump but walked separately, heads down, as they hurried to their destinations. It was not business as usual.

By now Elliot was sure that he had not contracted the virus, but after sitting so long with his own thoughts, he was less certain there was not some other sickness in him—some chronic avoidance of the real business of living. Perhaps he had always sensed it, without knowing what it was. If anyone would know, it was Dory, but he did not intend to ask her.

Dory had passed out of his life in a way he'd never dreamed possible. Their six-year marriage was unimaginable to him even though there was nothing to imagine—it had already happened. It was as though he had been somebody else back then, when the middling happiness of their life together was about as much as he believed he deserved. Mingling with her friends, mustering opinions about curtains and upholstery, and enjoying the thousand thoughtless comforts of home that he could just as easily forego—and had. Dory had always joked that she'd bullied him into falling in love with her, but the joke's kernel of truth had developed into a version of the past he couldn't escape. Not that he'd minded the idea of her being the leader in their partnership; it said something about his manhood, his own confidence in it. Or so he'd thought. He knew there must have been tender moments at the very beginning of their relationship, gentle and dizzying and insatiable, but he could remember none of them. It felt like another lifetime, a time when he had been blind to himself. He didn't understand, altogether, why he had done the things he had done in his life: donating sperm, becoming a cop, marrying Dory. Or why he had failed to do other things. Maybe nobody did. These days, when her name came up, he felt duped and a little embarrassed.

But even though it had been Dory's choice to leave him for Julia, Elliot still felt responsible for the dissolution of their marriage. To be divorced was to have failed. But then failure was good for the soul. It was humbling. More people ought to be humbled. He repeated this to his sister when she called him after Noah was in bed.

"You're awfully introspective all of a sudden," said Sarah. "I'm not sure I like it."

"Don't worry, it'll pass." He was about to spin his desk chair away from the computer when he saw a notification of another email from JKG. "One sec," he said, turning the chair back and clicking open the message.

Hi. I just wanted to say that I hope you're okay. Given everything going on, I really wish you would reconsider. JKG

Even ghosts were feeling the pressure. Elliot rolled his chair towards the window, once again debating whether to tell Sarah about the quarantine. The idea of not telling her broke over him in a wave of loneliness.

He cleared his throat. "Sarah."

"What? What's wrong?" He could already hear the concern in her voice. It wasn't often he entered into a serious register.

"I have something I need to tell you," he said. "I've been keeping a secret."

"So have I," blurted Sarah. "I'm so sorry. I should have told you as soon as I found out."

Elliot blinked. "Found out what?" He wondered if there was a way for someone in his building to have mentioned the quarantine notice to his sister.

"Dory and Julia are having a baby." Sarah let out a breath. "Isn't that what you were going to tell me?"

He was too surprised to offer more than a vague murmur of assent.

"I've actually known for months," she said in a rush. "Dory asked me to tell you. But I've been trying to figure out how to bring it up."

Elliot got up from his chair and sat down on the couch. He felt a slight irritation with Sarah's need to rehash exactly how hard it had been for her to broach the subject, then let the blow-by-blow swirl over him, feeling the ebb of some instinctive dismay wash away with it.

"I should have told you as soon as I found out, Ell, because the more I thought about it, the more it seemed like there was never a good moment. I was going to tell you at dinner a few weeks ago but then you cancelled, and I don't know . . . Have I even seen you since then? Is that possible? Honestly, I was on the point of asking Dory to just tell you herself. Except, of course, she thinks I did it ages ago."

The baby he and Dory never had grew in his mind's eye from a grey wisp to a silvery pink balloon. Faceless, it floated up and away from him, off into the distance, where it receded to a mere speck on the horizon of everything that might happen in a man's life. Then it popped.

When his own secret came out, it was anticlimactic. Sarah screeched and fretted and peppered him with questions, but he had lost any zest for describing the past two weeks.

"So do you know about this girl they're looking for? The one from the restaurant who might be infected?" asked Sarah.

"I think I might have talked to her," said Elliot, a memory stirring. "I spoke to a waitress there." He could still picture her solemn, unstudied beauty, the barbed and wary look in her eyes. If it was her, the photo didn't do her justice. He remembered having felt the sudden, uncharacteristic urge to impress her, as well as the sense that he hadn't quite pulled it off.

"Hmm, okay." Sarah seemed to be doing some kind of private calculation that came out in favour of dismissing whatever concern had surged to the fore. "Well, do you know her name?"

"Nah."

"So you're really okay? You're sure? But you still have to stay inside?"

"Just be grateful it isn't you, boxed into a couple of hundred square feet." He stood up and moved towards the treadmill. "You start to feel like a rat."

Quarantine Day Nineteen

As the quarantine wound down, Elliot came up against the limit of his own self-sufficiency. When the woman who delivered his food lingered for five minutes to talk from the hallway, Elliot cried in gratitude. The sight of his tears made her draw back down the corridor.

Quarantine Day Twenty

He was expecting another food delivery when there was a knock on the door instead of the usual text message alert. Curious, he peered through the peephole. It was a tall woman with long, blond hair and a huge bulge of a stomach under a paisley shirt. She looked both vaguely familiar and like an apparition in the dark hallway, her whole person bright with colour and something that bore a terrible resemblance to hope. Elliot opened the door a crack, keeping it on the chain.

"Did you read the sign?" he called, still behind the door. Everyone stopped to read the sign. He preferred to watch people recoil from him only through the funhouse mirror of the peephole. It was a lens that matched his current perspective on life: circumscribed but far-reaching, and consequently distorted. Exposure to a deadly virus had a way of helping you see the big picture, even as it simultaneously cut you off from doing anything about it.

She looked at the notice then. "Quarantine." She glanced down at her stomach and took a step back.

"So you can't come in, do you see?"

"I see." She took another step back, sideways this time, but didn't leave. "Elliot."

"Yes," he said, and before he'd closed his mouth, he knew who it was. Julia, Dory's wife.

"Dory misses you," said Julia Katherine Gibbs. JKG. "But she doesn't think she deserves to be forgiven."

"We have a lot in common, me and my ex-wife."

"You shouldn't blame her."

"I don't," said Elliot. "I blame you."

The faint smile that had already begun to bloom evaporated at once. Julia nodded. "Right."

"You went after her when she was already taken." It was Julia who had provoked the romantic and sexual awakening—in their breakup conversation, Dory had referred to it as a "flowering"—that had upended their lives. Elliot blamed himself, too, though it irked him that he couldn't get past it. Nothing major had happened to him besides losing his wife in the most anodyne way possible.

"It was wrong," said Julia. "The way it happened. And I'm sorry about that, I am. But it was the right thing for Dory. And for me."

"Sounds ideal," said Elliot. As Dory had said in that same conversation, as though it might actually be a comfort, their breakup had "nothing to do with him." According to that logic, he didn't need to feel bad about what had happened. And in fact, the past three weeks had dismantled some of the scaffolding of his resentment: his usual emotions on the topic came back to him as if through the wrong end of a telescope. He knew that there was no logical reason for him to keep feeling bad about his divorce. It was an insult to his dead friends and their families, to the terrible unfolding of catastrophic events the world over, to retain any feelings about it at all. "I guess I'm the only one who still thinks that vows are supposed to mean something. Or, you know, that words matter."

Julia seemed taken aback, glancing around as though she'd accidentally stepped into a yard with a snarling dog. "I do," she said, hesitating. "We both—"

"I saw your wedding announcement in the *Times* last year," he went on. He had allowed himself to wallow in a pleasurable fury about it for a day or two. *Dory Karen Applebaum and Julia Katherine*

Gibbs exchanged vows at four o'clock in the afternoon on the grounds of ABC Winery in Rensselaer County, New York. He and Dory had married in his parents' living room. "Congratulations."

"Dory wished you could have been there, but didn't want to invite you," said Julia, finding her voice and shuffling her weight from foot to foot. She probably needed to sit down. Strands of hair clung to her cheeks, which were shiny with sweat. "I mean, for you to feel like you had to come."

"Well, that's something." He leaned his head against the door and closed his eyes. Everything about her—her protruding belly, her clammy, beseeching face—made him want to relent.

"And I didn't want you there, if you were still going to be angry."

Elliot yanked the door open as far as the latch would allow and thrust his body forward in all of its possibly infected glory. He jutted his chin out above the chain.

"Sorry I'm tripping up your happiness." It came out more bitter than he intended.

"So am I," said Julia without flinching, and her smile showed a trace of teeth. "I guess I'm here to try to make things perfect. Isn't that stupid?"

"Let me guess: Dory doesn't like the idea of someone hating her." Even as the words came out, Elliot knew it wasn't true. Dory had never been bothered by that.

Julia shook her head. "She misses you. But she respects your feelings, and your space."

"But you don't."

"I guess not?" Julia shrugged and a hoarse laugh escaped. With one hand on her belly, she gazed down the hallway at the elevator, and Elliot realized he admired her for coming. For thinking that there was still something that could be done about him and the mess of regret that clung to him like a second skin.

"When are you due?" Sarah had taught him never to ask this, but it looked like Julia was hiding a beach ball under there.

"Five weeks or so." Maybe she sensed him softening then, because she said, "Look, you guys were close, weren't you? With everything going on, it might be nice to . . . make amends."

"Nice for her, maybe." He folded his arms. "Do you want that?"

Julia pressed her lips together as she declined to answer. "But it's okay, isn't it? That I came?"

"It's okay," he said. It was the longest face-to-face conversation he'd had in weeks.

She adjusted her cotton tote bag on her shoulder. "We don't have to be friends."

"We're not."

Julia nodded. Elliot watched her retreat down the hallway with wide, deliberate steps. When she reached the elevator she turned back to wave at him, her face unsmiling and inscrutable, as though signalling from a distant shore. And he waved back.

Quarantine Day Twenty-One

When twenty-one days had elapsed, Elliot put on a tank top and shorts and ran around the block. People stared and dodged him on the pavement. A mother walking grimly with her daughter jerked her child out of the way and glared as he sped by, even though Elliot had been nowhere near colliding with them. He called out an apology that was carried off on the breeze. He resisted the urge to strip, to feel the air on every inch of his body. The whispering scrape of his sneakers on the gritty sidewalk felt like a secret percussion to his victory lap.

As the sun began to set, he headed further afield, not stopping to plan a route or think about anything besides the cool air entering his lungs. Every green light was a path opening up, an invitation to surrender. Even the smog tasted good—sweet and salty. He was tempted to run to Sarah and Noah's apartment, but they lived too far, so he sprinted crosstown on a street he wasn't sure he'd ever been down before, feeling freer than he had in years. But the further he ran, the more self-conscious he became. The people he passed who weren't bent on some errand or destination began to look less like citizens and more like odd, willful loners, dangerous and suspect. The changes he'd observed through his window held true on the ground and began to weigh on him. He slowed, losing steam after his sprint.

When he'd run about four miles, he spotted a staircase to the High Line. The elevated park was normally too crowded for runners at any time besides the early morning, but it was deserted now apart from a few tourists who shot him nervous glances as he approached at speed. One couple in particular, with visors and fanny packs, appeared determined to see through their holiday, although their body language conveyed only a diffuse dread. They stepped nearer to one another as he drew closer, as if expecting something to happen. As Elliot dashed past, he thought he could feel the electricity in the air mount and then dissolve, as though the invisible line that might bind them all together in every possible future had been pulled taut, snapped, and tied off by some industrious Fate. He hoped, for maybe the first time, for nothing to happen. Not then, not ever.

They should all be so lucky.

August 26, 2020, 11:04 a.m.

Hi. This is Owen. Leave me a message and I'll call you back.

[beep]

Owen! It's Dory from Shillelagh. I wanted to congratulate you on *How to Avoid the Plague* being a #1 bestseller again after all these years! And thanks to the latest CDC alert, it looks like we'll be calling another printing any day now. Terrible about the virus, of course, but what a silver lining for us. There's a pile of interview requests coming in—print, TV, the works. So be sure to get back to Colleen soon so she can finalize your publicity schedule. And let's find a date for you to come over for a celebratory dinner before the baby's due. We've got another seven weeks until D-Day, and Julia has been cooking enough food for an army. Just drop me a line. Ciao for now.

OWEN

—

SEPTEMBER 2009

Owen booted up his computer, opened the file for his third novel, then circled the desk and dropped to the threadbare Mexican rug for a set of push-ups.

The nubbly inside of his worn grey track pants, the sagging ribbing of his white tank top: these were his controlled reality. These were the means by which Owen could travel to where he needed to go—to Rachel. Rachel as she used to be. He'd had the idea for this book a dozen years ago, when they were first dating and she'd told him about Chanoch, a gifted violinist who had followed her from Tel Aviv to Chicago before dying—tragically but nevertheless conveniently, from Owen's perspective—at the age of twenty-four, from a lung infection. Though she had only mentioned him once or twice in passing, Owen had often thought of Chanoch and his brief illness and the reckless singularity of his devotion, which back then he had found only too easy to relate to. But at the heart of the Chanoch story was the idea of love as a kind of salvation, and it was a feeling that Owen was having a hard time accessing these days. Even his lucky track pants weren't helping.

When he could feel sweat beginning to bead across his back, he stood up and returned to his writing desk, willing his mind to stay in that emptied, receptive zone.

"Thanks again for making dinner," said Rachel, poking her head into his office. She had been doing this every night for the past five weeks since they stopped having sex. Even their crisis had fallen into a predictable routine. "I'm going to bed now."

"Goodnight," said Owen. He waited a moment before lifting his eyes from the screen and was surprised to see her wearing the blue lace negligee (his favourite) under the flowered Chinese silk robe he'd bought her for Valentine's Day last year. "You look nice." Whatever his misgivings—about their marriage, about monogamy, about his stalled writing career—he felt compelled to pay homage to female beauty.

Rachel came around his desk and leaned down over him so he could see her breasts. She stroked his cheek, then down along the side of his jaw. "You could use a shave," she said, her voice soft and affectionate. Showing in so many small ways that she hadn't lost faith in him yet.

"I could use a lot of things," he said, and even to himself, he sounded angry. Put upon. He leaned back in his desk chair and stretched both arms up over his head before cracking his knuckles. "A plot, for instance," he said, letting his actual discouragement resound in the complaint, and the force of it made his voice shake.

"Don't worry," she said. "All things in good time." Rachel beamed at him, no longer wistful now that he'd tuned her into his problems, and with another quick smile she withdrew, closing the door behind her.

Owen stared at the screen, then got up from his desk and returned to the rug for another set of push-ups. He'd had a hard time concentrating since the start of the sex stand-off with Rachel. They'd stopped sleeping together the day she announced that she'd changed her mind: she really did want to have a baby after all.

It had happened after a baby shower for one of her graduate students. A girl who had no business having a baby, whose whole future was being derailed in the service of pointless procreation, but whom the entire department, students and faculty alike, had seen fit to celebrate nonetheless. For most of the faculty, who were older than Rachel, with children already grown, a baby was a novelty; for the other students—preparing with a frantic, punishing intensity for a dismal job market—probably even more so.

They had sipped lemonade and nibbled on baked goods of varying quality as the mother-to-be opened gifts and her unremarkable boyfriend handed around napkins. Rachel played a clapping game with a baby who belonged to one of the few non-academic guests. When Owen slipped into the kitchen for a glass of water, Rachel's department head, an older woman with a messy halo of coppery curls, seemed to detect something in his expression.

"It's a bit of a farce, isn't it?" said Gretchen, pouring herself a glass of San Pellegrino. "Celebrating this baby. You think so, too."

He did, but he found Gretchen's bluntness distasteful, so he only shrugged. "She seems happy."

"Young women shouldn't be allowed to fall in love." Her laugh was sharp and low. "But it might be for the best. Her candidacy paper was a complete disaster."

He followed Gretchen back into the living room, where he noticed one of Rachel's male graduate students appraising him. Owen knew that his wife attracted a certain type of interest from her students and colleagues. When they'd first moved to Lansdowne, he had attended all the departmental parties to make his presence known, until he'd satisfied himself that it didn't matter. Rachel wouldn't stray.

It was during their walk home that she mentioned the child.

"What a sweet little baby," she said. "And smart for eight months old, I thought."

"Yes, very cute."

"Maybe we should have one." She said it lightly, almost playfully, as though she were any other woman and not his Rachel, whom he'd always known as driven, level-headed, constant—the last person to break a promise.

When he didn't answer, her face fell, and the rest of the walk was silent and strained. Owen had been caught off guard, and he resented it, even as pain seemed to radiate from his wife in all the little twitches of her eyes and mouth. But for her to upend their whole life so casually, to test the waters with a joke, felt like a betrayal.

Now, Owen stood up and stretched before settling back on the rug for a set of crunches. The most galling thing was that Rachel had been the first to forswear children, and back then she'd been even more certain of her choice than Owen. They'd been at a bar after a midnight screening of *Rosemary's Baby* at the Sunshine Cinema on the Lower East Side when she'd twirled her glass by the stem, finished her Kir Royale in two gulps, then blurted out that she saw an upside to the movie's ending.

"I'd rather give birth to Satan's baby than have to look after a normal one." Her voice was arch, but Owen could sense her sincerity. She was wearing wine-dark lipstick and her chin was set and serious. "At least Rosemary has a whole coven to help her."

"You don't want kids?"

Rachel shook her head. "I want to be an auntie. And not have to feel guilty about how much I work." She was ambitious and came from an unhappy family. She said she was grateful for her life but did not think her parents ought to have had children.

And so he had ordered them two more drinks before running through a whole list of scenarios in which he predicted her changing her mind, grilling her with what he thought had been an exhaustive thoroughness.

"The very idea of me having a baby," he said. "It would be like splitting the atom. It would be a *fucking disaster*."

Rachel had laughed then—laughed as though a baby were the last thing she wanted, a joke. But it was a cruel joke to have used that to make him choose her, to let him dare to think that he could be safe in a relationship when he knew, when he ought to have known, that he never could be.

Owen felt the fibres in the Mexican rug clinging to the sweat on his shoulder blades, and a flush overtake his torso as his muscles warmed. He was in even better shape now than when he and Rachel had first met. A better lover, too. As graduate students at Columbia, they used to spend hours at home alone together. They planned movie dates, visits to MoMA, even trips to Cape Cod or Martha's Vineyard, but they rarely managed to get past the front door. Rachel cooked *shakshuka*, which she had learned to make in Israel, and *cholent*, a slow-cooking stew that she would usually prepare on Friday and serve on Saturday, even though she did not generally observe the Sabbath. Owen found himself picking up how to cook because he loved how these meals came together and the way he and Rachel moved around one another in the kitchen, never far from a buzzing awareness of each other's bodies. Sometimes, when he cooked dinner, Rachel would prepare a salad with tomatoes, cucumbers, and soft white cheese, which she arranged on a plate in a circular design that made Owen exalt in the superiority of women. Whoever was not cooking would pour two glasses of wine or beer or whatever they had on hand that was more special than tap water. After dinner, they would make love, and after that, they would have dessert. Owen got into the habit of buying fruit sorbets that he would scoop into a cut-glass bowl and bring back with him to bed, where Rachel would remain splayed on the sheets soaked with his sweat. She would open her mouth and close her eyes as he spooned tiny, teasing portions onto her tongue.

Rachel's body was different back then, too, though unlike the wives of many of his friends, she had not put on any weight in the past decade. If anything, the opposite. She had embraced gym culture and she was fit, toned, even stringy. The Rachel he had fallen in love with had been womanly and soft. Her stomach and ass were rounded, pliable. *She* had been more pliable then, more flexible in her ideas and in her openness to trying new things. Once, they had driven to Mexico on a whim—on *his* whim—and although the trip had not been an unequivocal success, she had laughed when they got lost, smiled through her food poisoning, and taken off her shoes to cool her feet in a fountain in Coyoacán that boasted a statue of two coyotes.

When they married, it was at City Hall, and Rachel wore a light blue dress shot through with silver, and she looked so beautiful that Owen had been uneasy about her assurances that she preferred to do things simply and quietly. But she expressed only radiance and a calm joy that soothed his own taut nerves, and she had not chided him for not wearing a suit jacket or for not remembering to polish his only pair of dress shoes.

They were happy. And for nine years Owen had been surprised but relieved. He had always believed that marriage was a part of normal life that would forever remain closed to him, like wearing a suit to an office during the work week, or a steady paycheque, or the hundred other ways in which his life was turning out to be different from what his parents had hoped.

There were few traces of that blooming woman in his wife now. She of the delicate hollows around her brow bone and beneath her eyes, like the faintest lavender bruises. Rachel's feet had startled him the other week, mere hours after their return from the baby shower, poking out below the bottom of an afghan. Pale and waxy and cold as the dead. He'd suppressed a shudder that seemed to travel into his stomach, bubbling up as indigestion. *This is the end, then,* he'd thought. The day he had feared for so long and even dared to think might never present itself. He was surprised his desire could be so quickly dismantled, but then it had arrived just as fast—in one sidelong look at her strong profile. Until now his hunger for her had never abated. Whenever he detected signs of it flagging, he'd allowed himself to yield to temptation with other women. The fear of getting caught and of Rachel divorcing him always rekindled his own red-hot desire for her. He had strayed in their marriage, it was true, but only in its service—to keep its flame alive.

When Owen finished another two sets each of push-ups and crunches, he stood up again and stretched. He tried to ignore the reluctance he felt as he returned to his computer. His wife could sit down at her desk and take up her work as though it were the easiest and most natural thing in the world. For Rachel, writing was no more than the logical extension of her thoughts on paper. She had come to him once, rubbing her eyes, screen-bleary after a stretch of four or five hours, one hand tugging to keep her wool shawl wrapped tight around her shoulders.

"It's a satisfying kind of thing, isn't it?" she said with a shy smile.

"What is?"

"Wrestling with words."

Her placid satisfaction in wrestling with words was a thorn in his side, though he tried—and failed—not to let it bother him. But Rachel, for her part, rarely assumed that her own process was at all similar to his. If anything, she was insecure about her writing, deferring to him on everything from syntax to word choice with almost comic humility. Even after the disappointment of his second novel, a critical darling but commercial flop, Owen remained the official writer of the household.

He saved a new version of the file on the computer, even though nothing substantial had been written or changed, and peeked out of the doorway to make sure there was no light showing through the crack under the bedroom door.

Inside the room, Rachel was asleep, only half covered by the quilt, her lacy nightgown slipping down from one fine, pale shoulder. His side of the bed was still made, and he slid like a knife into the sheets without untucking them or nudging the bare arm of his sleeping wife.

By the time Owen awoke, Rachel's side of the bed was cold. It was a Tuesday, one of Rachel's teaching days, which meant she went into campus early. He dressed quickly and picked up his gym bag and car keys.

On a day like this—clear and cool—he felt a strong call to the water. He'd taken up sculling in college and had been doing it ever since, though no longer as part of a team. When Rachel was first hired at Lansdowne University and they'd relocated to the town of the same name, he'd joined the rowing club in the next municipality up the river. Two years ago, she'd surprised him with the gift of his own refurbished ocean shell. Not the fastest boat, she'd said, but one of the safest. In the absence of children, all of Rachel's solicitude had been directed towards him.

At the rowing club, he got changed in the locker room and retrieved his scull from the boathouse. The stretch of the river outside the launch was still and wide, unlike in Lansdowne, where it was quick and narrow.

As Owen was pushing off from the dock, a quad racing scull was being taken down the boat ramp by four women. The one closest to the bow was studying him closely, as if she recognized him.

"Nice day," he said, catching her gaze head-on.

"It is," she said. She was in her early thirties and wore grey and fuchsia shorts that clung to her athletic form. "Enjoy yourself."

Owen steered away from the dock and soon put several boat lengths between him and the club. As he fell into a rhythm, his thoughts drifted back to the woman on the crew boat. The glance that had passed between them had been electric. He was sure she had felt it, too.

Ever since he and Rachel had stopped having sex, he'd been looking at other women without bothering to hide it. And he had been told more than once that the way that he looked at a woman was tantamount to a proposition. He remembered a locker room conversation in high school, when two of his buddies from the wrestling team were discussing their best pickup lines. "How about 'hello'?" is what Owen had said. When pressed, he'd offered up a partial list of the girls it had worked on, and it had gone down in legend as the ballsiest invention of any braggart seventeen-year-old. His friends still brought it up at the pub when he went home for the holidays, though he wondered what they would think if he told them the real tally he'd racked up over the past twenty years. Likely, they wouldn't believe him.

There were also certain women, he was sure, who would be surprised to know he'd gotten married. But Rachel, in the sheer, undeniable beauty of her person—both body and soul—would have been answer enough. And though at this point he took her intelligence for granted, it was her mind that had attracted him in the first place. She was now an associate philosophy professor at Lansdowne, and her research had been radically interdisciplinary even before the concept became a buzzword. She had a third book coming out in the spring, an elaboration on her dissertation, which had taken longer than expected only because Rachel had not wanted to publish it without expanding its scope to a significant degree. Owen knew that it was dedicated to him, though he did not think this was a normal thing in academic publishing, and it made him uncomfortable. He had dedicated his first novel to her, before they were married, but he did not expect reciprocation. Rachel had been his muse, in the old-fashioned sense. *Gracewing* had been a *New York Times* #1 bestseller and was featured on the *Today* show, where it was described as "a love story for the ages." The *L.A. Times* called it "a transformative story of redemption by an astonishing young novelist." Women who came to his readings always asked about Rachel but seemed eager to forget about her afterwards. In one sense, the novel was about a man who worshipped a woman who was a much better person than he was. If he had inspired *Being and Becoming: Change and Human Possibility from Heraclitus to Levinas*, he wasn't sure he wanted to know.

Owen breathed deeply as he pulled the oars. He tried to empty his mind and let in nothing beyond the rhythmic sound of the blades going in and out of the water and the knock of the oar handles against the locks on the rigging. Every once in a while he could hear the faraway sound of people on the banks as their voices carried over the water. The swift glide of the scull and the warmth in his muscles soothed him as the craft moved like a dart across the river.

Stopping to think about things was part of the problem. He was sure it was why he couldn't write faster. Wondering if the next book would sell. Trying to figure out what people wanted to read about. There was something counterintuitive about needing to be less thoughtful in order to be a successful writer, but it was a conclusion he'd come by honestly, through hours logged and hundreds of pages discarded.

After he'd returned to the club and his boat was wiped down and replaced in its rack, he headed to his car. In the parking lot, a woman was lingering next to a new-looking SUV, peering in its driver's-side window and frowning at a cellphone. She spotted him and waved. It was only once he met her partway across the lot that he recognized her as the quad boat woman, of the tight grey and fuchsia shorts. She was now dressed in a white blouse and black skirt, her black hair freed from its ponytail and brushing against the tops of her shoulders.

"Hi again," he said. "Everything all right?"

"Locked my keys in my car," she said. "And the rest of my crew is already gone." She gave a rueful smile. "Spent too long in the shower, I guess."

"Is there anything I can do?" He prided himself on his proactive willingness to lend a hand in any given situation. It might not balance the scales in the long run, but it couldn't hurt.

"Could you just give me a lift down the road?" she asked. "I have another set of keys at home."

"Sure. Not a problem."

"Thanks a lot. I'm really not far." She shifted the weight of her black bag as she gave him directions, before adding, "I'm Stella, by the way."

"Owen Grant." If she recognized his name, she didn't give any sign. She fell into step with him. "Are you new? I haven't seen you at the club before."

"Been around a while. I just tend to avoid all the social activities."

"A loner."

"Ha. Maybe." Owen unlocked his car. "I spend too much time in my own head, that's for sure." He thought he saw a heavy, prurient look in her eyes as he held open the car door for her, though it was possible it was only a badly calibrated expression of gratitude. Before he drove out of the lot, he slowed and asked, "How do you feel about a scenic route?"

"Sure," said Stella. "It's beautiful around here." He glanced over at her, and this time there was a definite curl to her smile, a gradual invitation to wickedness. He stayed on the smaller roads, following her directions, and when she suggested pulling into a clearing along a lonely wooded lane, the familiar spike of guilt was quashed by a roar of rushing blood in his ears.

By the time Rachel came home at seven, he had showered and put the chicken in the oven with some carrots, onions, and new potatoes. He'd almost made a Waldorf salad until he remembered that elaborate cooking was a sure giveaway of a crap writing day.

They sat across from each other. The food was bland by Owen's standards, and probably Rachel's, too, but she complimented it anyway, deploying positive reinforcement like any skilled parent or trainer. Ever since he'd begged off teaching freshman creative writing to all the would-be poetic geniuses at Lansdowne last year, Rachel had deemed it only fair that he take on a greater share of the household chores. It was a reallocation made with ironclad logic, but the iron aspect had stoked his eagerness about as much as a pair of manacles.

"How's the novel?" she asked.

The novel was nothing. The novel was a non-starter. There were thirty-seven pages and twelve of them were nothing but dialogue.

"It's okay," said Owen.

"Just okay?" she said.

"Well, it's coming along."

"That's wonderful." Her whole face transformed with her enthusiasm, and Owen felt sickened at how incapable she was of discerning even his most obvious lies. "Are you going to be able to send Andy a draft soon?"

Andy was his agent, at least on paper. Owen was hesitant to contact him in case the only thing that was preventing him from being dropped was the fact that Andy had forgotten about him.

"No, not *soon* exactly."

"Did you turn the corner on that problem you were having?"

"What problem was that?"

"Of David's father?" David was Owen's stand-in for Chanoch. "The fight they were going to have on the telephone as soon as he arrived in Chicago?"

"Right." He'd forgotten he'd mentioned that much about it. The story had petered out as soon as his protagonist had reached Chicago and discovered his violin had been stolen. "I haven't figured that part out yet," he said.

The truth was that in the past few months he had not done much more than move things around. He had changed everything from first-person to third-person and back again. He had spent time looking at porn and online reviews of his earlier novels, and he had priced Caribbean vacations even though they did not really have the money to go anywhere. He had also looked up the fertility chances of a thirty-seven-year-old woman. The chances were, unfortunately, still quite good. But not for much longer.

"You will," said Rachel. Her confidence in him was singular and terrible, a constant balm as well as a reproach. "Now, what do you say to some dessert?"

Owen had noticed the new container of peach sorbet in the freezer when he'd gone searching for ice cubes for an afternoon scotch.

He stood up. "I think I'd better get back to work."

Sitting on the overstuffed armchair in the corner of his office, his back to the shuttered window, Owen angled the lamp to illuminate the gathering dust on the piles of books on his desk. He tore open an envelope that had arrived a week ago, which he already knew contained a royalty statement from his publisher, a statement that was several hundred dollars into the negative. It was demoralizing how many copies of his second novel, *Blue Virginia*, were still coming back from bookstores a full three years after its release. Surely there ought to be a cut-off for how long the stores were allowed to return them.

The new novel was stagnant. His protagonist, aimless. He could scarcely bring himself to describe the Rachel character, let alone muster the prose to steer David towards her. What he needed was a crisis that would throw everything into upheaval. Owen envied those writers who set novels during wartime, though he had never felt the urge to do so himself. The Second World War had been rendered so many times in fiction that it ran the danger of seeming more like a symbol than a tragic set of real human actions and consequences. A symbol of ignorance and hate, and an opportunity to showcase the human spirit in the face of adversity. It was terrible, really, the way one could start thinking about catastrophe.

And then he was thinking about catastrophe. The pressure it would force upon his characters. There was no reason it had to be a war. No reason it had to be in the past, even. His thoughts drifted to the real story of Chanoch and the unexpected pneumonia that had killed him so far from home.

Owen stood up and stretched his legs, cracking his knuckles behind his back. Then he sat down again, with an excitement he had not felt in months.

At four in the morning, he lay down on the couch in his office and napped for two and a half hours before getting up to put on the coffee. Without waking Rachel, who slept like the innocent, he stripped off his sweatpants, showered, dressed, and returned to his computer.

At eight, he saved the file, then emailed it to himself and printed out a hard copy to be safe.

"You look happy," said Rachel, knocking as she entered his study.

She was putting up her hair in an elaborate chignon, something she always amazed Owen by doing without a mirror. And then she noticed his clothes. "And, oh my goodness, you've gotten dressed." She was teasing him, smiling as her gaze met his eyes and travelled down the cut of his shirt and his trousers.

"I have," said Owen, standing up. He felt a charge on his skin, and he wanted to turn her over the back of the couch, dig his hands into the sides of her skirt and yank it up to expose her pale, slim thighs and her firm white ass. But there was the smell of that musky perfume he liked, and along with it, the whiff of a trap. She had been on the pill, but her doctor had recommended stopping after she'd suffered some recent migraines. There was no way to know anymore if her desire was for him or a baby.

Owen shoved his hands in his pockets, which felt like the only safe place for them. "Have you thought any more about what we talked about?" he asked.

Rachel's eyes widened. "Sort of. Have you?"

"No. I mean, I haven't changed my mind. It's just—"

"What?" Cutting him off, she shook her head as something seemed to close down in her expression.

"I want you, Rachel." Fuck, his cock was practically tingling with his need for her. Sometimes he tuned in to nature programming during the day, just to be reminded of the extent to which animals would go to propagate the species. Really, it was a miracle he ever managed to get anything done at all. And even more astounding was what one good writing day could do for his libido where his wife was concerned. "But I don't know . . ." He was trying very hard not to say what he was feeling. *But I don't trust you.* It was terrible, the way she was searching his eyes again. "I don't know if we have any condoms."

———

Without meaning to, he agreed to go buy some. The two of them hadn't used condoms together in years, not since Rachel had gone on the pill. But thinking of buying them made his cock stiffen again in his jeans, as though he was orchestrating some secret tryst. He usually bought condoms somewhere far from home, always in cash and never at the same place twice. He only allowed himself to keep a few in his car, in a compartment obscure enough to offer plausible deniability by implicating the previous owner.

From habit, he'd grabbed a cloth bag before heading out as if he were picking up groceries. But he ought to have grabbed an umbrella. A light drizzle was intensifying into a shower, and he turned up the collar of his jacket to keep the raindrops off the back of his neck. Two twenty-something girls huddling under an umbrella passed him, hurrying in the other direction. The one with dark hair like Rachel squealed as her foot splashed into a puddle. Her friend, a redhead, kept pulling her along by the wrist, with a laugh crescendoing into a shriek. He turned around to look at them as they moved away from him, half thinking one of them would turn around, too, but neither did.

The closest place to stop was the drugstore, which was one of those franchises he used to hate—the big corporate chain that had put two small family pharmacies out of business. But the convenience of it was undeniable. They had a grocery section and two snack aisles. Even a couple of shelves of DVDs. More than once, he'd run out in a hurry before Rachel came home, to pick up a frozen lasagna for dinner.

The condoms were displayed at the end of a rack at the back of the store, facing the pharmacist's counter. He took down a box of the ultra-thins and headed straight to the cash. Two registers over, he noticed a woman in line who had the demure sultriness of Catherine Deneuve in *Belle de Jour*, buying a carton of milk and some Tylenol.

She was wearing a khaki trench coat over a low-cut black dress, and her blond hair was swept back in a clip.

He gazed at her with intent, and a few seconds later she raised her eyes to his as though she could sense him watching. Owen gave what he knew was the barest crinkle of a smile—a twitch at the corner of his mouth and a slight crook of his left eyebrow. The woman smiled back at him, but her gaze was distracted and vaguely curious. Then, without warning, she bent down so her head was hidden from view by the aisle. When she arose, she was carrying a toddler on her hip. The child seemed to be a boy, based on the little red and black sneakers and the truck on his T-shirt. His long blond curls fell over his ears, and his luscious lips pouted as he caught sight of Owen.

As the cashier rung up her purchases, the woman pulled out an apple from her purse and took a bite before holding it out to the boy, who sucked in his lips, shaking his head until, coaxing, she brought it right up to his mouth. As she held out the fruit to him, he took a small bite, and then she took another before passing it back. Their eyes never left each other as they traded bites, but though they said nothing, they amused one another. Then the boy let loose a delighted laugh, and a bit of apple fell from his mouth and landed on his chin. His mother flicked out her tongue and lapped it up.

Owen looked away as the woman in front of him in line asked for cigarettes. She was a heavy-set black woman with a huge bosom that intrigued him as his eyes passed over it.

"Sorry this is so slow," she said, as the cashier took a key from the register and headed for the glass cabinet behind the customer service desk.

Owen waved her off. "I'm in no hurry," he said, returning the courtesy. She had kind, watchful eyes. "Don't worry about it."

When he looked back to the blond woman in the other lineup,

she was already picking up her bag. She smiled over her shoulder at him, but her ear was bent to her son. The cashier in Owen's aisle returned with a king-size package of Marlboros. The woman in front of him said, "You smoke?"

"No," he said, wondering what would happen if he said yes. "Thanks, though."

As the cashier counted out her change, he pocketed his wallet, left the condoms on the counter, and headed for the exit.

"So?"

"They were out." Owen let the lie come out flat. He hung up the empty cloth bag on the coat rack inside the front door. "Can you believe it?"

Rachel blinked at him. Her mouth opened as though she was going to say something, but then she turned her back on him and went into the kitchen.

"I'm sorry," he called. "I'll be in my study."

Even with his office door closed at the top of the landing, he could hear her washing the dishes. There was recrimination in the sound, in the almost indistinguishable clatter of plate on plate. The water running into the sink might as well be a bucket of tears.

He turned on his computer and opened a couple of the sites he'd bookmarked the night before: the National Centre for Disease Control and the National Institutes of Health. If the novel was going to be as gripping and frightening as he imagined it, he had to get the details right about the risks of contagion and the safest way to avoid infection during a global pandemic. He jotted down some facts and some phone numbers, too, for when he was further along.

He wrote in a concentrated burst for forty-five minutes, until his shoulders started aching. Standing up, he paced from one end of the room to the other, swinging his arms back and forth in a stretch. He knew he was on to something with this imagined disaster in the near future. It was liberating to free himself from the constraints of the past, the historical record. He sat back down at the computer and scanned through the pages he'd written.

Midway through his reread, the door to his study swung open without a knock.

"Can we talk later? At length?" The question cut through the room like a command. Rachel rarely got angry, and even more rarely at him, but when she did it brought a strangled precision into her voice. And for reasons he didn't quite understand, her anger, no matter the cause, always provoked his own.

"About what?"

"About this dismissal of my idea of having kids," said Rachel. "And what it means for us, and the future." She paused and let the threat hang over them. "It's too big for you to shut down with a word."

He gave a curt nod, and, with a tight face, his wife stepped back and pulled the door shut.

It was impossible, what Rachel was doing to him. It wasn't fair. No matter which way he looked at it, he was the bad guy, and yet somehow, in spite of everything, he was the one who had kept faith with what they had promised one another. It didn't matter how many women he'd slept with here or there since they'd been married. They had promised the rest of their lives to each other alone. She was the cheater.

Now Rachel wanted a different future, and without a baby, he wasn't in it. He could already see how it would go. For her, the future was children. But children would be the end of their relationship, the end of his writing, the end of his days alone. Children were like a plague upon the Earth, eating up everybody's time and freedom.

And then he knew what was going to happen in the novel.

Owen had always thought lust was the most powerful fuel he'd ever find for his writing, but it turned out that anger at Rachel left everything else in its wake. Once he'd started with the new direction for his story, his fingers could hardly keep pace with his ideas. The ire that had kindled the plot burned itself up in an ecstasy of absorption, as all his old distractions receded. He was pleased with what he'd accomplished, so pleased that after days of working almost non-stop, almost without thinking about the rest of his life, he'd brought the first section of his new novel to Rachel to read with a bursting kind of pride and excitement.

She accepted the pages with a show of reluctance that reminded him they were in a fight. "So this is why you've been too busy to talk," she said.

"I guess you could say that." He hadn't been putting her off so much as forgetting about her in an all-consuming creative fog. In the meantime, she'd been spending more evenings out with friends and, when she was home, having long phone calls with old confidantes from out-of-town. But if she'd wanted him to notice or comment on her new independence, he'd disappointed her.

She sat on the couch with a frown of forbearance and told him to go do something else. "I don't want you to watch me," she said. "I'm not in the mood to explain my every fleeting thought."

Owen grabbed his keys, but though he had energy to burn, he was too impatient to drive to the rowing club. Instead, he went outside and paced the streets near their home, wondering and worrying what Rachel's keen intellect would make of his newest project.

He came back just as she was turning over the last page of what he'd given her, everything he'd written in the past week. She tapped the pages against the coffee table, shuffling the edges flat.

"It's wonderful," she said. "And horrible."

"Horrible?" He tried to read her expression. The new story was already more sprawling with characters and less ornate in its prose than his other books, but he'd expected her—his best and most faithful cheerleader—to be excited by the sheer drama and ambition of its plot.

"Well, I suppose this is your way of telling me you're not going to change your mind," she said. "Millions of kids dying in a pandemic." She pressed her lips together and then sighed. Her fingers with their pale pink polish drummed against the table.

Owen put a hand to his forehead, grimacing. He felt like a cardboard cut-out of a man. He'd lost himself in the story somewhere along the way, which he supposed was both a good thing and a bad thing. "You're much smarter than I am, Rachel."

She brushed past the concession with nothing more than a raised eyebrow. "I know." She lowered her face, which was starting to flush. He thought it was possible she was about to cry, and he wondered with a sudden panic if this was going to be the moment when everything changed. The moment when he truly failed her—the final treachery after a hundred smaller betrayals.

He reached out and put both of his hands on hers, even though the romance of the gesture was something he found faintly galling. It was a gesture reserved for one's wife. "It's not that I don't want a child with you, Rachel. I don't want one with anyone. That's just not something I can do, remember? We're talking nuclear fallout. It's impossible."

"I understand." Rachel was just a curtain of hair across the table from him, her chin dropped down almost to her chest.

It was horrible to see her sad—his sunny, positive Rachel. It was even worse than he'd imagined, and he'd imagined it every time he'd thought there was a chance he was going to get caught with another woman. To see her fine figure brought low was a travesty against her classic beauty. Owen remembered the tenderness between the mother and child at the drugstore, the intimacy that had excluded him so completely. But the trust and adoration in the little boy's expression was something that Rachel deserved. It was what he felt for her himself.

"Do you want to leave me?" he said, and he could feel his face spasm. "You deserve to have a child. You deserve to have everything you want." He felt the truth of this, and an answering echo at the back of his mind confirmed he had already failed her. "If you want to leave, I'll understand." The words strangled in his throat.

"I don't," said Rachel. His wife's face as she raised it to him was fierce and without tears. She stood up and, coming around the table, kissed him full on the mouth. "I want to work on splitting the atom. On making the impossible, possible."

Up close, the old poles of their magnetism still pulled. His desert rose. His only hope. The kiss was a beautiful lie, as beautiful as his wife. The lie that he alone could be enough for her, or that there might be a life in which he could compromise and still be happy. He kissed her back and felt the truth, waiting to be spoken, as heavy as a stone.

"Have you seen this woman?"

How one doctor's request led to a worldwide furor

September 21, 2020

NEW YORK—The jokes are all over social media. ARAMIS Girl dragging people into the sewer. ARAMIS Girl wants YOU for U.S. Army. She even has her own meme, popularly known as "Dead-Eye Girl Doesn't Want to Be Found."

The notoriety of the so-called ARAMIS Girl began during a September 2 press briefing, when Dr. Keisha Delille, Associate Director of Infection Control at Methodist Morningside Hospital, released a low-quality photo of a woman in her late teens or early twenties with Asian features who had worked as a server at cipolla, the Italian restaurant on the Lower East Side now known as the site of the first ARAMIS infection cluster in North America. "We have a strong interest in locating her," Dr. Delille said at the time. "We need to alert people she was in contact with who may have been exposed to the virus." The only catch: nobody was sure of her name.

But more than two weeks after the photo's release, the identity and whereabouts of ARAMIS Girl remain a mystery, sustained partially by the ARAMIS-related deaths of co-workers who knew her, as well as by a loss of paper records when cipolla was firebombed on August 20, an unsolved crime authorities believe is linked to the outbreak. cipolla's owner, restauranteur Paolo Fabbrini, says her name is Naomi but he does not recall a surname. He believes she was only a visitor to New York City, possibly a summer college student who left shortly before the CDC investigation began in earnest.

But the idea of someone remaining unidentifiable and un-locatable in our current information age has captured the public imagination. Self-styled online detectives have tried to track down the mystery woman, so far to no avail. People all across the globe are now actively looking for ARAMIS Girl via a massive virtual research collaboration. Known in China as the "human flesh search engine," this type of information crowd-sourcing for the purposes of pinpointing the identity of a wrongdoer or other social offender is a long-standing practice in that country and is becoming increasingly prevalent worldwide.

The writer Owen Grant, who has become a household name due to his prescient novel *How to Avoid the Plague*—one of the bestselling novels of the past five years—commented via email that he believes the public release of the photo was irresponsible. "We're living in desperate times, and people are scared. With over 2,000 confirmed cases of ARAMIS in New York at the time the photo was released, I'm not sure what practical purpose it served to launch a manhunt for this young woman. The virus had already found a foothold in the city. It seems like a classic case of the authorities overreacting to make up for being caught off guard."

Elsewhere, sympathy for ARAMIS Girl is thin on the ground. Many blame her for the spread of the virus to New Jersey, Connecticut, and Pennsylvania. There is a popular belief that ARAMIS Girl is a kind of modern-day Typhoid Mary, well aware of her disease and recklessly infecting others. According to Dr. Delille, this is highly improbable. "Given everything we know about ARAMIS so far, this woman has most likely been hospitalized or has already succumbed to the virus. I want to emphasize that there have been no observed cases of healthy carriers, only incubatory carriers, and the median incubation period of the virus is five days, with a range of two to 14 days. If this woman is still alive and asymptomatic seven weeks after exposure, she remains of interest to us from an epidemiological standpoint only."

But false information continues to proliferate online, where an informal poll on CNN.com revealed that 66 per cent of respondents incorrectly believed ARAMIS Girl to be the original index patient in North America. Experts from the WHO have identified the first carrier of the disease from rural China to the United States as Zhihuan Tsiang, a visiting martial arts expert from Yunnan province who spent eight days in New York City before he died in Beijing on August 2.

This widespread misapprehension may trace its origin to a darker theory about ARAMIS Girl. Users on popular conspiracy sites have seized on the fact that ARAMIS Girl's initials (A.G.) are the same as the abbreviation for *antigen* (Ag), short for *antibody generator*: a toxin or other foreign substance that binds to an immune receptor and induces a defensive response in the body. Based on this coincidence, online theorists have speculated that ARAMIS Girl might be a biological warfare agent activated by the American or Chinese governments. Fake news stories promoting this connection have proliferated on social media, which many believe has contributed to an alarming spike in the negative public perception of ARAMIS Girl and the Asian-American population as a whole. At least three dozen incidents of anti-Asian hate crimes have been documented in 14 states across the country since the photo went viral, ranging from verbal assaults and acts of vandalism to serious physical attacks.

Dr. Delille continues to defend the decision to release the photo. "We were trying to reconstruct the spread of the virus, both from a containment point of view but also for information-gathering purposes." She points out that, thanks to the rapid efforts of the Department of Health, all of the other restaurant patrons and employees were located and either treated or quarantined within weeks of the first infection cluster on July 31. "There was no reason to believe that taking this simple action at a small news conference was going to result in such misinformation or violence. The 24-hour news cycle should take responsibility for feeding the idle curiosity of internet troublemakers."

Whether ARAMIS Girl will ever be found, or whether she will simply become another forgotten obsession of the viral internet age, is unknown. Dr. Delille admits that in light of the current number of infected patients, locating ARAMIS Girl is no longer essential to reconstructing the spread of the disease.

"But if this young woman is still alive, I hope that she receives the support she needs. We seem to have forgotten that there's a real person at the bottom of all this."

EDITH

—

JULY 2020

Edith is not the name of a pretty girl. It is an old-fashioned name, an old woman's name. People hear her name and think of grandmothers, of loosely gummed dentures and brown shoes squared off into stiff, orthopedic contours, of starched doilies and handwritten notes in medical charts that read *No heroic measures*.

Edith grasps this fact about her name at the age of ten and begins insisting that she be called Ed. It is not very much of a change, she explains, not very much to demand of the people who brought her over from China and have defined her very existence with a word so unsuitable, so revolting, as to make her almost despise herself. It is only the softening of a vowel and a shortening in full. It is not as though she is asking anyone to call her Xiaolan, the name on her birth certificate and adoption papers. Still, her father resists.

"Edith was my mother's name." He has a tendency to become mawkish, crying over outgrown dresses and broken dolls.

Edith's mother is game for anything. She says, "It'll be one in the eye for the old lady." Even though the old lady has been dead for ages, Edith's mother still likes to think of putting one over on her.

———

Ed has been known as Ed for eleven years when she begins an affair with a middle-aged novelist named Owen Grant, who is the writer-in-residence at Beaton College in New York City, where she is taking a summer course. She meets him on the first day of June at one of his readings, after he signs her well-loved copy of his second novel, *Blue Virginia*. There are notes to herself scribbled in the margins, thick pencil lines under particularly beautiful sentences, paragraphs hugged by stubby, eager exclamation marks; Ed only realizes they are embarrassing as Owen flicks through the pages and raises his eyebrows, which are crinkled and wry, before drawing a line through his printed name on the title page and signing underneath.

"I really love the character of Naomi," says Ed. "She's so forthright and principled." Owen is wearing a white T-shirt under an olive button-down dress shirt, and as he nods, she can see the sinewy muscles of his neck. "She's like a beacon to everyone around her," Ed adds, already blushing.

"Do you think so?" he says. Delight transforms his chiselled features. His ice blue eyes are mischievous but somehow still sincere. "That's exactly how I imagined her when I wrote the book."

He asks Ed to have a drink with him and she accepts without hesitation. His voice is a gravelly baritone that plucks at the base of her spine until she feels her every nerve strumming. Just before making love to her the first time, he tells her that he is married.

She writes a great deal in her diary during the early days of their affair: filmic reports of their sexual encounters, and snippets of song lyrics which have begun to seem meaningful. She stays up late worrying about his wife and the integrity of her own soul. There's a line from the new Dove Suite single that she can't get out of her head: *A woman in the small hours / waiting in the dark*. She tells herself that there is a kind of nobility in being reduced to the emotional banality of pop music. In becoming so absolutely simple. Girl wants boy. Boy is trouble. Love hurts.

Outside of the fleetingness of Owen's touch, she exists for his words. Fragments of things he wrote before meeting her, the graphic longings and stunning compliments he utters when they're in bed. *Pretty lies*, she reminds herself, a Joni Mitchell lyric she copies out in swirling cursive. Still, his words creep in, envelop her, trap her in the impression of wanting him, inspire an urge to get down to the source of his language, his vision, his point of view.

And beyond that, there is the invisible pull of Owen's celebrity. Ed is drawn to the aura of fame as though it might catch her in its glow and light her up from within. And then, maybe, people will finally see her.

When the affair starts to cool off after just a few weeks, she mopes, reads the *London Review of Books*, buys herself chocolate and stockings. Counts it as a good day when she goes half an hour without picturing Owen naked, kneeling over her in his final exertions, falling into the moments when words fail him. Their trysts have become sporadic and unpredictable; somehow he always sends her a message just when she has made peace with never seeing him again.

She stalks the campus with a view to finding a replacement, stopping whenever she sees a man broad in the back with a book in his hand. But she fears the men she might bring to herself this way, with her hungry, sidelong looks. She worries everyone can hear it: the pulsing call from her groin. She imagines it as a kind of current, a sucking sound. A tongueless mouth aiming for speech.

———

Ed gets a job at a new restaurant at the beginning of July to pay for her extra expenses. Living and studying in New York City is more expensive than going home to Boston, even with her scholarships. She dislikes waitressing, but it's better than having to endure a whole summer with her parents and her little brother, and spending the break in Lansdowne, Massachusetts, her tiny college town, is scarcely more appealing. For some reason, the city feels twice as real to her as any place else. In New York, Ed skips lunch to pay for breakfast at Balthazar and to be anywhere she's liable to catch sight of someone she's seen on television. By the time she interviews with Mr. Fabbrini, her bank account is down to fifty dollars.

Fabbrini waves away her resumé until she tucks it back into her bag. "I go with the gut," he says. "Not paper." Then his gaze moves over the neckline of her sundress and her bare shoulders, and Ed tries not to flinch.

"We already hired a full staff for the summer," he continues. "I can't put you on the payroll until September." His hands are small with dark hair on the backs, and his fingers worry the fabric of his pants across the knees.

"I'm happy to just cover the occasional shift until then," says Ed. She will be gone by the last week of August, anyway, though there's no need to mention that now. "Whatever you have."

"You seem like a nice young lady." His eyes are leering, but he has the beneficent smile of an old grandfather. "Okay, we'll call you when we need you. Cash at the end of the night." He asks for her phone number and copies it into a little notebook he keeps in his jacket. "Remind me what your name is, dear?"

Ed thinks about the protagonist in Owen's second novel. Her fearlessness and calm virtue. "Naomi."

When Fabbrini shakes her hand, he cups it between his palms and pulls her in close to kiss her on both cheeks. His skin is as soft and dry as a Kleenex.

So a few nights a week, Ed puts on eyeliner and a tight black dress and kitten heels to go to the restaurant. She lets down the hair that she usually wears pulled back, styling it into face-framing waves. Maybe she should have looked for another kind of job. Maybe being a waitress in New York City is a cliché almost as tired as a restauranteur hoping to make it big with a new word-of-mouth eatery on the Lower East Side. But Fabbrini's restaurant, cipolla, has stayed at the top of the weekly rankings in *New York* magazine since its opening in May. It turns out that Fabbrini is the uncle of a trendy designer who came up with the concept (country Italian remix), floor plan (cozy urban bistro), and a decor that taps into the naturalistic yearnings of thirty-something hipsters who've grown up in the urban jungle. There are antlers in the entryway, wooden barrels in the restrooms, and antiquated farm tools embellishing the walls above the wainscotting. The niece has somehow even managed to make everything match the expensive rug and the reproduction Art Deco chandeliers that are evidently beloved by Fabbrini. And she has pinpointed the right fonts for the logo and the discreet, rusticated sign: small serifs, lower case, oblique. Ed has a pet theory that the importance of fonts in a restaurant's success has been wildly underestimated, a view she airs to the talented niece, who thrills and vindicates her by agreeing, but then quickly surpasses her interest in the topic by enthusing about the benefits of manual kerning.

Fabbrini got lucky in the hire of his chef, too, who is coming off of a run at Enoteca Bella. In fact, if one didn't know Fabbrini personally, you'd be forgiven for thinking he was a canny entrepreneur with a prescient eye for the next big thing. The downside is that Fabbrini believes the restaurant's success is due to his own ingenious management, rather than—as far as Ed can tell—in spite of it. Fabbrini's main gift seems to be in catering to his rich and influential patrons—the wealthy with no taste who will follow a trend off a cliff. Though he struggles with the hip power set under forty-five and the arts and media types with cultural capital who have put his restaurant on the map, they at least think him a charming throwback, with his musical accent and waxed moustache.

Still, cipolla started making an absurd amount of money almost immediately. Anyone who manages to get seated is only too happy to make a night of it: tasting menu, wine, the works. For a waitress working under the table and living mostly on tips, the evening shift at cipolla is about as good as it gets.

Owen writes to Ed regularly, even though they have stopped sleeping together. His emails are terse two-liners dashed off while his wife is in the shower. He makes inquiries after Ed's studies, sly references to their encounters, and repeated requests for nude photos.

She fumbles in the bathroom to pull off her shirt, and her hair sticks up in staticky bunches. In her reflection, her eyes are either the only part of her that is still, or the only trace of movement. She thinks about Owen and shudders run through her; a quivering begins again below her navel. With her back to the mirror, she holds the cool silver totem of the phone at eye level, and when the fake shutter-sound clicks there is a flash as she commits her small breasts to the memory card. The light reflecting in the mirror obscures her face like a blazing sun, her whole head disappearing into a halo.

Later, when she looks at the photo, she realizes for the first time that her right breast is slightly larger than the left. She decides not to send it.

ᵐᵢ|||ᵢᵐ

Ed would rather be a hostess, but all the hostesses at cipolla are white girls. Hostesses wear nice outfits of their own choosing: silk blouses, wrap dresses, statement necklaces. All the waitresses wear the same tight black dresses with no jewellery but lots of makeup.

Late on Friday and Saturday nights, the restaurant becomes a hot spot. On Friday nights especially, one of the main job requirements of waitressing at cipolla is enduring comments from men in suits who have had too much to drink. Like the man at Table Two who cups Edith's ass and suggests they get married. As she steps out of reach, he asks her the word for "pussy" in Chinese.

"I don't speak Chinese."

"Sorry, sweetheart." He looks predatory and foolish but not sorry. "Korean? Thai?" He drops his voice. "Can you do that ping-pong ball thing?"

Fireworks of humiliated fury explode behind her eyes, but all she says is, "I'll be right back with your drink." Rebuffed men are bad tippers.

"Temper, temper, Naomi," says Alondra as they fall into step on their way to the bar. The words hiss out with a chuckle. "Smile now, go shoe shopping later." Ed forces her face into something like a smile. Naomi is the kind of person who lets all the crap roll off her back.

Alondra is one of the waitresses she is friendly with. When Fabbrini told Alondra she had to either tame her afro or quit, Ed sympathized and joined her in calling him a cunt behind his back. Now Alondra has a close-cut cap of hair and a modelling agent, and together she and Ed roll their eyes whenever Fabbrini goes on about how much more beautiful he has helped her become. Alondra is quitting in a few weeks, too, as soon as she has enough saved up to move to L.A.

When she settles up with Table Two, Ed gets a smaller tip than expected, along with a phone number that she incinerates over the sink in the kitchen.

"You should save those," says Tia, one of the other waitresses. "I have a whole pile I'm going to give to my little cousin for prank calls." Ed laughs.

At the end of the night, the music gets turned up and cipolla transforms into a private club for the staff. It is Ed's favourite part of working at the restaurant, when spouses, boyfriends, and girlfriends start to materialize, and the frustrated shouting in the kitchen finally comes to an end. Tip-counting time.

Lawrence the bartender sets out a tray of shots for the wait staff. Judging by the generosity with which he pours, right to the lip of the glass, he has already had a few himself. Ed downs one with no chaser. She remembers how Owen told her tequila could be savoured just like whisky, but to her it still tastes like burning. Not seeming to notice her revulsion, Lawrence slides over another. Ed swings her hair back, brushing it out of her eyes, and drinks the second shot. Naomi, she has decided, is less serious and more fun than Ed. Naomi is totally normal.

Alondra, who apparently skipped supper, gets drunk and loud fast. She laughs hysterically about how much of a lightweight she is, as she slings an arm around Ed.

"Somebody help!" Ed calls out jokingly, as they both start staggering, setting each other off into further peals of laughter. "Al, you're only a lightweight in one sense of the word."

Tia hurries over, giggling, to lend a shoulder until Alondra calms down and pulls herself up to her full five foot ten. "Come on, ladies," she says. "We look hot tonight. Larry, take a picture."

Lawrence obeys, pulling out his phone and coming around the bar. "One hundred per cent babes," he says, snapping a photo. As far as Ed can tell, he has a thing for both Tia and Alondra.

"Print me a copy of that," says Fabbrini, who has turned up without warning to verify the take at the end of the night.

Lawrence nods, edging along the bar to block Fabbrini's view of the tray of empty shot glasses. "Will do, boss."

Fabbrini squeezes Ed's shoulder. "I'll keep it at home, to remind me of my beautiful girls. So international."

It's as if the only people who can see Ed are the creeps, the lechers, and the users.

"Hi there!"

The man who calls out to Ed from behind the kiosk in the Arts & Science building is standing in front of a banner that reads *Campus Esperanto! Speak the Universal Language* in hand-lettered blue tempera paint. From the way his eyes occasionally pop with wariness, she suspects he does not have permission to set up a table.

"Hello," he says, when Ed steps up. "I'm glad you heard me." He has strange skin—fair around his neck, and irritated, bubbling pink along his jaw. In other places, as along his hairline, it is tanned dark as wet sand. He looks to be at least thirty, not a student at all.

"Hi. Esperanto's the made-up language, isn't it?" she asks, hoping that she does not sound unkind. "I remember my high school Latin teacher mentioning it. He thought it was kind of a joke. Too artificial or something. You know?"

"Some people think Latin is a joke," says the man. His voice is serene, a warm tenor that makes her think of oak casks and aged wine, of deep flavours being slowly released.

She nods. "Dead language and all." She studies him intently, adjusting the strap of her black bag on her shoulder. Up close, she can see his thin-framed glasses and can tell that he has shaved badly, missing a patch of stubble just visible on the underside of his chin. "My Latin teacher was also very down on the French Academy," she says. "Trying to prevent French people from saying *le hamburger*."

"They'd have a field day here in North America," he says. "Have you ever been to Montreal? A day there would bring them to their knees, don't you think?"

"I do," says Ed, and she hears a high, coy lilt in her own voice, challenging. She has never been to Montreal, but that doesn't matter. She gets the idea. "So you agree that language can't be controlled."

The man seems thoughtful, like someone who might never rise to the bait. "I suppose," he says. "But I also believe that things can be imagined and made new. Made better."

He has longish, curly hair that flops onto his face as he reaches down to pick up a flyer from the pile in front of him. Ed notices a gathered corner of his striped shirt poking out from the top of his fly, which is not quite zipped.

"I'm Jericho," he says. "Take a pamphlet?"

Ed gloms on to Jericho like wet spaghetti to a strainer. They meet at various cafés across campus, where Jericho drinks green tea and Ed always has two sugared coffees. Jericho talks about his ideals, his dreams of global cooperation through a network of Esperanto speakers. He has a conversational mildness that pleases her, and she likes the way he leans his head to the left when she talks, like a bird listening.

Looking at him in his neatly ironed shirts, his knobby ankles prominent below short pants, Ed feels her anxious cravings ebb away. In the presence of his simple niceness, something loosens around her hips, and she is struck by a sense-memory of what she used to be like, near enough that she can almost grasp it and shrug it on. An easier version of herself: hair long and held back with a plastic headband, spine hunched from the weight of a purple knapsack loaded down with books. Before boys made an impression on her mental landscape. Before she ever stopped to wonder how and where she belonged.

Ed also loves how Jericho always gives the kindest interpretation possible of what she says, and never makes her feel like a bad person. He is a little like an alien, a bespectacled, motley-skinned being with a superior temperament. And so Ed vents her spleen: railing against the professor of her summer class, and examining her ongoing grievances with Owen without ever mentioning his name.

When Jericho asks about her own name, he surprises her with his guesses. "Short for Edelina? Edelweiss? Edwarda?"

"Edith," she says.

Jericho shakes his head. "You're neither an Edith nor an Ed. You're something more like Feina." *Feina*, he tells her, is the word for "fairy" in Esperanto.

Ed's hands fly to her cheeks and she flutters her eyelashes, feeling pleased but also slightly embarrassed. "How many bitchy-ass fairies are you acquainted with?" she asks.

Jericho pulls her hands away from her face with the barest touch, and sets them down on the table.

"Feina," he says, and from then on refuses to call her anything else.

In late July, Ed goes to one of Jericho's Esperanto workshops in the evening after her summer course. She finds a strange assembly of six or seven who look to be regulars and a few wary newcomers, standing diffident and apart at the back. Three guys sit on the tops of desks at the front, surrounding an emptying cookie tin of home-baked lemon bars, taking turns reading incomprehensible dialogue off photocopied sheets.

"This is Feina, everyone," says Jericho.

A girl in a wool sweater raises her head as Ed offers a smile. The girl has a neat binder set in front of her, with tabbed dividers in a rainbow of colours, and a sharpened purple pencil. Her eyes are fixed on Jericho.

"Esperanto means 'one who hopes,'" says Jericho, "and I hope we'll all get a lot out of tonight's session. Why don't we go around the room and introduce ourselves, for everyone here tonight who's new?"

Afterwards, Jericho tells Ed that he has been leading the workshops for four years. She is hole-punching her scrawled notes from the class, putting them into a binder with her handouts, determined to at least give the appearance of someone attempting to learn the language.

"And how many more Esperanto speakers do you think there are now?"

He looks startled by the question. "You mean, because of me? I don't know. Maybe one?"

"Only one?" Ed is surprised. "And you don't think that's kind of sad?"

"Don't you think one person can make a difference?"

Ed considers it. "I guess I do, sure."

"Well, one by one, that's how change happens. And then imagine if there's a catastrophe, like another flood or an ice age or whatever happened to the dinosaurs." Jericho speaks in the calm tones of a flight attendant pointing out the emergency exits. "We'll need a way to communicate with people all over the world."

"What about English?" Ed blurts out. It is a question she has been attempting to repress for weeks.

Jericho looks disappointed in her. "Just think of its colonial past." Then he crooks an eyebrow. "You know who doesn't need to be convinced of the need for an alternative? The frontman of your favourite band." One side of his lip curls with this last remark; he claims not to be a Dove Suite fan himself.

Now Ed is the one who is startled. "Stu Jenkins speaks Esperanto?" Jericho nods. "I've never read that. And I swear, I have read every single interview."

"It's true. At least, he has expressed an interest in it to me, via email." Of course it is too good to be true. "Ah. Email."

Jericho has a curious expression on his face. "You don't believe me."

"I didn't say that." Ed doesn't want to pry into the details of how exactly her friend has been catfished. She changes the subject without asking any more questions.

When he isn't promoting Esperanto, Jericho works part-time as a veterinary assistant. He claims that the animals speak to him.

"Not so much in words," he says, "or sounds like *woof woof* or *meow*. But with their eyes, the way they breathe. The way their fur moves."

Ed is skeptical and calls him the "dog whisperer," but Jericho doesn't laugh. He says, "I can make my own fur move. See?" He holds his forearm up to her face like a crossbar between them and closes his eyes. After a minute his skin ripples with goosebumps, the fine dark hairs standing on end in one slow but definite motion, like the raising of a drawbridge.

"That's incredible," she says. "What a trick! How do you do it?"

Jericho is fervent but grave, shaking his head. "No trick. I think about the animals. Put myself into an attitude of complete sympathy. Then it just happens."

She's reminded of a story she heard on the news, of a zoo worker who was killed after entering the enclosure of her favourite tiger, convinced it wouldn't hurt her. Ed decides not to bring it up.

That Friday, Ed is lingering near the corner of the bar where the waitresses pick up their drink orders when she sees Alondra approach, distress flickering at the corners of her mouth.

"Naomi, do me a favour and take that table, please?" she says, nodding at the next table over, where two older gentlemen are having dinner with half a dozen athletic-looking young men and women. "My ex, Lucas, is over there." Alondra points out a black guy with a shaved head and a button-up shirt. "It's his kung fu group. Look, I'll trade you for Table Four."

Table Four is a bunch of Wall Street types, already drunk. Big tips for sure, but probably with some unwanted phone numbers and groping thrown in.

"Deal."

The kung fu group is loud, shouting good-natured in-jokes up and down the table and ordering an astounding amount of food. Ed appreciates that they are not cipolla's usual clientele, and definitely not Fabbrini's preferred demographic of wealthy, well-connected social climbers. As Ed refills their water glasses, she gathers that the older gentlemen are kung fu masters: one, the head of a local kung fu school; the other, a visiting expert from China. The younger people are their students.

Later, as they're settling up the bill, a uniformed police officer comes in and joins the table after a swift appraisal of the room. Like her, he is alert, poised with potential energy. Ed's thoughts fly to the envelopes of undeclared cash handed to her at the end of each shift, though she banishes this thought as the officer is hailed by some of the younger guests and the head of the kung fu school gives him a smiling nod. A guy sitting next to the visiting Chinese master slides over a half-finished beer, and the cop downs it in a single swig.

"I'm off-duty, I swear," he says to Ed, when he notices her watching the table. "Just had to say hi to my pals." She likes the congenial, unvarnished way he observes her, as simply another human being or perhaps even a fellow citizen. Not the late-night stare of a patron with the mistaken impression she might be on the menu.

She's about to ask if he wants a drink when a lout from Table Four waves an empty glass in the air and shouts over the din, "Can I get some freaking help over here already?"

The officer spins around in his seat. "Maybe you should watch your tone with the wait staff." With a sour look, the customer falls silent as Alondra hurries over.

Ed enjoys the intervention but knows Fabbrini would not. "Haven't you heard?" she asks the police officer. "The customer is always right."

"Nobody is always right." He adds five dollars to the pile of cash amassed on the table before getting up to leave.

"What's that for?"

He grins at her before replacing his hat. "To make me a customer. I wouldn't mind being right, for once."

Ed and Jericho are having ice cream, and she is back to obsessing about Owen, having slipped up and met him for a drink that turned into a quickie in an alley.

"Everything I know about his childhood I read in one of his magazine essays," she says. "Do you think that's normal?"

"I don't like to use that word, *normal*. It creates a false dichotomy of social acceptability."

Ed spears the plastic spoon into her mound of ice cream like a flagpole at the summit. Shrugging back into her green sweater, she waits for an answer.

Eventually, Jericho says, "No, not really. I guess not." He is always reluctant to pronounce judgment, as much as he seems to want to please her.

"He's a withholding son of a bitch," says Ed.

Jericho's face is solemn. "That may be, Feina," he says.

Ed thinks Jericho must be on a mission to cheer her up, to keep her from falling into her aggrieved and sordid thoughts about Owen. He spends the next few days taking her out for more ice cream, for bike rides, for long walks. He takes her to a series of concerts put on by NYU's Department of Music—the examination pieces and free recitals. Seizing her hand at key moments, he fumbles for words to describe his elation at certain passages. The satisfaction that comes in a sonata; hearing the recapitulation of the theme in the original key. He tries to relate it to rock music, for Ed's sake.

"It's like that moment when a drumbeat finally kicks in at the second chorus. Like in that Dove Suite song you love."

Ed nods, noticing how when Jericho's face is animated it bestows an unexpected unity on his strange features. And that his eyes are huge, brown reflecting pools of intelligence and sympathy.

"Maybe you should make up a word for it in Esperanto," she says.

He frowns. "I can't just do that, Feina. There are rules about those sorts of things."

The music starts up again then, and when Ed is about to press her point, Jericho leans over in the creaking auditorium seat and whispers, "Okay, maybe. I'll look into it."

Fabbrini has been on edge all week because of a visit from the health inspector. Eight patrons have fallen ill with a mysterious illness following dinner at cipolla the Friday before. There is to be no end, it seems, to Fabbrini's outrage over the matter.

"It's a travesty, targeting us! Why didn't everybody get sick, if it was the food? Why not the whole restaurant? Almost everyone ordered the *zuppa*, and one-third the *osso buco*." He knocks a pile of folded napkins to the floor. "*Dio mio!*" Ed has noticed that Fabbrini has begun mixing more Italian phrases into his regular speech over the past month. His clientele seem to appreciate this extra touch of authenticity. "They can't hold us responsible for the common cold and the promiscuity of our customers."

It's just like Fabbrini to impute the outbreak to some sort of post-prandial orgy among the afflicted. Behind him, Alondra picks up the jettisoned napkins and rolls her eyes at Ed, who struggles to suppress a smile.

"I think it's a little worse than a cold, Mr. Fabbrini," says Ed. From what she's read in the newspaper, the eight individuals are being closely monitored by local health authorities after one of them was admitted to hospital for respiratory problems. She was disappointed the article didn't mention anything about the restaurant. She gets a second-hand thrill from all the cipolla media coverage—just another instance of fame and fortune lurking around every corner of the city. Though she supposes in this case it wouldn't be good for business.

"Whatever it is," Fabbrini grumbles, "it wasn't the *osso buco*."

Ed is browsing at the campus bookstore after class when she overhears two women talking about Owen Grant. The remaining signed copies from the reading two months ago are facing out in a thick stack on the shelf across from where she's standing.

"I'm telling you, he's hot," says a blonde in a pale, summery dress as she pulls out a copy of *How to Avoid the Plague*. She is carrying an enviable shoulder bag of soft, brown leather. "Have you ever seen him?"

"Oh yeah," says the other, who looks Korean and sports a cat-print sweatshirt and dark-rimmed glasses. A funky nerd aesthetic. "In the flesh. He used to live in West Mass, like my sister."

They flip to the author photo. "This guy. Brutally hot."

"Well, I heard his wife left him three or four years ago," says the funky nerd, with insider authority. "He didn't want kids, so she had one on her own. Sperm donor."

"Yikes. You think it was about the kid?" asks the blonde.

"Nah. I think she found out he'd slept with half the town. Even a bunch of people in her department."

"God, that's cold."

"Yeah, my sister works at Lansdowne as an administrative assistant. She fooled around with him, too, actually."

"What a dog."

"And now he's off the leash. I feel sorry for whoever dates him."

Ed only has fifteen days left in the city, a realization that prompts her to create a spreadsheet of top New York activities compiled from over a dozen bookmarked websites. Then she spends the weekend working her way down the list, determined to visit at least some of the attractions alone. Ed fears that she has been seeing too much of Jericho in the past couple of weeks. She worries he has done something to her by giving her a new name, fettered her in ways she cannot consciously combat. She is afraid of leading him on. She knows from her experience with Owen that it doesn't matter how well-informed everyone might be about who is or isn't available for a relationship. It is not enough to say the words; romantic disinterest needs to be shown in brief flashes of cruelty, and hinted at with a degree of reticence, a reluctance to confide. Words are never enough to make the situation clear. She tells herself that the most important thing will be to remember not to kiss him. Then everything will be okay.

Over the next week, Owen sends Ed five longing texts, ostensibly while his wife is at Zumba class. Ed tries hard to believe in the existence of said wife but agrees to meet him at a motel across town. She spends her subway ride uselessly vowing to turn around, and when she at last spots his car pulling up to their motel room, she is trembling and still resentful.

For some reason he refrains from his standard dirty talk, and in the absence of their usual collaborative and profane narration, they lapse into silence, leaving only grunts and the moist sounds of slapping as their words fall away. With Owen's hands on her hips, Ed closes her eyes. The din of their lovemaking begins thundering in her ears until she drops to the sheets, muffling her head in the pillow. Owen's deep breaths are a Morse code of exhalations on her neck and shoulders. Ed realizes they are having a cold conversation: a back-and-forth of when they will finally end it.

"The way that you talk about Owen makes me think that you still love him," says Jericho.

The day before, after a marathon session of movie-watching at his tiny apartment, Ed finally leaned into Jericho's patient, looming face—and into the kiss that had always seemed inevitable. It was better than she thought it would be. Soft and insistent, urgent and sweet. But Jericho has seemed sadder since the kiss, as though whatever his daily burdens, they have become harder to bear.

"I don't," she says. She never loved him, but Owen is still with her, the thought and shape of him, the things he says and writes. He seems to linger in these ghostly traces, like something that might show up in a photograph—a dark mark, a smudge somewhere behind her head. Though their affair was already bound to end in a matter of days, when Ed returns to Lansdowne, Owen has abruptly cut off contact again. This, more than anything, has shaken her. Before, she had his words to cling to, if nothing else. But it is as though by kissing Jericho she has severed whatever invisible and improbable thread used to exist between her and Owen. "It's not that at all."

"I know." Jericho turns his head away. They are at his apartment again, just two blocks away from cipolla, and lying close together on his mattress on the floor. It's the only place to sit, apart from his desk chair. "In my heart I believe you, but the things you say make me doubt my true instincts."

"I'm sorry," says Ed, and she is. She knows Jericho is preoccupied by her imminent departure, though they've avoided mentioning it since the kiss. "I don't know what else to tell you." She reaches for one of the cold beers they brought back from the bodega downstairs and takes a sip. The cool, blank white walls of Jericho's apartment seem to stretch up forever towards the ceiling.

"Don't you see?" His eyes are fixed on the floor, a pink and blue Afghan carpet swirled with rings of roses. "It's what you've told me that's the problem. We shouldn't have to say anything to one another."

His books are stacked around the room, surrounding his mattress in piles divided according to subject: Buddhism, evolution, philosophy, opera, Esperanto. Ed sits up and examines them, running her finger along each title in turn, pretending to be absorbed. Earlier, she thought it might be convenient to stay over, given how close Jericho lives to the restaurant. Now she is starting to reconsider.

"Let's put on some music," she says, and she can hear him moving behind her, getting up, heading for the computer. "Do you have any Dove Suite?"

He makes a strange, choked noise in his throat. "Told you before—we don't share that particular obsession." He puts on an electronic album by a band she's never heard of.

Later, when Ed asks Jericho about old girlfriends, he is pleased and fair-minded. Returning to the mattress, he lists his few significant relationships, offering a fond and considered analysis of their break-downs. Stroking her wrist with his thumb, he mentions one desperate unrequited love, for a classmate during his undergraduate degree.

"I did something I'm not proud of," he says. "On some level I thought it would be good for her to know how much she really meant to me. To show her."

Ed shifts closer to him on the mattress, feeling worried and a bit diminished. She ignores her beer, which is growing wet with condensation on the rug. "What do you mean? What did you do?"

Jericho shrugs. "I guess you could say I tried to become someone else entirely."

Ed says, "I wouldn't want us to become quite so desperately in love with one another as all that." She is suddenly tired. She thinks of Owen, her foolish notebooks, and a sigh escapes her lips.

Finishing the last of his beer, Jericho gets up in silence to place the empty bottle on the desk.

◄‖‖►

The radio is turned on low in cipolla's kitchen, where Fabbrini is perched on a step stool, waiting for the hourly news update. His anxiety is veering into panic. He has had two more visits from the health inspector, followed by a call from the CDC, who are apparently coming in to do health screenings of the staff. According to the advisory released the day before, all eight of the hospitalized patrons have now died of their illness, and another two hundred people in New York have been infected. The restaurant has been officially cleared of wrongdoing—the people who got sick are suffering from a respiratory virus, and apparently nothing food-borne—but given that everyone who died ate at cipolla three weeks ago, it still wouldn't play well for business if word got out. According to Alondra, Fabbrini has been using all of his influence to keep the name of the restaurant out of the papers.

When at the top of the hour the newscaster begins by announcing twenty confirmed new cases of the mystery virus, Fabbrini claps his hands together and shakes them reverentially at the ceiling, while the line cooks exchange nervous smiles.

"How is that a good thing?" Ed asks, glancing at the door as Alondra slips in to join them. "People getting sick from a dangerous virus?" It occurs to her that she hasn't seen Tia in a while, or Lawrence, or the friendly hostess with the jade necklace. She has an involuntary vision of a pandemic-ravaged planet and a new global culture that will have her doing a Skype call in Esperanto with someone in China.

"Don't you see? Now nobody is worrying about cippola," says Fabbrini. "And that son-of-a-whore health inspector can go get fucked in the ass." Everyone cheers because it is a treat when the old man lets loose his tongue. Then, as the laughter quiets down, the announcer's voice cuts through: "Officials are investigating whether any of the new cases can be traced to the first infection cluster at cipolla, a trendy bistro on the Lower East Side that officials have pinpointed as ground zero for the infection."

Fabbrini begins swearing again, but this time nobody is smiling. He flings a baking sheet to the floor and lunges for the cellphone he wears in a holster on his belt. The cooks begin to edge away and return to their cutting boards. Ed, too, sees this as a good opportunity to check on her tables.

Alondra pulls her aside on the way out, flashing a wicked grin.

"I called someone at the *Post*," she whispers, dark eyes brighter than normal. "That little fucker is finished pinching asses for good."

⸺⫷⫸⸺

Two days later, after her final class, Ed heads to the Esperanto workshop a little late, carrying coffee and all the notes she can find. She hasn't been going regularly, as the workload for her summer course started piling up towards the end. When she enters the classroom, she finds only three people sitting around the front, each separately muttering something from Jericho's large-print Esperanto handouts.

The girl with the meticulous binder looks up at her. Her eyes are wide and shrewd. "Is Jericho sick or something?" she asks.

Only then does Ed realize that he is not there.

Ed avoids passing by cipolla on her way to Jericho's place, noticing the traffic backed up along that block, the cacophony of honking horns propelling her down a side street. With the pungent taste of smoke hanging in the air, she waits for him to answer the buzzer as a couple of guys outside the bodega discuss the rising price of fire insurance. When a man leaving the building holds the door open for her, she hesitates for only a moment before going inside. Upstairs, she finds Jericho in his unlocked apartment, curled up on the mattress.

His eyes are open and glazed, his glasses folded on the floor beside him. His hair is greasy, clinging to the sides of his face.

"There's no word for it," he says. "What I feel. For you. You'll never understand." His voice is raw. "And I know we're breaking up when you leave."

Ed crosses the room to join him, trying to keep the surprise from showing on her face. She'd imagined something long-distance, coming to New York to visit him or hosting him in Lansdowne, but now her whole body is flooded with relief.

"I told you," breathes Jericho, as though she has said something.

Ed blinks. Then she lies back on the mattress, face to the ceiling, and he rolls over until their arms are touching. Taking his hand in hers, she exhales in a long, slow rhythm, and when he squeezes her palm, she squeezes back, again and again, until the pressure starts to feel like a message, or maybe a question, and then a release.

Dove Suite Announces ARAMIS Fundraising Concert

September 9, 2020

VANCOUVER—Platinum-selling rock band Dove Suite have announced they will be headlining a music festival in Canada in support of ARAMIS relief. Dubbed "To America With Love," the day-long event will be held in Vancouver on Saturday, September 26.

Frontman Stuart Jenkins, who founded the indie rock quartet with his wife, Emma Aslet, commented that "a crisis like this has a way of making people feel powerless. We decided to take that feeling and do something with it." A donation link for ARAMIS relief organizations has also been set up on the band's website.

Dove Suite rose to prominence in 2010 with their first album, *WhisperShout*, which was certified triple-platinum. Their fourth album, *Beads*, was released in June to favourable reviews, but a planned worldwide tour was abruptly postponed earlier this spring for "personal reasons."

The charity show will feature mostly Canadian performers, with Dove Suite headlining the evening portion. Event organizers promise that the full lineup is sure to thrill concertgoers and that "there will be something for everyone."

Further details to be announced.

STU

—

SEPTEMBER 2004

On the day he left for college, Stu Jenkins's mother tucked two twenty-dollar bills into the pocket of his leather jacket before he headed out in a cab to the Greyhound station.

"For notebooks and things," she said. Her hair was unbrushed, and the breeze blew it out in wisps around her face. "Okay?"

"Okay, Ma." He kissed her on the cheek.

He knew she was sorry that he had to take out a loan. But only a little sorry, and not sorry enough to say so in front of his father, who had already said goodbye inside—a clap on the shoulder in front of the television and a gruff exhortation to *study hard and don't forget who you really are.* During dinner the night before, he'd asked Stu if he thought going to college was going to make him a better person. Stu had stared at his lap. His mother had said, "It's going to help him get a better job."

Stu was the first person in his family to go to college. Though none of them had acknowledged the milestone out loud, their mutual avoidance had created its own unspoken pressure. His parents had saved, he had saved, and it still wasn't enough. His education was already a kind of failure that he felt compelled to put right.

"Be sure to look out for Jericho," his mother said. Jericho and Stu, as their mothers never tired of reminding them, had met in a Mommy and Me play group in the park when they were toddlers.

"I'm sure Jer is going to love college, Ma."

Stu did not look back before the cab turned the corner, in case his mother was still standing there in her robe, watching him go, and because he couldn't decide whether knowing that for sure would make him happy or sad. The worst part was that he only sort of wanted to go to college. School was just a way of buying himself some time.

On the bus to Lansdowne, Stu pulled out his lyrics notebook and wrote *Don't forget who you really are.* He'd started out writing protest songs, but now he was gathering snippets of overheard conversations: telling phrases or tiresome, mangled platitudes or painful truths that rattled his heart with their very ordinariness. Over the summer, he'd spent time eavesdropping while he worked nights at the same steel factory as his dad, gathering bits of lives and other ideas he could use. So far, he had a song about a man whose wife couldn't have a baby, another about a man whose daughter had stopped speaking to him, and one about a man who only met his kids once they were grown.

The money Stu earned went into the bank, and it meant that next year there might not have to be a loan at all. When he'd told his father that, expecting to elicit a little pride, his father had said, "Don't boast, Stu. It isn't Christian."

On the first day of classes, Stu crossed the Lansdowne University campus feeling like an actor plopped down onto the wrong set. He recognized the quad from the brochure: the grey stone buildings nestled on the rolling green lawn, the perfect blue sky vaulting overhead an exaggerated symbol of unlimited horizons, though the colours in real life seemed muted. But standing there on the bustling, tree-lined path, he was surrounded by strident birdsong that rivalled even the lively conversation of the other students who streamed around him, carrying book bags and coffee cups. He followed the path to the river that wound its way around the edge of the campus. Its steep, muddy banks were clumped with reeds and wildflowers, and there, too, he was struck by the sheer noise of the water rushing past. Even the river was in a hurry to get somewhere.

As he headed to his first class, Stu found himself trailing a young woman into the room. She was slight with dark hair, and her smile was warm as she propped open the door. Stu was ready to follow her into the rows of desks, but she dropped her leather satchel on the large table at the front of the room, then went to the blackboard and wrote *Professor Rachel Levinson* in neat, cursive letters that bled chalk dust. Stu blinked and took a seat near the door, as did the student walking in behind him—a skinny guy with red muttonchops and an Anti-Flag T-shirt. Stu was just thinking of Jericho, who was wiry like that but taller, when Jericho himself loped in and sat down at the desk beside him.

"So you're in this class, too," said Stu, hoping Jericho couldn't read his disappointment. For one whole minute there, he had imagined himself saying hello to someone completely new.

"Probably in all of them." Jericho extracted a sharpened pencil from his bag. "Memory loss, much? We have the same major."

Stu tried to assess his friend as though he wasn't someone he had known all his life. He thought Jericho looked like the sort of guy who studied Klingon (he was) or who spent hours creating elaborate D&D campaigns (he did). But like Stu, he lionized Chomsky and had memorized the transcript of *Manufacturing Consent*. Unlike Stu, he owned a unicycle and three hamsters. Since the dorms didn't allow pets, Jericho's mother had promised to email him every evening with an update on their well-being.

A pretty young woman came in and sat down at the desk in front of Jericho. Her long, strawberry blond hair hung straight down her back, and she wore wide-legged magenta pants over a pair of black combat boots. Under the fluorescent lights, Stu could see her zebra-print bra through her cream blouse.

Jericho half stood up then sat back down. "Hello," he said. "I'm Jericho."

"Sarah," she said, looking startled as she turned around in her seat to find him staring at her.

Stu wasn't sure he'd ever seen Jericho notice a woman before, but then there hadn't been anyone quite so noticeable in their high school.

"Welcome," said the professor. She was soft-spoken, with the slightest hint of an accent she explained was Israeli by way of Chicago. She passed out a syllabus and said that they were going to study the very origins of philosophy and critical thinking itself. "But first," she said, eyes glinting, "we play trivia."

Professor Levinson divided the class into teams and pitted them against one another. Stu, Jericho, Sarah, and Truscott of the red mutton-chops became a group and soon dominated. Jericho, who'd spent the summer studying everything on the reading list, kept shooting his hand up, and Sarah seemed to know just as much. Truscott, who turned out to be British, managed to call out a few answers as well.

"I'm already failing the class," said Stu, "and it's only the first day." He was joking, but his ignorance felt like evidence of just how far he was overreaching.

"Both my parents teach philosophy here," said Sarah with a touch of apology. "I can't help knowing this stuff."

As Professor Levinson confirmed the right answers, she spent a few minutes explaining each one, sketching out in miniature the trajectory of Western thought. Her cheeks flushed and she spoke quickly as she bounced from one topic to the next. Stu wrote down what she said until he noticed he was the only one. He put down his pen.

At the end of the game, Stu's team was declared the winner. He high-fived the others without sharing in their jubilation.

"Thus concludes the fun part of the course," said Professor Levinson. She tossed their team a bag of Skittles that Truscott caught in one hand. "Just kidding. It's all going to be fun. See you on Wednesday."

As the professor erased her name from the blackboard, Stu accepted a handful of Skittles from Truscott. Each one tasted as sweet and sickening as mediocrity.

⸱⵬ⵛⵛⵉ⸱

At the end of the following week, Stu's mother called and proposed an arrangement she had discussed with Jericho's mother.

"Jericho needs to switch rooms, honey," she said. "So we thought maybe he could move in with you?"

Jericho suffered from insomnia, and his roommate had complained to the resident advisor that Jericho stayed up all night reading and laughing. Stu knew the laugh, which was more of a bark—an exultant cry of excitement that was symptomatic of one of his more irritating moods.

"It's better for both of you this way," said Stu's mother. "Now neither of you need to share with strangers."

"Okay, Ma." Stu's assigned roommate was a quiet young man majoring in religion whom he'd barely seen.

Now Stu sat on his bed and strummed his guitar while Jericho arranged his figurines on the bookcase. He turned a miniature Luke Skywalker to face Stu and wiggled him slightly.

"I'm not going to go to the philosophy welcome party," said Luke Skywalker in Jericho's voice.

"Oh no?" said Stu. He watched as his new roommate expanded Luke's posse with a wizard, a Stormtrooper, and the Incredible Hulk.

When they were kids, Jericho had been the deviser of all games and chief explorer of imaginary lands. Stu would return from playdates at Jericho's house with the disorienting sensation of having spent three hours inside his friend's brain—an odd place filled with fantastical lore and the peculiar detritus of Jericho's current obsessions. Stu wondered if it was still the wild place it had seemed then.

"No," said Jericho. Having positioned one final winged superhero, he extracted his linguistics textbook from a pile on the floor and hunched on the bed to read it.

"You might meet some girls," said Stu. Before they graduated from high school, they used to joke about Jericho's virginity as his incurable condition. But Stu wasn't sure Jericho would find it so funny anymore.

His friend grunted without looking up. "Lots of studying to do."

"Sure," said Stu. "It's the first party, though. It might be good to make some other friends besides me." He regretted how it sounded, but Jericho didn't flinch. He had always regarded Stu's high school drift into the orbit of the popular kids as nothing more than a naive lapse of judgment.

Jericho grunted. "Busy." Then he cringed as Stu began rehearsing a song. "Can't you see I'm concentrating?"

The house party was in full swing by the time Stu arrived. Motown was playing on the stereo, and the kitchen and living room were full of people. He squeezed past some guys he didn't know and helped himself to a beer from a cooler in the kitchen. There was a sign posted on the wall that said ONLY CONSUME ALCOHOL IF YOU ARE 21+. Over the din, he could hear Truscott in the far corner talking to some girls about spending his summer on tour as a replacement guitarist for a band Stu was surprised to realize everyone had heard of.

"Good money for a summer gig, but I couldn't stand those pricks," Truscott was saying. "They wouldn't know real art if it bit them in the arse."

Stu moved into the hallway, where Professor Levinson was sitting on the landing of the central staircase, wearing jeans and an Emma Goldman T-shirt. In casual clothes, she was nearly indistinguishable from the older graduate students milling around.

She stood up as he approached. "You're in my Presocratics class, aren't you?"

He was both thrilled and alarmed that she'd addressed him. "Yeah, I'm Stu."

"You can call me Rachel," she said. She sipped from her plastic cup of red wine. "Outside of class, anyway."

"I like your shirt," said Stu, nodding at Emma Goldman. "Are you an anarchist?"

"I'm skeptical of power," she said, shrugging. "And, you know, the *system*." Her voice was gently ironic. "But I vote."

"Hey, Chomsky votes, right?" said Stu.

"Right! Exactly." Rachel finished most of her wine in a single gulp, then frowned a little at the tiny cup. "And are you a musician?"

Stu wondered if he was giving off some palpable creative vibe. "Guitarist. How'd you know?"

Her dark eyes were full of fun. "The pants are a giveaway."

Stu peered down at his skinny black jeans. "Right. Ha. But I'm a songwriter, too," he added. "Though I haven't written much since I got here." He hooked his thumb into his pocket. "Everything sounds trite when I try to play it in my dorm. Or maybe it's because my roommate hates my singing."

Rachel looked thoughtful. "You know, there's an open mic at Birdy's. You could sign up, get some audience feedback."

"Oh yeah?" said Stu, vaguely embarrassed by the parental tone of her encouragement. "Maybe I'll do that."

"You should. Put things out there." The front door opened as more people arrived, and Rachel shivered in the draft. "And how do you like Lansdowne so far?"

"It's great," he said, after a pause, struggling to sort out his impressions. "Really different . . . from high school." As soon as the words came out, he regretted them. Everything he said was stupid.

Her eyes were sympathetic and a bit glassy. "It's actually my first semester here, too. I've only been here a month."

"You're lying to the boy," said a voice behind her. "It's been five weeks." A tall blond man with a chiselled jaw and the approximate physique of a Greek god ambled up and girded her shoulders with a possessive arm. Rachel only came up to his armpit. Next to him, she suddenly seemed ordinary, a mere human.

"Okay, five weeks," she said with a laugh. "I was lucky I could bring someone with me. Stu, this is my husband, Owen. He's Lansdowne's Distinguished Visiting Writer this year."

The Greek god shook his hand. "Owen Grant."

Stu nodded, embarrassed into silence, unsure if he was expected to say hello or, like Owen, simply repeat his own name. Another professor approached and Stu slipped away and got himself another beer. He wanted to pound them back until he'd expunged the whole end of the conversation from his memory.

Several beers later, Stu wandered past the living room, where the general party din was lowered to the level of quiet discussion. Owen was holding forth from the arm of the couch, as a group of students listened, seemingly rapt. Stu lingered in the doorway, self-conscious until he realized no one was watching him. Then he made his way over to an empty spot beside the writer. He noticed his ethics professor,

Gretchen Howe, sitting in the wingback chair opposite, dispensing advice to two young women. The heavy-framed turquoise eyeglasses by which he usually recognized her were pushed up atop her mass of caustic red hair. After a minute, Sarah plopped down in between him and Owen.

"Hi," said Stu.

"Oh, hi." Sarah bumped into his shoulder then slid over, out of the dip of the couch. "Oops. Having fun?"

"Yeah, not bad," said Stu. "Though I don't really know anyone." But Sarah had already switched tracks, her focus trained on Owen.

"After all, wisdom is an aphrodisiac," the writer was saying. He turned to include Sarah in his address, as well as the people looking over from the next room. "And the transmission of knowledge is an erotic act." The book-lined walls felt close, almost stifling, while Owen seemed larger than life, magnified by the admiring gazes of Sarah and the other young women. "Even if it's not physical, it can be incredibly intimate," said the writer, capping the remark with a half-shrug. "Inconvenient but true."

"Come now," called Professor Howe from across the room. Her voice was sharp. "Let's not get into all this here."

Owen waved her off. It was obvious in that moment that he held sway in the room. "I'm sure you've felt it, too, Gretchen. What about when you were a student? I know I still feel it when I encounter work that challenges me." He rested his hands on his knees. "That intense desire for someone else's take on the world. And the hunger to possess it."

"I think it's true," Stu spoke up. He remembered the way he'd felt when Rachel lectured, how her exhilaration about ideas seemed to light her up from within. "Learning can be kind of sexy."

Owen turned and noticed Stu for the first time since he'd sat down. "Exactly! When learning is effective, there's an erotic charge. It's unmistakable."

"For God's sake, Owen. Stop saying 'erotic' in front of the students." Professor Howe put down her cup and threw off her shawl. "I'm going to find Keelan. I've half a mind to shut this party down right now."

A gentle smile crinkled the writer's eyes. "Oh, Gretchen. There's no orgy about to break out. We're just having a conversation."

Stu opened his mouth to chime in, but Sarah tugged on his sleeve. "Don't get involved," she said in a low voice. She stood up and pulled him out of the living room, letting the conversation continue without them. "My mom is on fire tonight. She's going to root out every last person who dares to disagree with her."

Stu glanced back. "That's your mom?"

"Yeah, remember I told you? Both my parents are profs." Sarah pointed across the foyer to an older man talking to Rachel. A silvering blond ponytail poked out below his tweed deerstalker. "My dad's here, too. And that's my brother, Elliot." Stu followed her gaze to a dark-haired young man who was chatting up a girl in the dining room. Her voice lowered to a whisper. "He just dropped out of grad school," she said, in the relishing tone of hot gossip. "And my parents still don't know."

"Holy . . ." said Stu. "So I guess you're the one who's following in their footsteps." It occurred to him that she looked like an exact blend of them both: reddish-blond hair, bookish, vaguely bohemian.

"I'm more like a splinter than a chip off the old block. Or blocks," said Sarah, her voice returning to normal as she led the way to the kitchen. She grabbed two beers out of the cooler and handed one to him. "Just taking some electives to keep them happy until Elliot breaks the news. They're definitely going to freak out. Even though he's the one who wants to go out into the world and, like, *live* the ideals of justice and benevolence they've been teaching." She used the bottom of her shirt to protect her palm as she twisted off the bottle cap. "But I guess everyone's family is a bunch of weirdos, right?"

Stu was about to respond that he wished his was weirder when Sarah said, "Be right back." He watched as she went to join Owen, who had risen from the couch and was now standing by himself. They clinked beers, and Sarah tossed her hair over her shoulder as Owen spoke to her with a grave, attentive focus. Stu chugged his beer, hoping someone would come talk to him, but nobody did.

Once the dance music on the stereo was turned up, Stu picked up his jacket. As he slipped it back on in the foyer, he was surprised by Owen sidling up to him with a friendly nod.

"So how do you know my wife?" he said. "Shawn, was it?"

"Stu. I'm in her Presocratics class."

"Ah. And what's your story?"

"My story?" Stu thought about his conversation with Rachel. "I'm a songwriter."

"Cool," said Owen. "Do you have an album?"

Stu was taken aback. "No, not yet."

"Why not?"

"Just taking some time to figure things out." When Owen didn't nod or otherwise acknowledge the statement, Stu added, "And, you know, learn some things."

Owen put his hands in his pockets and leaned up against the wall next to a large framed painting of a goat playing a violin. "Where are you from?"

"Philadelphia."

"That's a long way away from here."

"Only a few hundred miles."

"Still," said Owen.

Stu felt himself being sized up, though not unkindly. "How about you?" he asked. "Where are you from?"

Owen shook his head as though it didn't matter. "And where are you hoping to end up?" He took a drink from a glass that appeared to contain straight whisky. "It doesn't sound like anyone has drawn you a map."

"I don't think anyone has a map," said Stu.

"Of course they do," said Owen. "Most of the people at this party do." He nodded at the students and professors locked in conversation or dancing to Justin Timberlake in the now almost impassable foyer and the living room beyond. "Their parents gave them one."

"The music industry isn't that straightforward—"

Owen continued as though he hadn't heard him. "Listen, if you really want to make art, you have to be all in. And nobody is going to give you anything. You have to take it for yourself."

Stu stepped aside to let a couple of partygoers slip around him and out the front door. He wasn't sure if he was being patronized or not, which made him uneasy. "Take what?"

"Whatever you need." The writer waved his whisky. "Time. Freedom. The means of doing your creative work."

"Just take it," repeated Stu.

"That's what I'm saying. Leave behind your expectations of a conventional life. Art is too important to come in second to marriage or kids. If you don't feel that responsibility, you probably shouldn't be making it." Owen stepped back towards the party. "Oh, and if you don't have a map, find someone who does."

Jericho was still awake when he got back. "Did you see Sarah?" his roommate asked, bent over his desk, reading Nietzsche.

"Yes." Stu studied Jericho's face. It had always been hard to tell what he was thinking. His eyes were hawkish behind his glasses, and his jaw was grim. He was an Easter Island head with a pair of wire spectacles. "If you like her, why didn't you come?"

Jericho turned the page without glancing up. "I don't like parties."

Stu kicked off his jeans and pulled on a pair of flannel pyjama pants. He'd stopped bothering to keep his half of the room tidy after his friend moved in. Jericho was the only person he had ever met who was a fastidious slob—who would press a shirt even as the legs of the ironing board crunched down on dried-up pens and empty Cheetos bags. "Do you think knowledge is erotic?"

"No."

Stu slipped into bed. As his head hit the pillow, he could feel the room spinning when he closed his eyes. He was drunker than he'd thought. "Why not?"

"If it was, I'd definitely have had sex already."

◁▏▎▎▏▷

"How's Jericho holding up?" Stu's mother asked on the phone.

"He seems fine, Ma." Stu returned his guitar to its stand.

"He doesn't really know how to be in the world, does he?" she said. "He's so sensitive."

Stu thought she had it partly right. "Don't you mean *in*sensitive?"

"He feels things deeply," his mother said. "Karen and I talk a lot. Jericho's all she has, you know."

"I know." Worry had become his mother's chosen pastime, her natural vocation—except, it seemed, when it came to her own son. After Stu turned eighteen, it was as though all of his choices had suddenly moved outside of her power to influence or even discuss. Likewise, any concern for his inner life or private doubts seemed to have evaporated. The only person who worried less about Stu was his father.

"Stuart," he said, when Stu's mother passed him the phone. "I hope you're learning a lot." His voice was gruff. Like so many men of his generation, he hadn't learned how to carry on a telephone conversation. He half shouted, as though into a walkie-talkie or a tin can.

"Plenty," said Stu.

"Like what?"

Stu hesitated. "Like, what is the nature of What Is? Is What Is all good? And what about What Is Not?" A short silence followed in which he felt faintly ridiculous.

"Anything you can take to the bank yet?"

Stu frowned, then remembered something that Rachel had said on the first day of class. "I'm learning how to think."

"Uh-oh," said his father. Stu could hear him handing the phone back to his mother. "Good thing the boy already knows how to tie his shoes."

And yet, sitting in Rachel's classroom, Stu felt a connection not to the philosophers themselves but to the followers he imagined sitting at their feet, suddenly alive to the mysteries of the universe, the mind, the soul. It was the first time in his life he had encountered thinking— the deliberate thinking of difficult thoughts—as a thing to be encouraged, rather than staved off or endured.

And with every class, he noticed that Rachel got a little more comfortable. *Like a flower in the sun*, as he'd written in the chorus of a song that was never quite finished.

"According to Heraclitus," Rachel was saying, "you can't step into the same river twice. Has anyone ever heard that saying before?"

A few people nodded in response to the question, including Sarah. Jericho was listening without taking notes. Truscott said, "Heraclitus just needed a better GPS."

Rachel smiled faintly. "We perceive objects in their *becoming*," she said. "Because change is constant. The river for Heraclitus is no different from everything else in its state of flux." Her hand dropped to her hip as she beamed at the class. The more abstract and challenging her lectures, the happier she seemed to be.

"People, too," she added. "It's easier to see change in people than in a table or chair. We are all *becoming*." She seemed to look right at Stu. "Nobody is static."

At the beginning of November, Stu signed up for the Saturday-night open mic at Birdy's, the campus bar. While he waited for the emcee to call his name, he made a concerted effort not to drink too much, even as more and more pitchers of beer arrived at their table.

Truscott scrutinized the performers. "Utter disaster but I'd shag her," he said after the first act, a ukulele player. After the next act—a singer-songwriter who Stu thought was pretty good—Truscott put his head down on the table in mock despair. "Is she accepting donations for voice lessons?" he asked. "My bleeding ears. God."

Jericho was silent, probably wishing he was back among his textbooks in their dorm room. Stu did his best to breathe normally and ignore the stage. He and Sarah ran their thumbs over the letters cut into the surface of the long wooden table, which was varnished well into the next century. There were dozens of names—sometimes twinned initials love-locked into a heart, but more often the gouged declaration of a lone male, usually with a three-letter moniker. LOU, BOB, and TOM had all been moved by the spirit of Birdy's to commemorate their time there.

"Look at all the other legends who got their start here," said Sarah. "Reed. Dylan. Petty. Posterity starts now."

Stu laughed. "You're drunk," he said. They all were. But he liked the idea of doing something with his hands, which felt shaky. "Anyone have a knife?" he asked. But nobody did.

By the time Stu finally took to the stage, all of his friends were wasted.

"Crack a leg," said Sarah, before bursting into giggles.

Stu could feel Truscott's eyes on him as he tuned his guitar. Looking out at the crowd, he recognized Owen sitting at a table with a few girls Stu knew from his classes. He'd heard the writer had become a regular fixture at Birdy's. Rachel was nowhere in sight.

Closing his eyes, Stu shook the dread out of his fingers and let the sense-memory of the music take over. His voice was nothing special but he could carry a tune. He opened his eyes and saw Jericho's implacable face, then closed them before he had to encounter anyone else's expression. He moved on to the next song without stopping to pause.

"*I feel like I've been sorry for a thousand years*," he sang, and there was a catch in his voice that caught him off guard. As it was, his upper arms ached with how tightly he was holding them steady. The fact that his body was recoiling from performing made him wonder if the lyrics were personal after all, even though when he'd written them he'd imagined they were about politics, or other people: his mother, his father, workers at the plant.

He got through his four songs, and when he stopped, everyone clapped.

Or almost everyone. When he opened his eyes, he saw Sarah's lips on Jericho's. He was so startled he almost jumped when Truscott grabbed him by the shoulders as he stepped off the stage.

"You're good," he said, as Stu swung off his guitar. "Let's collaborate. Come over tomorrow night."

———

Their collaboration already had a name by the time Stu arrived at Truscott's off-campus apartment.

"Let's call it Green Screen," said Truscott. He ranged around the room, closing windows and turning on amps. "Let's hear what else you've got. Anything new?"

"Since last night?" But Stu played a new song he'd written over the summer, and Truscott listened with a faraway smile playing on his face.

"Lovely," said Truscott. "But a bit conventional, don't you think?" He got up and plugged in a series of guitar pedals. "What we're going to be doing is well beyond boy-meets-girl. I mean, pop is already in its death throes."

"I'm not sure it's entirely done for," said Stu.

Truscott continued as though he hadn't spoken. "I'm not much into lyrics myself, mate," he said. "Better to say nothing than rhyme *heart* with *apart*, know what I mean?"

Stu didn't think he had rhymed those words during his set at Birdy's, but suddenly he wasn't sure.

"Check it out," said Truscott. He grabbed a pick off the table and started playing a dense pattern of syncopated power chords over a looped drumbeat. When he was finished, he threw his guitar down on the couch. "I want to make music that makes people go crazy," he declared, pulling on his hair as though it was itching him. "Change the way they think. Cut in on their boring inner monologues and force them to confront their pathetic, privileged lives."

Stu was dubious. But Truscott had singled him out, had *seen* something in him, something that Stu was starting to realize he had been waiting for someone to see. Never mind that with Truscott he wasn't quite sure what it was.

Later, his ears ringing and his enthusiasm kindled in spite of himself, Stu returned to his room. When he got there, he found the door slightly ajar and heard Sarah's voice coming from behind it.

"I really like you as a friend," she was saying. "I'm sorry if I gave you the wrong idea."

Stu backed away from the door and went to watch television in the lounge. When he came back to the room an hour later, Jericho was alone, reading Wittgenstein's *Tractatus Logico-Philosophicus*.

"How was your night?" Stu asked.

"Fine," said Jericho. "Boring."

On Monday, Jericho wasn't there at the start of class.

"Where's Loverboy?" said Truscott.

"Oh hush, you," said Sarah. "I'm worried about him."

Stu yawned. Jericho had spent all of Sunday night with the light on, reading and barking, as Stu dozed in and out of a fitful sleep. When he awoke, Jericho was gone.

"Did you keep the poor boy up past his bedtime?" said Truscott. "Naughty girl."

"I was wasted," said Sarah. "That kiss shouldn't have happened." Her cheeks flamed as though she'd been slapped. "I feel awful."

She looked down at her notebook as Jericho came in and took his seat. Stu noticed his friend was wearing the same clothes as the day before but was missing his socks.

Rachel picked up from where she had left off last class. "Did everyone manage to read Parmenides's *On Nature*?"

There were two distinct thuds as Jericho's shoes fell to the ground one at a time. Half of the class turned to stare as he tucked up first one bare foot and then the other into his cramped plastic chair.

At the lectern, Rachel raised her voice above the murmuring Jericho had set off. "Parmenides is in some ways the most difficult Presocratic philosopher because there is so little consensus about his work. And all we have left of him are fragments." She moved to an overhead projector in the centre of the room, where she began to arrange transparencies. "But metaphysics effectively starts with Parmenides, as well as all subsequent investigation into the differences between appearance and reality."

Stu flinched as Jericho snorted. Ahead of him, Sarah sank down lower in her seat.

"Parmenides maintained that all appearance of change is an illusion," said Rachel, flicking off the lights and projecting a translation of one of the fragments onto the screen. "We may think that things are changing, that the world is in motion around us, but Parmenides believed that knowledge gained from the senses is unreliable." She twisted a knob to bring the text into focus. "He only trusted logic. And—"

"He was right." Jericho didn't bother raising his hand. "The world is a lie. Just like all the lousy people in it." He was bristling with tension, his tone combative.

"That's interesting," said Rachel. "I wonder—"

Jericho cut her off again. "So why do we even bother?" He began smacking the surface of his desk. "War." Smack. "Famine." Smack. "Heartbreak." Smack. "Everything bad in the world has always been here and it's never going away. *Change isn't possible*."

Stu realized he was holding his breath, as were most of his classmates.

Rachel stepped away from the lectern. "That's a good point, Jericho." She was composed but watchful. "Can you elaborate?"

"Isn't it clear?" Jericho's eyes flashed with disdain. "If nothing can change, what's the point of anything?"

Rachel's eyes zigzagged over the rows of tense faces, assessing the collective patience of the rest of the class. "I think a lot of people would agree with you. Some philosophers as well."

Jericho snorted again. "Forget it," he said. "It doesn't matter anyway."

"I think it matters, Jericho," said Rachel, before segueing back into her planned lecture. "I'm glad you do, too."

As class ended, Rachel handed back a quiz and Jericho mumbled something about the grades. "I need to go see Professor Levinson," he said, blinking behind his glasses at Stu's A minus. His own test, which had received a B, lay on the edge of his desk, as though he were afraid to touch it.

"Just because I got a better grade than you?" Stu wasn't really insulted; he was relieved Jericho was talking to him.

"Not *just* because, but yes." Jericho picked up Stu's test and examined it. "Something is disordered in the universe."

"So go."

"You're coming with me." Jericho was counting up the marks allotted for each question. "She needs to look at them both in case she made a mistake."

"Thanks a lot."

"This is numerical, Stu," said Jericho. "Not personal."

Office hours started half an hour after class. As they walked over to Rachel's office, Stu said, "What was all that shouting about? That was nuts."

"Was it?" Jericho peered at him. "I want to learn what really matters. Things I can use. Like, if the Presocratics are wrong, why bother studying them?"

"I don't know, Jer. Maybe we're taking the wrong courses." A similar thought had crossed Stu's mind more than once since he'd started college, though he would never have had the nerve to express it. On the contrary, he'd worried that even thinking it was a sign he didn't belong there. "By the way, I'm sorry about what happened with Sarah. I know she still wants to be your friend."

"I know," said Jericho. All the cold contention from earlier returned to his voice. "She told me herself."

"Right, of course," said Stu. He hadn't intended to be condescending. "I'm sorry."

"You know, you've changed since we got here," said Jericho. "You're a little bit nicer now. And smarter."

Stu suspected Jericho knew he still felt guilty for the times he'd ignored him in high school or ditched him for his more popular friends. "You've changed, too, Jer," he said. Though he wasn't sure it was true.

When they arrived at Rachel's office, the door was partially open but they heard someone inside and so waited on a bench in the hallway. Stu recognized the voice of Gretchen Howe, Sarah's mother.

"I'm not saying you need to pick sides," Gretchen was saying, "but it would help to have a unified front at the meeting."

"You're talking about challenging the Chair of the department."

"He won't be the Chair forever, Rachel. And we have a duty of care to our students." Gretchen's voice got louder, as though she was pacing closer to the door. "The whole atmosphere of that party was unacceptable—the drinking, the casual innuendos. I've had enough of it, myself."

There was a pause before Rachel answered. "I don't think that codifying relationships between students and faculty is going to change anything." In the hallway, Stu felt a film of sweat on the back of his neck. "Or teach our students what we want them to learn about freedom and responsibility."

"I wonder what you'll say by the end of the year," was Gretchen's dark response. She took her leave without noticing them, striding past in a swoop of batik shawl and clattering heels.

Rachel gave them an unsteady smile as they came in.

"Is everything okay?" said Stu.

"Fine. I'm just new here." She held out her hand to take their tests. "And apparently I still have a lot to learn."

◄┤┼├►

Essays piled up as the term went on. When Stu stayed up late in the computer labs working on papers, Jericho just kept on reading, a constant fixture in their increasingly rank dorm room. Stu was grateful for the nights he played music with Truscott, though Green Screen practices had begun to require ear plugs. They had tricked-out amps and a wall of pulsing, clamorous, exhilaratingly unpredictable sound. Stu wasn't sure he liked their growing set list, but he enjoyed playing it. Jamming with Truscott felt like a kind of harmless violence, a cathartic release of all his academic anxiety.

Stu tried to joke about it with Jericho when he came home. "Truscott calls it 'texture,' but I think the technical designation is 'long-term hearing loss.'"

Jericho barely cracked a smile. He had started missing classes and, Stu felt sure, assignments.

"You okay, bud?"

His roommate spared him a dark glance. "Is it okay with you if I'm not?"

The phone rang, and when Jericho didn't react, Stu answered. It was Sarah, calling to ask if he wanted to study together. The midterm exam for Rachel's class was the next day.

"You could come to my dorm if you want. I have a single and it's quiet here." She paused. "Jericho, too, if he wants."

"I'm going to Sarah's to study," Stu said after he hung up the phone. "Do you want to come?"

"Do what you want," said Jericho, his voice frosty. "Like I care if you guys date."

"It's not like that, Jer," he said. "We're just friends. And she invited you, too."

Jericho remained silent and flipped the page.

"Suit yourself," said Stu. "See you later."

"Later," said Jericho, without looking up.

Sarah had a dorm room even though she could have lived at home. "It's a compromise with my parents, to keep me in school," she said.

"Nice," said Stu, though he was shocked by both the extravagance of the expense and the implied bribery. "I like what you've done with it." There were half a dozen thriving plants, some colourful wall-hangings, and a collage of photos mounted above her desk. Stu thought he recognized the brother she'd pointed out at the party in a few of them, but most were snapshots of young children. "Who's this bunch?" he asked, pointing.

"I'm a nanny in the summers," said Sarah. "My specialty is knock-knock jokes."

There was a picture of Sarah doing a one-legged yoga pose on some rocky ledge. Stu leaned in and saw mountains in the back-ground, a fringe of sky, her hair burnished to gold and red where it caught the sunlight. Someone had written CHOOSE across the bottom in silver marker.

"My brother took that photo," she said. "On a family trip."

"Did he write that at the bottom?" asked Stu. "Or you?"

"I did. I just thought . . ." She paused so long that at first Stu thought she had finished, until he turned and saw that she was staring off into the distance. At length, she sat down on the bedspread and said, "How do you know you're living the life you were meant to be living? You have to choose it for yourself, if you can." Her pupils were looming large as she pressed her lips together. "Think how many people never even get the chance."

When the tea was ready, they studied and ate rice crackers. Every hour or so, Sarah boiled more water while Stu went through her CD collection. They stayed up until two-thirty in the morning, quizzing each other and listening to music. After Sarah dozed off mid-conversation, Stu lay down on her couch and fell into a deep, undisturbed sleep.

The phone was ringing when Stu returned to his room the next morning, but Jericho wasn't there. It was Stu's mother.

"Where's Jericho? Karen couldn't get a hold of him last night for their usual call."

"Ma, I know that you wanted me to—"

"Look out for him," his mother finished. "You said you would."

Stu could picture his mother's honey-coloured hair and the way she sat when she talked on the phone, with her legs crossed at the ankle, leaning an elbow on the kitchen counter. She kept a pad of paper where she doodled triangles and daisies. The daisies always reminded him of squashed spiders.

"Yes, okay. I will. I promise."

Stu checked the lounge, the dining hall, the library. He headed over to the philosophy department and poked around the hallways and offices. Truscott had pinned up lime green notices for their first show on all the departmental bulletin boards: GREEN SCREEN / BIRDY'S / TONIGHT 9 P.M.: FREE YOUR MIND.

Finally, he went to class, hoping Jericho would show up for the midterm exam. Hunched over her test, Sarah caught his eye and nodded at Jericho's empty seat. Stu shrugged.

He lingered after class, shouldering his bag only once he was the last student left in the room. He approached the front as Rachel finished stacking the tests.

"Where's your friend Jericho today?" she said, slipping the pile into her satchel. He snuck a glance at its contents: a turquoise wallet, *Totality and Infinity* by Emmanuel Levinas, a Twix bar.

"I'm not sure."

"I hope everything's okay with him."

Stu wondered why all the women he knew interpreted Jericho's silence as weakness and sensitivity, rather than indifference. It wasn't so long ago that men were praised for being strong and silent.

"Me too." Stu took a step forward and his sneaker squeaked on the floor. "By the way, my new band is playing a show tonight. At Birdy's." He grinned. "Maybe you saw the posters."

Rachel ducked her head as she zipped up her bag. "Oh, I think I'll be busy marking," she said. "But thanks." Her voice was light and friendly but frosted with professional distance. Stu realized in a rush of humiliation that Rachel had zero interest in seeing his band.

"You know, I notice your husband there a lot," he said. "With other women." He left before he could take in her reaction.

Truscott's bizarre posters seemed to have worked. Birdy's was packed with his classmates. As usual, Owen was there, lingering at the back of the room with a beer in his hand. When Stu joined Truscott on stage to set up, he spotted Jericho standing in the crowd. He raised a hand in greeting but Jericho didn't acknowledge it. His friend was focused on Sarah, who was laughing at something with some girls Stu didn't know.

Stu plugged in his guitar, already feeling electric with anticipation. This time, he was only nervous that they might blow a speaker. They had practised until they had all the formations—Truscott refused to call them songs—flawlessly memorized.

Truscott counted them in, cuing his electronic drum track, and Stu scanned people's faces as they played their opening bars, as loud and discordant as a mistake. But as he and Truscott hit their stride, it became obvious that they were tight—tight and relentless and unpredictable. People were nodding their heads and rocking out to the music. Only a few people had their fingers in their ears. But everyone was watching them. Whether or not Green Screen were any good, they were at least too loud to ignore.

As they moved into the second half of the set, he saw Sarah standing with Owen at the very back of the room. Everyone had their eyes on the band, so Stu was the only one who could see that the writer's hand was on her waist.

During their second-last song, their chord progressions became more and more elaborate, multiplying and turning back on themselves like a fugue on acid. As Truscott flailed rhythmically, his red locks thrown forward in an orange blur, Stu noticed Rachel enter the bar, locate Owen, and use her tiny frame to slip through the crowd. When Rachel arrived at her husband's elbow, Owen extracted his arm in a swift movement and angled his body away from Sarah, who spotted Rachel at the same moment. Shame and disappointment flashed across his friend's face.

As they began to decrescendo the song in its extended, teasing, stutter-stop rhythm towards silence, Stu saw people turning around to stare as Rachel and Owen faced off, voices raised. Eventually, the writer pulled her away from the crowd and out of Stu's sightline. Sarah had already disappeared.

When the set was over, people clapped and whistled. Stu packed up his guitar, wiped the sweat from his forehead with the towel he'd brought, and pushed his way towards the bar for some water.

Sarah ran up to him, her face pale. She clutched at his T-shirt as though he might slip away. "Have you seen Jericho?"

"Yes, earlier. Why?"

Sarah was looking around the room as though still hoping to catch sight of Stu's roommate. "He came up to me just after your set ended and said something about the river." She was distraught. "I think he might try to hurt himself."

They ran down the dark path that Sarah said was the fastest route to the river, through a treed area where students liked to make out when the weather was nice. Further along, there were streetlamps where the path came closest to the river bend.

"If anything happens," said Sarah, sounding close to tears, "will it be my fault?" She raked her fingers through her hair in a nervous motion. "I know I was drunk, but I swear I thought I was doing a good thing. Like, maybe a little make-out session would build up his confidence, you know?"

"Tell me you didn't say that to him." As far as Stu knew, it had been Jericho's first and only kiss. "What, did you think it was going to change him into a prince or something?"

"I didn't want to lie to him." She seemed shaken by Stu's anger. "He's my friend."

"No, he's *my* friend." It came out cold. In a sick shift, Stu felt the gravity of the situation come into focus. He swallowed back the taste of bile rising in his throat. It had been hours since he'd eaten anything.

"I shouldn't have stayed over at your place. That's the real problem."

He wasn't sure if Sarah had heard him. "There!" she said, pointing. In the glow of the streetlamp, they could see where the reeds had been trampled.

Stu clambered down the slope, his sneakers sliding in the mud until his feet were in the river, his socks and shoes soaked. The water was freezing. Sarah followed more slowly, picking her way from rock to rock.

The moon was up and the water reflected its light. A few yards away, Jericho was standing in the current, just a thin shadow holding his arms up to the sky. He was still a few feet away from where the river ran deepest, but the water was already up to his waist.

Stu cupped his hands. "Jericho!" he called.

His friend turned to face him, his eyes wide and wild, his glasses missing. "We both step and do not step in the same rivers," he shouted, quoting Heraclitus. His face was twisted in anguish, stark white in the light of the moon. "We are and are not."

The river rushing past made Stu dizzy. The current was known to be swift—signs posted along the banks warned off swimmers. He took another step in and braced himself as the freezing water hit his calves, the cold registering as sharp pain shooting up and down his legs. He grabbed the branch of an overhanging tree and inched closer to Jericho.

"How long have you been standing there?" he yelled.

Jericho's teeth were chattering. "How long does it take to become a different person?"

"Jericho," Sarah yelled. "Stop scaring the shit out of us!" She had now reached the edge of the water but was facing the riverbank. "You two!" she shouted then. "Go get help!"

Stu turned and saw Owen standing on the bank, with Rachel beside him. They had come to the river path to continue their argument.

Sarah gasped as she stepped fully into the water and made her way towards Stu. "Here," she said. She'd taken off her scarf and was passing it to him, her upper body hunching convulsively against the cold. "Throw the end to him so he's got something to hold on to."

The stabbing pain in Stu's legs had already begun to subside into a dull ache. He wondered how he would keep his footing once his legs went numb. He moved further into the river's depths, keeping one hand on a branch that narrowed to not much more than a twig—a reassurance, more than a safeguard. His heart was racing, and with every step he offered up a prayer to adrenaline, hoping it would give him enough strength to reach his friend. When he thought he was close enough, he threw one end of the scarf towards him, and Jericho caught it.

Sarah screamed in exultation, and the piercing sound seemed to rouse Jericho. A sob broke from him. Hand over hand, they drew him closer to the bank, encouraging each stumbling, unwilling step back to safety.

When they got him out of the river, Jericho's clothes were dripping muddy water and his whole body was quaking. Stu gave him his jacket, and Sarah rubbed his back. By then, Rachel and Owen had returned to the riverbank with campus security and the medics.

"Thinking is a sacred disease," said Jericho, as he sat in the back of the ambulance. He was wrapped in a silvery emergency blanket and his lips were bluish. His head wobbled back and forth as he stared beyond them at something neither of them could see. "And there's no cure."

"It's a little cold for a swim." Sarah's voice was stiff and barely audible. "Why were you trying to hurt yourself?" The medics passed her an emergency blanket, and another to Stu.

"I wasn't doing anything, really," said Jericho, his gaze still wandering high above their heads, somewhere beyond them.

"You could have died," said Stu. A tremor in his own legs began as he said it. He didn't know if it was the river or fear that had turned his limbs to ice. If anything had happened to Jericho, their mothers would never forgive him. "You fucking idiot." He kicked a rock off the path and it landed in the river. "Fucking Heraclitus!" Sarah put a hand on his arm.

When he turned around, Rachel was staring at him with a pained expression. Owen's arm was around her, protective and possessive, as though there had been no fight, no flirtation, no room for doubt. The way she leaned into him, Stu realized that marriage had strength embedded in its very architecture, a resilience that beat back the usual threats. Given his parents' union, he'd always thought of marriage as something more like resignation, a contractual obligation of last resort. But he now saw the hope of it, the faith in the promise itself.

"Is he going to be all right?" asked Rachel.

"We're going to take him to the hospital," said the medic. "Make sure everything's okay. He was in there for a while."

"But was it me in there?" Jericho asked. "Or the person I used to be?"

Stu brought Sarah back to his dorm room, where they changed into dry clothes. She perched on the very edge of Jericho's bed, wrapped in Stu's comforter.

"You can lie down," he said, and Sarah inched back on the mattress. She had gone oddly quiet. "You must be tired."

When his mother answered the phone, the eagerness in her voice gave him a pang.

"Mom, call Karen."

"I'll tell her," said his mother, after he explained what had happened. "Maybe it wasn't the right time for him."

Stu said his goodbyes and hung up. "So that's done," he said. He collapsed back onto his unmade bed and slipped between the sheets. "I've never felt so exhausted."

"Would you come with me to visit him tomorrow?" said Sarah. She was still sitting up, a twitchy, staring huddle. "Maybe we could bring him something to read."

"That's a nice idea," he said, flexing his thawing feet. "You're a good friend." But when he looked back at Sarah, her cheeks were wet.

"No, I'm not," she said. "He nearly died. And it's all my fault." She squeezed her eyes shut. "And weirdly I almost get it now. What are you supposed to do with all these feelings? It's unbearable. I wish I could just clobber myself until they go away. Or, say, jump in the river."

"Don't joke about that." Stu was unnerved by the way she was rhythmically clenching her fingers into her palms. "Anyway, it's not your fault."

"How can I be sure? How can I ever be sure that something I do isn't going to turn out to be a terrible mistake? I've been so focused on my own choices, I never stopped to think about what they might mean for other people. What if I hurt someone else?" She swallowed, her eyes still closed. "Would you play something? I think it would help me calm down."

"If you like." He got out of bed and reached for his guitar. When he finished, she opened her eyes.

"Can you keep going?" She flipped up the hood on the sweatshirt she'd borrowed and leaned back on Jericho's pillows. Tears were still leaking down her face. "You know, that's the kind of thing you should play. Not like that stuff with Trus before."

"Oh?" The Green Screen set already felt like another night. "How so?"

"It's very . . . proficient." Diplomacy lingered like a stray hair on her brow. "But I couldn't really get into it. I guess I prefer songs with lyrics."

Sarah's gaze was too tender for Stu's taste. It hinted of pity. He felt a tremulousness building in his gut, the tension of an unresolved chord. He smiled so brightly that it almost felt real. "Fair enough."

"You know that stuff you played at Birdy's by yourself that first time? *That* was good." Sarah sat up again and used her sleeve to wipe her eyes. "It reminded me of Neil Young a little bit, the way you had songs in the voices of specific characters. Though I think you could try writing in your own voice, just about normal things, and that would be pretty interesting, too."

He felt the truth of what she said. After the events in the river, the night had taken on a new vibrancy. "Everything is a song in one way or another," he said.

Sarah nodded. "Just play. Please. It helps." Her eyes were closing.

A melody was starting to tease the back of his mind, as he thought about a girl's jangly laugh echoing across an alley. The patterns of frost on his bedroom window. The strong, blunt fingers of his father, shared by Stu himself. And just sitting there in quiet camaraderie with Sarah after midnight, wondering if having no map might be fine after all.

Excerpt from "Empty Grave"
Lyrics by Dove Suite

No one cares what they know
They just try to behave
Till the day they catch sight of
An empty grave

And that river rose
Oh, my river rose

And no one remembers
The promise I gave to
Keep you one step away
From your empty grave

Keep it waiting
Keep it waiting

OWEN

—

AUGUST 2020

The restaurant is a mix of diner and bistro, kitsch and chic, French and American, old and new—and at all hours of the day they serve eggs and burgers, waffles and salads, nibbles and entrees, and, from time to time, the occasional four-course tasting menu. It is all things to all people, at a low-to-medium price point. Harriet's casts a net wide enough to catch Owen, the early-morning corporate crowd, the mid-morning grannies, the old men with non-ironic moustaches, the young mums and babies, and the rest of the neighbourhood hipsters who are already more conversant with Arabica growing altitudes and avocado varietals at the age of twenty-one than Owen will ever be. Every so often, he considers finding another breakfast place that is more authentic, that is less obviously *pandering*. But the restaurant can only survive for so long, with its foie gras toast triangles and its greasy grilled cheeses, so he might as well enjoy it while he can. Though there are always lineups now.

Once he's seated, Owen awaits the server with an impatience that nettles him all the more for being unexpressed. He straightens a crease in his paper placemat, noticing at the same time that there are words on the back. He flips it over. The reverse of the placemat is for kids: a picture to colour, a maze, a tic-tac-toe grid, and a connect-the-dots puzzle with so many dots crowded together he can make out the image at once—a grinning fish with a bow tie.

Owen tries to catch the eye of his preferred waitress, while wondering if connect-the-dots is a lost art. When he was a child, there was an old book of them around the farmhouse from the forties or fifties, and he remembers doing them with his cousin, and how far apart the numbers were spaced. The pictures remained unfathomable until they began to trace lines in arcs across the page to reveal a dog, a hatching chick, a Christmas stocking. With another look at the puzzle in front of him, he wonders if he has only forgotten what it's like to be a child, how not to see at a glance the shape of an ending before you begin. Before images, ideas, events, and even people began to be as predictable as the alphabet. Maybe a child today would find this puzzle just as difficult. If only there was one near at hand he could ask.

When the waitress comes—an acerbic redhead about whom he occasionally fantasizes—she sets down a cup of coffee and confirms his regular order. Poached eggs, sourdough toast, an arugula side salad. During the first forty-three years of his life, he never ate poached eggs, and he never ate arugula, at least not on purpose, though he consumed it willingly enough if Rachel put it on his plate. But Owen, through no inclination of his own, is the recipient of a new life, a new start. Perhaps not really so new anymore, four years in, but only now does it finally feel like his own. A new apartment, new furniture. No new friends, but he has managed to keep the few he had, which is more than most men his age can say. He has a new book out that is also not really new, but it is still being talked about because of its tenacious snail's pace up the bestseller lists. It is what his agent calls a phenomenon, mainly because he can't understand how it became such a success, though Andy has alternately tried to attribute it to excellent word of mouth or, given the subject matter, existential despair. Five years ago Andy was surprised to hear from him again, but now he is busy making esoteric deals for Owen's phenomenal book that Owen barely even comprehends, like the one with the video game studio he's going to visit after breakfast.

He has a new routine, too. His small-town homebody ways from his years in Lansdowne are gone. On mornings he has appointments, Owen likes to go out for breakfast at this diner-bistro. On other days, he gets up early and goes over to Greenpoint, where he keeps his ocean shell, the same one that Rachel bought him when she still loved him, and rows out from the creek into the East River, going up and back or down and back, depending on the current. Even the river here—really a saltwater tidal strait—is more dynamic than what he's used to. It changes direction every six hours.

While he waits for his breakfast, he searches in his bag for a pencil and then traces through the dots until the fish and its bow tie are clear and defined, sealed within their own outlines.

After breakfast, Owen takes the M train into Manhattan. A mother with a small baby sits next to him. The baby is asleep in a carrier, its tiny head lolling to the side in a purple knit cap.

When Rachel decided she wanted a baby and Owen refused, she'd stayed with him anyway. She had loved him that much. And for seven years, Owen tried to be a better husband, and failed. He tried to make it up to her in other ways, and failed even worse. Of course he had. That kind of sacrifice on her part was obviously too much love. People who loved like that were bound to be disappointed.

And during those years when he was working at the marriage, he was slogging away at the novel, too. Looking back, he wonders if his ardour for one outranked the other. At any rate, only one of them was a problem that could be solved with words. His extra attentiveness to Rachel merely allowed him to track with heartbreaking precision the diminishing tenderness in her eyes when she returned home from campus every day. As time went on, he began to think of his declarations of love as an ill-conceived engineering project, like digging graves along a shoreline; they could neither withstand nor contain her sorrow, nor his growing sense that he was no longer enough for her.

He can still picture Rachel during that last month, uncommonly quiet and listless, bound to her disappointment and to him, his whole existence just an unwelcome burden. No wonder she cut him loose so fearlessly, without looking back. Ever since signing the divorce papers four years ago, she has ignored all his messages.

He understands, too, that in the grand scheme of things, he exited his marriage as a winner. He has his freedom, his savings, a career. Everything he could want except for Rachel, who has cast him out, not just from her love but from her life. He knows it is a punishment for wanting too much, for not stopping her from sacrificing her needs to his. If he had let her go when she first brought it up, when her chances of conceiving a child were still that much higher, she might never have discovered that he was cheating. They could have parted as friends.

And now that Rachel has had a baby by herself (what that means exactly, he isn't sure), his conscience has even this reprieve: that she finally has everything she wanted, in spite of him. Every so often Owen thinks about the baby—whom he knows is named Henry although he's never met him, and who is now no longer a baby but a toddler—and considers providing for him in some way: possibly a trust fund from some of the proceeds of the book, which after all he wrote while he was with Rachel, even if it was only published while they were breaking up. But he has yet to figure out the details, and Rachel continues to shut him out.

Owen only truly confronts what he has lost when he is sitting down to write, or during a rare wakeful hour in the middle of the night. The rest of the time he is careful to be preoccupied with the demands of other women, his work, the shape of his new life. He knows this is because he is a coward, and because Rachel is everything, morally, that he is not. It is what all of his books have been about, and why Owen suspects women enjoy them—they love that a man can recognize just how terrible he really is and express it on paper. It is a common human mistake: misinterpreting words for action. It is a mistake he often makes himself.

When Owen stands up to get off the train, the baby opens her eyes and stares at him, her gaze at once innocent and reproachful.

At the studio, he is greeted by Josh and Ryan, both white men in their thirties wearing glasses and superhero T-shirts. Josh has a mass of curly hair and Ryan sports a beard, details Owen absorbs for the purposes of distinguishing them.

"Great to meet you finally," says Josh, pushing his curls behind an ear.

"Love the book," adds Ryan. His beard is long and wizardish.

"Nice to meet you guys," says Owen. He has been dubious about the project ever since the studio bought the rights. His involvement was stipulated, but Andy warned him that the process might be painful.

"Just remember it's a very different medium," Andy had said. "There's got to be some give and take."

Owen tries to keep this spirit of exchange in mind as he follows Josh and Ryan down a hallway into a galley kitchen. A girl with electric blue hair offers him a soy meal-replacement drink from a fridge that appears to be exclusively stocked with identical glass bottles filled with chalky-looking liquid.

"No thanks," says Owen. She shrugs and takes one for herself.

He follows the young men into a brightly decorated and aggressively casual meeting room, where they settle around a table. Owen chooses an orange leather armchair that seems less saggy than the others, but finds himself sinking down further than expected. The blue-haired young woman is with them, though Owen has somehow missed both seeing her come in and getting her name.

"So, as you know, we've been in preproduction for a while now," says Josh of the curly hair. "We've got our own ideas we're excited to show you and some concept art, but right now the question we're wrestling with is how the player actually wins."

"Wins? By staying alive, I guess," says Owen. When nobody responds, he adds, "As in, not dying?"

Ryan shakes his head. "Not specific enough."

"Everybody dies," says the blue-haired girl. "Eventually."

"I think it *could* be enough," says Josh, considering. "But we need to complicate it."

"You're basing this on the novel, right?" Owen asks. "The plot is already laid out there."

"Sure," says Josh. "But we can't just follow the book beat by beat. It has to be interactive."

"It's about agency," says Ryan. He spreads his hands out on the table and Owen can see he is wearing a series of dark metal rings shaped like dragons. "People want the illusion of control. They want to feel like their choices are meaningful, even if they're not."

"So, like life, then," says Owen.

"Exactly," says Ryan, as though Owen has not made a little joke, or possibly the joke is so little that no one deems it worth acknowledging.

"In real life, the best way to survive a plague is to be alone," Owen offers. "Just go off somewhere away from other people."

"But that doesn't make for a very interesting game," says Ryan.

"Well, that's what David does," says Owen. "In the book."

"That's not all he does," says the girl, tapping a pen on her notepad.

Josh stands up and moves over to a wall-mounted whiteboard. "Okay, so part of the goal is to be the last man standing." With a dry-erase marker, he writes LAST MAN STANDING. "And maybe something else. Maybe something harder?"

The girl tries again. "Well, the kids are the ones getting sick. That's the heart of the book, isn't it? The player character should have to save as many kids as possible. That's the challenge."

Josh points the uncapped marker at Owen. "Tell us more about the player character. The main character, I mean. David."

"He's a science teacher," says Owen. "A microbiologist by training. He's overqualified for his job, but a lifelong learner. And he has an interest in pandemics, kind of as a hobby, so he's able to guess what's happening a little sooner than everyone else."

"So he puts it together himself," says Josh.

"Not all by himself. But he has the opportunity of seeing things unfold up close. And, like I said, he takes an interest. He tracks the warnings coming out of the World Health Organization and the Centers for Disease Control." Owen takes out his phone. "They post health advisories and alerts of new infection clusters worldwide." He pulls up the CDC page and starts reading out the titles of some of the bulletins. "*Salmonella Outbreak in Utah; Pneumonic Plague in Madagascar; Mystery Virus Being Investigated in New York City.*"

"New York? Look out," says Ryan. "It's starting."

Josh laughs.

"Huh," says Owen. The conversation continues around him while Owen clicks on the advisory, posted just that morning.

August 10, 2020: Twenty-eight reported cases including four deaths attributed to a suspected coronavirus in Manhattan. Unidentified respiratory virus with possible airborne infection. Foodborne pathogen ruled out. All surviving patients hospitalized, with one-third in critical condition.

"You still with us, Owen?"

"Yes," says Owen, putting down his phone.

"I think . . ." begins the girl, clearing her throat.

"So I'm thinking we should have an ongoing tally," says Josh, "of how many kids he saves. That'll be part of it."

"Right, great," says Owen. "That makes sense."

The girl with blue hair gets up with a glare of loathing and leaves the room. Josh and Ryan exchange a puzzled glance.

Owen turns his attention to Josh's scattered scrawls on the whiteboard. If they have been working on the project for months, how are they only just now having these sorts of conversations? He says something to this effect.

"We usually do the story last around here," says Ryan. "It's the fastest part."

Josh, perhaps catching Owen's look of alarm, says quickly, "The VR environment build isn't quite ready, but if you come back next Monday, I'm sure we'll have something to show you that will really knock you out."

Though he's unsure of what he is being told, Owen nods. A visible relief permeates the room.

Afterwards, Owen catches the subway, gets a seat near the door. Standing close by is a twenty-something model-thin blonde, chic in jeans and a white T-shirt. Then a woman sitting opposite catches his attention: a fiftyish brunette with a battered briefcase and terrible fashion sense, totally absorbed in a highbrow, prize-winning novel that until as recently as last week outranked *How to Avoid the Plague* on the *New York Times* bestseller list. Almost certainly an academic. But he appreciates the seriousness of her face, the slight flare of her nostrils as she frowns at the page. Her lack of self-consciousness as she shifts in her seat, sending the lower flounces of her tiered jade skirt cascading over the feet of the next passenger. Women are always surprised to discover that Owen has a very expansive sense of the beautiful. Younger women in their twenties and thirties. Older women in their forties and fifties. Every woman is a secret waiting to be unlocked. And the key, the tantalizing key, is sex, and the means of getting it.

With an intellectual like the brunette sitting across from him, Owen's conversational gambit might be something about the inadequacy of reason in the face of primal urges. It was a tactic that worked before, and had the advantage of being something he actually believed. Owen would lean in, and at a certain attentive moment would run his index finger over an inch of her wrist and contend that it is neither laughter, planning, nor cooperation that define humanity. Rather, a Cartesian project of mind and body separation has undermined the unity of how human beings see themselves, to their detriment. Owen would muse, as if for the first time, that the culture is only sex-obsessed because it is essentially prudish, and that sex is human and natural and not to be controlled or repressed—in fact, the instincts they share with the so-called lower orders are valuable and profound. Though it was also possible, Owen would acknowledge to her, with a longing and complicit glance, that he was just rationalizing.

The subway car slows and lurches as it enters the station, and Owen sees the blonde coughing into her hand. Then she grabs at the pole to steady herself before hurrying through the doors, leaving behind a smear so wet it seems to sparkle under the light.

He stares at the smear, then gets off at the next stop and starts walking the fifteen blocks to his apartment, trying to avoid thoughts of the mystery virus. When he stops at an intersection, he pulls out his phone and sends a message to Edith. He knows she would prefer to be called Ed, which he finds absurd, so he avoids calling her anything at all. *I need you*, he writes. *Do you have time this afternoon?* He might as well meet her; the day has been squandered and he's too agitated to write, anyway.

By the time he gets home, Edith has written back: *Okay.* When he sees her response, he gets into his car rather than going inside. He tries to avoid driving in the city, but the train ride has unnerved him.

Edith is a good example of Owen's comprehensive taste in women. She is of average height, average prettiness, though with a nice body and an intelligent face. She is of Asian heritage, a fact he notes only for his record, which is diverse. They met at a book signing ten weeks ago. She was a fan and made that fact known. He made it known in turn that he found her attractive. The normal things ensued. Then an abnormal thing ensued: a repetition of the normal things, over and over again, with Edith.

In his old life, he would have avoided repeat encounters with the same woman to protect his relationship with Rachel. But one irony of his divorce is that he is still a liar, except now he tells women he is married in order to protect his solitude. Rachel left behind a space in his life, and Owen doesn't want it filled by anyone else. And Edith does not require seduction, only satiation. It is simply more efficient to continue sleeping with her rather than spend time pursuing more conquests. It is a conservation of energy. It is good for the planet.

He is meeting Edith at a motel he found online. He has asked her to get a room, though he will of course pay her back. It is an elaborate ruse, as well as an indulgence. And though it is a bit ridiculous, the pretence gives him a rush—one he chooses not to examine too closely in case it gives off a hint of his own sexual neuroses, which are bound to be as small and sad as everyone else's.

At the motel, Edith is stunning and tremulous in her desire. He usually talks dirty to her when they are together—it is his secret gift, this filthy commentary—but this time he is silent, which seems to bother her. But he likes her better when she is bothered.

The sex is hot, spectacularly so. It is one for the ages, like something out of a porno, except that, as usual, Edith refuses to perform or accept oral sex. Nevertheless, he knows how to make her come.

When they drive away from the motel, he steels himself for the inevitable conversation.

"Do you want to get something to eat?" she asks. "I'm starving."

"I have to go home and write," he says. He is technically in the middle of a new novel, though its progress is slow. "I'll drop you at the subway." He never drives her all the way home.

"Cool," she says, turning to gaze out the window.

Edith is not the kind of girl he could love. Woman. Whatever. She exists too much on the surface, like most young people. She conceals nothing, keeps nothing back. If she has an inner life, it is as thin as a magazine. She thinks she can get to know him by quizzing him. He does admire her seeming independence and her willingness to go after what she wants even with minimal encouragement. At the same time, he wishes they could dispense with these exchanges. She talks about books she reads and asks him for recommendations. (He declines.) Then she begins filling the silence with talk of her life, her summer class, her waitressing job, and her boss, a conceited, foolish sort of man. The kind of man who is so small, in his vanity, that he is actually beneath them to mock. Owen resents that Edith does not understand this, and that certain details about this man have become etched in his brain. His variable accent. His waxed moustache. Now she is telling him that health inspectors have visited the restaurant.

"And, like, more than just health inspectors are coming tomorrow. Some government people. I think it's actually going to be on the news." She looks over at him, her face so eager and animated that he cannot help but stare back. "Mystery virus," she says, over-enunciating.

Owen's ears, which he was willing closed, now pop open. He can hear his own breathing over the muted rumbling of the car and the traffic. "I think I may have read about it, earlier today," he says.

"Well, it all started with us, if you can believe it. They thought it was food poisoning at first, but not anymore."

"Did you serve the people who got sick?"

Edith seems not to catch the severity of his tone, or maybe she thinks it is born out of a natural concern for her well-being.

"Maybe." She is nonchalant. "I mean, I was working the night they've been asking about. But I don't know who got sick, or if they were at any of my tables or not."

If the traffic wasn't so bad, he would pull over. It is almost too much, the day's relentless insinuation of the virus upon his consciousness. But logical enough, he supposes, given his book. It is his own work that has invited the conversations. His back stiffens and his hands tighten on the steering wheel. This she notices. After the past couple of months, Edith is attuned to his body in ways that keep surprising him.

"I'm not sick!" she exclaims. "God, relax." Then she laughs. "You would definitely already have it by now, if I was." Her eyes are teasing, sexy, inviting him to laugh with her, but all he can manage is a grimace.

When he gets home, he turns on his computer and visits the CDC site again. The infection alert is still there, and seeing it in larger type makes it even more horrifying and unreal. The urge to shower again crawls over his skin like a spreading rash.

Shoulders twitching, he logs into NextExtinction.com, an online forum he joined when he was researching his previous book. Back then he logged in daily, posting comments and asking questions like any survivalist newbie trying to learn the ropes. He found the best places to buy N95-rated face masks and other protective gear. He followed links to sites that sold crates of canned goods and bottled water at deep discounts. Owen even learned how to buy bitcoin and access the dark web to purchase antiviral medications in bulk, though he was too uncomfortable with the idea to actually try. In the end, he came away with a handful of useful details for the book and an uneasy acquaintance with the culture of fear.

He shares the CDC alert in a new thread on the disease monitoring board, adding that he has heard about it first-hand from someone who was at the initial infection site.

Someone he used to chat with messages him almost immediately. Unlike some of the right-wing kooks on the forum, GERTIEBIRD is a kind soul who only recently rejoined society after dropping out in the seventies. She posts tips on the proper way to use water purification tablets, and how to build a natural shelter out of native Californian trees, and other bits of off-grid advice relevant to the interests of a fringe group of paranoid internet users.

\<GERTIEBIRD\>

I hope you and your friend are doing okay. Still feeling well?

\<GRANTER\>

I think we're infection-free for now, thanks.

\<GERTIEBIRD\>

Are you feeling lucky? You should buy a lottery ticket.

\<GRANTER\>

Quite the opposite, actually.

\<GERTIEBIRD\>

But think of the odds. You've already had a brush with the virus, and you're fine.

<GRANTER>

Might be too soon to tell.

<GERTIEBIRD>

Maybe. But I have a good feeling about you. You like dogs, right?

Owen reminds himself that he is talking to an actual nut—a lucid nut as far as nuts go, but a nut all the same. A few of GERTIEBIRD's posts suggest she spent decades believing herself a survivor of a nuclear blast, afraid to emerge from hiding for fear of capture or radiation.

<GRANTER>

I used to have a dog, when I was growing up.

<GERTIEBIRD>

See? I thought so. You're an animal person.

<GRANTER>

Is that supposed to mean something?

<GERTIEBIRD>

No. Except that maybe you're sympathetic to the forces at play . . .

<GRANTER>

You're going to have to spell it out for me, Gert.

<GERTIEBIRD>

These viruses usually come from animals, don't they? Usually when their habitat is under threat from humans. That can't be a coincidence.

<GRANTER>

Ah.

<GERTIEBIRD>

Mother Earth is trying to restore some balance. Stop global warming and overpopulation. Maybe it's a battle we're going to lose? I don't know.

\<GRANTER\>

So we die, she wins? I thought this site was about us winning instead?

\<GERTIEBIRD\>

You think so? I ended up here after I first came out of the forest. It was a place for me to connect after being alone for so long. It showed me how people could cope with their fear and how I could help by sharing what I know. I think it's a nice group of folks, overall.

Owen wants to laugh. Only the most deluded Pollyanna could imagine the survivalists of NextExtinction.com as altruistic. If they are ever generous to one another, it is only from a sense of allegiance to their shared paranoid ideologies. They are nothing more than a self-selected community of outcasts.

Before Owen logs off, he checks his original post. A user named FLUDAD, one of the site's most active members, has written a response. If FLUDAD's posts can be believed, he has a bona fide bunker completely stocked with six months' worth of supplies and equipped with its own ventilation and water treatment systems. He used to be a moderator over at MushroomCloudPreppers.net. Once he was finished preparing for nuclear war, he started to consider the implications of a new strain of bird flu.

Checking with my man Li in China, Jorg in Germany, and a few other people I know in research around the country. We'll get some answers soon.

FLUDAD's email signature is *Buy more ammo!*

Just as Owen is about to turn off the computer, he thinks better of it and instead sends a message to Rachel: *I know I'm the last person you want to hear from, but I'm worried about you and Henry. Keep a close eye on this new virus, okay?*

Owen stays in that evening, eats leftovers out of his fridge. When he gets a text from Edith, he ignores it for an hour before asking her again to send him a photo of her breasts. One of these days she's going to give in and send one. But when she suggests meeting up instead, he jerks off and goes to sleep.

The next morning, he wakes up with the notion of the virus still vexing him, like a sentence left unfinished. He gets up, goes to the bathroom, then moves around his apartment without a clear sense of purpose. He feels the call of the water and the urge to lose himself in something rhythmic and mind-emptying, but the rowing club has been inhospitable of late.

He'd underestimated the women. The club is close-knit, its members all neighbours, friends, confidantes. He slept with one too many and now when he shows up he can sense a current of hostility thrumming like a transformer as soon as he walks through the door. Once women talk amongst themselves, there is not much room for someone like him to manoeuvre.

Opening the fridge, he takes out the orange juice and pours himself a glass. He ought to work on the new manuscript but knows he is too tense. Without his scull, he doesn't know what to do for exercise. He doesn't want to have to find someplace new to go.

After his split with Rachel, he'd tried to stay in Lansdowne. He was still teaching an advanced fiction workshop once a week and co-supervising an honours thesis, so he rented an apartment near campus. But most of their mutual friends had shunned him, either passively or actively, and after the ex-boyfriend of a student he'd slept with spoke to the Chair of the English department, there began to be rumblings that a spousal hire who was no longer technically a spouse might not belong on campus anymore. So he'd left, before more of the women started talking and before the bureaucratic bomb could blow up in his face. But it is an uneasy thought always lurking at the edge of his mind: that there is a whole town in America where Owen is *persona non grata*.

He quells the rowing urge with a few sets of push-ups, making a mental note to order some new weights. Then he finds himself sticking close to home, monitoring the news and the chatter on NextExtinction. com. As the only active forum member in NYC, he is the subject of more than a few unsolicited messages either asking how many weeks of non-cook food he has laid by or urging him to get out of town. When Owen goes silent on the thread, FLUDAD posts a notice asking people to lay off GRANTER and stand by for more information.

Once the message board quiets down and he gets into a good groove with one of his chapters, Owen tells himself this is why he's staying in. To get some work done. He tells himself the same thing the next day. And the next.

The following Monday, Owen drives back to the gaming studio, braving horrific crosstown traffic and forking out an exorbitant sum to park in a lot three blocks away.

This time, the meeting feels like a pitch. There are more people in the room, most of them projecting a youthful vibe accentuated by jeans and pop-culture T-shirts. The blue-haired girl is nowhere to be seen. Owen keeps his hands in his pockets throughout the introductions, nodding at each new face, realizing that he is old enough to not even believe he was supposed to stay young. He takes a seat at the far end of the table and accepts a maple-flavoured soy meal-replacement drink, making a note to mention the product on the message board.

Curly-haired Josh starts the meeting and thanks Owen for his input to date. He takes him through a quick slideshow of some background artwork samples, then brings them back to a discussion of gameplay.

"So we were trying to think about what's different with this IP in particular."

"IP?" says Owen. There are a lot of acronyms flying by.

"Intellectual property. I mean, it's not the first disease game, not by a long shot." Josh nods towards the other end of the room, which has been cleared for a demonstration. "We've got something novel with the VR, but we want the goal to be more than just evasion."

"I can't help it if that's what happens in the book," says Owen.

"Of course not," says Josh. "But our job is to make it entertaining. Playable." He shoots a look at his colleague, who stands up. "Over to Ryan for part two."

"Well, we've got the kids he's saving," says Ryan, taking Josh's place in front of the meeting table. "That's great. But we want to complicate the mechanics in another way," he adds. "Morally."

Owen waits, as it is clear they are leading up to a talking point. He sees a few of the team members exchanging glances.

One of the older guys says, "We're thinking the player character will have access to an arsenal and the ability to add to it, but they will also have a humanity bar tracking them. If they do good, their humanity meter goes up."

"And violence lowers it," says Owen.

Ryan is watching his face. "Do you see where we're going with this?"

"Guns?" says Owen, feeling the start of a dull headache. "You want there to be shooting."

"Well, it's more active, for one," says Ryan. "I guess the question is whether you can see your guy doing that. If necessary. Let's say his family is threatened."

"Maybe," says Owen. "I guess I could see that."

"Then once he collects the children, he'll have to find enough money to buy the boat and make his way out to the water."

"Maybe he fights his way through some panicked citizens?" suggests someone else.

"Look," says Owen. "I'm not going to be okay with random murder, under any circumstances."

"Noted," says Ryan. He grins. "Thanks for being such a good sport about this."

"We'll show you the environment we're working on," says Josh, possibly to change the subject. He goes over to the desk on the far side of the room and holds up a large black headset. "Showtime."

Everybody gets up and pushes in their chairs. Josh gestures to Owen to go first.

"Can we wipe it down?" says Owen when he gets close. "Can't be too careful."

Josh shrugs. "Sure." He puts the headset back on the desk and rubs it all over with an antibacterial wipe.

"Sorry," says Ryan. "He was supposed to do that anyway."

Ryan and Josh both help Owen put on the headset, which completely covers his eyes, and a large set of headphones that engulf his ears. And all at once it is dark. Owen blinks and finds himself outside. It is nighttime, the darkness softened by streetlamps. He looks to the left and sees grey concrete scrabbled with graffiti. Owen steps forward and knocks into something invisible. The pain, in its incongruity, disappears for a moment but throbs back as though coming from far off, just like the suppressed chuckles he can hear in the real world.

"Sorry," he hears faintly, followed by the sound of a desk chair rolling away. "Meant to move that."

He is in an alleyway. A puddle ahead of him reflects the moon. When he tilts back his head, he can see it rising high above him, bright and cold, in a sliver of sky between buildings trimmed with fire escapes. In the distance are the sounds of sirens and traffic. And much closer, a whimpering. Owen turns the other way and sees someone huddled in the alley, crouched beside a dumpster. A child. A little boy, by the looks of it. Just about the age of Rachel's son. He takes a small step in his direction, feeling queasy as the scene zooms forward more quickly than expected.

Breaking into his dream, he hears an instruction from Ryan: "Just move slowly. You've got lots of room."

He hears the echo of his own footsteps, mismatched to his own stuttering pace. He is a soul in a new body, struggling to take control. And the little boy is ahead of him, still whimpering. Not looking up. As Owen draws closer to the child's hiding spot, he feels a chill spreading across his shoulders and the overwhelming urge to speak to him.

When Owen is a foot or two away, the area around the boy begins to glow. He can make out a striped T-shirt and grimy arms and legs. The boy's face is buried in his knees. As Owen reaches out to the boy, the soundscape changes abruptly. He can hear panicked shouts and footsteps approaching. He takes a step backwards before stretching a hand out to steady himself on the dumpster, but his fingers pass through and he stumbles to the side. There are the sounds of helicopters and approaching sirens, and a distant wailing, as if of the bereaved, overlaid above the boy's uninterrupted sobs. Owen knows he is supposed to act, to make a choice, but he feels nothing but a conviction that something bad will happen no matter what he decides. That he is forever doomed to do the wrong thing. He resists the frozen terror of his body by closing his eyes and reflexively starting to push upward on the headset. Almost at once, he hears flustered voices and feels other hands reaching to help remove the expensive equipment.

"That was fast," says someone.

"Were you dizzy?" says Josh. "That can happen."

"Was it like seeing the future?" asks Ryan, grinning.

Owen shakes his head. He feels alien and adrift, like a shaman coming out of a trance. He mutters something about being late, exchanges dazed goodbyes with the development team, and finds himself sitting in an armchair in the lobby, hunched over and with his head in his hands, before he has even processed leaving the room.

He exhales slowly, trying to calm down. The developers are probably upstairs laughing at him, a middle-aged man freaked out by five minutes of a game prototype. He'll send them a note later, when his heart stops racing and the queasy, light-headed panic has ebbed away.

He pulls out his phone to do something that feels normal and sees that he has a notification from the NextExtinction.com board. FLUDAD has revived the thread about the mystery virus, and forty-four messages have been posted within the last hour.

Heard back from my friends. I think this is it, folks. There's a province in China with a weird flu. Practically a whole orphanage of kids infected. Same symptoms, insanely contagious. All the nurses and doctors who've gone in are sick now. No official word yet but you can bet the WHO is tracking where all the NYC patients have been recently.

Buy more ammo!

Then, in his next post, FLUDAD has shared the link to a new advisory from the CDC, citing over two hundred new cases logged at hospitals across New York's five boroughs. The Department of Health is urging anyone with direct exposure to an infected patient to self-quarantine and report themselves to authorities.

Another user has posted a computer simulation of a pandemic spreading across global networks. To Owen, it looks like a firework exploding in slow motion.

Many of the messages are addressed to Owen directly, asking what he plans to do or requesting that he keep everyone updated. In the absence of any immediate response from GRANTER, a number of users have taken it upon themselves to suggest what he ought to do, or what they would do in his situation. All in all, Owen has never seen the users of NextExtinction.com quite so worked up. He suspects it is not only the dreadful excitement of a potential Big One, but the idea that they have pieced it together themselves. They are, if not ahead of the WHO, then at least in step with them.

Owen writes another quick message to Rachel: *You don't need to write back, but I'm getting more information that this virus could be really bad. Please take care.* He gets back in his car and drives out across the bay to Rockaway Beach, where he knows there is a marina. He and Rachel saw it once, not long after they got together, when they walked the boardwalk hand in hand and ate fish tacos and were happy together in a simple, summer way.

He parks the car in the first spot he finds, anxious to stretch his legs. When he finds the marina, it looks just the same as it did all those years ago when he was with Rachel, though this seems impossible given how hard the whole area was hit by Hurricane Sandy. There is a sign on the side of the main building that says *Berths & Storage, Rentals, Repairs, Hands-on Training.*

Owen opens the door and goes in. "I need private sailing lessons," he says to the man behind the desk. "Intensive. With your best instructor." He pauses while the man glances up at him, slow and wary. "Money is no object," he adds, feeling foolish as he says it.

The man puts down the magazine he is holding. "We don't really do that here anymore," he says. "Maybe you'd be better off in the Hamptons."

Owen suspects the man has taken a dislike to him, and wonders if he is refusing lessons out of some secret anti-elitist sentiment. Lingering by the door, he considers pressing the issue but worries that if he angers the man, something bad will happen. Paranoia pulses around his every decision now. Owen puts his hand on the doorknob, almost as unnerved by the irrationality of his own thought process as by the thoughts themselves.

"Thank you," he says. "I'll do that." He will do that. Owen thinks about the firework exploding in New York City. How long might he have before one of its sparks rains down to touch him with its tongue of fire?

He walks away, longing to check his phone again but afraid of seeing the latest virus update. Afraid that if he looks, he knows what he'll find. Afraid that if he thinks it, it will happen.

"No," he says aloud. He's just being spun around by too much information. Running his fingers through his hair, he forces himself to breathe slowly and sort through what he knows. He is not overreacting—he is reacting appropriately, given the facts. Also, he is not thinking magically. He is thinking rationally. Though he isn't entirely put at ease by his own assertions.

He continues along the boardwalk, which has been repaired since the hurricane. The storm came and battered the shore, destroying buildings and livelihoods. But the storm was forecast, and people who were sensible and had the resources to leave the city planned accordingly and left. There was nothing magical about reading the signs in that case.

With the water at his back, Owen heads away from the beach, keeping an eye open for any familiar landmarks he might recognize from that day with Rachel. The bench where they kissed, scandalizing a group of tourists, or the neighbourhood bar where Rachel was thrilled by the tiny piña coladas in Styrofoam to-go cups.

He hopes Rachel is happy now. Of the two of them, she was always better at being happy, though he had perhaps benefitted from lower expectations. He knows that happiness is not a state of being. It is a knack. It is like hitting a baseball or skating backwards; there are certain tricks to it that some people can never master. A Buddhist he had sex with once told him that "desire is suffering," but Owen has considered it and is sure she was wrong. Desire is electric. It is what keeps him alive.

What else is there? Only denial, which is death.

A few blocks inland, set between a surf boutique and a taco hut, he comes upon a squat concrete building painted turquoise that seems like some contractor's idea of what he could get away with. A neon hand glows pink in the window, above a crystal ball next to a hand-lettered sign that says *Sister Francesca's Cosmic Consultations*. A magic shop. It strikes him as a fitting rebuke for his own irrationality. As he pauses in front of the door, a woman opens it and emerges from inside.

"You look lost," she says.

"Oh," says Owen. "No." He turns his hands over in a vague motion to acknowledge that he does appear lost, tarrying there and staring off into the distance. The people waiting in line at the taco hut are talking and laughing in a way that seems incongruous with an impending pandemic. "Just trying to decide what to do next."

"Do you want to come in and get your bearings?" The woman is leaning up against the doorframe. She is wearing tight black jeans and a black leather motorcycle jacket crisscrossed with silver zippers.

"Are you Sister Francesca?"

She makes a dismissive gesture, either implying that she *is* Francesca or that it is absurd that he should think so.

"I'm Owen," he says. She rolls her eyes at him and disappears inside the shack.

He estimates the chances are at least even that something might happen between them, and this surge of confidence feels normal, much more normal than anything else he has been thinking all week. Keen to endorse that version of reality, he follows her inside.

When the door swings shut behind him, it is so dark that it takes his eyes a moment to adjust to the candlelight. The whole place is not much larger than a garage, and the walls are draped with red velvet curtains. Then the woman steps towards him and her hands, strong and cool, are on his wrists, pressing him into a seat. She sits down in a chair opposite him, across a small wooden table. She is wearing long earrings now and her hair is covered with a scarf. Her eyebrows are thick, pointed, and dark. She appears like another person entirely, and the effect has been brought about so quickly he almost feels as though he has been plunged into another virtual reality.

"Just so you know," she says, "this is for entertainment purposes only."

He must seem puzzled, because she adds, "Fortune-telling is illegal in the state of New York." Her face is arch. "Except for entertainment."

"I am definitely only looking for entertainment," he says.

"Good. Tea, palm, or cards?" she asks. There is a sideboard nearby with a teapot, a kettle on a hot plate, and several china teacups.

Owen has no desire to drink any concoction brewed in this witch's shack. "Cards, I guess." He hopes she will hurry through the charade. The novelty is already gone and he feels only a growing shame to be in here with her at all.

She takes one of his hands and passes it above a pack of cards she has produced from somewhere. Then she withdraws a card from the deck and sets it on the table between them. It has a knight with a chalice on it.

"Tell me about your parents," she says, still holding the rest of the cards.

"I thought you were supposed to tell me things?" She narrows her eyes at him. "Fine, my parents," he says. He has not spoken to anyone about his childhood in so long, not to anyone except Rachel, that he has no idea how to do it. "They were good people. Decent, church-going." Both of his parents are dead. They died of cancer before he got divorced, within a year of each other. He has a vision of Rachel at their funerals, wan and tear-streaked, her arm linked through his. It makes him ache for her plain, kind touch.

"And you're not."

Somehow he doesn't think she's asking if he goes to church. "No, I'm not."

She puts down the cards and takes his right wrist, turning it to expose his palm and pressing his hand upon the table.

"Hey," says Owen. Her grip is strong. He came into this hut hoping for a distraction, for some sort of contact to make him forget about his fear of contagion, but the touch he is receiving is entirely unwanted.

"There's something wrong with you," she says. Her finger is tracing a line he can't see. "Something that you need to fix." The woman pokes him in the centre of his palm and the jab zings straight into his brain.

He does understand now—in a profound way he did not before Rachel left—that there is something wrong with him and the things that he does. But he cannot stop himself. Right now it is too difficult to stop. Right now it is enough that he is a person who understands that there is something wrong with the things he is doing. He has to believe that. If he didn't believe in his own redemption, he thinks he would implode from the inside, like a potato in a microwave, with all his excuses just as bland, middling, and half-baked. Most days he does not enjoy being himself anymore, now that he can no longer pretend to be the man that Rachel believed him to be.

"So what should I do?"

The woman's face twitches as though the question has startled her. Owen will think about this moment later, many times in fact, wondering why he listened and why she seemed to know what he was asking before he did. And how even if she was only trying to frighten him, it was as though she were offering him some kind of salvation.

The woman's lips have fallen open. Her eyes are as dark and impenetrable as the future.

"You should stay away," she says. "Stay away from them."

September 9, 2020, 2:24 p.m.

Hi. This is Owen. Leave me a message and I'll call you back.

[beep]

Owen. It's Dory. Colleen and I have been trying to get a hold of you for over two weeks now. I know you're busy, but we've missed out on *Late Night* and the *Today* show, and God knows what else. You're turning Shillelagh into a joke and making it impossible for Colleen to do her job. And Julia is extremely pregnant, in case you've forgotten, so I've got bigger things on my mind right now. What is going on with you? Call me back. I mean it.

SARAH

—

SEPTEMBER 2020

When she finally got to the office, Sarah slunk past the receptionist and straight into her cubicle, where she deposited her face mask and transit gloves into a desk drawer. Swabbing her sweaty face with a tissue, she once again regretted sleeping in. Noah was not a child who was easily hurried, which meant another hour of daycare money down the drain, only to be followed by the resentful glares of those dried-up crones who thought interrupting snack-time was like starting World War Three.

Snack-time reminded her of the turkey sandwich in her purse, so she got up and put it in the staff fridge before filling a tall glass of water from the cooler.

The phone in her cubicle was ringing when she got back.

It was her boss, Dory. "Where were you? I've been calling all morning." In the ten years Sarah had worked at Shillelagh Press, Dory had risen from senior editor to publishing director and finally to vice-president—a figure of fearsome competence who responded to all urgent messages in five minutes or less. "Never mind. Can you meet me in the upstairs break room in five minutes?"

Dory's summons were often abrupt. Sarah slipped first one foot then the other out of her sneakers and into her cherry-red work pumps, feeling something swell and throb in her head as she leaned forward. Last night's celebration of the end of Elliot's quarantine had gone later than expected. "Maybe I should respond to a few emails first?" She clicked open her inbox and saw the usual smattering of messages she felt little interest in answering.

Her boss snorted. "Just get up here."

Dory always preferred their tête-à-têtes to take place in private, as though on guard against any accusation of playing favourites. She had hired Sarah at a time when the only entry on her resumé was "part-time nanny on a Bolivian commune," but Sarah thought the precaution was silly: she'd never even been given so much as a promotion. The only reason her former sister-in-law had offered her a job in the first place was to get Sarah out of her and Elliot's apartment, where she'd been crashing since she'd returned to the States.

"Thank goodness," said Dory, handing her a latte from the automatic espresso machine. "I needed to see a friendly face." She was wearing a houndstooth skirt and buttoned blazer, with black-framed glasses that had slid partway down her nose. Even in three-inch stacked heels, she was shorter than Sarah.

"What's the matter?" asked Sarah. It wasn't often that Dory appeared vulnerable or expressed an emotion beyond mild annoyance or impatience with the world at large. "Is everything okay with Julia?"

"Jules is eerily calm for someone who is eight months pregnant, but I feel like one of us ought to be worried. So I guess it has to be me?" Dory sat down at the table and motioned for Sarah to join her. "Honestly, I feel like I can't win. *How to Avoid the Plague* is back on bestseller lists thanks to this horrible virus and ARAMIS Girl, and Owen Grant has chosen this moment to go AWOL. Doesn't want the attention."

Sarah took a sip of her latte and scalded her mouth. "That doesn't sound like the Owen Grant I used to know."

Dory's eyes popped a little, then narrowed. "You've met? How did I not know this?"

"I only knew him a bit, back when I was a freshman in college and he was a visiting writer." Sarah shook her head, nursing her sore tongue. "It was almost nothing. A flirtation, I guess." Owen's then-wife had been her professor. Sarah remembered being surprised, at the time, to discover they were married, then less surprised, years later, to find out they'd divorced. Of all the things from her youth that she regretted, she felt perhaps the most shame for how thoughtlessly she'd accepted Owen's attention as no more than her due, the just reward of somebody young and beautiful. "Anyway, what happened to Colleen?" Colleen was the senior publicist, who up until now had handled everything to do with Owen Grant.

"There seems to be some problem with Colleen." Dory frowned. "Or with Owen. It's not working." She spun sideways in her chair and stretched out her legs, rotating each foot in turn as though her ankles might be sore. "I warned her not to fall for his act . . . at least not until he agreed to a good dozen or so events. And now he won't even return my calls."

A woman carrying an empty mug poked her head into the break room and Dory turned to glare at her. "Occupied," she snapped. "Five minutes." When the woman retreated, Dory got up and locked the door behind her. Twice she opened her mouth as though to say something before closing it again. It wasn't like her to leave silences in a conversation.

"Do you want *me* to try with Owen?" Sarah asked.

Dory looked almost as surprised by the offer as Sarah was to have made it. She straightened her glasses. "Oh, I didn't mean to suggest you needed to—honestly, I'm not sure what you could do."

"Yeah, of course." Sarah let out a breath she'd been holding and watched as Dory paced the room. Then her boss stopped in front of her and crossed her arms.

"But it could be an amazing opportunity for you," Dory said slowly, seeming to scrutinize her. "And it would really help me out."

Sarah swallowed, wondering if Owen would even remember her. "Then I'm happy to do it." Encouraged by Dory's growing enthusiasm, she added, "And remember when you asked me about reading manuscripts? I think I'm finally ready."

"Sarah! That was years ago." Dory drew back, then returned to her seat and leaned forward across the table. "Look, part of the reason I called you up here was to brainstorm how to keep you on. They're canning your current position."

"Oh." Somehow, in spite of her best intentions, Sarah always seemed to coast under the office radar, while everyone else was moving on, getting ahead. *Glorified intern*, she thought with a sudden clarity. And then, *So what?* Publishing wasn't exactly a growth industry, although she'd thought that with the latest spike of infections in New Jersey, a few positions might have opened up.

"But you taking on Owen Grant's publicity could solve everything," said Dory. "As long as you watch yourself with him. Seriously, though. No more broken hearts allowed at Shillelagh."

Sarah was already regretting her offer to help. "So what exactly am I supposed to do? Owen's already been profiled everywhere." She was sure she'd seen a think piece about *How to Avoid the Plague* and the tortuous relationship between fiction and reality in a recent issue of *The New Yorker*. "And I've been doing my part on the subway this month, wearing my kit." Her transit gloves and face mask were among the thousands that Shillelagh Press had purchased and branded as promotional tie-ins for Owen Grant's novel after the official federal advisory of the virus was announced in mid-August. A Shillelagh Precaution Kit, as they were marketed, came free with the purchase of every copy of Owen's book, and sold separately for $4.99 on the company's website, undercutting the drugstores. There had been the predictable social media backlash against the cynicism of the marketing plan, but Dory had insisted they weather it out and her gamble seemed to have paid off. These days, Sarah estimated three-quarters of the people on her morning train wore personal protective gear, and at least half of those were Shillelagh-branded. She'd even given Elliot a few sets last night as a get-out-of-quarantine present.

Dory sighed. "It's only going this well while ARAMIS is making people nervous. And it would be better not to have the company's fortunes tied irrevocably to a global pandemic, don't you think? We don't want every sale tied to the outbreak. We have to assume there will be some people left to buy books."

"Dory," said Sarah.

"Look, the problem is that Owen Grant has started bailing on his responsibilities. Everyone wants him, especially with that tie-in video game coming out, and now he's stopped picking up the phone. At least when Colleen or I call. But this is his moment! You've got to get him back on board and make him take care of his book."

"If he doesn't listen to you, why—"

"He'd better listen to you, Sarah. Or, like I said, you're out."

All afternoon, Sarah tried and failed to call Owen from her cubicle. The truth was that she could think of no good reason why he ought to speak to her when he wouldn't even talk to Dory. It was only once she was at home and Noah's giggles had finally subsided into sleep that she felt the day's failures recede. She registered a fleeting triumph in Noah's long lashes curled against his soft cheek as she lowered a kiss onto his forehead. It was something, to be raising a son so joyous he could laugh himself to sleep. Then she sank into a corner of the couch, dialled Owen Grant's number on her cell, and hit Call before she could change her mind.

"Hello?" A warm baritone.

"Mr. Grant?"

"Yes?" The word seemed inflected with an air of indulgent patience, as though she had already begun to waste his time.

"Hi. My name is Sarah Bailey."

"Hello, Sarah. I'm Owen."

"I . . . I know." Was Owen Grant giving her a lesson on proper phone etiquette? As she hunched into the back of the couch, her thigh pressed against something hard and oblong wedged into the cushion. The television blared to life.

"Fuck me," she said. It was the goddamn news, with the volume on max. Every night, the same thing: the investigators in hazmat suits; the masked nurses of the mobile ARAMIS clinics; the eyes of the newscaster growing wider and wider as she announced another 10,000 people had been diagnosed in New York City alone, bringing the global tally of confirmed cases to nearly 300,000. Sarah thought it was reckless to show that much panic on television. She fumbled for the remote, tucking the phone up to her chest as she did so to dampen the sound. Once the TV was off, she returned the phone to her ear.

"Sorry," she said.

"What was that?"

"Oh, the news. You know, horror and mayhem. I don't like to watch it anymore."

"But you should." His voice had the weight of authority. Owen Grant was giving her some free advice. It was what all of his readers wanted. She ought to be taking notes.

"Why's that?"

"To stay informed. Stay alive."

"Right." In spite of herself, Sarah felt a lonely feeling unsettle her stomach and quicken her pulse. She recognized it as fear.

"Sarah Bailey," said Owen. "I'm looking at a picture of you now. I see you work for my publisher." If he remembered her from Lansdowne, he gave no sign of it.

"You're googling me?" She tried not to feel flattered, and failed. "Yes, I'm from Shillelagh. We have lots of things lined up for you. Interviews, appearances. Bigger than anything you've done yet, and it's going to be huge for the book."

She heard him sigh.

"No."

"No?"

"I'm not going to be doing anything."

"But why not? Mr. Grant, I'm sure we can come up with a publicity plan that will be to your satisfaction. It doesn't have to be everything they want." *They*. She wasn't strategically trying to distance herself from the publishing house—it just came out that way. Probably subconsciously linked to her imminent firing when she couldn't deliver. "Please, we'll do everything your way."

"Because, Sarah. Sarah, because." Though she could see her job security slipping away, she couldn't help smiling at how tenderly he repeated her name. As an undergrad, she probably would have been swooning by now. "Because it's a matter of life and death."

Sarah thought about their exchange in her cubicle the next day, as she picked up her phone and debated calling Dory to confess she'd failed. Owen Grant had condescended to her and refused to meet her in person. He had urged her to quit her job and stop going outside. And between warning her against taking the subway and flying on commercial airlines, he had also refused to do any media appearances whatsoever.

She hung up the receiver once she realized she would only be putting herself out of work. And she had almost nothing saved in the event of a layoff. Rent, food, daycare, health insurance—very few of her expenses were luxuries. Somehow, she had to convince Owen Grant to listen to her.

She studied the juddering jacket art of his latest novel. It had a striking typographic design with bold red and yellow chevrons radiating outwards from the title. If you squinted, the colours almost seemed to be moving, flashing in high alert. Sarah had seen the cover of the new paperback edition, which was black, subdued. A novel in disguise as a survival guide.

She picked up the book but was reluctant to open it. Office osmosis had revealed so much of the plot she could write the back cover copy herself. *When a mysterious virus strikes an elite Manhattan private school, lovelorn science teacher David Gellar works to stay one step ahead of a pandemic that infects most of the city's children.* She reminded herself that it was just the book's title and the eerie similarities between the novel's pandemic and the current ARAMIS crisis that had made it seem relevant to a terrified public. That and the fact that there were children getting sick. But that was normal, too—children were always more susceptible to viruses. Just because nearly all the children in the book died did not mean that would happen with ARAMIS.

She put the book down and called her brother to ask for his advice.

"Aren't you at work?" Elliot said, right after "hello."

"Yes, you know I am." Her brother still treated Call Display as a novelty, and he flagrantly abused the feature when it came to fielding calls from their parents.

"So this is when you're catching up on your messages?" His voice sounded faint and windblown alongside the roar and rush of passing cars.

Sarah ignored him, as she knew his teasing was more of a reflex than a barb. "Where are you? Can you talk?"

"We're on food delivery duty today, if you can believe it. In between active calls." The street sounds quieted and Sarah could hear Elliot's partner Bryce talking to someone over an intercom. "A hell of a lot more people in quarantine now."

Sarah felt the usual queasiness in picturing her brother on duty, in harm's way. "I guess it's a nice change of pace from patrol?"

"Nothing nice about it." In the background, a sardonic laugh of agreement from Bryce. "There's a lot of panic out there. People can't afford to get sick anymore. Some seem more worried about losing paycheques to a Q-notice than they are about catching the virus. Anyway . . ." Elliot seemed to want to change the subject. "I'd like to see Noah tonight."

"We'd love that," said Sarah. "Now, tell me what you think about something."

"Can't we talk when I come over?" Elliot's breathing became laboured, as though he was climbing stairs.

"No." Once Elliot was anywhere near Noah, Sarah might as well be invisible. Her father Frank said they got along like peas and carrots, but it went well beyond side dishes as far as Sarah was concerned: they were each the other's favourite person in the world. It didn't hurt her to acknowledge their bond, because they were both her favourite people, too, and she loved how much they loved one another. But she wanted Elliot's attention while she had a hope of holding it.

"I need advice on how to handle someone." She quickly told him about Owen Grant, and Elliot listened without interrupting. He and Noah were the only members of their family with that particular gift. "If I can't get him on board, I think I'm out of a job."

"Tell him that," said Elliot. "Show him his actions affect other people."

"No thanks. I already feel pathetic enough."

"Suit yourself. But it's a lot easier to get what you want if you just ask for it."

Sarah heard someone clearing their throat, and when she looked over her shoulder, Dory was standing there and frowning at her in a pair of red-rimmed glasses. Owen's book fell out of her lap and clattered to the floor.

"Gotta go," she said quickly to Elliot, then she hung up and spun around. "Dory! I wasn't expecting you." Her boss was rarely spotted in cubicle territory.

Dory unfolded her arms, seeming amused. "Did you get Owen on the phone?"

"Yes." Sarah nodded, more emphatically than necessary. "We had a great chat last night."

"Really? That's wonderful." Dory sounded surprised but willing to take Sarah's success in stride. "You know, Colleen is convinced he's pulling a Salinger or something. Becoming a total recluse," she said, already walking away.

"Not at all," said Sarah, raising her voice as Dory retreated. "He's actually working with me on a plan I think you're really going to like."

When Dory was out of earshot, Sarah dialled Owen from her cellphone, sure he would recognize the number and pick up. But this time the phone just rang and rang.

After Elliot left that night, Sarah tried Owen again, but her calls continued to ring into the void. She put Noah to bed with a sinking feeling that if she couldn't make Owen talk to her, she was doomed to forfeit the little sliver of life she had built for herself and her son. She pictured herself handing out resumés, screwing up job interviews, her bank balance racing ever faster towards zero. Then: packing up their tiny apartment, moving back to Lansdowne, living with her parents. Becoming known as the single mom who ordered takeout three nights a week. What she valued about the city was its protection of her solitude. The only people privy to her decisions were the ones she'd chosen as friends. Back in her hometown, she would always be her parents' disappointing daughter. The feeble-minded Bolivian-brainwashing victim.

She held open Noah's book, turning the pages automatically, only half listening as he lisped out the words. The women at the daycare always wanted to talk to Sarah about Noah's development, as if they couldn't quite believe that she might already understand his special gifts. Or as if they couldn't believe she was his mother, period.

"Mommy, the story's over." Like his reading, Noah's conversation was precocious, but his occasionally lisping pronunciation made it hard for others to understand him. He tapped on her wrist until she picked up the next book, which she opened with a long, slow exhalation that failed to release the tension in her chest. Even a tender moment such as this one was being overshadowed by her anxiety over Owen, her job, and the virus.

By the time Noah was asleep, Sarah was ready for bed herself, exhausted by her panicked imaginings.

As she drifted off, she had a single buoyant thought about Owen: their mutual interest in one another when their paths had crossed years earlier. Maybe if she could meet him in person, she would have more leverage. Just last week she had read something online about pheromones, how they functioned on a microscopic level to affect people's brains and bodies, leading to attraction or repulsion according to nature's unerring plan for genetic diversity. Given the chance to play a role, Sarah thought, maybe nature would lend a hand.

◦◦|‖|◦◦

On Monday morning, recharged by caffeine into a less fatalistic estimation of her prospects, she called the office for the mailing address they had on file for Owen Grant, then grabbed her purse and caught the train out to Bushwick.

Owen's address brought her to a slim, modern building in grey and white, a steel-and-glass anomaly rising above the mostly two- and three-storey brownstones and turn-of-the-century houses Sarah passed on her walk from the subway. She stepped into an entryway with floor-to-ceiling windows and dialled the apartment number she had written down in her notebook.

"Yes?"

"Mr. Grant, it's Sarah Bailey from Shillelagh Press. Can you buzz me up? I'd like to talk to you in person about the publicity plan. I've worked out a proposal for the next few weeks."

"Sarah," he said. "I'm sorry, but as I mentioned the other night, I'm too busy to do any promotion right now."

"It won't be time-consuming. Or onerous in any way. We can be strategic."

"Strategic," he repeated. "Yes. That's right. I'm being strategic about what's really important."

"Owen." She had counted on seeing him face-to-face, within pheromone-firing distance, and now she'd forgotten everything she planned to say. All she wanted was to delay any finality of a refusal. She noticed a camera mounted in an upper corner of the lobby. "Can you see me? Do you have a screen?"

"I can see you."

She glanced up at the camera and waved. Then she addressed it directly. "Look, can I get you anything? While I'm here?"

There was a moment of silence. "I wouldn't mind a coffee." He seemed to hesitate. "A cappuccino. There's a place around the corner."

Jolted by the promise of success, she raced down the street and spotted the café, slipping ahead of two people hovering in the doorway. While she waited in line, she smoothed her hair and double-checked that her voice recorder app was working. She was back in Owen's entryway within ten minutes.

"One cappuccino coming up!" she said when he answered. She had a hand on the inner door, ready to pull it open when he buzzed her inside.

"Great." Owen sounded distant. "You can leave it there on the table."

Sarah's hand dropped from the door. Her pulse thundering in her ears, she stepped over to a narrow table and set down the cup next to a vase holding a bouquet of convincing fake orchids. She turned with slow deliberation to make one more plea to the camera. "Please, Owen. Mr. Grant. I just want to help. Please, *please* call me if you change your mind."

"Thank you for coming, Sarah," he said. "I appreciate it. But don't come back."

The casual authority of his tone spurred her natural defiance as she stalked out of the building. No, she wouldn't come back, but neither would she leave. Retreating to a bench a few paces down the sidewalk, Sarah pulled out from her bag a magazine emblazoned with the now-ubiquitous ARAMIS Girl photo, and in an all-too-earnest impersonation of a bad private eye, kept watch on the lobby from behind it. If nothing else, it would be a story to make Elliot laugh—probably while he loaded her things into a rental van and tried in his laconic way to convince her that moving back in with their parents was not a defeat or even a disappointment, but merely sensible planning on the part of any single mom who wanted the best for her son.

Fifteen minutes later, a man emerged from the elevator, garbed in a floor-length hooded rain slicker, gloves, and a face mask—though not, Sarah noted, one of the promotional sets from Shillelagh. In spite of all the gear, she recognized him at once. Head lowered, Owen pushed open the inner door, claimed the coffee in one thickly gloved hand, and was back through the elevator doors just in time to be swallowed up by them.

Sarah was stunned. Owen no longer seemed like a celebrity jealous of his privacy or an artist too consumed by his craft for the trifling racket of peddling books. He seemed like a man who was mentally ill.

She remained on the bench for the duration of the day, puzzling about Owen and flipping through his novel. There was an outside possibility he knew she was still waiting for him, that the slicker costume had been nothing but an act to make her go away. He could be watching her even now, if his windows faced front. But somehow she didn't think it was an act. Sarah imagined him inside, bleaching his shoes, pouring his coffee into a clean cup, looking up infection data. Possibly writing, if he wasn't too bonkers. Jerking off. And if he really was as afraid as he seemed, she felt for him. She knew what it meant to be paralyzed by doubt and indecision, and the terror that could lead a person to seek refuge indoors. She briefly considered calling Elliot before deciding to trust herself and stay the course, vague as it was.

It wasn't until she noticed the bustle of impending rush hour and her stomach began to spasm from hunger that she rose from the bench with a strange feeling of accomplishment, simply from not having given up.

She buzzed Owen's apartment again. This time it took longer for him to pick up.

"You're back." He sounded tired, and possibly, as Sarah dared to hope, resigned.

"I never left." It was starting to feel natural, talking to him through the intercom. "You're frightened," she said. "That's why you won't see me. You're scared to leave your house."

"What?" said Owen. "No. Look, I did a lot of research for the book. You might say it made me paranoid enough to assume things will get worse before they get better."

"So you're not afraid—you're careful."

"Exactly." There was a pause. "It doesn't help that everything that happened in my novel seems to be coming true. You know, the virus from China, the aerosol transmission, the kids getting sick . . ."

"Do you really think things are going to become as desperate as in the book?"

"Sometimes," he said. "Sometimes not."

Sarah waited to see if he would go on, but when he didn't, she continued. "Okay, well, I've been thinking about what you said, about what's important."

"One always should."

"So hear me out. Your book is full of good advice," she said. "And so are you. Since talking to you and reading your novel, I've caught the earliest and latest trains, to avoid crowds. I've taken my temperature twice a day, and most of all, I feel . . . I don't know . . . less paralyzed. You've helped me feel capable of protecting myself. And I think you could help other people, too." She was fudging some of the details, but not the spirit of the thing. He *had* changed her way of thinking, just by forcing her to consider whether he was a genius or a crackpot.

There was another long pause. Two people exited the building separately, giving her curious glances as she stood in the entryway, waiting to find out if she was still talking to Owen. Finally, the intercom crackled to life again.

"If you call me tonight, I'll answer the phone," he said. "I promise."

Once Sarah had him on the line that evening, she wasted no time in getting down to a list of prepared questions. "These are all things I really want to know," she said. "Both as a reader and as a person who wants to survive."

"I'm glad you mentioned survival, as I wanted to highlight that it isn't necessarily unethical to look after yourself in a plague situation." He paused before continuing with greater emphasis. "Selflessly caring for a loved one while neglecting your own safety might feel like a moral decision, but preserving your own health is also a public good that helps prevent the further infection of others. We should all be doing our best to take care of ourselves. Designate a sick room or area in your home if caring for ill family members. Be responsible and prepare accordingly. Stock up on N95 masks and enough food and supplies to shelter at home for a few weeks."

They spoke for an hour, and Sarah spent the rest of the evening transcribing and condensing her notes until she had nine hundred words ready to post at seven a.m. The Q&A with Owen became one of the most shared articles that day across all social media platforms. Sarah's inbox was flooded with new interview requests from NPR, the *New York Times*, the *Washington Post*, and four different television news outlets.

KEEP IT UP, read a rare encouraging email from Dory.

Sarah got Owen on the phone again and read out all the inquiries that had come in. "You see how easy it can be?" she said. "Everything on your terms."

"That's quite the list."

"I'll be your filter," she said. "Your gatekeeper. All you have to do is answer the phone every once in a while from the comfort of your living room. And maybe write the odd blog post. I'll supplement."

For the next three weeks, they spoke twice a day, once mid-morning and then again in the evening, after Noah was in bed. Sarah was getting used to the low, grave sound of Owen's voice; how the flattened vowels of his Midwestern accent emerged when he was flirting; how empathy shaded his voice when he spoke of the ARAMIS victims and the bewildering hysteria around ARAMIS Girl. And how when he sounded annoyed he was usually just excited and in a hurry to move on to his next big idea. Sarah continued the series of Q&As and acted as an intermediary for various print and online magazines. She set up phone calls for radio interviews, and talked Owen through setting up Skype on his laptop, since he wouldn't visit television studios.

Occasionally, their conversation meandered off-topic to Sarah's favourite authors (Virginia Woolf and André Gide), her hometown, her shelf full of sailing trophies from when she was a teenager and still had dreams of winning the America's Cup. Though she was the interviewer, Owen had an innate curiosity and in certain moods would ask her nearly as many questions as she posed to him.

One night, he said, "Does Noah spend any time with his father?"

Sarah's hands froze above her keyboard. "His father isn't in the picture, never was."

"I'm sorry," he said, seeming to hear the sudden wariness in her voice. "I didn't mean to pry. I only wondered if you ever got a break."

"My brother helps," said Sarah. "I couldn't do it without him."

"My ex-wife is a single mother, too," said Owen. Then added, "Not by me. But I've been thinking of setting up a fund for her boy just the same. Henry is right around Noah's age. Do you think you can help me do that? Look into how to get the process started?"

"Okay," said Sarah, slightly bewildered. It would be bizarre for Owen to have suggested the idea merely as a way to gain her trust, but she couldn't help thinking it all the same. "I'll do my best."

Another part of her job was to moderate the interactions on Owen's newly minted blog, and respond or forward as necessary. Half were scams hawking so-called ARAMIS cures or protection spells being offered by sketchy online pharmacies or Haitian witch bloggers, and the other half were messages from female fans looking to strike up a correspondence.

Dear Mr. Grant,

Your book is the #1 most-requested book in our city library system. I've just put in an order for thirty more copies. I've been recommending it to everyone, and I wanted to personally tell you how much your work has meant to me over the years. We'd love to host a reading at our local branch the next time you visit the West Coast.

Sincerely,
Laura C.

Hi Owen. I saw you on television and remembered our night at Jiminy Peak all those years ago. Nice to see all the success you've had. Let me know if you're ever in D.C.

xo Angelica

These messages Sarah forwarded without comment, though they embarrassed her and she was relieved she hadn't reminded Owen of their previous flirtation. But she became uneasy when Owen asked her to start deleting them. She sent a quick note to Dory seeking advice, but Julia's due date was only a week away and all she received back was a terse message that read *Don't respond or erase. Don't do his dirty work for him. Just do your job. D.*

Later that morning, Sarah called Owen, and after the usual hellos she launched right into the day's questions, typing his answers directly into an HTML editor. "Is the virus progressing the way you imagined Xi-RV-5 in your novel?"

"No," said Owen. "And thank God. Xi-RV-5 was designed to be an efficient and straightforward killer, suitable for mass fatalities and extreme drama. Its mortality rate among those under twelve was over ninety per cent, unrealistically high for any known type of coronavirus."

"Much worse than ARAMIS, then? And especially for kids, right?"

"So far, yes. Children are more vulnerable to ARAMIS, but by and large these pediatric infections are resulting in comas, not death. We'll have to wait and see what the long-term prognosis might be, but I think there's reason to be hopeful these kids will pull through. ARAMIS is fulfilling the expectations of experts who predicted a pandemic, but you'll notice, if you compare it city by city, its progression seems highly dependent on response and preparedness. Voluntary quarantining in the five boroughs seems to be slowing the spread here in New York City, where you might imagine infection levels could quickly become catastrophic. Yes, thousands of people are sick, but just think of the population here."

"You support that initiative then?"

"Absolutely. But I will say this: I don't think voluntary quarantining is enough. I think it should be mandatory and endorsed from the highest levels, so that nobody risks losing their job for doing the right thing. But if people follow the recommendations, if they are really scrupulous about staying home if they've been exposed, the strategy should help. We need to keep it from going exponential."

"You might get your wish," said Sarah. "From what I've heard."

"Is that what Elliot said?" asked Owen, interested. "He would probably be on the front lines, enforcing it. I don't envy him that particular assignment."

Ever since she'd mentioned her brother was a cop, Owen had been asking about him. In a way it was nice, but it usually had the effect of making Sarah more nervous for Elliot's safety. Over the years, she had mostly inured herself to the usual dangers he faced in the line of duty, but a virus was different from a bullet. Plus, the outbreak had changed things. She'd seen on the news that there had been a surge in petty crime, as well as an increase in anti-police sentiment: through their relief and containment efforts, the force was becoming associated with the virus and its spread, though the worst and most irrational contempt was still reserved for ARAMIS Girl.

As Sarah finished typing, her phone flashed with a call from Noah's daycare. "Sorry, Owen, just a sec."

It was Iona, one of the educators, who began by reassuring her. "He's fine, Sarah, just a bit of a fever. But it's the new policies. We can't be too careful. Just come and pick him up, and I wouldn't be surprised if he's better by tomorrow."

Sarah had already slipped her feet back into her shoes and grabbed her keys when her cellphone buzzed inside her purse. She seized it, expecting a follow-up from the daycare. A turn for the worse. Her imagination was spinning out that fast.

It was Owen again. "We got cut off," he was saying. "And I actually wanted to ask you a favour."

"I'd love to help. Really." She had already moved through the office and was jabbing the button to summon the elevator. "But I have to call you back."

At the daycare, Sarah repented for every mean thought she'd ever had about the trio in charge. They'd reprimanded her in the mornings when she dropped Noah off late, and they'd scolded her at the end of the day when she was the very last parent to arrive for pickup. They'd pressured him to clean his plate at lunchtime, against her explicit instructions that Noah never be forced to eat something if he didn't like it, and she had maligned them so often in conversation with her friends Corinna and Hilary that a series of cruel nicknames had evolved: Wages (short for "Wages of Destruction," aka Waverly), No-Neck (Nellie), and Pigeon Pie (Iona). She was fuzzy on the exact etymologies, but even though the aliases were not solely her invention, Sarah felt a wave of guilt when Pigeon Pie hugged Noah tightly in the vestibule, as if to show she really wasn't afraid that he had It. They'd bundled him up in his naptime blanket with the trains printed on it, since he'd said he was cold.

"Don't worry, Sarah," said Iona. Her calm was genuine, and Sarah felt comforted. "He's not doing too badly at all." Sarah took Noah's hand and he looked up at her with a smile that spoke of his delight at being wrapped up in the train blanket. He had been asking if he could bring it home ever since Elliot bought it for him when he'd started daycare.

"Thanks," said Sarah. "I'll give you guys a call in the morning."

When they got home, Sarah let Noah change into his airplane PJS, then took his temperature. "How are you feeling, baby?" She sat on the closed lid of the toilet and contemplated her son. He seemed 100 per cent normal.

"I'm fine, Mommy," he said. Then he threw up.

She cleaned up the sour-smelling mess in a distracted panic, trying to remember exactly how the virus presented in children. Persistent high fever, headache, muscle pain. Vomiting was only a symptom in the disease Owen had invented. The more time she spent immersed in the world of his novel, the less she was able to distinguish between the real facts and the invented ones.

"I'm better now," Noah said, even though he was still crying. "Nellie made me eat tomatoes at snack even though I told her I don't like them."

So that was it. The last time he had been made to eat tomatoes, Noah had thrown up when he got home, too. She wouldn't be surprised if the fever had broken now that they were out of his stomach.

"Did you tell her I didn't want them to force you to eat anything?"

Noah nodded. "They said the rules were for everybody." He wiped his eyes with his sleeve. "I'm sorry, Mommy."

She held him, feeling her usual rage against No-Neck welling up. The woman must be psychologically damaged to be engaging in an ongoing power struggle with a three-year-old. "It's okay, baby. I'm not upset with you." She rubbed his back and shoulders. "Next time you have to tell her you're allergic."

She put him to bed despite his protests, holding his hand until he fell asleep. It took less than five minutes.

With her other hand, she called Owen back. "I'm ready to help." She kept her voice to a whisper. "What do you need?"

"I'm going to the marina this afternoon to look at a boat, and I'd like you to come with me. From what you've told me, you're a top-notch sailor."

"The marina," repeated Sarah. "To look at a boat." She eased herself off Noah's bed, smoothing the comforter with its gridlock pattern of cars and buses. Why put a traffic jam on a child's sheet set? But then, she was the one who had bought them.

"I'm in the market for a big purchase," said Owen. "And honestly, I could use an advisor."

Sarah paused as she pulled Noah's door halfway closed. "You're buying a yacht?" She felt stupid asking again, but then he had said the word *advisor*. She kept her footsteps quiet as she padded down the hallway to her bedroom.

"I'd like to just call it a boat."

"Wait, isn't that what happens at the end of your book?" In the last third of Owen's novel, after his love interest dies, David Gellar buys a boat and takes to sea with his students and their parents, to escape the disease ravaging everyone on land.

"Yes," Owen said. "I'm following my own advice."

When Sarah heard him chuckle, she allowed herself to laugh, too. "For real?"

"Yes, for real."

"Does this mean you're going outside?" Ever since the great apartment stakeout, she had avoided mentioning Owen's agoraphobia. She had never revealed that she'd witnessed him descending to retrieve the coffee like a bloodless vampire terrified of the sun.

"Yes," he said. "I do still go outside from time to time, for things that matter."

"I haven't been sailing in years," she said. "And I've never been yacht shopping."

"So we'll be in the same boat, so to speak."

"I'm sorry, but my son is home with me."

"Oh," said Owen. His tone changed. "Is he sick?"

"He—" She heard a small sound behind her in the hall. "One sec," she said, covering the phone. When she turned around, Noah was standing in the doorway, holding out the digital thermometer, which flashed green behind its numeric display. A normal temperature.

"Please, Mommy. Let's go see the boat."

Sarah and Noah caught a taxi and met Owen in the parking lot behind his building. He was dressed normally this time, no giant raincoat, but like her and Noah, he wore gloves and had a face mask slung around his neck. She'd forgotten just how tall he was, but standing in his presence she was reminded of his loping walk and a particular gesture of ruffling his own hair while he was thinking. His hairline had receded, but only slightly, and his jawline was more pronounced.

She didn't think she'd changed much in the past sixteen years, at least not on the outside, but still he gave no sign of recognition. She noticed that he stood back while she strapped in first Noah's car seat and then Noah himself. Before Owen got in the driver's seat of the Jeep, he lowered the windows and put on his face mask.

They pulled out into the street, and Noah fell asleep in his car seat almost immediately. There was something about moving vehicles that relaxed him. Planes, trains, and automobiles. Even if he wasn't in la-la land, he was sure to be docile and happy.

"You know, we've actually met before," said Sarah. "In Lansdowne, when I was at college. You were the visiting writer that year." She watched as Owen's head inclined sharply, though his eyes stayed focused on the road. "And my parents taught there. Well, they still do. Gretchen Howe and Frank Bailey."

He shifted into second gear as traffic slowed. "I remember your parents," he said, his voice somewhat muffled by the face mask, "but not you." Sarah wanted to laugh at how little an impression she must have made on him, even though back then their brief interactions had felt loaded with import. When she told him truthfully that she'd loved his second novel, *Blue Virginia*, his eyes looked a little haunted.

"Thanks," he said, glancing over at her for the first time since they'd exchanged greetings in the parking lot. "You and all my closest friends."

Sarah couldn't think of anything to say to that. No wonder Shillelagh Press had wanted to fire her.

"There's a lot of traffic," she remarked, raising her voice to be heard over the street sounds. The open windows were making things loud. She wished she could find a way to tap into the effortlessness of their phone conversations.

"People are avoiding the subway," said Owen. "You should, too, as I keep telling you."

"I would," said Sarah, "but it would take me four hours to walk to work."

They fell silent as they entered the Lincoln Tunnel. Her hair whipped around, strands of it blowing in her eyes. She tried to roll up the window, but the child lock was on. "Do you mind putting the window up?"

"Sorry," said Owen, raising his voice over the echoing sounds of the other cars. "It's better to keep them rolled down. Less chance of infection."

"From me?" She was used to thinking of other people as the threat.

"I don't know where you've been."

"I guess you're right." Then she glanced back at Noah, who was still sleeping. It was true she couldn't confirm what either of them might have been exposed to in a given day. The WHO had recently issued a travel advisory deterring tourists from visiting the city, but there were still millions of New Yorkers carrying on with their regular lives. Only now they could buy personal protective gear from every newsstand and vending machine.

"God," said Owen. "It feels good to be on the move." They had entered New Jersey, and he navigated along a road parallel to the river.

After Owen parked the Jeep, he took long swift strides across the gravelly parking lot, pausing every few seconds to let Sarah and Noah catch up. "Sorry," he said, after his fifth stop-and-wait. "I can't seem to make myself go any slower. It used to drive my ex-wife crazy."

"It's okay," said Sarah. She remembered Rachel and how petite she was: a slim sprite who'd easily commanded the class's attention with a magnetic intelligence. At length, Sarah said, "I meant it when I said I don't know much about yachts."

"That's okay. I know more than I let on. I pretty much know what I want."

"You think it's getting worse, don't you?" said Sarah. She came to a stop and looked over at Noah, who immediately crouched down to examine some ants on the ground. "So bad that you need to leave?" She paused. "Maybe I should be working from home. And keeping Noah home with me." There was no reason she couldn't. It was stupid to risk their lives out of convention, or because she was too nervous to ask for what she needed. "I wish I could be sure."

"That's just it," said Owen. "It's the uncertainty of every action. Every choice is a threat. I don't want to stay shut up in my condo, trying to decide if a breath of fresh air is worth risking my life. I'm going to leave while I still can."

"Wow." She envied him the wherewithal to make and enact such a bold plan. She waited for her son to take her hand before she started walking again.

"Yes," said Owen. He paused behind her to tie his shoelace, but then he was quickly strolling apace. "It's kind of a 'wow' thing."

Noah started babbling his amazement as they approached the marina. Dozens of moored boats bobbed in their slips, and the water dappled in the afternoon sun. Manhattan's skyscrapers gleamed across the Hudson. Noah wanted to dash ahead, but Sarah kept a tight hold on his hand.

"No running," she said.

"Okay." For a second, he pulled on her arm like a swinging monkey, but then he began walking normally. There was no sign of the morning's illness. They waited while Owen spoke to a man in the office, who came out with a packet of papers on a clipboard and a key that he used to lock the office behind him.

"You won't find better in this price range," the man said. He had a gruffness that Sarah found suggestive of honesty as he shook her gloved hand. His button-down shirt was open at the collar. "You're looking at three cabins, two convertible berths in the dining area, and a ton of hidden storage."

He was peddling the features, not the boat, Sarah decided. When the man started citing fuel capacity and nautical miles per hour, Owen launched into an elaborate series of questions. He was taking a lot of notes in a worn leatherbound journal.

"Why are the current owners selling?" she asked.

The man shrugged. "It's a lot of work owning a boat," he said. "Especially if you don't use it much. The current owner is retired, but his health isn't so good."

They followed him along the docks until they came almost to the end, where a smallish ketch sailboat was moored. White with navy blue trim, the name *Buona Fortuna* swirled on its side.

"'Good luck,'" Sarah translated aloud, though she knew she didn't need to. The sunlight glinted off rigging that ran in perfect geometry from its two masts to the deck. "It's really kind of beautiful, isn't it?"

"It is," said Owen.

"Forty-two feet," said the man. "Steel hull." He had a beard, another detail which Sarah considered and weighted on the side of integrity. Being put into the position of an advisor for a major expenditure was making her listen to her instincts rather more than was warranted. "It's Dutch construction," he went on. "Nothing more reliable than that."

"Is there a transferrable warranty?" asked Sarah.

"No, it's too old for that by a long shot," he said. "Though we could check on some of the upgraded components." He glanced at Owen, who was considering the boat, arms folded. "It's very seaworthy. A family of four sailed her all the way around the globe." He turned back to Sarah. "This was their only home for years, so as you can imagine you can make it quite comfortable for yourselves."

Sarah realized the man assumed she was Owen's wife, and Noah his son. When she looked at Owen, there was the crinkle of a smile around his eyes.

Aboard *Buona Fortuna*, Noah climbed in and out of the berths and dragged Sarah in to see the miniature bathroom. After, she stood in the middle of the tiny galley kitchen and marvelled over its design.

"It's so clever," she said. She fingered the faucet on the small double sink before running her palm along the handle of the miniature oven. "I think it might be more functional than the one in my apartment." She glanced at Owen, wondering if he could guess how little use she made of it. Surprised, too, by the sudden guilt she felt. Noah knew all their favourite takeout menus by heart. But what did it matter? He was happy and healthy. And Owen was busy poking around.

"I have to go to the bathroom," Noah said in his lisping way to the man. "Is that okay?"

"What's that?" The man stared. "What did he say?"

"He's wondering if he can use the bathroom," said Sarah.

"Aren't you polite! Go ahead." The man handed Owen the clipboard with the pricing folder. "I'll leave you to think about this as a family. Just drop the info packet back at the office before you go."

Once he was gone, Sarah turned to Owen, expecting the same conspiratorial smile as before, but instead he seemed thoughtful.

"Your son is a lovely little boy, isn't he?" he said. "Very sweet."

"Yes. I think sometimes we forget that boys can be sweet."

Owen nodded, his eyes still lingering on the door of the bathroom. "Aren't you afraid for him?"

"Of course I am." A lump formed in her throat almost immediately. "But our lives can't just come to a grinding halt because there's a virus on the loose."

"But that's exactly what will happen. Don't you see?" His voice was curt, or maybe only urgent, but Sarah's temper flared even as her eyes brimmed.

"I do, yes. I do." She tried not to blink, which would only send the tears spilling down her cheeks. The energy she was already putting into dampening her worry could power a small car. All she wanted when she closed her eyes at night was to pick up her son in her arms and retreat to some high mountain cave—free, alone, and safe at last.

Owen was giving her a hard look, and Sarah was surprised as he ran his fingers up through his greying blond hair, his palms slowing as they crossed his face. "It's strange," he said, "being treated like a prophet. As though I could actually save anybody."

Sarah considered the strain of his position, the burden of a kind of imposter expertise. "You will," she said. "All the press you've been doing . . . people are really listening. You're doing amazing things with the platform you have."

"Right," he said. "Maybe. I hope so." He put his hands in his pockets. "You know my ex and her little boy? Henry? I've been trying to convince them to leave, either with me or by some other means, but she's cut me off completely."

Sarah nodded, unsure of what to say. She had put Owen in contact with an estate lawyer to set up a trust for Henry, but as far as she knew, Rachel hadn't responded to any communications. Sarah and Owen spent the next few minutes in silence, watching Noah as he climbed into every cubbyhole he could find.

"Hey," said Noah, clambering into the furthest corner of one of the berths. "Hey, look at me, Owen, I'm sleeping." He closed his eyes, but he was grinning.

"I see you," said Owen, "but I think you're awake." Noah giggled.

"That's impressive," said Sarah. "Not everyone can make out what he says." They slid into seats across from one another at the central salon table. "I'm worried about you being out there, alone on the ocean."

"I've been taking sailing lessons," said Owen. "For almost two months now."

"Good," she said, relieved. "On a real boat?"

"Yes, a real boat. Though there's also an autopilot." His eyes were still on Noah, who was giggling as he pretended to snore. "I'm worried about your boy. I'm serious about keeping him out of school. Think about it, okay?"

"I will, I promise." She put a hand on the table to push her seat back and realized all the furniture was bolted down. "Won't you be lonely? Or afraid?" She could picture herself in the dark of the open water. A sky full of stars. She wondered if there were people who were meant to be apart from the world, and if she might be one of them. And she knew, in the next instant, what she wanted.

"I've never been lonely in my life." Owen swung his legs out from under the table, stood up, and offered her a gloved hand to help her out. "It's partly why my ex-wife divorced me." His laugh was not exactly bitter, but it was not self-deprecating either. "I suppose I'll probably be afraid, though. That seems to be the human condition."

Sarah took a deep breath. "So let us come with you. Me and Noah." She summoned a confidence she didn't feel. "Sailing classes are one thing, but experience is what will save your life out there."

Owen said nothing for a long minute.

"If you just leave, I'll lose my job, anyway." She meant to say this as though it were a joke, but it did not even remotely sound like one. She wondered what molecular messages might be rising off the surface of her skin, and if something in him might be responding to her the same way he had so many years ago. "You know you need my help."

The silence continued, and she thought Owen must be angry, but his eyes were sober. "Okay, come with me," he said. "You and Noah." His voice was low and intense. "Then I'll know I've done something. More than just put words on a page."

She felt a prickling along her spine, a thrill that was half fear, half triumph. "What about Rachel and Henry?"

"There's room enough if they decide to come," said Owen.

Sarah stared up at the varnished wood of the cabin, the clever net baskets swinging in the corners, and the high bookshelf with its metal railing. How many other major life decisions had she made this way— vertiginously, emotionally, seemingly in reaction to what other people expected of her? Quitting school to work on the farm. Running away from Living Tree. Having Noah all by herself. But it had been years since she had done anything risky, since she had managed to overcome the ever-present doubt that hung over her life like a fog. It was exhausting, to always be second-guessing herself. Besides the handful of people who had never let her down, there was nobody she really trusted. Least of all herself.

But the idea of leaving Elliot behind began to spread across her body like a heat rash. She would ask if he could come with them, but she knew that as long as there was a job to do in the city, something he still construed as a duty, he would want to stay. Closing her eyes, Sarah exhaled slowly. The slight sway of the boat didn't help with the bright dizziness ringing in her ears. A trip with a near stranger, a man about whom she had many misgivings. But the dangers on land were clear and certain. She opened her eyes. "I need to protect my son."

"This is the best way," said Owen. "I'll tell Dory I need you to keep me on track writing the sequel."

"The continuing adventures of David Gellar?"

"David Gellar on a beach," said Owen, his voice ironic. "David Gellar making friends with the dolphins. David Gellar . . . still crazy after all these years."

"It'll make a great story," she said, thinking of the publicity plan.

"A great escape," said Owen, correcting her. "A great life."

October 9, 2020

Without prejudice

Lambert, Chase, & Rider
Attorneys-at-Law
206 Florence Street
Lansdowne, M.A.

Re: CEASE AND DESIST

Dear Mr. Grant,

Please be advised that this office represents Rachel and Henry Levinson. Kindly direct any and all communication concerning Rachel and/or Henry Levinson to our attention at the address listed above.

As you are aware, Ms. Levinson has declined to respond to your emails and calls since your marriage was dissolved and a divorce granted on January 28, 2016, by the Supreme Court of the State of New York. While she acknowledges that your messages may not originate from a desire to cause harm, she nevertheless finds them emotionally distressing and an intrusion on her privacy.

Ms. Levinson has further asked us to advise you that she has received your invitations of September 30, October 4, and October 8 to join you on a sea voyage departing October 12, 2020. On behalf of herself and her son, Henry Levinson, she unequivocally declines said invitation. You can expect this to be her final communication to you.

Sincerely,
Monica Rider, Esq.

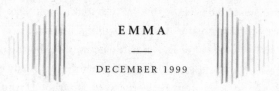

EMMA

—

DECEMBER 1999

Domenica was running along the beach, away from *Buona Fortuna* and her family. She sprinted across the shore, her bare feet compressing the sand with every step, so that it looked to Emma as though her sister was running and sinking at the same time. As though she were intent on speed to avoid becoming trapped in the shoreline.

Was it quicksand? Emma was eleven and still excited by the thought of quicksand, which was every bit as real as tornados, man-eating sharks, and Komodo dragons. Ogres and black magic might be fairy-tale inventions, but the world was still wild and untamed, full of danger and possibility.

Domenica was almost at the water. As she stopped running, her golden hair blew forward over her shoulders. Emma stumbled after her, clutching at her aching sides, knowing her sister would never turn around and acknowledge her, never stop to let her catch up. But Dom was so still and elegant standing there at the edge of the ocean—her cotton dress white and pristine against the deep bronze of her skin—that Emma's heart ached with the beauty of it. Domenica was four years and a lifetime older. Emma would never reach or overtake her.

While Emma stopped halfway across the beach to take a breath, Domenica stepped into the ocean and, bending her knees, trailed her fingertips in the cool water. The hem of her dress spread flat and floated forward, seized by the motion of the waves. And then, in one fluid dip, she plunged under.

Emma had paused near the ruins of yesterday's sandcastle, slumped into a heap only its creator would recognize. The water was already slurping away clumps of walls and battlements, wave by steady wave. The tide was relentless, as unyielding as the current already carrying her sister off to some remote territory of adulthood. And before Emma could take another step, Domenica emerged from the ocean, wet dress clinging to her slim hips and thighs. She walked slowly this time, her dripping feet safe from the scorching heat of the Fijian sand, and all Emma could do was watch as her sister stalked by without a word.

Back aboard *Buona Fortuna*, Domenica wrung out her sopping wet hair until a puddle formed on the boat's deck. Then she swung it around her shoulders, where it cooled her neck and dripped down her back. Emma was nowhere in sight. Domenica took a certain satisfaction in the fact that she'd outstripped her altogether, though competing with Emma was a pointless exercise to begin with. Her dreamy sister might just have stopped to poke at beach debris or sing a song to a sea turtle.

Domenica slipped down the companionway towards her cabin. At the communication station just opposite, her father, Harold, was reading something on the computer. Her parents liked to catch up on correspondence and the news when they were anchored at a marina. The shortwave radio they used for email on the boat made the internet speed onshore seem luxurious by comparison.

Her father was absorbed, oblivious. Feeling wicked, Domenica began to tiptoe towards him, taking her wet rope of hair in her hands, imagining how a sudden dribble of cold water down his back would make him yelp and provoke a chase, a tickle fight, a bout of silliness. He had been tense and serious lately, and she wanted to make him smile. As she closed in, she saw his shoulders shaking—he was already laughing. But the giggle rising in her throat died when she heard an unmistakable sob. Not laughing. Weeping.

And just as she was about to step forward to ask what was wrong, there was her mother's voice, complaining, "Where did all this water come from? What a mess! Domenica?" Her mother's feet were visible on the deck. In a second, she would come down and find them.

Domenica backed away, sidling into her cabin. She held the door open a crack as her mother joined her father at the desk.

"Harold," said Faye. "What's wrong?" Domenica could hear her own bewilderment echoed in her mother's voice. "What's happened?"

"Just some bad news." His voice sounded strangled, hiccupy. Domenica steeled herself for some terrible announcement.

"Oh my God. Is it my parents? Your parents?"

"No, no, nothing like that," said Harold. "It's Annie Gibbs. The art consultant. She died. She told me she had cancer, years ago, but I guess I'd imagined she'd beaten it."

Through the crack in the doorway, Domenica saw her mother's face harden. Harold's chin quivered and there were wet smears on his cheeks. His expression was too vulnerable, too unlike him.

Swift and silent, she shut her door and put in her Discman headphones, pressing play on her Lauryn Hill CD. Whatever was wrong with her father, her mother would take care of it.

As they prepared to leave Fiji, Harold listened to Faye discuss the Y2K bug again. For months, she had been talking about the computers all over the globe that hadn't been built for the future, and the mayhem that might ensue when they tried to flip from 1999 to 2000.

Still, he was grateful she had so quickly abandoned the subject of Annie and had switched to this well-worn track. Her fretful rant and his diplomatic reassurances were as scripted as a play by this point.

"It's not only the possibility of power cutting out or satellites failing," Faye was saying, "but missiles accidentally being deployed, stock markets crashing . . ."

Harold turned off his ears as he checked all the ropes and lines for chafe. His wife always grew more anxious as they prepared for a crossing. He could almost see the strain in the muscles of her neck and face. Nerves made visible via frown lines.

"Harold, are you listening? We need to take some precautions."

"My dear, it's a computer bug." He made a mental note to cut more plastic tubing to protect the rode where it came around the bow of the boat.

"What if our autopilot goes down?" said Faye. "Or we lose our GPS?"

"We'll handsteer. We'll navigate by the stars. We'll do as the sailors of yore. Not to mention we'll be in Sydney by then." They still had three weeks to make the journey to Australia, though they ought to have had six. They had tarried too long in Bora Bora, then again in Tonga. He resented how their itinerary still tormented them like a bad dream, even though they had agreed in principle that they needed to remain flexible. Boats that didn't account for vagaries of the weather ended up at the bottom of the ocean. "With any luck we won't have to be steering or navigating at all." Just last night they'd reviewed the plan: one week to New Caledonia, four days at the marina, then another week to Australia, with three days to spare before New Year's Eve and the millennial midnight countdown. The weather was the biggest variable, but Harold was feeling good about their chances. It was pretty much the only thing he still felt good about.

"Don't talk to me about luck," said Faye. "I mean it."

He turned to her. Her brows were knitted together and there was an edge to her voice. He couldn't tell if there was more to her anger than her usual pre-departure unhappiness. "Do you want to double-check the provisions? We could go get some lettuce before we set off, if you like." Faye got temperamental the longer she was deprived of fresh produce.

His wife made a face, then nodded and headed for the galley.

Faye counted the remaining cans and dried goods, all the pre-portioned meals double-bagged against moisture. She didn't actually need to count them, because she had a running tally of everything stored on the boat—food, batteries, books, Christmas presents, birthday presents. She kept the master list tucked away in a series of protective Ziplocs, but at this point she had it memorized. And she knew that what her husband really wanted was for her to go away. Sometimes it surprised her, how she knew more about that man than she could ever have imagined. But she had been majoring in Harold 101 ever since "Silly Love Songs" by Wings was a Billboard hit.

She'd met and fallen in love with Harold during an exchange year to Syracuse—his handlebar moustache and polyester slacks notwithstanding. They'd bonded over Lasers and catamarans, as Faye was from a sailing family, too, back in England. She'd cheered him on at every regatta before cooking him savoury rice and lamb dishes in a tagine. Eventually, their love of Moroccan cuisine led them to travel through Casablanca and Fez. Then it was *kaeng phet pet yang* and a month in Thailand, where Faye took a cooking class and shopped for rambutan and fingerroot in the public market.

They married after graduation and settled down in Montauk near his parents, who had a summer compound they'd taken to living in year-round. When Faye hinted to Harold that he could make himself into more than just a shareholder in his family's company—more than a frequenter of his parents' grand weekend house, a member of their yacht club, and captain of his father's racing sloop—Harold said she was right. So he bought a full-keel, forty-two-foot cruising yacht of his own. It was a rejoinder, of sorts, though not the one she was looking for.

They named their boat and their firstborn while Faye was still in love with Italy—when she still served grappa at dinner parties and kept an Italian guidebook in their peach and white bathroom, on top of Harold's stack of back issues of *Cruising World*. They sailed around Sag Harbor on *Buona Fortuna* almost every weekend when the weather was nice, and Domenica was an angel who slept through all of their dinner parties.

When Emma was born, they made a plan for a five-year circumnavigation that would take them from Panama to Australia to South Africa and back again, with time built in for sightseeing, relaxation, and boat repairs. The girls would come and Faye would homeschool them. She had laughed out loud when she'd heard that part. It was a crazy plan, Harold's insane dream, and one which could be endlessly refined and discussed—and delayed. She was terrified of taking her children to sea, but with every year that went by, she watched her husband's good humour dwindle as the course of their lives inevitably narrowed. She wondered how much longer she could stall before he began to resent her, and the calculus became one of a known unhappiness balanced against an uncharted bliss. And then, even after they'd decided to pick up and go, it took time to make the arrangements: sailing lessons for everybody, calculating food storage, educational materials to keep the girls on track with school, and refurbishing *Buona Fortuna* to make her seaworthy for a cruising family of four.

It wasn't until Domenica was ten and Emma was six that Faye was finally ready to quit her job at the travel agency, rent out their house, and leave the comforts of home to begin circumnavigating the globe *en famille*. And now, after nearly five years away, in the final stretch of their incredible journey, she longed for home more than she had ever imagined possible. Hearing Annie's name again had been like a cold bora wind stirring up waves. Maybe she had been naive to think that the sea could save them. How could the two of them stay the same when the ground was ever-shifting beneath their feet?

When Faye calculated that she and Harold had each been alone long enough to shed their mutual irritation, she went back on deck and poured herself a drink of rum over crushed ice. Ice was the great commodity of *Buona Fortuna*, doled out even more frugally than their stores of eggs and fresh veggies in between anchorages. The tinkling of cubes in a glass could still thrill her with anticipation of the spiced relaxation to come.

Then she gave the girls her usual speech about sea crossings: *stay in the cabin, look after each other, and don't bother me or your father with trivialities.* "And I want you to actually do your lessons for once," she added.

Fiji had not been a great place for making headway in the workbooks. There was too much to see, too many unforgettable, once-in-a-lifetime opportunities for first-hand learning, just like everywhere else they'd travelled. But the girls were keeping pace, more or less, with other children their age, and that was all that really mattered, Faye thought. She had enough to worry about in terms of staying afloat. Every day that they had tarried in Fiji, waiting for the weather to change, she became more anxious about making it to Australia before Y2K. Plenty of people said that intervals of calm weather in November and December were some of the safest times to make the passage to Sydney, but they would have done better to avoid cyclone season altogether.

She struggled at times under the burden of all her research and knowledge. Always install netting on a yacht with small children. Always have children clipped into tethers when a boat is underway. Always have at least two methods of communication available in case one should fail. All children in personal flotation devices at all times. Never swing the boom while a child is above deck. Never set sail without checking at least three different forecasts. Never step out of your role. That was how everything could fall apart.

And though Faye had more than once confided to Harold over the past few months that she was ready to pull the plug on their trip and go home, he had insisted with a strange intensity that they stay the course. He said if they went back to Montauk now, they'd live to regret abandoning their dream. They shouldn't give up just because it was harder and less luxurious than the life they were used to. He had shown a mettle and resolve she hadn't known he had when they set out. It was possible he'd changed. Maybe they both had.

She remembered something their friend Luisa Hall had said when they were anchored together in the Galápagos. They were exchanging war stories of broken alternators, leaking hulls, malfunctioning auto-pilots. "It's a slog sometimes," Luisa told them, "and it can be scary as hell. But it's an adventure that we're so lucky to be able to enjoy."

But was an adventure really an adventure if it was only an escape? Somewhere along the way, Faye thought, she and Harold must have blurred the line.

As she finished her drink, she noticed the girls kept right on reading their books as though she hadn't spoken.

"I'm serious," said Faye. "Math worksheets. Now."

"Yeah, yeah," said Domenica.

Yeah, yeah. Faye's nostrils flared. Everything with that girl was "yeah, yeah." As though now that she was fifteen she'd suddenly heard everything before.

"Yes, Mummy," said Emma.

Faye heard an apology for her sister in the primness of her younger daughter's response. As in, *please don't get mad right now*. She wondered how much the girls had noticed the tension between her and Harold, and their not-always-coded conversations about the itinerary and planned ocean crossings. She could scarcely sleep from imagining their boat in a storm off the coast of Australia, foundering on the reefs, unable to call for help because Y2K had crippled their communication systems.

So she refrained from getting mad and biked to get groceries instead, while Harold checked the lines. Emma and Dom didn't bother pretending to do their homework until their mother came back, by which point she didn't care anymore either.

Later that evening, Emma and Domenica were confined to the cabin as Harold raised the anchor and Faye assisted him in casting off and motoring out of the harbour. In the galley, Domenica heated up a bean and pasta soup with buttered rolls for supper.

Emma could hear her father calling above deck: "Hoist the spinnaker on my call! I'm bringing her about."

"Why are boats always girls?" she asked.

"Because captains are always men," said Dom, wrinkling her nose in distaste.

As they moved out to sea, Emma used her spoon to tap on a floating piece of pasta that reminded her of *Buona Fortuna* with the wide, wild ocean beneath it. She took turns counting how many taps until the little shell submerged for good.

After they'd eaten, Emma sat poised in the salon with her pencil and her calculator, her workbook open on her lap and her eyes on the window. They had set off to make the crossing with reassurances of fair weather from both the satellite map and the forecast roundup they'd picked up off the SSB radio, but Emma could see dark clouds on the horizon signalling a squall.

Her father liked to say, "*Buona Fortuna* has already weathered more storms than we could ever face as a family." She was made of steel and came from Holland, where she had first taken to the water on the blustery North Sea, proving herself to be a sailor well worth her salt. Emma knew every inch of her, from the chain locker in the bow, to the rigging at the top of the mizzen mast, down to the storage area below the cockpit. When Emma was very small, she had hidden there while playing hide-and-seek with Domenica during an ocean crossing. She still measured herself against the canny little boat nooks she used to squeeze into. Her mother called her a chipmunk, and her father joked that one day she'd get stuck and he would have to pull her out by the hair with his heavy-duty pliers.

As Emma watched, the cabin windows became painted with a film of raindrops. She turned on a reading light as the sky darkened, abandoning her math lesson to flip through a book about sea adventures. In every story the captain was a man, just as her sister had said. Dom was stretched out on the narrow salon couch with a vampire novel, having already given up all pretence of studying.

Although Domenica had described what regular school was like, Emma couldn't imagine so many children assembled together in one place. Most of the other yachties they met were retired, or young couples without children. But there had been a few memorable friendships: Mireille, a red-headed girl from Nice whom she met in Sicily; Steph, from North London, with whom she had tried to speak to an enormous sea lion in the Galápagos; and Jacqui, whose parents had let her dye her hair purple and whose boat, *Rain Dog*, had been anchored next to *Buona Fortuna* in the Azores. These friendships had been both sanctified and spoiled by their fleetingness. Most alliances were created out of convenience, and Emma longed for a friend she could really choose and who would choose her. Her mother had promised that once they arrived in Australia, they would stay put long enough to enroll Emma and Domenica in regular classes, starting in January. This was what was going to sustain Emma during the days they would be anchored in New Caledonia, waiting out the storms that lay between them and Coffs Harbour in New South Wales. Cyclone season was upon them, and they were already supposed to be en route to Australia. Now they were aiming to get there in time to ring in the new millennium in Sydney Harbour. Mummy had promised fireworks, the biggest ones they'd ever seen. And then, at the end of the school term, they would finally return home.

When Emma was younger, Domenica used to entertain her by making up new constellations or telling her stories of life on land. Emma was six when they left Montauk to sail around the world, and she had only vague memories of living in a house. She didn't remember what it was like to not always be slathered in sunscreen, or to run around on grass like it was no big deal, or be sheltered by trees instead of forever gazing ahead into the dazzling, endless distance of the ocean. Solid ground was as novel to her as the swaying of the moored boat was to their occasional guests at the marina.

Domenica, she knew, did not feel the same way. There were things that her sister missed—memories she now only spoke of during the most difficult crossings. The corner store that sold sour gumdrops. The playground. Her friends from school. Emma remembered some of these things, too, but they did not feel real to her. They were like pictures in a storybook: bright and flat and static.

As the waves picked up, Dom went to the toilet to be sick. Emma brought her a glass of water and a Dramamine from the medicine cabinet.

"Tell me about our house, Dom," she said. It was her favourite story, the one that never got old. Emma could listen to her sister talk straight through a whole night of rough seas, while her parents took turns manning the wheel and throwing up. Usually Domenica would have to throw up, too.

"Our house had, like, a dozen rooms," said Dom, when the rolling of the ocean was less intense. "And we had a ping-pong table in the basement. And we were happy. Mum and Dad—they were happy then. I wish we'd never left."

Emma felt a tightening in her stomach, the same ache she always got whenever her sister started talking about their life on land. The fact that Domenica knew more than she did—about things that Emma herself had said and done in the time before she came into possession of her own memories—gave her an uncomfortable sensation she felt compelled to seek out, like a kind of irresistible torture.

"What's a ping-pong table, Dom?" she asked, even though she already knew. And as the sea churned beneath them, Emma held back her sister's hair and prodded her to continue her story in between her retching. There was something to be said for having her sister's undivided attention. Dom wiped her mouth with the back of her hand and spoke about ping-pong, and their lost backyard with its tree swing and the herb garden, and the heady, sweet smell of the lilac bushes that used to catch on the breeze and waft straight up through their bedroom windows.

After Dom told her about the lilacs, Emma went to her cabin and wrote a poem. It read: *Like Mummy's perfume on the shelf. / Like the memory of purple itself. / A flower in the spring / doesn't mean anything / on the ocean.*

The next morning, her mother made pancakes, Emma's favourite, so she knew that everything was going to be okay. When the weather was bad, nothing got cooked at all. Emma had eaten crackers for breakfast at least a dozen times that she could remember.

Faye turned on the SSB to listen to an amateur broadcast that was a family favourite. It was a show about cruisers: other yachties like them who were making a life aboard their vessels and travelling the world. During a crossing, the radio felt like the only thing still lashing them to shore and the rest of the human race.

The first news reported was that the *Maggie Mae* of England, a vessel owned by Mark and Luisa Hall, had been attacked by pirates off the coast of Somalia.

It was a boat they knew well. Faye and Harold had had the parents over for drinks when they were moored together in Panama and again in the Galápagos. Emma and Dom had spent hours sifting sand on the beach and counting sea lions with Steph and Katie, Mark and Luisa's children.

The family had been taken hostage and brought ashore, and though they were rescued a few days later, the *Maggie Mae* had not been recovered. The Halls had returned to London, cutting short their planned three-year trip.

"At least they're all alive," said Faye. Her voice was tight.

"The poor kids," said Harold. "It must have been terrifying for them. Well, for all of them really."

"What if pirates attack us?" asked Emma. She was scared, but everyone knew that the Indian Ocean was where most of the pirates were, and *Buona Fortuna* had already crossed the Gulf of Aden in a sort of impromptu convoy with seven other cruisers. Though there were other places in the world where yachts had been preyed upon.

"I have a baseball bat for emergencies," said her father, with unusual vehemence. "I'll hit the pirates on the head until they're dead."

"Harold," said Faye.

"Until they can't hurt us anymore," he amended, relaxing into a smile. "Better?"

But Emma had seen the dark glint in his eye and the determined strength in the curl of his fist, and she was frightened all over again.

Harold always took the first and last watch on a night crossing, and Faye in counterpoint put the girls to bed and woke them up to a cooked breakfast. It was good for him and Faye, he thought, to have the time apart. Night watches were the only solitude to be found once the boat was underway.

He wondered if he had overreacted earlier. A panic had been building in him ever since he'd received an email from the family lawyer two months ago. The subject line—*Bad news*—undersold the contents. It turned out that his father, Walter Aslet, director of the family foundation and trustee of a series of funds set up by Harold's late mother, had been outed as a fraud. Millions of dollars were missing. Millions more were owed. And Walt himself was gone, too—the United States would try to have him extradited if they had any idea where he was. The compound in Montauk had been seized by the bank, including the house Harold and Faye had been living in and were now renting out to tenants.

But though the title was seized, the renters had not been evicted. And whether through oversight or error, the rent money was still being transferred into Harold's personal account, though he had no idea how much longer that would last. Only the boat was theirs outright. Even if they wanted to go home early, they couldn't. Worse, he had yet to confide the bad news to Faye, whose ignorance he now found touching, like a quaint souvenir from a bygone era. After almost five years away, his wife had fallen out of touch with most of her Montauk friends. But it was only a matter of time before she found out the truth.

Soon he would have to reveal they had no home to go back to, and then they would have to decide what to do next. He wasn't sure they could even afford to complete their sojourn in Australia and the last leg of the journey home.

And now Annie was dead, and Faye had caught him crying at the computer. Even though she had never said anything, Harold had sensed that she knew about the affair. His wife's antagonism registered more as a kind of absence than anything else. It was possible that one day Faye would have removed so much of herself from their relationship that he would suddenly find himself alone. But for now they were together, never further than a few feet apart.

The affair with Annie had been sixteen years ago. It had lasted a year. A little longer if you counted the time they'd known each other professionally before they gave in to the attraction that Harold, at any rate, had felt right from the start. Annie had done some art dealing for his parents and arranged the sale of a Chagall sketch that his mother had left to him in her will. She lived in a college town somewhere in Massachusetts, where her husband taught, but often travelled to New York and the Hamptons for work. She was slight and pale, with the kind of translucent beauty that wouldn't survive long on deck, hauling lines under a tropical sun. But she was charismatic enough to sell a Picasso to a pauper, and had a better sense of humour than Faye— she could laugh at life's dark absurdities.

Soon after they'd broken it off, he'd heard she was pregnant. He'd worried a bit about the timing—he couldn't help doing the math— but Annie must still have been sleeping with her husband, too, at the end of their time together.

Faye had fallen pregnant with Domenica not long after. A lucky coincidence given how he'd felt himself drifting away from her. The pregnancy brought him back to himself, to the life he had chosen. To Faye. And it was the choosing that had made the difference, that was going to redeem him in the end. He had to believe that.

Harold checked the radar and updated the hourly log. The rows of handwritten entries painstakingly recorded by him and Faye stretched down in neat columns on page after page. No balance sheet, yet he knew that every entry brought them closer to a final reckoning. But, for now, Harold returned on deck and waited for his eyes to adjust to the darkness.

⊶||||⊷

As a kind of protest against her parents and her whole frustrating, constricted life, Domenica would only speak to Emma when it suited her. And it usually only suited her when she was sick. As *Buona Fortuna* sailed through the second bout of stormy weather between Fiji and New Caledonia, Domenica found herself laid low again, her bare knees bruising against the cool bathroom floor.

"Do you know about Annie?" she said, taking a tentative sip from the glass of water Emma handed to her. While her sister was despicable for her absolute insusceptibility to sea sickness, she really was helpful during the times when everyone else was incapacitated.

"No. Who's that, Dom?" said Emma.

"The ghost of *Buona Fortuna.*"

"*Buona Fortuna* doesn't have a ghost."

"We do, too." Now that Emma's jaw was set and resolute, Domenica began to warm to her story. "Annie was a friend of Daddy's. A *good* friend, if you know what I mean." She noticed the growing blankness of her sister's face, an empty canvas she could never resist. Domenica liked to make an impression. She plunged on. "She came over once when Mummy had to go out. And she was nice—she brought us presents. You got a book about the Pied Piper that you were obsessed with."

"What happened to her?"

"Daddy had to hurt her." Domenica's face was solemn. "He had to hurt her to make her go away."

Emma was studying her closely. "No, he didn't. Daddy wouldn't hurt anybody. Not on purpose."

"Yes, he would. To protect his family." Inspired by her own performance, Domenica felt tears pricking her eyes. "Daddy was jealous that I liked her so much. She said I could stay with her instead of going away on the boat." Despite the absurdity of the story she was telling, Domenica broke out into an unexpected sob. Every once in a while, she uttered a lie she almost wished were true. It was so unfair to be stuck on a boat with no friends and nothing to do, while her life was passing her by. She folded her arms over the toilet seat, laid her head down, and cried, shaking with a genuine misery that even her sister could not mistake.

"So what did he do?" asked Emma.

Domenica took in a shaky breath and looked at her with pity. "You're just little, Em. Are you sure you don't want me to stop?"

Emma opened her mouth, then paused and shook her head.

"Annie came over to talk to Daddy late at night while Mummy was at a fundraiser for the opera." Domenica stared off into the distance, conjuring the scene in her mind's eye. "She had long dark hair and a blue dress and was as beautiful as Mummy's print of the nymph that's hanging up in the galley. Annie brought me a pop-up book about Cinderella. Then Daddy drove us all to the marina. You were there, too, but you were only six."

Domenica closed her eyes and remembered her father kissing Annie on the deck of *Buona Fortuna* when he thought that she and Emma were both waiting in the car. It was a passionate, consuming kiss—the kind of kiss she had rarely seen between her parents. If ever. She cleared her throat. "And then, when they got down to the water,

Daddy pushed her and she fell in." Domenica shuddered. Her own imagination was sometimes a terrible place to be these days.

"No." It was Emma's one small protest, but it lacked all resolve.

"Yes," said Domenica. "Daddy had to do it, to keep us together."

"No, he didn't. He didn't do it!"

Domenica allowed her sister's determined glare to persist for a moment longer. "And he never even tried to get her out. And so she drowned. Everyone thought it was an accident, but it wasn't."

"Poor Annie!" cried Emma, her voice rising to a wail. "But Dom," she said, "couldn't she swim?"

"Don't you remember Daddy's pirate bat?" said Dom. "It's come in handy for all sorts of things."

Domenica's stomach was calm now. The story had allowed her mind to move along with the swells of the ocean. She felt nimble. Light as a bird. "I'm going to bed," she announced, muting her triumph somewhat in deference to her sister's misery. She rose, rinsed out her mouth at the sink, and washed her face with a pink washcloth. She took one step over her sister to reach the door, then paused. "Don't ask Mum and Dad about this, Em. It's a sore point between them. Mum doesn't like thinking about Annie and everything that happened."

Emma only nodded, her knees pulled tight to her chest under her turquoise nightie. Domenica left her like that, a small huddle on the floor.

By the next morning, Emma felt compelled to substantiate some part of the horror that her sister had told her.

Eventually, she found it, tucked away in the sail locker between the pantry and her parents' cabin. The fact that the bat was hidden away seemed to support Domenica's story. Emma could only imagine that Daddy must feel terrible about what he had done and didn't want a daily reminder.

She peered at the bat closely to look for traces of blood or damage. Emma knew murder weapons were not always things like daggers and revolvers. She thought through the array of other death-dealing objects that figured in her favourite board game, Clue. The candlestick, the wrench, the lead pipe, the rope. Most of those items could be found aboard *Buona Fortuna*. But the bat did seem more potent than those precious miniatures. When she tried swinging it, it slipped from her grip and hit the floor of the locker with a loud thud.

"What are you doing in here, chipmunk?" asked a mild voice right behind her, causing Emma to drop the bat again and her mother to step back to avoid its falling weight.

"Playing," she answered, as the bat clattered to the floor.

"Darling," her mother said. "Tell me what's on your mind. What are you worrying about?"

Emma's eyes widened. She shook her head. Maybe it was best to just blurt it out. Domenica's story could not be left unchecked. Emma tried to point to the bat, but she felt her movement was exaggerated, her elbow a massive hinge threatening to swing loose. Finally, she cleared her throat.

"Mummy, is our boat haunted by a ghost named Annie? A friend of Daddy's who drowned?"

Her mother looked at her a moment before replying: "Yes." Then, "Don't you want to lend your father a hand in the cockpit? I'm sure he could use your help."

Then her mother returned to her couch in the salon.

Faye could never understand why she helped to sustain Domenica's lies. There had been other times when Emma had posed her a seemingly innocuous and random question, usually related to their life in Montauk, and Faye's unwillingness to expose what she knew must be one of Dom's fabrications had always resulted in a slip of the tongue, a *yes* where there should have been a *no*. Perhaps she only wanted to prolong Emma's adulation of her sister a little longer. At times, her younger daughter reminded her of an exotic pet removed from its natural habitat. She worried that the girls, especially Emma, had been away from regular life too long.

She could not be certain what transpired between the girls late at night during the rough passages, when she was too focused on helping Harold in the cockpit, or occasionally too ill. But she suspected that Domenica must be trying to relieve her own passionate boredom. And Faye, who loved travelling but had grown to despise the sea, could hardly blame her.

And in this case, it was really only half a lie. Annie was haunting her as surely as any real ghost ever could.

She wondered exactly what Domenica knew or pretended to know about Annie. God forbid Harold had mentioned her to the girls. The online obituary he had been crying over mentioned a vibrant career in curation and art dealing. A bereaved husband, Keelan, and a daughter, Julia, who was the same age as Domenica. Annie's ashes had been scattered in the Columbia River, near a wooded area that she had apparently liked to frequent as a young woman.

Faye thought of her often, this woman whose unexpected death had brought Harold to tears. And who had brought to Faye an unwilling awareness of a hesitation, a vagueness at the centre of a love that had once felt so secure.

So far she had kept secret her awareness of the affair for nearly as long as Harold himself had hidden it. Was that not its own kind of betrayal? However the lie had begun, she was now almost as complicit as Harold. As Annie.

Just last night Faye had traced the Columbia River on a map to see whether, in fact, its waters emptied into the sea.

·ı| | |ıı·

It was first watch when Emma joined Harold in the cockpit. Small for so long, she'd at last begun to spring up into a coltishness that made her look scrawny in the summer clothes that she'd practically outgrown. The morning light revealed dark circles under her eyes as though she hadn't slept, and Harold wondered if stress could be contagious, if his own disquiet above deck had diffused into his children's bunks.

It was more of a burden than Harold let on sometimes, being the captain of a small vessel with his whole family aboard. Their lives were in his hands. And all their fates were tied to *Buona Fortuna*. His youngest daughter's ease with sailing still made him nervous in a way he couldn't quite explain. It made sense, after all, given she'd spent more than a third of her life at sea. She found endless enjoyment in using the depth sounder, the radar, and the compasses. She pored over any chart spread out on the table in the salon. But with WASPish logic, Harold reasoned that the best way to cultivate this sort of talent was to make as little of it as possible, treating her as he would a son, or a hired crewman. Probably what he was really afraid of—more than bad weather, more than any Y2K computer glitch, more than being broke, even—was that he would come to rely on her.

"Morning, Em. It's a lovely day, isn't it?"

Emma nodded, squinting her eyes and frowning in the sunlight. She could see the island nation of New Caledonia beckoning in the far distance. A haze of red soil and green trees. She longed to shout *Land ahoy!* the way she probably would have yesterday. Had it been an equally lovely day when her father hit Annie with the bat and pushed her into the water?

Her father glanced at her again, and Emma squinted at the face that was so familiar to her but now so strange. How mild he looked.

"Have you come to give me a hand?" he asked.

This time Emma shook her head. Her small brow furrowed as she thought of her sister's tears, her mother's terse confirmation, and the woman who had been sacrificed so that they could all live on the sea.

"You don't need my help," she said, hands pulling at the sides of her dress. "And you never listen to my weather updates. You don't need me to take the wheel because it's on autopilot right now."

"Well, that's not quite—"

Emma cut him off. "You know, Mummy could just cook breakfast and peek outside every five minutes and it would be pretty much the same thing."

She watched her words register on her father's face. Emma recognized her statements as true, but she could not remember thinking them before. She wondered how much knowledge it was possible to possess without knowing it. She had few memories of living on land, even though she had, for six whole years. Perhaps a part of her even remembered Annie—the part of her that was sad and, all of a sudden, a little afraid.

"Baby," he began.

"I'm not a baby!" She swallowed to keep the tears from coming.

"No, you're not. But you're acting as nuts as your sister these days."

This was too much for Emma and her eyes overflowed. The back of her throat ached, but only one sob escaped. She didn't want them to say any more horrible things to each other. Some words, once heard, couldn't be forgotten.

When Emma got below deck, her eyes were stinging. She curled up in her bunk, even though it amounted to hiding in plain sight. She used the end of a pencil on the inside wooden railing to sketch a tiny bicycle made of stars, the first constellation her sister had helped her pick out of the night sky. The bunk was the only refuge she had left. There were no nooks she could fit into any longer. There was nowhere to get away to when you were in the middle of the ocean. She wondered if people who lived on land knew how free they really were.

Her father had called her a baby, but Emma didn't feel like a kid anymore. When she remembered things now, it was like looking back on someone else's life. She remembered the first time the hot sand had burned the soles of her feet and how her mother had complained about her standing there and screaming instead of running to get off of it, as any normal person would have done. The skin on the bottom of her feet had blistered and peeled. What her mother didn't know was how unfamiliar the ground had seemed that afternoon. How unsteady and dangerous, as the Earth heaved and spun around her.

That spinning on land didn't happen anymore—*mal de débarquement* was what Daddy called it, after Emma had finally made him understand she wasn't exaggerating. That was another sign that she was no longer a child.

As Harold motored *Buona Fortuna* into the anchorage at Nouméa, Faye was keeping a lookout, something her daughters usually liked to do when they made landfall. But both of the girls were sulking about something. She had left them below deck after extracting a promise they would do some homework.

Faye had spent most of the morning making contingency plans for Y2K, and her heart felt lighter the moment they dropped anchor. The squall they had encountered on the last passage had made her long for solid land and other people. It wasn't normal for a woman of her age to be trapped for days on end with only her husband and her two children for company. At least, it shouldn't be normal. With Domenica and Emma, she felt the need to remain parental, in control. With her husband, she felt compelled to fill all roles: shipmate, cook, wife, buddy. She had prepared so many miserable meals on their hotplate that *Buona Fortuna*'s anchor might as well be attached to her ankle, complete with its two hundred feet of galvanized chain.

Nouméa, the capital of New Caledonia, was very French, and Faye, remembering the glamour of the Riviera, dug out a dress that was less threadbare than most of the shirts and shorts she usually wore. Harold muttered something about needing to look for another alternator and stalked off without making plans to meet for lunch. She wondered whether his bad mood was really related to Domenica, or if it had something to do with Emma, who'd seemed upset earlier. It was a delicate dance, managing four personalities on a forty-two-foot boat. These days, she couldn't be bothered.

A few evenings later, they set sail for Australia. The crossing could take over a week, depending on the weather. Emma's parents had spent the better part of two days listening to Inmarsat satellite weather reports and calculating the fastest route to Sydney that would avoid the low-pressure zones. The palm trees waved, the sandy beach enticed, but they were wrapped up in the uncertainty of what might happen in the next few hours, few days, few weeks.

In and out of sleep, Emma dreamed of exploding computers, sharks clubbed to death by bats, and her parents kissing and being attacked by seagulls. Around midnight, a sudden lurch of the boat woke her, and she would have tumbled from her bunk if she had not remembered to attach the lee cloth before going to bed. When she looked out of the porthole, all she could see was water.

Clambering out of her bunk, Emma rushed from her cabin to make sure all the hatches and windows were closed. It felt as though

Buona Fortuna was keeled right over almost onto her side, while being tossed up and down on the roiling swells like a carnival ride. Emma could scarcely walk—she had to grab at the bolted-down furniture to move through the salon. Her parents were not in sight; she guessed they were in the cockpit, trying to steer by hand. She could feel the boat being battered by the waves. It was much worse than the last storm they had weathered; she knew that much for sure. She wondered if she should go to Domenica, who would certainly be awake and scared.

Before Emma could decide what she was going to do, her father stumbled down the companionway into the salon. Dressed in his complete foul-weather slicker suit, he was soaked. He moaned, then staggered to the bathroom, water pooling in his wake.

"Help your mother," Emma heard him say between retches.

Domenica had by this time emerged from her cabin, her eyes wide and frightened. Her hair had lost its sleek perfection of the day before, and her cheek showed the indentations of a creased pillow-case. She stood there silently, staring past her sister to the darkened portholes of swirling ocean.

"It'll be okay, Dom," said Emma, snatching up a blanket from the salon sofa, where her mother had left it earlier. She wrapped it around her body, swathing herself from head to toe in its soft fleece. After checking that she could still move her arms freely, she rushed up the companionway and through the hatch to the open cockpit, her sister trailing behind her.

The sight that met her eyes seemed to justify Domenica's petrified silence. The sky was as black and furious as Emma had ever seen it. A huge wave loomed above them, foam at its crest, but just when it looked as though it was going to break over them, sweeping them into the ocean, *Buona Fortuna* was lifted up violently, foam rushing onto the decks and flowing down into the cockpit.

"Close the hatch!" Emma yelled, terrified the water would swamp the cabin. Still lingering on the companionway stairs, Dom slammed the glass door, latching it shut between them. Emma turned to her mother, who was taut with an intensity she had never seen.

With water pouring off the surface of her yellow raincoat, Faye's face was pale and strained, her hair drenched and clinging to her cheeks in wet strands. Leaning her whole weight into the wheel, her knuckles white and her feet braced against the base of the post, she tried to retain control of the boat.

Since power steering allowed even the girls to take the helm in fair weather, Emma understood that the hydraulic system and maybe even the autopilot had either failed or could not be trusted in such dangerous weather. If *Buona Fortuna* were steered wrongly, the waves could get the better of her. Emma rushed to join her mother at the wheel, grabbing on as firmly as she could and helping wrench it around in the direction they wanted the bow to point.

Her mother shook her head, shouting something about a harness, and Emma quickly strapped herself into the gear that her father had just vacated and secured herself to the stanchion. Then she took hold of the wheel again, summoning all of her slight strength to aid her mother.

Faye immediately felt the effects of Emma's assistance, and her arms began to relax even as she tried to maintain tension in all her muscles. She had no idea how long she had been holding *Buona Fortuna* on course. It might have been ten minutes or three hours. When Harold had been out on deck, he'd had the difficult task of bringing in all the sails—something that they would have done before the storm set in had it not come upon them so unexpectedly. Once he had finally pulled in the jib, nearly slipping into the water as he did so, he had retreated below to succumb to his seasickness. She knew that she ought to have called out to him, explained how hard it was for her to hold the wheel on her own. She hoped that her pride wouldn't cost her family their lives.

Through the driving rain and wind against her face, Faye tried to force her eyelids open, through what seemed like a torrent of water pressure trying to fight them down. The pitch and roll of the boat was making her head spin; the roar in her ears made her feel as though she were already underwater.

"Chipmunk," she said, not knowing whether Emma could hear her. "I don't feel well."

When she felt her mother's strength on the wheel dissipate, Emma threw the weight of her whole body into the pull. She remembered her father telling her about the adrenaline that allowed mothers to pick up whole cars under which their children were trapped. She hoped she had that, whatever it was. She screamed for her sister and father as loudly as she could.

Her gaze fixed on the compass, Emma did not see or hear anyone joining her on the deck. Then, from the corner of her eye, she recognized her father's foul-weather suit and its hard-brimmed hood bending over her semi-conscious mother, gripping the wheel with one hand and easing Faye into one of the deck seats behind them. Emma readied herself to relinquish her spot at the helm. But she didn't feel the release of as much tension on the steering as she would have expected; she was still straining to hold *Buona Fortuna* on course. She turned to greet her father and saw Domenica's terrified face looking back at her beneath their father's hood.

"Dom, don't worry," she yelled, feeling protective of her sister. Emma watched the streaks of lightning illuminating the sky in the distance. Black squall lines were still rushing towards them over the darkened horizon. Emma's blanket was soaked through, and her teeth were knocking together.

"Dom," she yelled again, shaking her head to remove some of the water streaking down her face. All her muscles ached. But Domenica kept her eyes down, looking at the deck rather than at the waves engulfing their small boat, and Emma realized her sister could not hear her.

She wanted to tell Domenica that they would never abandon one another, that she would never betray her like their father had, or ignore her like their mother. Or try to keep her to herself, an ocean away from real life. "Everything's going to be okay," Emma shouted, though in that moment she wasn't sure she believed it.

If Domenica heard her, she didn't give a sign. The girls held on tight.

Thank you for your messages, everyone. I'm thrilled so many of you responded to my tentatively expressed hope for some lively commentary on the blog. I feel as though I've been seen off by scores of well-wishers.

A few of you have requested more details about the process of setting to sea. Jim in Homestead, Florida, asked for a list of yacht upgrades, and Sam in Ayr, Scotland, wondered about provisioning for a long-term offshore cruise. First of all, let me say that you should only undertake this type of journey if you're a qualified sailor. But with that disclaimer on the record, I don't mind sharing some details about my preparations.

I've brought onboard a lot of necessities: food, fuel, spare parts, tools, manuals, an extensive medical kit with four bottles of seasickness pills. The bottom of the boat has been freshly painted with anti-fouling paint to keep off the barnacles. New solar panels have been installed, as well as a new watermaker, new communication systems, a wind generator, and underwater lights for night swimming.

I've also discovered that more food comes in powdered form than I'd ever imagined. Case in point: powdered butter. But don't worry . . . I'm opting for canned. Yes, canned butter!

Another thing I've learned: you have to think about buoyancy, the weight of everything you've put aboard. Water and other liquids (ahem, beer), with a stockpile of food and fuel laid by, can actually affect the overall weight so much that you may need to adjust your waterline.

Of course, I'm carrying aboard a lot of cherished hopes and plans as well. This isn't just about avoiding ARAMIS. It's an excuse to follow a dream that I've had since I was a little boy—simply getting in a boat and sailing away.

One thing I don't have: plants. I'd mentioned a potted fern and a cactus in my first post and a couple of you warned me that real sailors won't stand for such things. Apparently, plants shouldn't come to sea; they seek the earth. Call me superstitious, but I've thrown the poor things overboard. Better them than me.

Dove Suite Band Members Announce Pregnancy

Sept. 12, 2020

NEW YORK—Dove Suite band members Emma Aslet and Stuart Jenkins are expecting their first child. Frontman Jenkins made the announcement during a press conference to reveal the full lineup of performers for To America With Love, the sold-out day-long music festival in support of ARAMIS relief that Dove Suite will be headlining in Vancouver on September 26.

Now based in Austin, Texas, Aslet, 32, and Jenkins, 34, were married in 2009, one year after founding the successful indie rock quartet in Philadelphia with bassist Jesse Luxton and drummer Ben Grainger.

Jenkins spoke to *Rolling Stone* about the couple's excitement: "It's beyond thrilling, to be honest. We've been waiting for this for a long time."

Rumours of the pregnancy have been circulating online since the abrupt cancellation of Dove Suite's worldwide tour in support of their fourth album, *Beads*. Jenkins confirmed the rationale for the touring hiatus: "Starting our family has meant shifting priorities for the time being. But I'm sure we'll get back out on the road before too long."

Jenkins admitted the couple was erring on the side of caution. "I'm sure we could go on tour and everything would be fine, but honestly it's just easier this way. I don't think we could live with ourselves if we took any unnecessary chances."

According to Jenkins, the baby is due in November.

Aslet was not available for comment.

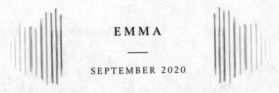

EMMA

—

SEPTEMBER 2020

Emma slipped her hand into her pocket and pulled out her phone. Reflexively, she snapped a photo of the half-deserted terminal and sent it to her sister. *Surprise upside of terrifying worldwide epidemic: no epic lineups to get through airport security!*

She and Stu and their bandmates were waiting in a newly designated pre-screening area, as six ceiling-mounted monitors tuned to the same news network flashed synchronously high above. In a couple of hours they would be flying into Canada by special dispensation to headline an ARAMIS benefit concert in Vancouver.

It was only a few weeks ago that Emma was lying on the couch in front of the television saying, "ARAMIS sounds like something nice to catch. Much less disgusting than swine flu."

Stu was on the rug, playing with an old theremin he'd found at the Salvation Army and repaired with the help of how-to guides on the internet. "They should name all the flu variants the way they do hurricanes." His hand cut through the air above the theremin and a hypnotic sound thrummed across the room. "They're like the chorus of a song, the way they come around every year. It would sound like a much friendlier way to die, getting killed off by Flu Henrietta or Flu Kevin."

Back then, she'd laughed. Now she checked her phone for a response from Domenica, though the time difference made it unlikely.

Her sister had moved halfway around the world and married a man named Ahmad, who was actual oil royalty from the U.A.E., and with whom she had two little girls, Aliya and Leila. Emma and Dom communicated mainly via text—or, more frequently these days, highly staged photos annotated with emoji reactions.

"Looking up baby names?" asked Jesse. "I nominate Jessica."

Ben shook his head. "Way too eighties."

"This may come as a shock," said Emma, "but you guys actually don't get a vote on this."

Stu grinned and leaned over to place a gentle palm on her belly. "How are you feeling?" he asked. "What did the doctor say?" Stu was tender, careful with her these days. The baby was precious cargo and Emma was the courier, the protective packaging. She was the Styrofoam peanuts. No matter how close they were, the baby was between them now.

"The baby is fine," said Emma. At least, the baby had been fine at last week's appointment. But this morning, while Stu assumed she was enduring the clinic's usual battery of tests, the premier tattoo artist in Texas had looked at her stomach like it was a dude who had cut in front of him in line.

"Absolutely no way," he'd said from behind the counter, and he shook his head so minutely it was as though he didn't want to give her anything—not a tattoo, not an apology, not an inch. "It's just too risky for the baby," he said, crossing his arms. Each one sported a forked-tongued scaly dragon licking its way down the back of his hand. "You've got the risk of preterm labour. Risk of infection. And pregnant women's skin is different. More elastic. It holds more water. So there's a question of the quality of the tattoo. Stretch marks. Scarring."

Emma suspected that tattoo artists liked saying no because they were the last people on Earth that anybody expected to have limits. Especially tattoo artists with tattoos on their *faces*. Yet she had apparently found a line that this leather-wrapped, forehead-pierced professional with two symmetrical cheek tattoos and a handlebar moustache was unwilling to cross. And then the baby had kicked up its feet into her side, as if in celebration of her disappointment.

Emma knew it was a morbid streak inherited from her mother that made her want to follow through on major life decisions before heading out on a journey. During the years her family had sailed around the world, at every port of call her mother had tried to take care of all the serious business that occurred to her as their boat lurched in the horrific swells of some Pacific storm. That was what Emma wanted: to take care of the serious business of defacing her God-given temple before the baby came to do it for her.

Plus, if anything ever happened to her, they'd be able to identify her body.

"You're sure you don't think it's too risky?" Stu asked now. "Did the doctor say anything about flying at seven months?"

"It'll be fine," she said, glancing down at her phone so he wouldn't see her face, unsure of what expression he would read there. If she was too afraid, or not enough. ARAMIS seemed distant and far-fetched compared to the more pressing concerns of a feeble bladder and broken sleep. The truth was that Emma already felt as though she'd contracted an affliction that was wreaking havoc on her body and mind.

But ARAMIS was alarming enough that there were travel advisories in place. The E.U., Mexico, and the United States had gone so far as to ban their citizens from travelling to and from China. In retaliation, China had called for certain debts to be repaid, and the President of the United States of America had gone on television and tried very hard not to say that his country couldn't quite afford to buy enough antivirals for everyone who might need them. The media, however, had no compunctions about spelling it out. Sales of guns and generators were through the roof all over the country, even as the overcrowded American ICUs reported a survival rate above 60 per cent for adults—a statistic that Emma did not find altogether comforting. They had no comparable data for children, who by and large remained comatose. But so far, there had been no cases reported in Canada. Or in Austin, for that matter.

Emma waited a beat before turning to grin at Stu. "Besides, the doctor said I needed more freedom in my life. And more fun. He actually *recommended* a tattoo. Can you believe it?"

Stu frowned, but she just kept smiling as though she'd somehow forgotten last week's fight, when she'd shown him the sketch of the tattoo she wanted. Stu had barely glanced at the design before pushing it back to her along the kitchen counter.

"I really don't see why you need one," he had said, dismissive. "Do you want to look like every other washed-up musician in twenty years?"

He was dead set against her getting a tattoo, but only nominally for the baby's safety. There was something ever-so-slightly uptight about Stu, a purity streak, or maybe just some strain of aspirational upper-middle-classness that made him think tattoos always had to be trashy, like a type of body graffiti that the taxpayers were going to have to pay to take down. As if her body were a kind of monument that the public could reasonably expect to be unsullied. All the more reason why she needed to reclaim it for herself.

Emma had looked over her drawing, a dove foregrounded by four blooming roses, petals unfurled and stems intertwined. Amateurish as it was, she was proud of it. "And why exactly will we be washed up by then? I intend to keep writing songs until I lose my marbles." She folded the sketch and pressed it back into her notebook, trying to shrug off how hurt she really was. "Listen to yourself. Stop telling me what to do like some fifties husband. You're oppressing me."

It was supposed to be a joke, but Stu's face had clouded over. "Don't say things like that. There's nothing funny about not respecting women."

Emma thought her eyes might roll right out of her head. "God, you're such a Boy Scout. It's crazy that people think you're some kind of rock god, when deep down you're completely conventional."

Stu scowled and threw down the book he'd been reading. "As if tattoos weren't the most conventional thing possible for someone in a band. Careful you don't become a cliché yourself."

Emma's cheeks felt as though she'd been slapped. "How about the cliché of running your mouth off to any reporter willing to sit down and listen? You're such a . . . a . . . a blabbermouth," she finished, feeling lame.

"And you're selfish and completely wrapped up in yourself." His tone was calm and diagnostic as he stood up and pushed in his stool. Then, seeing her face collapse, he softened. "Em, why can't you understand that the choices you make affect me, too?"

The argument had continued, but Emma had let it peter out, nervous at how far they'd coasted from the familiar shores of their relationship and out into some uncharted sea of cruelty.

Now Emma tried to keep her voice light, avoiding any of the Republican comparisons she'd resorted to last time. "You know it's my decision, right? You actually can't tell me not to."

"Just wait a few months, until the baby's born," said Stu, wrapping his arms around her waist. Emma wondered if he was being affectionate because the others were there or if he really was less rattled by their last fight than she was. He leaned in and smelled her hair. "And who knows? You might change your mind by then."

"When have you ever known me to change my mind?"

He laughed. "You're right. You're an abominably obstinate woman."

"Thank you." When Emma glanced up at the TVs again, the news was airing another story about New York City's so-called ARAMIS Girl.

"Oh, I want to see this," she said. Stu patted her hand as they listened to pundits speculate about how many people ARAMIS Girl might have infected.

"She's an example of a broken public health authority," an analyst from a Washington think tank was saying. Emma stared at the now-familiar photo of the smiling girl, frozen in time before her face and life got blown up out of all proportion.

"I feel so bad for her," she said, watching the rabid discussion of ARAMIS Girl's possible movements. Emma tried to imagine the down-sides of sudden fame without any of the perks. "She must be scared stiff."

"If she's even still alive," said Stu. The program switched to a con-versation about infection avoidance and an interview with one of the station's new commentators, the writer of a bestselling pandemic novel. He appeared onscreen via a low-quality video feed. "Oh my God," said Stu, sounding oddly vehement. "This guy. Can't they find an actual expert? Or is real science taboo now?"

Emma squinted at the TV. "Why is he so grainy?"

"Because he's Skyping in from home. He's saying we should all stay inside, too."

"Easier said than done." A few months earlier, Emma had read the writer's novel, in which all of the world's children caught a deadly virus and died. At the time, it had seemed preposterous. The baby began a fury of kicking.

"Maybe we ought to call someone," said Stu. He rested his hand on her belly again, his eyes watching the ticker at the bottom of the news program as it tracked the confirmed number of cases of ARAMIS worldwide. "Let them know we want in on the special secret bunker for the rich and famous. Ha."

"Don't worry about ARAMIS," said Emma. "Believe me, I'm not going to."

Emma had met Stu at a concert—a story she had vowed to stop telling after it appeared in a sidebar in *Rolling Stone*. It was the first Philadelphia show of a band that had two decent college radio hits at the time, but who were now more well-known for having played the show where Stu Jenkins met Emma Aslet.

The story was that Emma had been knocked down by a falling crowd surfer and Stu had helped her to her feet. Then they had squeezed their way out of the scrum, bought six shots of Jäger, and found their way up to the roof, where they stargazed and more or less immediately fell in love. Somewhere in there, they had sung the song "Victoria" by the Kinks at the tops of their lungs, which was a detail Emma regretted revealing after people began requesting it during the encore. That was when she realized there were some things they needed to keep for themselves.

And Stu. In those days he used to make her forearm the neck of his guitar, closing his eyes while she lounged in his lap and let him press their songs into her, one chord progression at a time. Her skin would tingle under the rough calluses of his left hand as she closed her eyes, too, feeling her way to the sweetest harmonies. He told her he had never sung without his guitar in front of anyone but her.

When they met, Stu was working in a bike shop, writing music at night. He'd done a philosophy degree at a liberal arts college in Western Massachusetts before moving back to Philadelphia with the idea of putting together a band, though he hadn't actually talked to anyone about it yet. A year later they were married, and Emma had dropped out of Bryn Mawr and moved into Stu's studio apartment in Fishtown, where she started them on a schedule of writing songs and recording demos. It was Emma who found Ben and Jesse at a party full of students from the Curtis Institute of Music. Both studied classical guitar, but Ben had played drums in high school jazz band and missed it. Jesse landed on bass. The four of them fell to work on the band as though it was the thing that mattered most. Before long they had an easy rapport in which the thousands of tiny decisions that took forever to explain to other people became simple, silent, subsumed into the music itself.

Emma booked shows for them at all the clubs within a day's drive, hawking their self-titled EP and keeping track of how much money was left on the inside back cover of their road atlas. And then, just before she had to figure out whether they could afford to fix the air conditioning in the van, they got picked up by Matador, released a full-length record, and watched as, one after another, the big music mags dubbed it the album of the year. Before they'd even started their first national tour with a real bus, MOJO had declared that Dove Suite might save rock and roll. No pressure.

Emma used to think she liked the pressure, the way it sharpened her nerves and reflexes. The focus it seemed to bring to all her decisions. The drive it gave her to write better songs, give more intense performances, and build the life she wanted from the ground up— brick by brick if she had to. But once she got pregnant, the pressure felt like it had no outlet, no purpose. She was like a kettle set to boil, forgotten on the element, just whistling Dixie until she burned dry.

Even before she'd started to show, Stu had summoned everyone to a band meeting to announce the pregnancy. Then he'd gone ahead and called off the tour indefinitely. Time was when he'd never make a decision about the band without checking with her first.

"You don't know how you're going to feel, Em," he'd said, and Ben and Jesse had sat around and nodded, and nobody had sided with her when she'd said that maybe, just maybe, they would be fine figuring it out on tour. Being the only woman in the band was something more profound than just a *drag*. It was a dive, a drop. It was like falling down a well into a world where she was half her normal size. After so many years of keeping the band's wheels turning on her own, maybe she should have been happy that Stu was finally making decisions by himself. Instead, she felt like telling him to play to his strengths and stick to the music.

But the baby had kicked her in the side and insisted she do the right thing, which she understood to be giving in without a fight. Forget about what she wanted. Forget whisky. Forget beer. Forget touring. Forget sleep, for that matter. Every night since they'd cancelled the tour, Emma had lain awake for hours, staring around their bedroom that felt cavernously large and nondescript in the dusky light filtering in through the blinds. It was only after she'd reached out to her Canadian promoter cousins and set things in motion for the benefit concert that she'd managed to get some rest at night. Her bandmates had been caught off guard by her sudden commitment to the charitable fundraiser, but they'd followed her lead. As usual. And for a few days she almost felt like things were back to normal. But then Stu had to go blabbing to reporters about the baby.

The pregnancy had made Emma feel as though she were preparing for a journey—*lift-off* was how she thought of it—a launch into the great beyond, where time moved differently. And yes, Stu would meet her there, on the space station or something, looking clean and well rested and wearing, for some unaccountable reason, an immaculately pressed beige suit. But he would get to teleport there unchanged, whereas she was supposed to be conditioning herself to exit the Earth's atmosphere with the pressure of a hundred rockets. *Blast off.* The least he could do was wait for her to announce the pregnancy herself, when they were both ready. Preferably after the child's safe delivery.

And just like that, all serious interest in the album and concert had been diverted into baby mania. The latest tabloid image of Emma circulating online was a paparazzi shot taken outside a drugstore in Austin, paired with an outsize zoom-in on the baby bump. In the second photo, they'd cropped off her head. The article was headlined IS THIS THE END OF DOVE SUITE?

⊶⊪∥∥⊪⊶

On the way to the security screening, Emma placed her shoulder bag in the top basket of a metal cart already loaded with the rest of their luggage. She began pushing it down the hall as she and Stu walked through the terminal. Ben and Jesse strolled a few paces behind, each with their own cart, deep in conversation about the best noodle places in Vancouver.

"Here," said Stu, reaching out for the cart's wide handle. "You shouldn't be doing that."

"It's okay," said Emma. She was enjoying the slight exertion of keeping the unwieldy vehicle moving forward in a straight line. If a stroller complete with baby weighed less than a weekend's worth of outfits, motherhood was going to be a cinch. "I've got it."

"Just let me do this for you," he said. Then, taking control of the trolley, Stu propelled it at a rapid clip down the wide, empty corridor. One of the front wheels began a high-pitch squeaking. "After all, you're going to be running around after our kids soon enough."

Emma slowed. "Kids? Plural?"

Stu stopped and gave her a half-grin. "Freudian slip?"

She caught up to him and seized the cart handle. "And why exactly am I going to be the one running around? What are you going to be doing?"

"Dad stuff." Stu furrowed his brow, squinting at her. "Come on, Em. It's just a figure of speech." He glanced over at Jesse and Ben for support.

Ben only shook his head, a warning look in his eyes. Emma saw something pass between them and realized she'd underestimated just how traditional Stu really was. She could see the future all mapped out: Stu spending more and more time in the studio, while she'd be expected to divert her energies to the baby. The only thing standing between her and the brute slavishness of motherhood was money.

"Just go," she said, lifting her hands off the cart and backing away. "God."

As Stu went ahead, Emma pulled out her phone and texted Jenna, the terrifyingly efficient young woman she'd hired to be the band's virtual assistant. *Can you go through that list of Vancouver tattoo artists I sent you and set something up* ASAP? *Make sure they're okay re: pregnancy and don't tell Stu. It's a surprise. Thx!*

Halfway down the corridor, Stu called to her over his shoulder. "Emma, you coming?" But he kept going without waiting for an answer.

With nothing in her hands, she felt too unencumbered, directionless. If there was anything that had changed in her over the years, it was that her rootlessness had deepened. All the travelling they'd done as a band kept bringing Emma back to her childhood at sea: all the countries she'd visited while always feeling from nowhere, or from a place more of the mind than real—half remembered, half described— and everywhere along the way picking up a phrase, a food, a new favourite thing. Markers and souvenirs. They might have been affectations, but maybe that was all character was anyway: an accumulation of affectations. The cigarettes were long gone. The bourbon still there—until she got pregnant. Sazeracs she'd left behind somewhere en route. She had come to enjoy a certain kind of unsettled, vagabond feeling, but the trade-off was always needing to know who you were. Otherwise, it was too easy to start drifting. If you stopped paying attention, there was no telling where you could end up, especially in the music business. That's what the tattoo was about. A kind of badge to show what she had been through. How far they had come and how much she had endured.

The baby was a badge, too, she supposed, though her foremost experience of the pregnancy to date was as a kind of weather. A fog of tiredness and uneasy sentimentality that veiled the fixed stars of her life. She was reluctant to complain to Stu. From what she could tell, her experience was normal. And though she'd wasted so many hours as a kid in pursuit of "normal," she had come to realize that her lack of that particular quality was what made her special. Special was the anti-normal. But having a baby was about as normal as you could get. Emma imagined their future child slip-sliding around in its uterine paradise, enlarging week by week through a progression of supermarket fruit benchmarks by feeding on precisely whatever it was inside Emma that used to make her different and unique. Since the onset of the baby weather, she had written three songs, all of them terrible. More than drifting, these days she worried she was actually lost. She wished she was at least carrying her purse.

At the departure gate, their tour manager Craig was sweating after rummaging in his briefcase for their medical certificates. Four all-clears, plus a waiver from Emma about the baby. Canada had no reported cases of ARAMIS to date and wasn't going to be held accountable for any lost babies.

"I had them last night," Craig was saying, glancing around as though hoping someone would chime in to say, *You did. They're in there. Keep looking.* Not that long ago, Emma would have been that person. Now she ignored Craig's public flailing.

Her phone buzzed with a message from Dom: *Freaky. But what I really want to see is a picture of your belly.*

Your wish is my command, Emma typed to her sister, then handed her phone to Stu, who had her pose sideways against a face mask dispenser.

"This isn't a mugshot," he said. "Smile, babe."

Emma made a face.

Then a security guard stepped out from behind him and snapped an identical pic, striding away before Emma could even blink or hold up a hand. She shivered.

Their first full day in Vancouver, there was a rehearsal scheduled for the afternoon. Gertie Colewick was pacing around backstage as another band played through their set, her hand jumping to her throat when one of the stage managers tapped her on the shoulder to ask for an autograph. She was wearing something that looked like a canvas mailbag, but her face was tranquil, her hair arranged into a precise and intricate wreath of braids.

Before she'd contacted Stu, Gertie was a forgotten treasure of the folk music scene who had been in the national missing persons database since 1975. She'd gotten in touch after she read an article in NME mentioning that "Tiny Hands," a song Stu had penned for their second album, was written about her. She'd mailed a letter to Stu, and folded within its pages were two tapes she'd recorded. Stu had called a band meeting to play them his favourites out of the thirty-odd songs that Gertie claimed were only about half of what she'd written since dropping out of the folk scene and, for all intents and purposes, off the planet.

"If you guys aren't behind it, I can go solo on this," he said. "I'm just really into her sound."

Emma had been surprised by the declaration. As long as she'd known him, Stu had avoided anything that required expending energy that he could be putting into his music instead. She used to joke that if she weren't there to make a plan for dinner, he'd end up starving until breakfast.

"I love her, too," she'd said. "So pure and unique." To Emma, Gertie still sounded exactly like she had in the summer of '73, when she'd recorded her one and only album in her parents' kitchen with the help of her younger brother. Back then, she'd seemed much older than twenty-two, singing about death and sagebrush and valley towns in California. "What if we do some orchestral arrangements?" Emma went on. "Or maybe ask her to collaborate on 'Bless Us' or 'The Moon'?" They were songs she'd written for *Beads* that hadn't made the cut. For the first time since they'd started making records, two-thirds of the songs on the new album were by Stu.

"If you don't mind, Em, I have a few ideas of my own for this one." Stu looked sheepish, proud, and—was it possible?—a little star-struck. "She wrote to me, after all," he said. Emma shrugged. In the first fog of the pregnancy weather, she hadn't felt much like pushing it. But it stung all the same.

Stu had gone on to produce the album, and Gertie had re-recorded twelve of the songs in their home studio. Her new breakthrough song was "Curious Fellow," which was generally assumed to be about her affair with a now-legendary folk singer who'd followed her from Greenwich Village to San Francisco. Stu had procured for Gertie something resembling her old homemade harp, and with Ben and Jesse, he had practised the arrangements they'd come up with in the studio so they could play backup on a few of the songs in concert. When Emma had heard this, she'd had to bite her lip to keep from pointing out, "Gertie didn't write to *them*, either." She wasn't sure she wanted to hear what Stu would say in response.

Gertie was now sitting cross-legged at the side of the stage. Her back was very straight, and the placidity of her face at rest was so open it was unnerving. Emma thought she looked like someone who had been living on the fringes of society, though the homeliness of her canvas-sack outfit no doubt played a role in this impression. Next to

Gertie, Emma felt ordinary. Diminished. A little foolish, too. It was the way she usually felt around vegans—who, Emma was sure, probably had it right after all. But Gertie was beyond vegan. Gertie probably strangled rabbits with her bare hands.

Emma tried to ignore the dustiness of the stage as she lowered herself to sit down next to the older woman. After she'd dropped out, Gertie had lived in tents, in shelters, and on the street. A floor probably counted as high luxury. "Did you ever get a tattoo, Gertie?"

"No," she said. Emma half expected a hippie screed about toxic ink, but the other woman only reached over and patted her hand. "I change my mind too much for that. Of course, I never had a baby either." Gertie's eyes were wide and sincere. She even seemed to blink less than other people. "Babies used to be a way to tame a woman. And I always needed to be free."

Emma flinched and glanced away, watching two roadies readying a piano in the wings. She didn't know what she'd expected to hear, but it had felt important to speak to Gertie, as though she were some holy woman come down from the mountain. Now Emma only felt nettled. "How'd that work out for you?"

Gertie's face was as mild as ever. "I got more freedom than I bargained for." Songs on her original album had hinted at a distrust of modern life, but she'd told Stu that her turn away from the world at large had more to do with a bad LSD trip than anything else. "You're braver than I ever was."

"I don't know about that." Emma hardly knew how to describe herself anymore. The pregnancy weather was a kind of separation that felt like it was as much from herself as from Stu. With every day that went by, she felt less in control of her own life. Deep in her bones, Emma feared the baby would force them off course. "It was brave of you to reach out to Stu. But it's bad timing for the comeback, isn't it? What with a deadly virus going around and all. Kind of a dangerous time to rejoin society."

Gertie pulled her legs up to her chest, wrapping her arms around them where they bulged up under her dress. "Maybe," she said. "I can't say I know much about joining or rejoining. I never even joined a band! Didn't want to compromise when it came to the music. Or anything else for that matter." She shifted her legs back out in a stretch, oblivious to any possibility of giving offence. "But the truth is I think things are coming to an end."

Emma closed her eyes. The poor woman had been living in the trees for years. There was no need to take her counsel about artistic integrity or anything else. But Gertie's words still felt like needles under her skin. "That's cheery," she managed.

"I shouldn't say that to a pregnant lady, should I? But we're too connected to keep going the way we have been. Everyone can see who has what and who doesn't." Without asking permission, she placed a hand lightly on Emma's belly as her face eased into a smile. "I might be a paranoid old hippie," said Gertie, "but it's time to come together, child."

⊷||||⊶

The pain was a trip, Emma decided. It was a trip because it was realer than real. It was an overload of new sensation. It was stinging and burning, a trial by fire. She was being born again, like a phoenix. Maybe that was what life should be about—change and challenge and new experiences.

"Are you sure about this, Em?" Ben was leaning up against the inside of the band's trailer with his arms folded across his chest, a pose that showed off both his defined drummer's biceps and his tattoos to best advantage. He shot her a worried glance.

"It's going to be a promise," she said.

"A promise? To whom?"

"Not to who," said Emma, ignoring the *whom* out of principle. "To what. To this. To music. To Dove Suite. And it's a surprise for Stu," she added. "So keep your mouth shut."

"Aha." Ben gave her one of his wide-open prairie smiles, but it dwindled as a buzzing sound filled the trailer again.

"Jesus fucking Christ, that hurts," said Emma. The desire to pull away from the tattoo gun was like an exhortation being screamed by every cell in her body. The baby was kicking, too: short, sharp blows to her side.

"Don't move," said Marisol, the tattoo artist. Her voice was low and intense, and Emma thought she might be able to draw some strength from it. She kept still but let her eyes rove around the trailer until they came to rest on the framed snapshot she always brought on tour: a photo of her family in front of their old boat. Her mother looking slim and strong in a sleeveless top, her hands on Emma's shoulders. Emma squinting, face scrunched, in a favourite pair of yellow shorts. Dom in her bikini with a sarong slung low on her hips, practising an alluring smile for the camera. And her father standing a little apart, sunburned in spite of his Tilley hat, his smile stiff and forced. But even from a distance, the relationships were clear. Nothing had seemed more enduring and inescapable than the four of them together on that boat. That impossible closeness that crumbled like a dry sandcastle once they returned home.

Inhaling in a slow, steady stream, Emma fixed her gaze on the picture, trying to experience the pain as any another benign sensation, like heat or cold. The photo itself was just as likely to provoke as soothe her at any given moment. Her childhood had been an idyll underwritten by anxiety. Her grandfather, Walt, was at least partially to blame, for embezzling from the family trusts and leaving them broke, but Emma remembered tense, miserable days in the last few months of their trip, listening to Domenica explain with evangelical persistence how wonderful their lives had been before they'd set sail. Whether Dom was right, or whether things had only fallen apart at the end, was something Emma still couldn't puzzle out. All she knew for sure were the plain facts: her parents' marriage had dissolved on the boat and was only rebuilt, years later, after they sold it. And after Emma eloped, Faye had the nerve to say that Stu was too idealistic and that marriage was only for the naive. Emma didn't think anyone who had fallen back in love with her ex-husband should be allowed the indulgence of cynicism.

"You know," said Emma, "people say you're selfish if you don't want kids. But what kind of world is this to be bringing a child into, anyway? That's selfishness, isn't it? That's sorrow. All the wars, the pollution. And now ARAMIS."

Ben looked perplexed. "Nobody is calling you selfish, Em."

"Well, maybe you should be." She exhaled then, and pictured calling in some of the roadies to hold her down. But all the guys out there were from a Vancouver company hired by the promoters. None of their regular crew was with them. She counted to one hundred and longed for Stu. She looked out the tiny window at a roadie smoking a cigarette, and her fear was spliced by a sudden nicotine craving curling out like a smoke tendril from the base of her reptilian brain. When her phone chimed in her purse, she told Ben to check it.

"It's your sister," he said. "She says she heard about the concert on the internet and wants to know how it's going."

"Take a picture," said Emma. "Send it to her." She smiled as Ben snapped some photos, then let her eyes close as he bent his head over her phone. She wished the time difference didn't always make it too late or too difficult to call Domenica. She wanted to hear her sister talking honestly about childbirth, motherhood, and whether she managed to hold any of her life back for herself. She wanted to hear Dom's voice on the phone, telling her, "Don't worry, Em, after all is said and done, you'll still be you."

The sound of the gun was the only thing keeping her on the ground. It was a song, and the gun was just percussion. Some strange new buzzing innovation by Ben. It was a performance, and she had to grit her teeth until the end.

"She's so pale," Ben was saying to Marisol. "Do you think she's okay?"

"I can hear you," said Emma. It was like that dream where they were getting ready for a concert and nobody could hear her saying she couldn't find her boots. "Can you hear me?" She forced her eyes open to make sure she was awake.

"Sing something, Em." Ben sounded calm, but his eyes were worried. "Would that be okay?" He looked at Marisol, who said it was a good idea as long as she could do it without moving. So they sang "Fixing a Hole" by the Beatles, Marisol smiling as Ben's tenor rang out. Emma sang quietly until she could actually feel the music pushing back against the pain. But as she got louder, Marisol told her to stop.

"Sorry, Emma, but you're actually vibrating."

The last five minutes were sound and fire and Ben holding her hand as she breathed in and out, counting up and down to ten in her mind as she inexplicably pictured Gertie Colewick rinsing clothes in a stream before rigging them up to dry in a wooded glade.

"All done," said Marisol after an eternity. "You're lucky. Greyscale is a lot faster than colour."

After Marisol left, taking all her equipment along with Ben's number, Emma stayed behind in the trailer, unsure of what her new pre-show ritual should be. She hadn't performed in front of an audience since before she got pregnant. How could she transform herself into the girl she was supposed to be onstage without the bite and heat of whisky down her throat, or the mellow buzz of a cold can of Pabst Blue Ribbon?

In the end, she decided to put on more makeup. There was a glittery purple eyeliner pencil somewhere at the bottom of her purse that had cost almost thirty dollars. It was about time she looked for it.

But first she angled herself on a seat in front of the mirror to peer at her shoulder again, carefully peeling back one corner of the loose bandage. Her upper back was bright pink. She jumped as the door opened.

"So you did it," said Stu. "And it's red as hell." He leaned down to inspect it, blocking the light from the window behind him. Emma felt like the trailer was shrinking around her. His face in the mirror didn't look happy, but she couldn't tell whether or not he was angry. "It's bleeding, too."

Emma refastened the bandage and stood up. "That's normal. That's what happens when somebody sticks a needle into you a thousand times." Then Stu's face started to swim in front of her eyes as her knees buckled, and she clutched at his arm. He grabbed her with both hands just below her ribcage.

"Are you okay?" he said, planting her back into her seat with less than his customary gentleness.

She nodded. "Head rush." Her mouth felt dry.

"For Christ's sake, there's only a quarter of a million people who showed up to watch you. Never mind the safety of our fucking baby." Stu's fingers tugged at the roots of his brown hair. "Goddamn it, Em. Where's your head at?"

Emma slid down in her seat, lip trembling. She put a hand to her side where she'd felt the baby's last kick. She hadn't felt it move since the tattoo. "Where it's always been," she said. "On the music, the band."

Stu lifted her crimson outfit off the back of the chair where Emma had draped it. "Stand up and hold up your arms."

As he slipped it over her head, she said, "I know how to dress myself."

"You also have a bandaged shoulder." Stu's breath was warm on the nape of her neck. "Talk to me. What the hell is going on with you?"

When her dress was fastened, Emma turned to face him. Even stern, he was so dear. His puppy-dog eyes half hidden behind his hair. His strong chin squaring off full, rounded cheeks. She decided to just say it, the thing she was so afraid of. "I'm worried I won't be the same after the baby." Stu only nodded. His calmness was infuriating. She wanted to shake him. "I'll be different and everything will be ruined. For us, and for the band."

"Maybe you'll change," he agreed. "Or maybe I will. Everyone is changing all the time. Even you, Em. That's what life is." He closed the distance between them and put his arms around her, careful to avoid her shoulder. "Didn't you tell me once that a plan isn't every-thing? You need to be ready to shift course when the weather turns." He chuckled with his eyes half closed, the way he did when he was embarrassed, and with the sound, Emma felt the baby move again. A sharp jab under her ribs. "I'm scared, too. Why do you think I've been talking about our progeny to anyone who'll listen?"

She swallowed her relief about the baby, not yet ready to step away from the outburst that felt like a lifting of the fog. "But why am I the only one who's supposed to change?"

"Haven't you seen me trying to step up in the band? Make my own decisions so it isn't all on you?" A wry, knowing smile at her astonishment. "Trust me, okay? We're in this together, I swear." Stu stroked her hair until she leaned in to feel the quick of his heart-beat. They clung to each other as it slowed and steadied, and Emma wondered if that could be enough for her—to set aside the frenetic drive of her own pulse and follow someone else's lead.

Emma watched Gertie from the wings as she played her last song alone. The sun had gone down, the floodlights were coming on, and the wind off the water had picked up. The banner across the top of the stage was lettered with the official name of the concert, TO AMERICA WITH LOVE, but it was too large to ripple in the breeze.

The boys, who had played backup during the middle section of Gertie's set, were buzzing about the size of the crowd and the vibe of playing such a high-profile event.

"I've been talking to Gertie about the song, about 'Curious Fellow,' and it's actually about a mad squirrel," said Jesse, breaking away from the others to join Emma. She could see he'd worked enough gel into his hair for it to defy gravity. "She thinks it whispered in her ear while she was sleeping in the woods."

Emma smirked. So much for famous love affairs and sultry California trysts. "Does Stu know?"

"No."

But when Jesse told him, Stu just hooted as a wicked grin spread over his face. "That's even better," he said. "It means it's about the music, not the bullshit."

When Gertie finished her set, she came backstage and kissed each of the boys on both cheeks, and Ben blushed, which made Emma laugh.

By the time the crew returned from setting up the equipment, their set was already fifteen minutes behind schedule. Impatient, the audience began clapping and chanting the band's name in rhythm. The boys couldn't help grinning. The applause was like the crackling of a fire gaining strength, and it felt just as warming. Emma wanted to go onstage and close her eyes in the face of its naked approval.

"Our turn," said Stu. "Let's do this thing." He brushed his hair out of his eyes and led the way onstage, one arm already extended in an outsize wave. When he got to the microphone, he leaned in and said, "Let's sing together, friends. Or for my Esperanto pals out there: *Saluton, miaj amikoj. Ni kantu kune!*"

Ben sat down at his kit and grinned at Emma as she crossed the stage. Jesse was on the other side of Stu, who was wasting no time in flirting with the front row. He was a light bulb when it came to an audience, and the bigger the crowd, the brighter he shone. This audience was a moving carpet of bodies as far as Emma could see, and everyone near the stage had their hands in the air as though the music might come upon them like rain in the desert. Around the edges, Emma could make out the bright turquoise of the porta-potties, like stalwart sentinels in the distance.

"Thank you for helping us help our country," Stu was saying, and a cheer went up from the crowd. Crowds always wanted to cheer for themselves.

"Thank you, Vancouver," yelled Jesse, and there they went again.

Emma tapped the sustain pedal of her Korg keyboard and leaned into the mic for the first song, just as she caught a sudden muddiness and stutter in Jesse's bassline as he tripped on a taped-down set of wires. They were a pretty ragged pack of saviours, if that's what they were.

They hadn't performed these songs in front of a real audience before, and as the boys played the first bars of "Cover Me Over," Emma wondered why they'd agreed to debut the album in front of so many people. It always took a while for the songs to gel, and it didn't help that they were standing so far apart from one another on the huge stage. They'd barely even played together since recording the album.

But as she sang the first words of the song, she knew it was going to be okay. The crowd was hot, ecstatic. Whatever reservations the promoters might have had about booking a sixty-nine-year-old woman as an opener, Emma could tell Gertie had managed to satisfy the inexhaustible cultural thirst for real experience. She was unadulterated, as organic as they come. And nothing could elicit #FOMO and other hashtag-worthy emotions quite like a rare performance by a reclusive artist. Emma registered an ambient happiness from the crowd, a contact high that was nearly as good as feeling it herself.

Then she felt the rhythm of the songs enter her body. When it came to music, she knew how to go with the flow, to be a part of the whole. Her voice sounded good, as full and clear in the upper register as it ever did. It could still take her by surprise sometimes, which was probably why people called it a gift. They moved from "Texas Rose" to "Century" and back into their catalogue, to the songs most of the people were there to hear. "Tattletale," "Bicycle," "Empty Grave." On "Lightning Heart," Stu strummed the opening chords in her direction, and Emma felt that surge of love that never failed to kick in when he looked at her like that onstage. Even over the monitor, she thought she could hear an *awwwww* rising from the audience. There wasn't a single review of any of their albums that failed to mention how cute they were as a couple. Indie or pop. Earnest or ironic. It was the one thing everyone could agree on—Stu and Emma. Even if Stu and Emma couldn't agree on much at the moment. Then it was back to the new stuff and she was leading off on "Opened Towers."

Her Korg on its stand felt like home under her fingers, even as her shoulder stung while she sustained the G chord through the chorus. But the pain from the tattoo receded as she sang the lyrics she'd written the night they found out she was pregnant. She saw now that it was the idea of a baby that had made the music seem smaller, less permanent—but the truth was they would always be bound by the music, no less than by a child or by the drawing buried and throbbing in her back. The music, she hoped, would outlast them all.

"*Is it fear or love? / We're none of us above / the doubt of why we're getting in / or out of this. / This bliss.*"

Emma swallowed at the end of the verse. She remembered the version she'd written, and how Stu had added a bridge with a key modulation that managed to capture both her hope and her uncertainty. Ben had added some syncopation to the pre-chorus, and Jesse had hit upon a riff with the digital delay that lifted the whole thing into a shimmering, elliptical thing of wonder. Together they'd made it better than anything she could have done alone.

When the song was over, Stu came up and placed his hand on her belly. "In case you didn't already know," he said to the crowd. "I'm ecstatic."

Emma stepped forward and grabbed her mic stand. "It turns out that everything with us is changing," she said to the audience. She tapped her stomach, a little telegraphed *hello* to her constant companion, who kicked back in response. She turned to Stu, who was watching her, frozen. "But I think that means we're getting better." In the roar of cheers and applause, he grinned and returned to his own microphone, then launched into the opening chords of their almost-dance number, as Jesse kicked off the heavy bass with his pedal. Almost instantly, Emma saw what looked like a wave rippling through the audience as they began to jump up and down en masse. But in the distance, she spotted a movement that was out of sync, as though a group of people were pushing in the opposite direction. Then she saw one of the turquoise porta-potties tumble down. And then another. She looked to her bandmates but none of them had noticed. She kept squinting out to the limit of the crowd and thought she detected a scuffle of security guards and concertgoers. It looked like people might be shouting, but she couldn't hear them over the music.

As she waited to come in with her harmonies, Emma searched the sea of faces closest to the edge of the stage, the young men and women clinging to the barricades who had waited for hours to be up at the front. They were pressed in tight together, sardines all the way along, and they had stripped off their sweaters and jackets in spite of the coolness of the evening. Their hands were up in the air, clapping or cupped around their mouths so their cheers would carry. She saw a girl a few rows back coughing into her hands then holding them up as Ben beat out the drum fill at the end of the verse.

Emma felt a new fear take hold in the back of her mind. They were all only helpless people trying to help. Yet maybe they were making things worse.

Then it was time for the chorus again.

Well-Meaning Disaster: Dove Suite's Doomed Fundraiser

Oct 12, 2020

VANCOUVER—It was meant to be the must-see live music event of the year, if not of a generation. The Canadian organizers of "To America With Love" promoted the event as a benefit concert to raise money for ARAMIS antivirals. With its lineup of popular acts, and featuring headliners Dove Suite in what would be their only live performance of the year after cancelling their fall stadium tour, the Vancouver-based festival seemed poised to become a blockbuster. A successful social media campaign, fuelled by Twitter trends, Instagram stories, and a few enthusiastic TikTok influencers, led to tickets selling out in minutes and a pre-concert buzz that likened the event to the next Woodstock. In retrospect, the music festival seems closer to Altamont—doomed to go down in infamy.

Sidney Reeve, 24, attended in spite of the high ticket price and the safety concerns of her parents. "I love Dove Suite and they haven't played Vancouver in years." She has been a fan of the Austin-based band since the release of their debut album, *WhisperShout*, in 2010.

For other concertgoers, the threat of the virus was more of a draw than a deterrent. Jason Harvey, 39, attended with a large group of friends and co-workers. "ARAMIS is really bringing home just how vulnerable we are as a species and how ill-equipped our governments are to protect us. Who knows what's going to happen in the future? And I just kept thinking, what if this is the last killer concert of my lifetime?"

But it was a killer concert in more ways than one. By late afternoon, rumours began to circulate about the presence of ARAMIS-infected attendees. A panic-fuelled stampede midway through the headlining set resulted in the deaths of eight concertgoers and dozens of injuries. Though the performances by artists such as SHÖR, Bakelite, and rediscovered folk artist Gertie Colewick earned rave reviews, hundreds of concertgoers began to fall ill within a week of the event. A second wave of the disease rippled outward across British Columbia and into neighbouring areas. All in all, Canadian health authorities estimate that up to 3,000 infections may ultimately be traced to the concert, a heavy toll for a country that, until recently, had largely avoided a public health crisis due to strict border protections.

Concert headliners Dove Suite issued a statement through their publicist: "We are grieving with the people of Canada and the families of the victims. Our participation in the concert was prompted by a desire to do good by fundraising for life-saving medication and equipment. Our hearts are broken that this attempt to help our country has brought about so much unintended harm."

The fundraiser succeeded in raising upwards of $4 million in relief funds. The United States has faced a shortage of antivirals and specialized medical equipment, due to an overburdened health care system and various diplomatic and economic issues with former allies.

To date, over 500,000 people have been diagnosed with ARAMIS worldwide since August. At least 175,000 have died.

Symposium Magazine

Where the internet comes to think

These days everyone is worried about ARAMIS, as the global death toll pushes health care systems to the brink and causes havoc in virtually every sphere of daily life. But the deadly virus poses other threats that rarely make the headlines. Keelan Gibbs, professor of philosophy at Lansdowne University, sat down with us to discuss some of the ethical considerations of living through a global pandemic.

Q. You became well-known in academic circles for writing about philosophy in times of crisis. You wrote these books decades ago as hypothetical frameworks for approaching different types of human catastrophe. Did you ever think they would become practical handbooks for real events?

A. I hoped they wouldn't. If I'd had to guess, I would have predicted my more recent work on climate change would have become critically relevant sooner.

Q. Can you describe your books for those who haven't read them yet?

A. *Ethics for End Times* outlines the choices faced by governments in times of crisis. For instance, should the government uphold the principles of free speech, or censor scapegoating and false science that could lead to vigilantism and further disease transmission? Classical liberals like John Stuart Mill made powerful arguments against censorship—Mill even believed that false beliefs could help lead to the truth through open debate—but could he have imagined how quickly untruths proliferate in our modern world and how easily they are believed? Similarly, the government may need to inhibit the personal liberty of exposed or infected individuals in order to promote the health and happiness of the greatest number of citizens. But what about non-compliance? Is the government within its rights to shoot people who violate quarantine? In *The Survivalist's Code*, I explore the dilemmas we may face as individuals. Do we need to obey the decrees of a government that has become unjust? If the government ceases to function, what are our responsibilities to one another? If an extinction-scale event occurs, are our previous social contracts dissolved or do we owe a duty of care to our neighbours? For this volume, I thought it was important to move beyond theory and engage with the practical problems arising from a global crisis. For the chapters on pandemics, I consulted with epidemiologists, disaster-preparedness experts, and infectious-disease specialists. For the chapters on environmental disaster and nuclear conflict, I offer a similar blend of historical theory and contemporary research.

Q. What do you think people might be surprised to learn from your work?

A. That most of our beliefs about disasters are myths. Study after study has shown that panic is actually uncommon. In almost all cases, people will act for the common good unless they have already been given reason to believe, either through prejudice or misinformation, that others will behave badly. The most dangerous type of panic, the one that can actually come to the fore in a crisis, is what sociologists of disaster have called "elite panic." This is the fear of those in power that the change brought about by disaster will undermine their authority, for disaster often precipitates transformation and renewal. When elite panic rules, dangerous and unwarranted measures may be taken in the name of preventing chaos or mob rule.

KEELAN GIBBS IS THE DUNHAM PROFESSOR OF ETHICS AT LANSDOWNE UNIVERSITY. HIS BOOKS INCLUDE *ETHICS FOR END TIMES* AND *THE SURVIVALIST'S CODE*.

THIS INTERVIEW HAS BEEN EDITED AND CONDENSED FOR LENGTH.

ELLIOT

——

NOVEMBER 2020

It was ten minutes before the start of his shift and Elliot was hungry. Half of the businesses in Washington Heights had shut down in early October, but the restaurant closures were the biggest pain in the ass. Elliot had been forced to revive cooking skills he'd repressed since college: scrambled eggs, pasta, sloppy joes. There was a booming commerce in food delivery for intrepid couriers, but sitting and waiting at home reminded him too much of his quarantine. Now even the grocery aisle at the drugstore was picked over. He leaned down to inspect a lone instant ramen bowl on the bottom shelf while a woman in a purple raincoat edged over to move away from him. He noticed she had peanut butter and pickles in her basket, and his stomach spasmed.

The centre display of Halloween candy at the front of the store was the one thing left untouched. Usually there'd be slim pickings the day after Halloween, but this year the mayor had called off trick-or-treating—just in case there was anyone living under a rock somewhere who still wanted their kids to go door to door in the midst of a pandemic.

Elliot grabbed a fifty-piece variety box with Kit Kats and Milk Duds. Better to get fat than to starve.

Bryce loved Kit Kats. Elliot's partner had come down with ARAMIS after they'd worked a quarantine relief shift at a big apartment building with sixty confirmed cases. Quarantine relief was a constantly evolving role that entailed food delivery, warning off visitors, and, increasingly, issuing tickets to people registered under a Q-notice who refused to stay home. Though quarantining was technically still voluntary, the city's top medical advisors had recommended enforcement given the long incubation period of the virus. For police officers like Elliot, this meant trying to strike a delicate balance between respecting the personal liberty of thousands, and guarding against the potential damage that could be wrought by a single infected individual on an ordinary day. What happened to Bryce was a reminder of how badly—and easily—things could go wrong. A feverish, stir-crazy woman adamant on leaving the building had pulled off his mask and coughed in his face to prove she wasn't infected. Forty-eight hours later, Elliot had watched as her body was carried out in a biohazard bag, while Bryce stayed home under his own Q-notice. A week later, he was symptomatic. Public visiting hours at all hospitals had been suspended, although according to the latest daily update from Bryce's wife, he was still conscious but breathing with a ventilator.

The self-checkout kiosk was slow; in the store's far corner, an idle cashier blinked up at a wall-mounted television blaring ongoing coverage of the deadly aftermath of the big ARAMIS fundraising concert in Vancouver. Even when people were trying to do the right thing, Elliot thought, things could still go spectacularly wrong. He stood well back from the person ahead of him in line. It was no longer considered polite to get closer than three feet of someone, though it made for some unruly queues that nettled his sense of public order. Behind him, there was a scraggly row of gloved and masked customers extending all the way into the shampoo aisle.

Everyone in line, Elliot realized, looked like they were steeling themselves for the worst.

———

"If four out of ten people with ARAMIS die, and eight out of ten people exposed to the virus get sick, and there are nine million people in New York City—"

"What's your point, Russ?"

"By all mathematical rights, we're fucked."

Elliot and his new partner Russ had just been assigned to maintain a cordon outside the Medical Science Pavilion of Methodist Morningside Hospital to manage the journalists. The outbreak had done more to sell papers and fuel the public appetite for news media than climate change and nuclear threats combined. As usual, fear was proving to be good for business.

"Why are you guys here, really?" Russ asked the journalist standing closest as they began their shift. "I wouldn't be anywhere near a hospital if it were up to me."

"This is the biggest story in the city," the reporter answered. "Children in comas. Parents dying. Nurses standing in for next of kin to make the kids' medical decisions . . . it's unreal."

Another journalist beside her said, "We've been covering the concert story for a month, but there's nothing new there. So we're waiting for the latest update from Dr. Delille."

"This is the worst," said Russ, ignoring the conversation he'd started and turning back to Elliot. "It isn't even our responsibility."

"Today it is," said Elliot, passing his partner a mask and a set of the gloves they'd been issued.

"I like driving," said Russ. "Not standing around."

Elliot remembered how, during the first few days of his quarantine, it had nearly killed him not to be able to just slip into his car and put miles of road between himself and the plain facts of his life. Even if you were going in circles, as long as you were behind the wheel, it still felt like you were going somewhere.

Russ took off his cap and, passing it to Elliot, stretched the elastics of the face mask over his head before securing it in place over his nose and mouth. "God, we look like armed surgeons or something."

Elliot peered into the underside of the hat, where a snapshot of two toddlers and a Saint Michael medallion were tucked into its inner plastic sleeve. "Think of it as a promotion," he said, handing it back. "This is life-and-death stuff we're dealing with here."

"So what else is new?" said Russ. "But this is putting my whole family on the line."

Elliot couldn't deny it. "I'm going to check on things inside."

"Don't leave me alone." The journalists were a calm bunch, but Russ was antsy, hooking his thumbs in and out of his belt loops. Then Elliot saw that his partner had shifted his attention to a man and woman who, in loud and desperate-sounding voices, were asking for directions to Emergency. Russ pointed them in the right direction before adding, "You know what I've been through." Like Elliot, Russ's wife had spent three weeks in quarantine, after one of her co-workers had fallen ill. Though Russ's family remained healthy, Elliot imagined his partner had gone through his own mortal reckoning.

"Just keep your mask on," he said.

"You've got to teach me some karate or whatever," said Russ. His fidgety hands had gone slack, but his voice remained tight. "I need to be more Zen, like you."

Elliot cracked a smile. "What is the colour of the wind?" His partner just shook his head, and Elliot noticed the dark circles below his eyes. "Hey, man." He clapped his partner on the shoulder and waited until Russ met his gaze. "We'll be fine."

Elliot went inside and followed the signs for the Infectious Diseases Division. He asked a nurse where the labs were and she directed him up to the fourth floor. He spotted Keisha as soon as he emerged from the stairwell. White coat, black hair, narrow hip swish, slight bounce on the toes. It was harder to recognize people in face masks, but being tall, she'd always had a very particular stride. She was headed to a set of doors at the opposite end of the hall.

"Keisha," he called out.

The woman who stopped to look at him was dignified, preoccupied, in a hurry. "Yes?"

"It's me," he said. "Elliot Howe. From college." He took off his hat because he knew it could be hard for people to see past the uniform. "It's good to see you," he added, in case she was on the fence. From what he could see, she'd aged better than he had, in that she hadn't aged at all. Shorter braids, still pretty, no makeup. "It's been a while."

"What are you doing here?" Her tone was, if not angry, then at least annoyed. She carried a slim metal briefcase under her arm.

"Keeping the journalists at bay," he said. "Though I wondered if you wanted to come downstairs and make a statement. It might be enough to make them leave."

She shook her head. "If they don't let me get on with my work, there won't be anything new to report."

It was clear she took no pleasure in her recent elevation to the status of media personality. She was as sensible as he had always known her to be, and he was glad she had achieved her goal of becoming a doctor and that there was a consistency to who people were over time. It reassured him to know that he hadn't been wrong to let her go back then, maybe only wrong to have gotten involved with someone as Type A as her in the first place.

"So you did it," he said, nodding at the name tag on her lab coat. "You're a doctor." Through her clear nitrile glove, he noticed a wedding band on her finger. "And married."

She nodded. "Nine years, no kids. He's a doctor, too. And you're going bald."

"Just a little." He put his hat back on. He could feel his back sweating. "Your patients are lucky to have you looking after them," he said. There was something wonderful and strange about speaking with her. He almost felt like he was twenty years old again, or that he had never stopped being twenty years old.

"Oh, I'm not involved with the patients," said Keisha, ignoring the gallantry. "I'm here for research."

"The cutting edge," he said. "That's awesome."

Her brow furrowed as though she was trying to figure out if he was joking. "Well, I'm looking at rates of resistance and survival in the patients here."

He spread out his hands. "I actually came up because I saw you on television. I wanted to apologize for being a jerk back then. What was it, nineteen years ago? You didn't deserve that."

"You're not sick, I hope?" Keisha sounded mollified.

"Not yet," he said. She raised an eyebrow but he didn't elaborate. "Just on a shift outside, like I said."

"Well, if you were sick, this is the best hospital."

"Good to know." Elliot felt the conversation coming to a natural close as Keisha glanced back to the laboratory doors behind her. "So, listen, I'm sorry again. I've been feeling bad about what happened."

"It's okay," she said. "I haven't spent the past nineteen years being upset with you. I got over it." She looked puzzled for a second, and Elliot remembered that expression from when he broke up with her—just before tears began filming her eyes and he'd felt that shameful uptick of pride that he had actually made someone love him. "I don't know how exactly, but I did."

"I'll bet it was easy," he said.

"Probably," agreed Keisha, but there was a smile in her eyes. "Okay, I've got to go. Tell the press I'll be down later."

"I will," said Elliot. "Thanks."

He turned and headed back down the staircase. When he got outside, he waved at the journalists as though he was actually the one they'd been waiting for, and a few of them laughed. The sun glinted off the roofs of passing cars, and Elliot felt restored and exhilarated, as though Keisha herself had examined him with her strong, practical hands and given him a clean bill of health.

·||||·

That evening, Elliot drove over to the unmarked building where the surviving students from his kung fu school had continued to gather on their own. Graham, a real estate broker, had found the place: an unrented loft space in a converted industrial building where renovations had been completed shortly before the outbreak.

Elliot waved a greeting to the others and stayed in his corner. After class, people would go online to talk and exchange news via group chat or private message. But for now, they maintained the unplanned silence with which their meetings had begun, as well as a vast distance from one another—more than was strictly necessary for doing the forms, but still in clear contravention of the new social distancing ordinances that forbade non-essential gatherings outside of a family milieu. Tonight's secret assembly included sixteen men and women of all levels, though most were kung fu students of long standing whose practice had knit into their identity. The weekly session was only a fraction of the regular training regimen that many of them were used to. Of his core group of friends from the school, Elliot was the only survivor, but of the cohort just behind them were Mina, Tariq, Jason, Sahir, Nalin, Hannah, and Brett. The rest he was getting to know little by little over the group chat.

One of the black belt students moved to the front and led them through a brief warm-up before the group moved through the forms in loose synchronization. Crane, snake, tiger. Resilience, speed, and strength. They'd shortened a standard two-hour class to about forty-five minutes, dispensing with sparring and all of the usual interaction that ARAMIS had rendered dangerous. The point of the gathering was to carry forward their practice, to remember their friends, the master, and all they'd learned. At the end of the session, the leader always read out a roll call of their lost members. But even before their names were spoken aloud, Elliot was thinking of Jejo, Cam, Lucas, Declan, Teresa, Paloma, Felix. The master and his wife. And he knew he wasn't the only one.

Afterwards, everyone shrugged their sweaty shoulders back into their coats where they'd dropped them, and held up gloved hands in farewell.

Outside, the city looked like it had been cleared for a film shoot. Most of the other cars on the road were police cruisers or ambulances. Elliot had heard from his friends on the evening shift that enforcing the new curfew was surprisingly easy. People wanted to stay inside after dark just as much as the authorities wanted them off the streets.

With two minutes to spare before nine, Elliot let himself into his building. Even with the makeshift decorating he'd carried out during his quarantine, his apartment had a spare, provisional feel, eased only by its slight messiness. One corner was full of boxes from Sarah's apartment that she'd sent over before leaving on her trip in mid-October. She'd packed in a mad rush. A few boxes were labelled MISC., STUFF, and ODDS 'N' ENDS. Right up until he'd seen her off at the marina, both of them putting on a brave face for Noah, he was sure she was going to change her mind. After all, the last time they'd ducked into a restaurant without first checking the online reviews, she'd been nearly too agitated to sit down. And when she'd considered switching mobile providers, they'd discussed it on and off for weeks before she announced she'd rather just keep her old phone and contract. It had been a long time since his sister had made such a big decision on her own. The step forward made him feel proud, uneasy, and a little bereft.

He opened a beer just before his parents called. In the midst of all the life-and-death situations he now saw daily on the job, he thought about them more than he'd expected. There were profound bonds of all kinds and of every sort, but parents and children, brothers and sisters, husbands and wives—they were the only ones acknowledged by the hospital in a time of crisis. This was the small circle of people who could visit a dying patient in isolation, who could legally accept the perilous risks of love and family.

"Hi guys," he said, picking up. His parents never called him separately, only at the same time on different extensions of the landline in the house where he'd grown up, as though he were a group project for which they were each determined to do exactly half of the work.

"We're worried about you, Ell," said Gretchen, once they had dispensed with greetings. Talking about ARAMIS no longer required a preamble. "It must be a living nightmare in the city."

"Anytime you want to come home," said Frank.

"Thanks, Dad."

With Sarah away, the three of them had been talking more than they had in years. She'd thrown the family balance into disarray, and now they were tilting into new angles and relations to one another. Though his parents had at first been alarmed by the departure of his sister and nephew on an ocean voyage with the writer and self-styled pandemic expert Owen Grant, their opposition was softening with each passing day of rising death tolls on land.

"I'll admit it now," said Gretchen. "I'm relieved they're out of harm's way."

"I just hope she knows what she's getting herself into," said Frank. "We're sure this isn't another hippie brainwashing group?" It was a point he raised almost every time they spoke.

"Sarah's the one who got herself and Noah on that boat," Elliot repeated. "It was all her idea."

"Well, Owen Grant is a decent writer," said Gretchen, as though making a concession. "Even if he's a total cad. He was a perfect monster to Rachel. I don't know how she'll ever trust anyone again."

"I just hope he's a decent sailor," said Elliot.

"Sarah can handle herself," said Gretchen. "Did you see the new photo? Captain Noah?"

"Yes, he looks like a natural," said Elliot.

Sarah had put them all on the same group email to share photos of her son on the boat, and his parents called after every new message to discuss Noah as if he were a celebrity in whom they shared a common interest. In the latest photo, Elliot's nephew was standing at the helm of *Buona Fortuna*, one hand on the wheel.

"So she's helping this fellow Owen write his weblog or whatever," said Frank, once again retreading previous conversational territory. "Though I can't figure out why anyone wants to hear what he has to say about viruses."

"Everyone's an expert these days," said Gretchen, sighing. "Have you seen Keelan on television, Elliot? He's been on all the networks, talking up a storm about rule utilitarianism and crisis management. The department is all in an uproar about it. Half of us are appalled and the rest are jealous." She sniffed. "But at least he's not a novelist."

"He might as well be," said Frank. "It's all very speculative."

"Is he saying anything so very wrong?" asked Elliot.

"What isn't he saying?" countered his father. "He'll talk to anyone about anything."

"The problem," said Gretchen, "is that he's advocating for a calm and collected acceptance of additional policing, instead of warning against the encroachment of civil liberties. First it's voluntary quarantining, then it'll be mandatory. Then they'll be shooting people who step out of line. That's the real danger."

In his twenties, Elliot would have taken his mother's remark as a personal affront, but now he was merely irritated, if not surprised, by her vehemence. "Mom, that's completely unfair."

Frank made a thoughtful sound. "Is it possible Keelan takes a less dim view of human nature than you do, dear?"

"That's funny, coming from you," Gretchen snapped back. "People are fine. But the state always works to preserve its own authority. First through economic factors, then through violence."

Elliot knew his mother was trying to pull him into the fray, but he didn't feel up to it and said his goodbyes. He had a feeling his parents would be continuing the conversation without him.

He felt grateful for their new routine. Elliot had seen more than a few stories on the news about estranged families reuniting during the pandemic crisis. Adopted children seeking out their birth parents. Birth parents reaching out to their children. Runaways coming home. Even exes reconciling, though he found that type of reunion to be the most wrong-headed and improbable of them all.

Elliot finished his beer and rinsed out the bottle. He was happy his parents were still together, that they had that kind of easy companionship. He wished he lived in a place big enough to have a dog. Then again, Noah was allergic. Elliot wondered if that was a gene Noah had inherited from his biological father, whoever that might be.

He turned off the overhead light. In a window across the way, he could see a candle burning in a small shrine, with clementines, bananas, and orange flowers laid out around a framed photograph of an older woman. A Day of the Dead altar.

He opened his computer and unwrapped a mini Kit Kat. He thought about the research centre where he'd donated sperm in college, and the bizarre resentment he'd felt after breaking up with Keisha. He'd wanted to drive away from his own life then, too—and the donations had paid what felt at the time like a fortune. He'd bought his Impala and enjoyed the freedom that came with a car that was wholly his own. But he wondered now if the donations had been about more than the money. If they were about feeling some simple sense of purpose, something tangible, away from the swirling mists of academia. And maybe, in retrospect, there had been a little perversity in the decision: the knowledge that it would horrify Gretchen and Frank. He didn't think the research project had had anything to do with artificial insemination, but then again, he didn't really remember what he'd signed.

He googled *Lansdowne research subjects sperm donation*, but he didn't find anything. Then he looked up *medical research Western Massachusetts sperm donor fertility*, and still nothing. He checked how long frozen sperm could remain viable and then shut off the computer.

He opened another beer.

Russ was donning his protective gear at the start of their shift. "Every day some new demotion from actual police work." He slipped on his gloves and snapped a face mask on over his scowl. "Next, we'll be changing bedpans."

They were still assigned to Methodist Morningside, where so many health care workers had developed the illness that they were running with a skeleton staff. The mobile units were practical for initial screenings, but at a certain point the very sick needed to be admitted to hospital for treatment. With every new wave of infection,

Elliot, like his parents, felt a fresh relief that his sister and nephew had set sail on their trip.

"Cheer up," he said to his partner. "It's our last day."

Their current assignment was to enforce order at the intake desk at Emergency. It turned out that families facing the life-threatening illness of a loved one didn't always follow the posted regulations regarding not asking the staff about wait times. In most cases, the mere presence of uniformed officers in the waiting room was enough to encourage calm. But their secondary duty was to help ensure the submission of insurance information, as families *in extremis* were also sloppy at completing paperwork. Elliot knew his mother would take a dim view of armed officers becoming involved in the bureaucratic enforcement of capitalism. He wasn't crazy about it himself.

Russ grimaced as he directed patients to the stack of clipboards on the counter. "You know, I thought I was okay with maybe being killed in the line of duty," he said, "but this is a whole other story."

Elliot adjusted his face mask, which had begun to slip down his nose. "Just follow the protocols and we should be fine." He said the same thing every day, and every day his partner failed to be comforted.

"Bullshit," said Russ. "I know what happened to Bryce. I'm praying we get moved to curfew duty next."

"He's not dead yet," said Elliot, though Bryce's wife had texted to say her husband had taken a turn for the worse. "He could be back at work next week."

As soon as their shift was over, Russ bolted for the doors. "Let's ride," he said, twirling the keys to the patrol car around a finger.

"Clock-watcher," said Elliot. "I'll catch up in five minutes."

He followed the signs around to the main entrance, where he paused to adjust his mask. He took his hat off and rubbed his head. He always began sweating the instant he started moving around inside.

His detour panned out when he spotted Keisha crossing the lobby.

He'd seen her a few times during his week at the hospital, and she often stopped to chat for a minute or two. He wondered if she felt as he did, that it was a balm to see someone from days gone by.

"How goes the battle?" he asked. He could read the stress of the past two months in the lines on her brow. Keisha had come under fire, first for the panic that arose after she released the photo of ARAMIS Girl, and then for the nationwide rash of hate crimes against Asian Americans that followed. So far, Methodist Morningside had stood behind her, but he could only imagine how devastated she must be.

"It's going okay," said Keisha. "We're working on developing a new drug with a few international labs."

They paused while a couple with two children burst into the lobby, looking frantic. The little girl was carrying a battered Elmo doll and the mother was crying. Elliot stepped forward and redirected them to the emergency triage at the Children's Pavilion.

"You know," said Keisha, "this is one of the most infectious places on the planet right now. Just walking through here could make you sick."

"I'm not worried."

"Then you're an idiot." She shook her head. "It's so weird to be seeing you all the time now," she said. "Come on, let's not stand here." He followed her out a side door leading to a small loading zone. A No Smoking sign the size of a shopping cart was mounted on the wall. "I feel better talking outside. Fewer germs."

"I thought this was the best hospital." He flinched as the door slammed shut behind them.

"Well, it is," said Keisha. "A prognosis here is better than anywhere else. We have protocols and we know how to use them. We've drilled. We have isolation rooms with separate ventilation. And we have more respirators than staff at this point." She looked proud but defensive. "We've had the most cases but also the most survivors."

"It's heroic, what you're doing," he said, and meant it. "Oh, hey. Here. A parting gift." He reached into his pocket and handed her a mini box of Milk Duds, their gloved fingertips briefly touching along the side of the package. "After today, with any luck, I'll be on curfew duty."

"I'm sorry you got assigned here," she said, slipping the candy into her lab coat. "We've had a few of your guys admitted, as I'm sure you know."

"I'm not worried," he said again, raising his voice a little to be heard over a passing ambulance with its siren blaring.

"Is this some sort of male invincibility complex? Because if so, spare me."

"Not at all," said Elliot. "Right before this rotation, I did seven weeks of quarantine relief. And before that, I was in quarantine myself."

"Really." Keisha raised an eyebrow. "Not many people would knowingly put themselves at risk after that."

"Well, that's the job, isn't it?" His shrug was a little self-conscious. "You know what it is to serve, too."

The door behind them opened with a clang as two nurses came out, cigarettes in gloved hands.

"I should go," said Keisha. She was looking at him oddly, as though he were displaying some symptom she couldn't quite diagnose. "Take care of yourself, Elliot."

After two days off, Elliot and Russ moved to the evening curfew patrol, as Russ had hoped. Away from the surging mortal fears of the hospital, the shift went by quickly. Until it was gone, Elliot hadn't realized the psychic burden of bearing witness to so much panic and grief. For the most part, people stayed off the streets. Elliot and Russ issued warnings and tried without enthusiasm to disperse the homeless, who had nowhere else to go but wanted to avoid what they saw as certain infection in the shelters.

When he got home, Elliot found a strange comfort in turning off his lights and opening the blinds. There was enough of a glow from the city for him to see his way around the apartment, though the nights were nowhere near as bright as they used to be. No more rivers of red tail lights slowing at the intersections, or white headlights blazing through in the other direction. Just streetlamps and neon signs and billboards illuminated by spotlights, because not even a plague could slow down corporate interests. As he poured himself a glass of water in the semi-dark, his phone rang.

"Keisha," he said. They'd exchanged numbers, but he'd never expected to hear from her.

"I got so used to seeing you every so often," she said, "it started to feel like something was wrong when you weren't there."

"It's nice to hear your voice." Elliot took his glass of water and sat down in the chair he'd pushed over to the window. "What's up?"

"I'm helping to supervise a clinical trial."

"A new drug already? That's fast."

"Not fast enough. The antivirals we have now cost a fortune and they don't work on everybody." There was a tinny echo to her voice, as though she was on speakerphone. "This could be the best hope some of these patients have."

"I'm sure you're right," said Elliot. She sounded prickly, which made sense after what she'd been through in the press. "I hope it goes well."

"Remind me how many weeks you were working with potential ARAMIS exposure?"

"One week at the hospital. Seven weeks on quarantine relief."

"And you said you were in quarantine yourself before that?"

"Yes, for three weeks." It was becoming apparent this was not a social call.

"What for?" she asked. He could hear a rustling sound, like papers being shuffled on a desk. "Can you describe your exposure?"

Elliot watched an ambulance speeding by on the street below. "Do you remember how it started? And where?"

"That restaurant on the Lower East Side," said Keisha.

"Go on," he said.

She took a breath, as though beginning a well-practised recitation. "Mr. Zhihuan Tsiang, the index patient, a visiting martial arts expert from China, infected everyone at his table, all members of a local gym. Mr. Tsiang died in China two days later, and the eight others developed symptoms within the week. All were dead within three weeks of the dinner, and six spread ARAMIS to their families." The timeline had been rehashed in news story after news story. "It came out later that Mr. Tsiang also infected a taxi driver, a hotel clerk, and the hostess of the restaurant, who continued to infect other staff members." He could hear a tapping sound: her forefinger on the desk, a tattoo of the dead. "Mr. Tsiang was what we call a super-spreader."

Another ambulance drove by with its siren on.

"Keisha, I was there," said Elliot, when the sound stopped. "At the dinner with Mr. Tsiang."

"No, you weren't."

"Yes, I was."

"No," said Keisha with some firmness. "We traced everyone at the dinner. And everyone working at the restaurant. And everyone who paid for a meal by credit or debit card. I would have remembered seeing your name. The only one we couldn't find was the ARAMIS Girl."

"It was just for a minute, but I was there. I told all of this to the Department of Health when I called in."

"Well, okay then," said Keisha. "A minute."

"I sat down. I shook people's hands. I drank directly from Jejo Galang's glass. He was sitting next to Mr. Tsiang."

Keisha's voice was quiet. "Jejomar Galang died."

"I know," said Elliot. "He was a friend of mine."

"So you went into quarantine," she said. "And you've been fine this whole time."

"Yeah, fine." It was a version of the truth. He'd doubted every decision he'd ever made, questioned whether his survival was a kind of punishment, and spent more time than he could ever have imagined considering matters of chance and fate. But still: he was alive. "I'm totally fine."

The sound of a door opening and a distant voice cut in on Keisha's end: "Dr. Delille? The patient's family has some concerns about the release form."

There was more rustling and some muffled conversation. "Sorry," said Keisha, returning. "I need to finish some paperwork to get the drug trial started. Can you come in tomorrow and let me take a blood sample?"

"Sure," said Elliot.

"Tomorrow, okay? If what you say is true, I don't want to lose track of you."

When Elliot hung up, he flipped on the television and saw Keelan Gibbs giving an interview. He looked older than Elliot remembered him, but not by much. Pale forehead, ruddy cheeks, limpid blue eyes. Had surely refused makeup. The professor actually stroked his long, white beard before commenting, "The only way a pandemic can be stopped is through international cooperation." Elliot clicked the TV off again. Then he turned on his computer and sent a message to Sarah and Noah. Their regular phone calls had been replaced with emails since they'd gone to sea. Sarah had a fair amount of time to write, and since they were being careful about putting ashore, she was limited in her company.

Hi guys. Thanks for the update. I printed out that last photo of
Noah and put it inside my hat. It's about time I had a new one
in there . . . in the Polaroid you gave me he's just a chubby
little baby!

He attached a photo of himself holding his police hat, flipped
over to reveal Noah and the boat tucked into its inner plastic sleeve.
His phone rang again.

"You're *sure* you were there?" It was Keisha.

"I was there."

"And you don't have kids, right?"

"No," said Elliot. He stared out the window again, where the city's
diminished lights kept on glowing. "Well, actually. I might."

"You might have kids? Plural? You don't know?"

"It's uncertain," he said. "Everything about being a man is uncertain these days."

"If you say so." Keisha sounded skeptical in the extreme.

The next day, Elliot stopped by the hospital before his evening curfew
patrol. Keisha was waiting for him in the lobby with a spare set of
personal protective equipment, the same full kit worn by at-risk hospital staff: gown, respirator mask, goggles, gloves. "Put all the gear on,"
she said. "We follow protocol here, no matter who you are."

Elliot followed Keisha upstairs and tried to ignore the sounds in
the corridors, ranging from animated murmurs to ragged coughing to
the outright distress of wails and sobbing. Ahead of them were the
doors to the ARAMIS ward that his colleagues had been guarding just a
few weeks earlier, after nurses complained about difficulties enforcing

the new isolation procedures. The assignment had been called off after half of the on-duty officers developed symptoms and had to be hospitalized themselves.

As they passed through the ARAMIS waiting area, it felt forcibly quiet in comparison, as though a testy Fate had whispered to the huddled family members that any wrong word might provoke a final blow. Every mouth and nose was covered with a mask, and every set of eyes was trained on him and Keisha as they passed by. A white-haired husband and wife, two thirty-something women in colourful hijabs, and a skinny, teenaged boy who was there by himself, whose eyes met Elliot's in such naked terror as the door to the ARAMIS ward clanged open that he was almost relieved to enter the epi-centre of contagion.

At first glance, the ARAMIS ICU was not so different from the other hospital corridors, though Elliot noticed that all the doors were closed, with visitor logbooks posted outside.

"Today's the first day of the trial," said Keisha. She looked keyed up, her eyes blinking rapidly, and there was a sharp edge to her voice. "This could be what helps us turn the tide."

She scanned a set of charts handed to her by a nurse, then passed them back with further instructions. The patients selected for the trial were all adults between thirty-five and forty-four. They were gravely ill, but still conscious and not on ventilators.

"We've assessed them as being the candidates for whom this new therapy could make the biggest difference," said Keisha. "They're also at the bottom of the scale if there's a new wave of patients."

"The scale?"

Keisha explained the controversial point system for gaining access to antivirals and specialized equipment that had come into effect at the beginning of October.

"Additional points for being married and for having children, exponentially increasing with each child. Mandatory subtraction of points for adults over sixty-five, with more points subtracted with each five-year span."

"Wow," said Elliot. "What about kids?"

"Oh, kids take priority," said Keisha. "Hospitals tend to have more pediatric-enabled ventilators per population anyway."

They peered through a viewing window. Nurses in hazmat suits were administering the drug via IVs to six subjects in hospital beds under the supervision of a doctor. There were curtains set up between the patients, but most were not drawn. The large pane of glass for observers already undercut any sense of privacy.

Elliot felt the import of the moment—to be present at a discovery that might soon be reported around the world. "Do you sort of feel like it's fate?" he asked. These days he couldn't avoid a preoccupation with the concept. "Working on this drug? You know, like everything in your life has led you to this?"

"I believe in science, not fate. Obviously."

"Right, sure." He noticed that the teenaged boy and the white-haired couple had been permitted inside and were standing at the other end of the observation window. The boy pressed a gloved hand up against the glass and, within the room, Elliot saw the gesture returned in the upturned chin and slow blink of a dark-haired woman, who seemed to be summoning reserves of strength to reassure the teen. "Is it normal to move into human trials so quickly?"

"It's worth the risk," said Keisha. "Especially for the patients without health insurance. Not to mention the exponential difference the medication could make around the globe."

She brought him around the corner, past the nurses' station, and into a small office, where he rolled up his sleeve and she began to draw several vials of his blood, carefully affixing a label to each one as she placed them in the stand.

"I know it seems like a lot," she said. "But this way I can send it to other labs, too."

"Cool," said Elliot. He glanced away from the needle in his arm to a poster on the wall of a cute puppy. In large letters, it bore the slogan THERE IS NO SUCH THING AS A HYPOALLERGENIC DOG. "Huh," he said.

They heard a Code Blue on the intercom, and running feet. Elliot felt Keisha's grip on his arm tighten slightly, but she carried on. The sight of his own blood being drawn was at first curious, then dizzying. He switched his focus to Keisha, whose face had become grim and intense. She was capping the last vial when the door burst open.

"They're hemorrhaging," gasped a nurse. "All of them. Everywhere. Eyes, nose, mouth. The doctors can't stop it."

Keisha was already on her feet. "Get the families out of here. Get them out."

"They're all going to die," said the nurse. "I killed them."

"Go!" yelled Keisha, and the nurse departed, sobbing.

Keisha turned to Elliot. "You need to guard the ward," she said. Her voice was sharp. "The families can't see this."

He stood up and followed her, holding his fingers to his forearm and feeling light-headed. She was already at the nurses' station when he caught up to her, talking to a woman behind the desk who sounded like she was about to cry.

"Are there any orderlies without families?" Keisha was saying. "All that blood, it's going to be very high-risk." She exhaled and closed her eyes for a moment.

"I don't understand," Elliot said.

Keisha shook her head, her eyes still closed. "Their blood must have decoagulated. I don't understand either. It wasn't indicated—"

"That's terrible," he said. Elliot tried and failed not to picture what the nurse had described, imagining blood pouring from his own eyes. He wished he could take his mask off and get more air.

Keisha opened her eyes and looked at him. "Please go guard the door," she said. "If those families see this, it will make everything so much worse."

He turned the corner into a wall of sound, a cacophony of shouting and screaming, clattering equipment and guttural wails. The urgency of the situation, or maybe its futility, seemed to thicken the very air itself. Elliot couldn't tell how fast he was moving as he retraced his steps down the hallway, where the white-haired couple were clutching each other in front of the observation window, their eyes squeezed shut and streaming with tears. Just beyond them, a weeping nurse was trying to hold back the teen boy, who was hammering on the glass.

Elliot averted his eyes from the observation window, a swimming horror of red, and he touched the white-haired man on his shoulder. Their eyes met and Elliot nodded to the double doors at the end of the hall.

"Please," said Elliot. The man's chin quivered, then he began steering the woman, whose shoulders were heaving, towards the exit.

When the nurse saw Elliot approach, she stumbled back from the boy, who was screaming for his mother. The teen pushed and rattled the window, his gloved hands scrabbling, feet kicking the wall. Crying and swearing, begging and demanding, until he collapsed into a heap.

Elliot felt as though his uniform were just a costume holding him upright. He wasn't really a police officer, or a man, but a human being as frail as any other. He felt the loss of the blood Keisha had taken—there was so little flesh and blood holding him together, really. And almost none holding people apart. Less than ten metres away, the blood of six people who were dead or dying was pooling on the floor.

He thought he knew what it meant to be grateful, but all of a sudden he wasn't sure.

Elliot put his hand on the back of the teen's shirt and pulled him up to his feet, light and unresisting as a rag doll, even as he kept up the primal sound that churned Elliot's stomach. They followed in the wake of the older couple, and as a group they moved into the silence of the waiting room, where the ward doors clanged shut behind them and the faces of the remaining families turned to them in mute horror.

finally

Bailey, Sarah <sarahbearaohara@seamail.com>
To: Elliot Howe <elliotimpala@mailnet.com>
Sent: Fri, Oct 30, 2020 at 8:09 PM

Elliot,

We've made it as far as Ponce Inlet, Florida. Nineteen days aboard *Buona Fortuna*. We have a dinghy for going ashore but somehow we still haven't used it. We're staying safe and keeping to ourselves to avoid infection.

It's only been a couple of weeks, but I feel like I've lived an age on this boat, getting my sea legs back. Owen is a good first mate and learning fast. Noah is in heaven, with two doting adults never out of earshot. You would think he was born on the water, the way he's taken to it. Right now, we're still heading to Key West, where we'll wait for a good weather window to cross the Gulf Stream over to the Bahamas.

Being stuck on this boat reminds me of rainy days at the cabin. Reading all day, doing crossword puzzles, those ill-fated attempts at crafting that left me with glue all over my fingertips! It seems strange to think that Noah and I won't be at the cabin for Christmas this year.

Do you remember how embarrassed I was by Mom and Dad's whole anti-Christmas thing? I hated having to explain it to anyone. Isn't that silly? I wish I could go back in time and get rid of every thought and impulse I had that just came out of something as stupid as wanting to fit in.

Tell me you're being careful, too.

Lots of love from me and Noah,

Sarah

---

re: finally

Howe, Elliot <elliotimpala@mailnet.com>
To: Sarah Bailey <sarahbearaohara@seamail.com>
Sent: Fri, Oct 30, 2020 at 9:46 PM

Sarah,

Don't be so hard on yourself. There are worse things than wanting to fit in. There's probably nothing more human.

xo
E.

SARAH

—

DECEMBER 2016

The Impala nosed up the access road, and Sarah gripped the bottom of her seat as the old car jounced up and down in the ruts. The snow compressed in a muted crunch below the tires and her brother craned his neck as they passed each sign and its accompanying—now almost invisible—turnoff.

Elliot said, "It has to be one of these next ones."

Everything in the woods looked the same under the blanket of white. Sarah often thought that once they were able to drive to their parents' cabin without aid or difficulty, they would finally have reached adulthood. But they were both in their thirties now, Elliot divorced, or nearly so, and Sarah was five months pregnant. Although the pregnancy was still a secret from her parents, a butterfly heartbeat beneath her bulky winter clothes.

Elliot grunted and Sarah knew this meant he had spotted the sign for their cabin, as the car lurched left and down, slower but still bumping and skidding. Twigs bent from snow-laden branches skimmed against the windows at startling intervals, each sudden tap like a threat or a beckoning.

"Why do we always leave it so late to drive up?" she asked. The forest at night made her nervous, though no doubt it was safer than her neighbourhood in Queens by far. But most things in life made her nervous now. Compared to her tortured relationship with everyday living, the normal concerns of a healthy pregnancy were a welcome relief. But she still felt like a gymnast on all fours, cowering inch by inch across a beam. A beam she had once been able to dance across backwards, eyes closed, half flying.

"Because we're busy?" said Elliot. He stared straight ahead, driving with a rigid attentiveness that Sarah chalked up to her pregnancy. He'd kissed her on the cheek when he picked her up, his hand at her elbow. A gentle, strange thing, that kiss. "Because we don't want to go?" Another branch smacked the roof, but he didn't flinch. "Because you don't want to tell Mom and Dad about the baby?"

"That's true."

Elliot had made excuses for her at Thanksgiving, but she couldn't avoid her parents any longer. She looked out the window into a darkness that seemed even blacker beyond the guiding yellow of the headlights. She wished she'd seen her family's sign as they'd driven past. It was part of the ritual: catching sight of that elaborate wooden arrow nailed to the tree at the turnoff. Unlike the other signs, with only a name—*JOHNSTON* or *BLAIKIE* or *MACPHERSON*—dug out in straight and narrow lettering, theirs read *LARSEN CABIN* in broad, rounded letters, charred to appear rustic; the whole thing varnished to a neat and weather-resistant gold. It was something her parents had done in a sudden fit of craftiness when she and Elliot were still children. An ostentatious in-joke, since their name wasn't Larsen at all. Ridiculous.

"The road's been used recently," said Elliot, "so they're probably already up here." He maneuvered the last turn, easing the huge car forward into a partially cleared spot beside a red Jetta, which was still running. "Are they still in the car?" he said, and Sarah was alarmed for a moment as the high beams illuminated the silhouettes of two figures slumped in the front seat. But Elliot shut off the Impala's engine and Sarah got out to find her parents just sitting in the car, quite alive, leaning into each other in their down parkas, fiddling with the radio and clouding the windows with the heat of their breath, of themselves.

Their mother threw open her door. "Children! My beloved off-spring. You made it."

"Fruit of our loins," said Frank. "Greetings."

"What are you doing?" asked Elliot. "You haven't started getting anything ready."

"Not even a hello?" said Gretchen. Her voice was mild as she got out of the car, heading for the shovels they kept stored in the shed. "We've just been listening to the live broadcast from the Met. It's *Turandot*. We love *Turandot*! You just have to stop to take it in."

Frank said, "I can't believe *you* turned up so late, hoping to miss all the work. I'm on to your game now, see."

Sarah thought her brother should know better than to try to shame their parents, unless he wanted to pursue an actual ethical debate.

But Elliot shook his head. "I can't believe you'd sit there wasting gas just to teach us a lesson."

"Can't you?" said Sarah.

Gretchen returned and passed Elliot a shovel, then bent to begin digging out a path to the door. She was tall and fit, but awkward at most physical tasks.

"Oh, come now," said Frank. He got out and motioned for the spade. "Here," he said, holding the car door for Sarah. She got in. It was warm, and she began to sweat almost instantly. She pulled open the neck of her coat. They'd left the radio tuned to classical. Some opera. Puccini maybe. Perhaps that's what her mother was talking about.

Before her, the cabin huddled on its little hill, snow on the roof and halfway up the door. To the right, the ground fell away at a steep grade to the lake, and to the left, a narrow path wound upwards to the outhouse. Squat and square, the log cabin was pint-sized compared to the large summer houses that had sprung up around the lake. Frank and Gretchen had dubbed it Larsen Cabin after they saw *The Gold Rush*, a Charlie Chaplin movie set mostly in an old prospector's shack hanging half off the edge of a cliff. Black Larsen's place. They had bought the cabin when they were very young for an amount that had seemed like a lot of money, but which now struck everyone as an absurdity, practically an affront.

"Too bad Dory won't be coming," Gretchen said to Sarah as she got back in the car, shivering.

"Oh," said Sarah. "I guess."

"I think it's for the best, though," said Gretchen. "The split."

Sarah looked over at her mother. Driven and unapologetic, Dory had always been a great favourite of Gretchen's. "Me too," said Sarah. Elliot had confided to her on the drive up that Dory had left him for another woman.

"Dory and I went for a drink last week." Gretchen leaned back, shook out her sleeves until her hands disappeared. "I told her at least she'll be able to focus more on her work now."

"Right," said Sarah. "Well. Elliot, too." Her brother had worked the same beat for the NYPD for years, and Sarah knew that, like her, he was only ambitious when it came to personal happiness, not professional advancement.

She watched him with a vague jealousy as he snapped off the huge icicles from above the cabin door. He turned to grin at her before launching them like darts into the snow heap.

"Oh, honey," said Gretchen. "You know, I've never understood why you and Dory aren't closer."

"We're close enough." Though Sarah had always suspected her ex-sister-in-law didn't exactly like her, Dory and Elliot had taken her in when she'd turned up on their doorstep with nothing but a dirty rucksack and a wavering hope that she was finally thinking her own thoughts. Back then, Dory couldn't help bombarding her with unanswerable questions about why she'd joined Living Tree in the first place. But Elliot seemed to understand, without needing to be told, that Sarah just needed to be warm, and quiet. Safe. Still, she was grateful to Dory for never complaining within earshot about how she'd shredded the guest bedsheets to weave into rag rugs, or about the long, red hairs that had started to collect in all the drains. It wasn't until three months later that Sarah seemed to wake up and notice that the spot on her brother's couch she had been occupying around the clock had become a major depression in more ways than one.

Frank and Elliot had disappeared inside the cabin.

"And we're in," said Sarah, popping open the car door.

At some point in its history, her family's cabin had reached a fork at which it could have come into its own as either an affectionate or mocking tribute to old-fashioned cottages, or as something comfortable but plain. But with its mismatched furniture and crockery, bare wooden bunks, and incoherent decor, Sarah thought that it had somehow become both. Hanging around the walls were old pairs of catgut snowshoes that Frank bought whenever he found them cheap at a garage sale. Gretchen had contributed a couple of amateur oil paintings of nude women sourced from junk shops, as well as a terrible, motion-activated singing fish advertised on late-night television. Then there were all the rag rugs, and the shutters with a pattern of hearts cut out at the top.

They carried everything in from the cars and took stock of the food they'd packed. Elliot turned on the electricity, then put on the lights. There was no question of anything festive. No eggnog. No turkey. Frank and Gretchen had adopted their strict anti-Christmas stance in the seventies, shortly after they were married, when they decided they took a dim view of people who weren't even Christian but who still went in for all the hoopla. At first, they stayed in town, declining invitations to parties, inviting people over only to serve whisky and play jazz records. But the story was that once Elliot and Sarah started school, they became so disagreeable and demanding, always whining about not getting any presents, that their parents began the tradition of dragging them out to the lake, isolating the family in a holiday-free zone.

Frank and Gretchen had packed chicken breasts, spinach, four bottles of Perrier, one cucumber, and a large quantity of dried Italian sausage.

"I remembered to bring herbs this time," said Gretchen. "And olive oil and salt."

"And I remembered the essentials." Frank revealed two bottles of wine and one of Crown Royal.

Elliot had a cooler filled with steaks, bread, eggs, pasta, bottled tomato sauce, oatmeal, and peanut butter. Coffee and beer. All in quantities enough to share. He had also bought two four-gallon jugs of water.

Sarah bent to retrieve her bag of supplies, exhaling as a small spasm stung her back. As she straightened up, she caught her mother looking at her with a critical eye.

"Have you put on weight?"

"Yes," said Sarah. "I've really been letting myself go." She unzipped her bulky coat and let it slip from her shoulders, revealing her pregnant belly. She cupped her hands above and below the bump, emphasis and embrace, and Frank and Gretchen stopped moving. Elliot put down a carton of eggs.

"This shouldn't be a surprise," she said. "I'm thirty-one years old, and I've been saying I wanted a baby ever since I came back from Bolivia."

The comment seemed to unfreeze her parents.

"Well, you've been saying lots of things, honey," said Gretchen, and Sarah's eyes brimmed. When Elliot groaned, their mother turned up her palms like someone cornered. "What? She has."

Elliot ignored her and crossed the room to give Sarah a hug. His stubble grazed her cheek, which he kissed again. "May I?" he asked. Sarah nodded, and he put a hand on her belly. "This is big news." He said this as much to their parents as to her. A demonstration. "This is the most wonderful thing."

Sarah's heart went out to him in gratitude as she blinked back tears. She would think of this instance of kindness often in the years to come, as a foundational moment for everything that followed.

"Congratulations, sweetheart," said her father, though he still looked bewildered.

Next to him, her mother nodded. "Yes," said Gretchen, though it sounded grudging.

"I'll help you with this," said Elliot, taking the bag from Sarah.

Wiping her eyes, she followed him to the counter and arranged her offerings across it: cheese and crackers, ginger ale, chocolate, four large cans of yellow pea soup, a tiny bottle of dill pickles.

Gretchen tutted over her supplies, shaking her head as Sarah placed them on the table. "Rather a poor showing, my daughter. I had higher hopes." Her voice had returned to normal. "Do you remember that hunter's stew you brought last year? And the garlic-stuffed olives from Trader Joe's?"

"Are you kidding?" Sarah said, baffled that the conversation had somehow already moved on. "At least I remembered a can opener." There had been one or two bad years when everyone forgot. It would probably be another couple of years before her parents managed to buy one for the cabin.

Gretchen shrugged, then began putting some of the food away

into the cupboards. "No need to get upset," she said, unflustered. "That's the first thing you learn as a mother. Everyone expects you take care of them."

"I'm having the baby by myself," said Sarah, once they moved to the living room, determined not to let her parents' nonchalance set the agenda. Her knit woollen sweater was stretched tight over her stomach. She had taken to swathing herself in things that gave her belly the comforting aspect of a familiar old blanket or stuffed animal. Nubbly brown wool or plaid flannel to neutralize its bulging, disorienting effect.

"Having children is what produces adults," Frank said. "Or so the saying goes." He squinted at his wife. "Who said that, dear?" Gretchen shrugged.

Sarah turned her attention to her father. "Are you saying I'm too immature to have a child?"

"No," he said, looking alarmed. "Of course not."

Now, as they sat together, settled on the worn sofa and armchairs, Sarah switched her focus from Frank to Gretchen. "I thought you guys would be supportive. But you clearly don't even want to talk about it."

Her mother acted surprised. "Of course I'm supportive. Why wouldn't I be?"

But Sarah just stared at her, feeling her mouth settle into a hard little knot of resentment—what Elliot always called her "prune face"—but she could do nothing to stop it. "You haven't even asked if it's a boy or a girl." She realized it was just another way her parents could prove themselves extraordinary, by being extraordinarily relaxed.

Gretchen sighed. "Give me time. I can't be excited about something that doesn't exist yet." She leaned over the arm of the couch to rub Sarah's belly with a strong, circular touch that stirred the baby and struck Sarah as wise and intuitive. When the baby kicked, she withdrew her hand.

"I just wonder," her mother said, sitting back, "given the state of the world, whether we ought to be bringing more children into it." Next to her, Frank was nodding.

"Well, you had us," said Elliot, sounding exasperated. He was over at the stove now, feeding it more wood. "It's not like everything was a picnic back then either."

"No, but it's worse now. Plus, the idea back then was that having children would be good for your art." Gretchen had been a poet for a brief but fiery period before she was married. She started her academic career after Frank, though she had by now eclipsed him. "But the time constraints can be prohibitive, no matter your new depths of feeling for the human experience. Plus, you haven't even started your career yet, not really."

"I have a job, Mom," said Sarah. "I did my degree. What more do you want?"

"I want *you* to want more." It was an old conversation between the two of them.

"I want this baby," said Sarah. "That's what I want." Throughout all her years at Living Tree, it was the one and only thing that had continued to feel right: a baby on her hip, staring up at her with a dazzled, trusting face. A clarity of need and response. Giggly smiles and silly dances and nonsense reigning as the prevailing order among all the children in her charge.

"You know," said Frank. "I've never even met the father." In his voice was a kind of wonder as to whether this should appall or impress him.

"Neither have I," said Sarah. "I went to a sperm bank."

In any other family, she thought, there would be protests of disbelief or dismay. But she was known for her straightforward, serious bent. From time to time it had helped a joke go over huge, but now her parents just stared at her.

Elliot stood abruptly. "The stove," he said, moving towards it.

"I'm surprised you didn't want to wait," said Frank, who looked as though he was trying to puzzle it out. "For the right guy. I mean, you've still got time."

"Why should I wait?" asked Sarah. Her voice was a bark. The only thing she had been waiting for was this exact question. She'd had a feeling her parents were not quite unconventional enough to avoid asking it. "*Why* should I have to wait for a *man*?"

Frank, mild as always, only shrugged.

"What kind of a man donates to a sperm bank?" asked Gretchen, though Sarah could tell from her tone that it was neither a judgmental nor a rhetorical question. Her mother was huddled under the quilt, her chin bobbing in a thoughtful bounce on her knee.

"Someone generous?" said Sarah. "Open-minded?"

Elliot came back from the stove with red cheeks. "I did once," he said. "Actually, a bunch of times, in college. To buy my car. But it was for research, not babies."

"Are you kidding?" said Sarah, almost as tickled as she was bewildered. "Was that when you were dating Keisha Delille?"

"Yes, dating," he said. "And then dumping."

"Keisha?" said Gretchen. "I always liked her."

"But . . . why?" asked Sarah.

"Why did I dump her? She was too good for me, remember?"

They both laughed. "That's not what I meant," said Sarah.

"Did you look at a magazine?" asked Gretchen, with interest.

Sarah knew her mother had argued both sides of the feminist pornography debate, though more convincingly—to Gretchen's continuing chagrin—from a pro-censorship position. There were papers in academic journals using Howe (1981) to combat Howe (1997).

Elliot just shook his head.

"Wait. *Where* did you do it?" Sarah almost spat out the words.

He gave her a sharp look. "Back in Massachusetts. I think it's closed down now, though."

"Oh thank God," she said. She swallowed, leaned her head towards her knees. She'd gone to a place on West 59th Street, across from the park. The ginger ale in her glass tipped out onto the floor.

Gretchen began laughing until she nearly cried. It was a terrible laugh, thought Sarah, who was almost on the point of retching. "Stop it," she said, her voice croaking.

Her mother chuckled, throwing off the quilt. "Oh, come on. Really, what would have been the odds?"

"Pretty good, I should think," said Frank. "I just read about this in the *Times*. Now that more women are refusing anonymous donors, there's a shortage."

"Stop it, Dad," said Elliot. He smiled at Sarah from across the room and she immediately felt calmer. "It was ages ago."

Sarah was lying on her bunk, having kicked off her shoes, stretching her feet out in small circles and repeating under her breath what had become her new mantra: *All that matters is that the baby is healthy*. From the other room, she could hear Elliot and her parents talking about some friends of theirs from the university who were looking into buying property nearby.

"There goes your getaway," she heard Elliot say, and Sarah snorted. She imagined bringing her child here in the years to come, initiating them into all their bizarre family rituals—secular Christmas, paddling with Plato, keeping a sharp lookout for the Larsen Cabin sign in the dark—and by doing so, tacitly endorsing them. With her baby, she would finally have to decide whether she was part of her crazy family or not.

After all these years, the people up here still took them to be Larsens. Anybody would. Sarah's parents never bothered correcting anyone or letting them in on the joke. They were only ever up here in the summer or for the odd weeklong stretch, and they maintained their share of the road, which was all that had ever concerned the neighbours. Once, years ago, Sarah had been lying on the dock, the cabin perched high and derelict on the hill above her, and a woman had come paddling up, quiet and swift as a minnow. Shading her eyes against the sun with one hand, the woman had called out to Sarah, "You're that Larsen girl, aren't you? Is that where I am now? The Larsens' place?"

And Sarah, glancing up from her book with a mute and graceless look of panic, was caught between the guilt of exposing her parents' meaningless deception or the inanity of propping it up, which might be worse. In the end she only nodded, and the woman nodded back, dropped her hand from her face, and paddled away.

Gretchen was talking about her fear of the woods when Sarah returned to the living room.

"It's a perfectly natural phobia," she said, sipping red wine out of an ancient coffee mug. "Historically, dating to the beginning of agriculture, the woods have been outside of our arena of control."

Frank disagreed. "It isn't about some horror lurking in the dark. It's the terror of humans left to instinct. *Lord of the Flies*, et cetera." Her father always seemed to find his conversational rhythm more readily after a couple of drinks. "Society is the only thing preserving us from the state of nature. It's just a fear of our true selves."

"No, just bears," said Sarah. "And wood ticks." She started to sit down, then said, "I have to pee." She was surprised she hadn't had to go before. They didn't use the cabin toilet in the winter, though two years ago, on Christmas Eve, Frank had taken a single drunken piss without pouring antifreeze in afterwards and the bowl had cracked spectacularly. After pulling on her coat, Sarah picked up the flashlight from the table and pushed out the front door and up the path, taking slow small steps to avoid the places where there was an icy sheen on the rocks. She was more afraid of falling than of the hardy dismissiveness she imagined from her parents: her mother booming out an account of tumbling off a ladder with a belly full of Elliot, or some strange fact from Frank about the pregnant women of ancient times drinking lead and jumping over bulls. Spartans or some shit.

It was much warmer out than before and she was happy she'd left her coat open. When she reached the wooden door of the outhouse, she pulled at it and fell back, seeing a metal hook and fastener, a keyed padlock snapped shut. A drop of rain hit her hand before she felt more dripping down her forehead. Then she heard the noisy rustling in the leaves as it came down. Freezing rain.

"Where's the key?" she shouted when she was back at the cabin, her voice sounding high and needy in her ears.

"It was my project," said Gretchen, always happy to take credit for any inconvenience, any strange and insistent whim. "There were a few incidents up here of some teenagers getting into outhouses, throwing things down there, messing things up." She looked at Frank. "But the key . . ." She frowned. "I can say for certain that wherever it is, it is not here."

All together they trudged up to the outhouse, Gretchen pushing into the lead, hood raised to keep off the rain. "I'm sure we can just bust in the door," she said.

"Then why bother locking it?" asked Elliot. He rattled the door, then kicked at it with his foot. It splintered but didn't break.

"I really have to go," said Sarah. She was close to tears and frustrated with herself. If this was her breaking point, it didn't bode well for motherhood.

"Just go in the woods," said Gretchen, throwing up her hands. Inside her hood, her hair circled her face like the mane of a lion. "Didn't you use to live out in the wilderness with those people?"

"Come on," said Elliot. "Good thing you're wearing a skirt." He took Sarah by the hand and led her off the trail and into the woods, out of sight of their parents and the lake, to where the trees were younger and grew closer together. "This looks good," he said.

She rustled up her peasant skirt and tried to squat out of range of the underwear she pulled down. It was brighter out than Sarah had realized—a big moon.

"I can't."

It was pathetic. The urgency in her bladder seemed to spread throughout her abdomen, a miniature earthquake shooting nerves of fear across her body, and all at once she considered how much larger were the tasks ahead. She felt more alone on the path she had chosen than she thought it was possible to feel. Blinking up through the branches, she remembered the sensation of looking up at the sky in Bolivia, a salty layer of sweat crusting her face and forearms, and the sinking feeling of having gotten everything wrong. A few hippies with a land title could never build a perfect world. People were too flawed—too venal—for paradise. She wondered now if she would ever recover from the realization of how easy it had been to walk away from her life, how seamlessly the world closed up around the place where she used to be.

"I'm scared," she said. As if on cue, the baby kicked. "I can't do this."

"There's nothing to it," said Elliot. "Here, I'll start." She heard her brother unzip his fly and whistle a few bright notes as she stared down at her boots sunk in the snow, its smooth surface pocked here and there where the freezing rain had penetrated the trees and slipped cleanly into its layers like ice-cold seeds planted at depth.

From a few feet away, Sarah could see the steam rise and the snow falling back. "That's not what I meant."

"I know." There was a hint of teasing laughter in Elliot's voice. "But either way, you have to start by letting go." Then her brother turned serious. "And I'm here for you no matter what."

After a moment, she repositioned herself and sighed, and there was the sound of her stuttering stream joining his, then the rain getting heavier. Sarah closed her eyes and let herself go, spreading herself out until all of winter melted away.

Program:	*The Hugh Besnard Show*
Date:	**November 9, 2020**
Time:	**9:36 AM EST**
Duration:	**2 minutes 2 seconds**
Interviewer:	**Hugh Besnard**
Interviewee:	**Keelan Gibbs**

BESNARD: Professor Gibbs, the writer Owen Grant has gone on record saying that disaster preparedness is a moral obligation for those who can afford it. Since that time, the United States has faced shortages of N95 face masks and generators, not to mention antivirals. Do you think Mr. Grant got it wrong?

GIBBS: Preparedness isn't wrong in and of itself. But it's also critical not to give in to fear. It's fear that prompts people to hoard more resources than they need to survive—they're nervous there won't be enough for everyone.

BESNARD: What do you think is the biggest single ethical issue surrounding ARAMIS?

GIBBS: We're already talking about it: fear and the way it can subvert reason and decision-making. In previous flu pandemics, healthy people starved in quarantine because others were too frightened to bring them food. But these days, we have plenty of information on how to safely interact with those in quarantine while avoiding infection.

I'm also concerned that we will see this type of anxiety play out on a nation-by-nation level, right at a time when global cooperation is most required. The government has a responsibility to protect its citizens, but it must also continue to join forces internationally in offering medical resources and staff, monetary relief, and assistance in kind. For instance, we cannot close our borders unilaterally.

BESNARD: What is your personal philosophy, Professor?

GIBBS: Human beings are flawed, just like our leaders. Sometimes we make the wrong decisions. That's why it's important to think carefully and consider the consequences of our actions—not just for their impact on others, but on our own psyches. This is especially true during times of crisis. If we want to continue to think of ourselves as good people, we need to ground that belief in everything we do.

ELLIOT

—

NOVEMBER 2020

His last days in New York City were the only time in his life Elliot remembered being afraid. He had picked up a call for a burglary in progress in the Bronx, but when he arrived at the squalid basement apartment, it turned out to be a standoff between a mother and her teenaged son. Piles of dirty dishes overflowed from the sink onto a counter littered with all manner of human detritus: knapsacks, makeup, shoelaces, cigarettes. A mattress in the corner was heaped with garbage bags and there were no shades on any of the lamps, perhaps to admit as much light as possible into the cramped space. The woman and her son stood in front of a dresser with every drawer yanked open. Both were clutching knives.

"He says I'm too old," the mother said, appealing to Elliot and gesturing with the knife as though she were an actor breaking the fourth wall. She was wearing an oversized Metallica T-shirt over a pair of flowered leggings. "Says I'll slow him down. Can you believe it?" she said. "I'm fifty-two years old and being junked by my own son."

The word *junked* gave Elliot a quicksilver shudder of permeability, as though she somehow knew he had been thinking *junkie*. He felt outside of himself. Only the gun on his hip registered, like a lead weight tethering him to Earth. "Ma'am," he said, "this isn't about what I believe." Although he understood that, in some way, of course it was. "It's about the two of you putting down those knives you've got." He wondered if the boy really was desperate to flee the city or if it was only an excuse to get away from his mother. It was an interesting question, whether the world ought to belong to the young or the old. The young seemed to feel they were owed something—a life. But . . . well. Maybe it wasn't a question for the childless. He remembered that someone once said youth was wasted on the young, and when he saw the terrified expression on the face of that scared, snarling teen, it certainly seemed to be true.

A call squawked through on his radio. There was a request for backup at a brawl on Courtlandt Avenue. The 911 caller had reported gunshots.

Elliot felt the emptiness of his patrol car outside on the street. The force was bleeding officers who'd taken ill or left town. His own partner, Russ, had gone on indefinite leave after his youngest child was hospitalized at Methodist Morningside just a week after the end of their posting there. Most beats were run solo these days. The usual arrest targets had fallen away. The order of the day was avoiding martial law. As the chief of police had said, "For God's sake, just try to keep the peace, or else we'll end up kowtowing to the National Guard." His salt-and-pepper beard had snowed over since the start of the outbreak.

"He's taking all the money I have," the woman said. Elliot detected a note of satisfaction mingled with the outrage. She waved her knife towards a pile of dirty clothes on the floor. "He's stolen it right out of my drawer. I want you to arrest him for robbery."

An impatience flickered within Elliot, along with a powerful urge to strike them both, burn the money, and leave them to figure out their own mess—or arrest them for wasting his time. "Nobody's getting arrested," he found himself saying. "We're going to resolve this together." Even as he renounced the idea of it, he was reminded of the extra weight brutality could lend to authority. The boy and his mother just stared at him, her lip curling up in what Elliot interpreted as disappointment. But he could tell the boy was used to being bossed. He was only tired of being bossed by his mother.

"Give it here, son." It was a butterfly knife the boy was holding, with a filigreed handle. "Just the money," said Elliot, as the boy tightened his grip on the blade and came closer.

Elliot held out his hand, and into the centre of his dry palm the boy deposited the wad of crumpled bills. With his thumb, Elliot separated out seven twenties—why seven? who knows? fairness was a feeling: it came from the gut—and handed these back to the son.

"If you want to leave, leave."

It took nothing more than a curt nod in the direction of the door for the boy to pocket the cash and flee. The flush of pride Elliot experienced then reminded him of how he'd felt after his very first calls as a rookie.

But the mother was not as grateful as expected. She entered into a maudlin howling. "I'd have given him all the money," she wailed, "to stay."

Elliot's sympathy curdled. He sensed the limits of the temperament that made him, most of the time, one of the good ones. "You called the police," he said. "You get what you pay for."

⊸║║║⊷

After his shift, Elliot returned to the converted industrial building where he and the other students continued to practise kung fu. He waited a moment in his parked car before going in. Two weeks ago, in early November, a grey belt student named Cassie had stopped coming and had gone silent on the group chat. Nobody knew if it meant she had caught the virus or not. Then, last week, there were three more absent, though two logged into the chat to say they'd quarantined themselves as a precautionary measure only: they were afraid Cassie was sick and they'd all been exposed. A general discussion began about whether they ought to disband the weekly gathering, and just last night Elliot had weighed in before he could stop himself: *I don't know what I'll do without this, guys.* And without meaning to, he had effectively shut down the debate—possibly by embarrassing the others into silence. Elliot didn't often chime in on the group chat, and perhaps a trace of authority still adhered to him as the only surviving member of the advanced class, not to mention as a police officer violating the social distancing ordinances. Nobody had typed a word in the thread since last night.

Elliot put on a mask and a pair of gloves, then exited and locked his car with a tamped-down apprehension stifling the base of his throat. The likelihood was that no one else would be there. Without wanting to acknowledge breaking their pact, he suspected the others would silently absent themselves—signalling both a sympathy to his point of view as well as a wholly natural self-preservation. He had been irresponsible with his words: too candid, too desperate.

He took the stairwell to the third floor. The air felt stagnant and too thick. All the units in the large commercial building remained unleased. Without the influx of human activity, the building still smelled of paint, sawdust, the sickly off-gassing fumes of chemical sealants and treated wood. Elliot steeled himself in the hallway before going in. It made him heartsick to imagine their numbers continuing to dwindle, week by week. If that was their future, then the others were right: they should stop now. And perhaps they had already. The room where they had balanced and flexed and wept together for their shared and private griefs would be deserted. In short order, it would return to the anonymous sterility of stalled enterprise, unless he decided to continue visiting by himself. A lonely vigil of one.

Elliot pushed through the metal door and opened his eyes, just as he inhaled the boozy lemon scent of disinfectant and the acrid tang of sweat. There were a dozen people, the bulk of their group, spaced out across the warehouse, moving through their usual warm-up exercises. They all turned to look at him, raising gloved hands of welcome. He couldn't see their mouths behind the masks, but he could tell from their eyes that they were smiling.

꜌꜌꜌

The next day, Elliot responded to a robbery call at Saint Michael's Parish on Alexander Avenue. The carved wooden door swung open more easily than he expected, then slammed shut behind him with an echoing clang. He removed his hat, noting that the marble holy-water fonts to the sides of the doors were topped with wooden covers. Blinking, he waited for his eyes to adjust, savouring the abrupt relief from the sounds of the street. Colour pooled on the floor from the stained-glass windows, forming spotlights for towering motes of swirling dust. A handful of worshippers were scattered throughout the sanctuary, each in a separate pew.

A priest in a black cassock and clerical collar signalled to him from the front of the nave. Elliot nodded back, his gaze lifting to the vaulted ceiling where heavenly beings re-enacted stories about which he felt an uneasy ignorance. Elliot heard his steps echoing and became aware of an unexpected ceremonial gravity as he walked down the aisle. He wasn't often in churches.

"I'm Father Mateo," called the priest, as Elliot approached the front. People half shouted now, to be heard through their masks, though it wasn't usually necessary. "I placed the call." Elliot thought he detected the soft sibilance of a Latin American accent.

"Officer Howe," said Elliot. A video camera was set up, pointed at the altar. "What's all this?"

"A webcast," said Father Mateo. He had a smooth brown scalp fringed with thick, dark hair. The priest's baldness was more pronounced than his own, but Elliot noted that Father Mateo's robes lent it a certain natural graciousness. "Father Christopher will celebrate mass this evening for our parishioners online. One of the young ladies in the choir set it up for us. Very clever, I thought."

"I agree," said Elliot. He wondered why he was surprised that churches would change with the times. He imagined the Holy Spirit flowing like a meme through the internet. "So what's the problem, Father? Something's been stolen?"

"Follow me." Father Mateo led the way to a door in the elaborate oak panels girding the sanctuary. Elliot followed him along a corridor and down a set of stairs until they reached the basement. An elderly priest with slightly gaunt cheeks was lingering in a doorway.

"The police arrive faster than the ambulances these days," he said, spotting them. "Property before people, I suppose."

"This is Father Christopher," said Father Mateo, acknowledging his colleague. "Officer Howe."

"We come as fast as we can," said Elliot. "The whole system is overtaxed right now."

"Yes, but how did we arrive here?" said Father Christopher. He held up a hand and snapped his fingers, though the gloves cut the sound. "What systems did we choose to invest in in the first place?"

Father Mateo said, "Officer Howe is here to help us."

The older priest folded his arms. "I apologize, Officer. We have lost part of our flock, you understand. It's been very painful."

"Faith must be a comfort these days," said Elliot. Platitudes had a time and a place, and never more so than during a crisis. They were the shared language of well-meaning strangers.

Father Christopher nodded as though Elliot had said something profound. "It's difficult," he said. "Our congregation could use some solace, but we've had to suspend regular services, of course."

"The webcast seems like a good solution," said Elliot.

Father Christopher nodded again and stepped aside to allow the younger priest to lead Elliot into the storeroom. The small space was lined with shelving along each wall.

"Our food cupboard," Father Mateo said, raising a hand to indicate a level just below the full height of the shelves, as though it had at one time been nearly filled. Now there were just odd boxes of spaghetti, some cans that had rolled onto their sides, and a few spurned tins of Spam and sardines. "We always kept a bit on hand in case it was needed, then during the swine flu we thought it was a good idea to keep a little more. Just some emergency provisioning, so our congregation knew they had somewhere to turn." Father Mateo clasped his hands together in what appeared to be a habitual gesture. "There are times when the Church can do what the government cannot."

Elliot glanced at the door. "Was it kept locked?"

The priests looked at each other.

"No," said Father Christopher. "The idea was that it was to be distributed as needed. We didn't lock it because we received donations and requests at all hours."

"You see, it had to be one of our parishioners," said Father Mateo, drawing down his dark eyebrows as he shook his head. "Nobody else knows about it. And they must have been desperate."

The older priest remained in the doorway of the empty room. "But is it theft if people are starving?"

"I understand," said Elliot. "What do you want me to do?"

"Nothing," said Father Mateo. He spread out his hands, seeming bewildered. "Absolutely nothing. But it's my duty to report the crime, is it not?" The younger, anguished priest appealed to the elder, who continued to observe Elliot with guarded concern.

"Officer," said Father Christopher with emphasis, "there has been no robbery here. And certainly no looting, least of all." He exchanged a worn-out glance with his colleague. "At least with divine law, you can be sure of mercy."

Elliot nodded as he prepared to leave. He envied them their certainty.

HEPTOMCAT User since: Sept 2001 Posts: 2083 Forum Level: Admin	**Posted: November 11, 2020 at 9:18 a.m.** So the virus has finally landed in Denver. Three people sick, all members of the Chinese Evangelical Church. Surprise surprise. Looks like ARAMIS Girl paid us a visit. What I wouldn't give to throw her ass in jail.
RAGECORPS User since: Nov 2009 Posts: 4295 Forum Level: Elite	**Posted: November 11, 2020 at 9:33 a.m.** ARAMIS Girl is just the start. Every organized military in the world has mastered hypnosis!! Going forward, you can bet that *INFECTED CIVILIANS* programmed for soft targets will be the weapon of choice for governments overfunded by the liberal snowflake agenda. Need any more proof than the To America With Love concert? Stay vigilant!
GRANTER User since: July 2010 Posts: 19 Forum Level: Apprentice	**Posted: November 11, 2020 at 10:17 a.m.** You guys should know better than to believe all that nonsense about ARAMIS Girl. The arrival and dissemination of the virus on American soil has been well documented. AG is not and has never even been speculated by the authorities to be Patient Zero.
HEPTOMCAT User since: Sept 2001 Posts: 2084 Forum Level: Admin	**Posted: November 11, 2020 at 10:46 a.m.** Oh please. As if you can believe the official story on these things. The left-wing media is so politically correct they'd never point the blame where it really belongs. Next they'll be saying it was really a white man who was making everybody sick.
BLISTERBURN User since: Jan 2014 Posts: 761 Forum Level: Sage	**Posted: November 11, 2020 at 11:01 a.m.** Agreed. And if we don't take steps to defend what we have, there are people who will seize this opportunity to take it away. We can't let that happen. A few more weeks of ARAMIS and you can bet there will be violence, looting, chaos. Protect what you have or else.

GRANTER User since: July 2010 Posts: 20 Forum Level: Apprentice	**Posted: November 11, 2020 at 11:24 a.m.** Have you guys heard of elite panic? Keelan Gibbs talked about it on the news. It's when people with power and entitlement are afraid that any change to the current world order is going to spark a revolution and cost them their land, money & privileges. And all too often the elite are the ones setting policies, controlling the media, influencing the official response to a disaster. Don't fall into the trap.
BLISTERBURN User since: Jan 2014 Posts: 762 Forum Level: Sage	**Posted: November 11, 2020 at 11:54 a.m.** Been a while, Granter! Thought you were gone for good. Why do you even spend time here if you think we're all a bunch of right-wing nutters? Don't patronize us. Gertiebird isn't here to be your cheerleader anymore. Go back to rowing your little boat merrily out to sea while we deal with reality here on land.
HATBURGER User since: Oct 2016 Posts: 349 Forum Level: Wannabe	**Posted: November 11, 2020 at 2:09 p.m.** I for one think Granter has shared some very interesting ideas. Granter, do you think this panic is driven (deep down) by guilt? The elite suspect they have more than they deserve, so they think people are always trying to steal it?
LIEGEON User since: Sept 2020 Posts: 4 Forum Level: Neophyte	**Posted: November 11, 2020 at 3:24 p.m.** More likely they're the thieves. The rich are rotten to the core and so they assume everyone else is too. Let's face it: the whole antiviral shortage is probably a lie. Some billionaire is just stockpiling them in his ten McMansions while his neighbours are dying. God bless America!

KEELAN

—

NOVEMBER 2020

"So is this it for the human race? Is this the end?"

The television announcer had lacquered blond hair and a thick coating of makeup that made his face look like clay.

Keelan shifted in his seat, aware of the heat of the studio lights and a bead of sweat travelling down the back of his neck. "It's a very interesting question you pose," he said. He wondered how much of his usual Socratic method would be sacrificed in editing for a television audience. They'd told him this segment was part of an hour-long feature on the crisis to be aired after the evening news, and his interview would be intercut along with those of other experts.

The interviewer, Neil something, was still looking at him with expectation and a hint of impatience. It was all in the eyes. Once he'd asked the question, Neil probably knew it was safe to give these sorts of silent cues: to encourage, intimidate, compel. It was part of the skill set.

Keelan knew what the man wanted him to say. He wanted him to say, *I'm afraid it very well could be*.

"I'm afraid . . ." Keelan began, and it was true, he realized. He *was* afraid—of the virus, of whatever it was he might be about to say. He almost wanted to stop right there. But the interviewer's carefully groomed eyebrows shot up in anticipation.

"I'm afraid," continued Keelan, "it's too soon to tell."

Now Neil's eyebrows were crestfallen, dejected. Keelan had let them down, along with the television-viewing public, who needed to be told how to feel, what to think, what to do.

Relenting, Keelan leaned forward on the desk, closer to Camera 2, revealing the corduroy elbow patches on his tweed jacket. He made his eyes as owlish as he knew how. "But it might be, Neil. It just might be."

Keelan had made amends to the eyebrows. They were furrowed and intense as Neil seized on the bone he'd thrown. "When you say it's too soon to tell, is there anything we can do that might make a difference?"

"Absolutely," said Keelan. He dropped his voice to a suspenseful pitch. "How we conduct ourselves throughout this crisis might very well determine the future of the human race."

On his doorstep, Keelan fitted his key in the lock, sparing a look over both shoulders as he did so. He wasn't sure when this had become a habit—probably around the time he'd started shopping at the bulk stores. But the street was deserted, anyway. The street hockey kids, the toddlers on plastic tricycles, the old men raking leaves from their lawns. All of them gone in the wake of ARAMIS. Gone inside, anyway.

Keelan locked the door behind him and dropped his briefcase beside the umbrella stand, before frowning at the wooden receptacle with a picture of an umbrella and the word *parapluies* painted on the side. Peculiar artifacts of this sort, so limited and specific, seemed doomed to impeach their fading era of wealth and complacency. Umbrella stands, grapefruit spoons, nose-hair clippers: these were not things that ought to belong to a world in crisis.

In the kitchen, he slid a frozen pizza into the oven and set the timer on the stove.

He didn't think he had gone too far in the interview. If anything, he'd been cautious. The fact was that a worst-case scenario, while perhaps not statistically more likely than any other—they'd have to ask an epidemiologist about that—felt historically, or at any rate narratively, inevitable. As a species, they were well overdue for reaping what they'd sown.

And yes, maybe it was only because he was old that he believed things were coming to an end; his certainty might be nothing more than garden-variety solipsism. If Annie were still alive, she would probably point out something along those lines.

At any rate, the new Chair would be pleased; he was happy whenever there was something that the university administration called an "interface" with the public. Publicity was good. Being the expert, even on the end of the world, had a certain cachet. But there would be the usual blowback to contend with among his colleagues in the philosophy department. He'd been careful, though, not to simplify or dumb things down. He'd *streamlined*, perhaps. But that was inevitable, in a sound bite.

Keelan predicted a few of his younger colleagues would wonder, *Why him?* Or, more to the point, why not *them?* Perhaps if anyone said anything, he'd deflect with a joke about his beard being the real reason he'd become the face of philosophy on television. A long white beard was still a symbol of wisdom, if only archetypally. And television producers knew almost as well as scholars how the language of visual symbolism worked unconsciously on the viewer. In fact, it would almost be worth bringing one in for a guest lecture on the subject if classes were ever reinstated. For his own part, he had a feeling Owen Grant's recent departure on a sea voyage had created a vacuum of readily available television experts unbesmirched by the haughtiness of a white lab coat. As far as Keelan was concerned, Owen was the real charlatan when it came to peddling so-called pandemic expertise. Though he supposed it wasn't the writer's fault that public discourse was in decline.

The lights dimmed, and Keelan frowned. They had been flickering all week, and he'd littered the place with flashlights—a strategic move of which he was rather proud. Now, in case this was a signal of an imminent outage, he moved towards the computer in the den and turned it on. There was a new email from Edith, his research assistant. She had been busy but curiously absent since the start of the semester—a disembodied presence who emailed him articles and scanned documents. He wondered if the widely reported anti-Asian sentiment in the wake of the ARAMIS Girl debacle was causing her to lay low. A local Korean church had been graffitied and a new Chinese restaurant closed following a boycott. It was hard to imagine the inhabitants of Lansdowne behaving so abominably, but as a town it had the kind of ethnic homogeneity that Keelan knew could spell trouble in a time of crisis, when certain bigots would be prone to racial scapegoating.

I've got a new stack of material for you. Books this time. Should I bring them by your office? Or maybe to your place? I heard the department is pretty much closed.

Edith was an odd girl with a serious intellect but a restless energy. Keelan was grateful that he had never felt the need to imagine himself in love with her, which seemed like a free pass under the circumstances. She was Chinese-American, with tiny bones like a bird, and jet black hair that she kept pulled back off her face with an Alice band. She had soft, expressive lips that trembled when she was excited. Just like Annie. She had Annie's pretty ways about her, too:

the deliberate and graceful movements of a small female person. Keelan sometimes wondered what would have happened if Julia had inherited her mother's delicate genes instead of his own Ukrainian-peasant bones and Irish-boxer build. Would boys have liked her more? Would she have liked them?

At any rate, there was no doubt anymore that Julia really was his daughter. Among the many blessings of puberty had been the conferring of several unmistakable physical traits: his robust frame, his snub nose, and an identical pair of deep-set, serious eyes. Keelan had been a neglectful husband and distracted father, but he *was* her father, after all. It was possible that his fears on that front had made him a little less warm towards her than he ought to have been when she was small.

Keelan pulled out the chair and sat down, repressing a groan as his knees twinged. Age was a battle of will. Next to the computer on the desk was a small sheaf of handwritten pages that comprised a meandering letter-in-progress to Julia.

Dear Julia,

I made the mistake of answering the phone the other day. It was someone from CNN. You know why I answered the phone? I thought it might be you.

It wasn't, of course, and it was the start of this media roller-coaster. Maybe you've seen me on television? It's both thrilling and maddening that I've become the voice of their calamity. My inbox has shifted from a place of dread and avoidance to one of stimulation and anticipation. The student emails begging for extensions or for class notes for the lectures they slept through have been buried beneath hordes of messages from national news outlets and major websites. The other day I stayed logged in, refreshing every five minutes, which I think means that I finally understand the younger generations. I never know who might want me next. I'm even naive enough to suppose it could be you.

Oh, I'm a doddering cliché and I know it. I'm a sad old man who misses his daughter.

When those poor souls in New York got sick and this whole thing started, I almost picked up the phone to call you until I remembered last time, when Dory answered. All that unpleasantness she brought up and the things she said you were talking about in couples therapy. Is it true? I thought I'd apologized for all that long ago. I can tell you it isn't pleasant being berated for things that happened twenty years ago by somebody who wasn't even there. You've found yourself a zealous champion, at any rate. I hope the therapy doesn't betoken some chink in the armour.

It was a letter that never seemed to be finished, nor ever quite enough. Its tone veered problematically close to antagonistic here and there, especially in the mentions of Dory, but short of scratching out whole sections, Keelan wasn't sure how to make it more palatable. The sensible solution would have been to forego the attempt, but it was too late for that. It was a strange impulse that had set him writing, but it might take a stronger one to stop.

He shuffled the pages back in order, leaving the half-finished one on the top of the pile. Then he quickly sent an email to Edith, asking her to drop by with the materials the next day, and responded to a few more media inquiries.

The timer on the stove dinged and Keelan returned to the kitchen. Using a pot-holder, he removed the pizza to a cutting board, where he divided it into four slices using his biggest knife. Then he put all four pieces on a large plate, poured three tall glasses of tap water, and—setting everything on a tray next to a roll of paper towel—brought it into the living room.

He turned on the news. He was momentarily confused by the image of a crowded football game until the field gave way to a clip of a full classroom, then a busy shopping mall, and a large-yet-peaceful protest scene, with people carrying signs reading NO FRACKING and PLANET BEFORE PROFITS.

"The ARAMIS crisis has made images like these a thing of the past in cities across the U.S., from New York and Miami to Austin and L.A.," the announcer was intoning. "Regular life is on hiatus for millions these days. Public gatherings are still restricted. Schools, by and large, are closed. Most offices are allowing employees to work from home, and many businesses have either temporarily shut down or closed altogether. The only places that are still bustling are the hospitals, many of which are full to overflowing."

Keelan lifted a piece of pizza to his mouth and took a bite. The cheese, still hot, stuck to the roof of his mouth. "Mmmm," he said, chewing. He only noticed he was making a sound when he was forced to turn up the volume on the TV. This was how people became loners.

The program cut to a shot of a reporter in front of a hospital in downtown Boston, motioning to the busy ambulance bay. She wore a beige trench coat and a pair of tortoiseshell glasses that reminded Keelan of Dory.

"As hospitals become crisis centres for the virus, other patients are wondering if the hospital is still a safe place for procedures and recovery." The reporter held out a microphone to a pregnant woman in a wheelchair being brought through the front doors, who admitted she had some qualms about delivering her baby in a place where there were at least four hundred confirmed ARAMIS cases.

"I'm sure they're doing their best," the woman said. "I'd go somewhere else if I could, but what choice do I have?" The indignation of her husband was palpable even in his stance behind the wheelchair. Keelan reached for the remote and pressed the mute button before he began to speak.

He moved on to the second glass of water. There was an almost criminal amount of sodium in these frozen pizzas. He ought to have his blood pressure checked, but he didn't suppose doctors were much concerned with routine exams anymore.

"Dark days ahead," he said aloud. As the program cut to the next segment, he unmuted the television. A female guest introduced as a virologist was gesturing to several blown-up images of the ARAMIS virus rendered in blue and red and taped to a whiteboard. Keelan wondered if the real pathogen had a colour and made a mental note to look it up.

Dr. Delille was speaking on location from a university laboratory in New York City. She had an open lab coat and a mass of shoulder-length black braids that framed her face. "The antivirals we've been relying on are only partially effective." Her tone was matter-of-fact. "We also have to expect that the virus will continue to mutate."

Only a microphone was visible in the shot, as though the reporter holding it was disinclined to get any closer. "So we have no medical defence against ARAMIS?"

Dr. Delille's voice became emphatic. "Far from it. We have a net-work of top research labs all across the world working on the problem simultaneously. My team has been trying to see if we can pinpoint any natural immunity to the virus. That could give us a new starting point for a vaccine."

"Do you think there's any reason to be optimistic at this point?"

"Well, epidemiologists have noticed the progress of the virus has been quite erratic." Keelan observed how calm the doctor was in front of the camera, almost as though she didn't notice it was there. "It might have to do with different hospital equipment and protocols, or it may be related to protective immunity or resistance in certain segments of the general population. That's what we're looking into."

The off-screen reporter capped it off. "A word of hope from the front lines of science. Now let's take a look at the reported worldwide cases so far."

An infographic flashed on the screen. Colour-coded clusters of dots indicated confirmed cases, and large red circles marred Europe, China, Vietnam, and Hong Kong. Zooming in on North America, the major cities south of Columbus were inundated with overlapping red dots, and bigger cities north of the Mason–Dixon line appeared in various shades of high-alert orange. In Canada, the west coast was heavily implicated, with a few smaller dots in the east.

Keelan put down the empty glass and slid the tray further away on the table. Settling back against the couch cushions, he considered getting up to pour himself some whisky from the amber bottle beckoning from the sideboard. One of his students had given it to him at the start of term, in a bribe so brazen Keelan had almost considered declining it. Instead, he'd satisfied himself with a raised eyebrow and a reproving thanks. It was ten-year-old single malt from Jura, after all. But the temptation reminded Keelan of the last time he'd indulged, and the headache he'd endured throughout the next day's departmental meeting. Now that Gretchen was no longer Chair, the meetings could drag on forever. He had to acknowledge she'd been a worthy successor, though she'd followed his own fifteen-year term with a mere four. The new Chair was long-winded, unpredictable, and in the Dean's pocket.

"Now's the time to look sharp," said Keelan. "No messing about." He thought about the end of the world and reasoned that drunkenness was an appropriate response. But this, right now, was merely a crisis. He reached for the third glass of water.

There was a clip of a memorial service with all the mourners wearing face masks, a convention that had not yet made its way to Lansdowne. A Jacksonville family had lost a mother, father, and aunt, and all five children were still hospitalized. Keelan's eyes began to close.

A funeral director was talking about adapting mourning rituals to suit pandemic protocols. "It's really about showing respect to our loved ones," he was saying. "They wouldn't want their last rites to become a source of infection for their nearest and dearest." Keelan opened his eyes and saw that the man on television looked afraid.

He remained on the couch watching the news until all the lights and the television abruptly shut off. Then he groped for the flashlight on the table in the hall and lit his way up to bed.

The next morning, Keelan awoke late and in a panic, until he checked his watch and remembered classes were suspended. He had been dreaming of Julia again. The time she'd had the flu when she was a teenager and the fever had stripped away some of her toughness, and how his anxiety had done the same for him. She'd stayed home from school and he'd taken the whole week off—the first week of vacation he'd taken since Annie's death three years earlier—and the two of them had played Scrabble and read books and she'd even talked to him a little about her life, which had become a mystery to him. Or rather, once she'd started telling him about her life, he'd realized he knew nothing about it. Something could only really be a mystery if it had ever occurred to you to be curious about it. That week Julia had talked a great deal about her friend Leah, at first tentatively, and then with such intensity that Keelan began to deflect the conversations, confused by what he'd worried was some type of unhealthy obsession with the girl. Back then, he'd thought everything to do with Julia's emerging identity was connected to losing her mother—it was the lack of feminine influence manifesting in a misplaced need for female intimacy.

Julia had been such a good girl, so uncomplaining and diligent at school. She had never sulked or raged the way that he had heard other teenagers did. Or, he wondered now, had she sensed he wouldn't have been there to listen if she had? Keelan felt a sob rising, which shocked him. It was a curse of old age, this late-breaking sentimentality. This wanting to go back to Julia's adolescence—a time that he could barely remember. And why should he cherish it, when it seemed to bring Julia, and certainly Dory, so much pain?

He turned over onto his side, away from the window, then grabbed a pillow and covered his eyes. The map from last night's newscast kept coming back to him: the pulsing orange and red dots of Miami, Savannah, Austin, Los Angeles. Though it had started in New York, cities in the south were having a harder time containing it, which gave him an uneasy Yankee smugness he wasn't proud of. Boston, for whatever reason, was still amber. Lansdowne wasn't even on the map.

It was so sad, really. He wasn't sure if the tears threatening to spill over were for Julia or for the world, or for fear of ARAMIS. No matter what he said on the news about the importance of cooperative principles and natural empathy, he did not really think that the human race would come through with flying colours. Not ethically. People with power would fear losing it, fuelling unwarranted instances of panic that would no doubt be distorted out of all proportion by the media. At a certain point, all governments traded in utilitarianism, and surviving a pandemic would become a numbers game, with the penalties and restrictions that went along with protectionism. There might not be witch hunts and persecutions like during the Black Death, but there would certainly be civic unrest and related reprisals. Harsh legislation to deal with disorder, a spreading-too-thin of police resources, the breakdown of law enforcement. Vigilantism. The inevitability of roving looters was an idea implanted in his brain by Hollywood, but he knew it had taken root in the collective imagination all the same. Maybe he ought to buy a gun.

Keelan kicked at the sheets until his feet poked out the end. He always woke up sweating these days, even though it was November. Anxiety made him overheat. It was insane for Julia to stay in New York City through the ARAMIS crisis. There was no way of isolating oneself in a metropolis of that size. And Julia and Dory had no car. They relied on public transportation to get everywhere.

He sat up and pulled off his shirt—a dress shirt, he realized, now soaked and wrinkled—and threw it on the floor into a pile of dirty laundry.

"I'll go get her," he said aloud, "and bring her here." The cooler air of the room soothed him, lightening his mood. He felt as though he were shedding a layer of dead skin. "Both of them."

With his new resolve, the structure of the day settled into an intelligible form. He needed to get supplies for the house, and some gas, some snacks, a map. He ought to leave before it got to be too late, although he needed to time his arrival to avoid rush hour in the city, which he'd heard had worsened since people began avoiding public transit. He got up and dressed quickly, in the first items he took out of the closet. It was the beginning of each day that was starting to become tenuous, shaky. Ever since classes had been cancelled, Keelan worried his mental energies were dissipating under the stress of the pandemic. He was watching too much television, thinking too much about the past. In short, he was feeling his age. He was not exactly frightened of losing his routine, but it was the type of small setback he wanted to get out in front of. He could feel deterioration lurking like a coded disease in his DNA. Maybe it was the kind of thing he could write about: *The New Rituals of Normalcy in a Time of Crisis.*

On his way downstairs, Keelan paused, startled by the sound of voices in the living room. He remembered his fleeting, treacherous thought about the potential necessity of buying a gun. Hollywood narratives. Perhaps history wasn't bound to repeat—it was only the stories they told about it that they were doomed to re-enact. Human beings were always looking for a script.

But no, it was only the television.

"Power's back on," he noted, then cringed as a hint of an echo returned from the ceiling over the stairwell, like an affirmation of his solitude. *On . . . on . . . on . . .*

In the kitchen, he put on the coffee and poured himself a bowl of cereal. He thought he could get most of what he needed at the gas station down the road. Officially, he knew there were advisories in place against travelling to or from any city already in a state of emergency, or what the government had lately dubbed "pre-emergency." But it was unclear to Keelan if these were being enforced. There had been nothing on the news so far about roadblocks into New York City. Then his eyes lit up. "Not yet," he said aloud. "That's why now is best. Get out ahead."

He stood in the doorway of the kitchen, bowl in hand, calculating the length of the drive. The last time he had driven to the city was before Julia was born, when Annie was still working as an art dealer, though he had visited by train in the years that followed. He moved to the desk and checked the Amtrak website, but rail service had been suspended along all of the major corridors.

Glancing away from the computer, his eyes fell on the never-ending letter to Julia. He picked up his pen. There was always more to say.

Quickly—

Forgive an old man his self-pitying missives and his paltry grievances. The latest on television (you'd be revolted to know that I watch it compulsively, like any ordinary vain person, now that I expect to see myself on it) is that they fear a major power failure on the East Coast. Or so they claim. Now that I've seen how the news is made (out of people like me!), I am far from reassured by what I hear. Doubtless there are conspiracy theories springing up on either side, but I'm not quite savvy enough with the world wide web to bother finding out what they are. Probably something to do with suppressing information to avoid a large-scale panic. Certainly the power here in Lansdowne has been on the fritz. (And before Dory accuses me of discriminating against Germans with the use of that phrase, let me assure you that the origins of the expression have never been determined.)

You know, I'm beginning to enjoy opining on camera—perhaps you'll say this doesn't surprise you. With a competent host who can muster a flare of curiosity in his eyes, it isn't so different from the classroom. But don't think I'm too much of an egoist to realize that my new-found celebrity is in itself a desperate sign of the times. When philosophers are on the evening news, you can be sure society is in crisis.

He put down the pen. He ought to call before driving all the way down there. He could give her the letter in person; save the postage.

He dialled her number, but there was a strange nothingness on the other end—no ringing, no beep, no out-of-order message. He double-checked the number in the back of his address book, and the second time it rang. After twelve rings, an answering service picked up and Keelan left a message.

"Julia, this is your father. I'm hoping to see you very soon." He paused, wondering if he should broach his whole plan. He decided, instead, that it was better to reduce anticipatory objections. Then he worried he was leaving too long of a silence. "Give my love to Dory and the baby. The baby-on-the-way, that is."

He picked up the pen again to add a postscript.

My dear,

In case I don't make it to you and in case I ought to have asked before, I just want you to know that when you announced your good news via e-card I was genuinely curious as to who is carrying your baby, be it you or Dory. If I said little, it was from delicacy, not from lack of affection or concern. There are oceans of debate as to what is or is not a legitimate or polite question, these days. (For instance, whose egg was used? And whose sperm?) It's likely best if I wade in slowly, don't you agree? There is nothing I want less than to inadvertently insult you, or especially Dory, whom history has shown may be less inclined to forgive my shortcomings. I am delighted to reflect that when I arrive in New York City I will see one of you with the glow of motherhood, and I hope you believe me when I say that any response to the above questions will overjoy me.

It was possible, he had to acknowledge, that they would not want to come back with him. Dory, he knew, was quite the workhorse at her publishing company, and Julia would probably defer to her. It was the safety of their unborn child that he had to press to his advantage.

He hoped it was Julia carrying the baby. He had felt prehistoric even thinking it (where was the ledger where he could get credit for this silent self-shaming?), but it was something he wanted for her: motherhood, and the physicality of it. Annie had carried Julia with such humour and laughing grace that it made him bristle with indignation to hear people talk about childbearing like it was all stretch marks and spider veins. But Dory would tell him—they both would, wouldn't they?—that motherhood was more than pregnancy. It started afterwards. It was like the difference between a wedding and a marriage. Everybody knew that. And thank God there were no adoptive mothers around to hear his offensive and hurtful comments that implied that they were somehow different, lesser, left out. Keelan wondered if his own voice had come to be the vicious conscience in the minds of his negligent students in the way that Dory's had become, in his, the soundtrack of all that was mean, querulous, and condemning.

He hoped not.

Keelan supposed it was his own bias that had turned her into the person against whom he was most inclined to dig in his heels. But it was all pretty rich. Even though Dory was only lately a lesbian, she'd made herself into the homosexual acceptance police. She used to be married to a man, for God's sake—the son of two of his colleagues, actually. He'd even met her before, at some departmental holiday party or other.

The doorbell rang, and Keelan shuddered, startled. Somehow he had acquired the reflexes of the guilty—as though the very shame he rejected had taken up residence in his bones. And though it may not have been Dory's fault, he blamed her anyway.

He opened the door after a quick glance downwards to verify that he was fully dressed. Noticing a hole in one of his socks, he slipped his feet into the brown loafers on the mat.

"Hello, Professor," said Edith. She liked to be called Ed and he obliged her, but the mental modification was beyond him. Using her hip, she insinuated herself inside without waiting for him to open the door any wider, and consequently he felt rude, old, out of step with time.

"Good morning, Ed," he said. His voice, at least, wasn't rough. There was one advantage in talking to oneself. He could feel himself smiling.

"Where would you like me to leave these?"

Keelan watched as the pile of books and photocopies Edith had cradled in her arms began to sag lower. "You can put the materials on the chair by the desk." He regretted directing her so close to the letter, but though he saw her glance at it, she didn't stop and stare.

"That was heavy." Edith wiped her hands on her jeans and adjusted the black baseball cap she was wearing in lieu of her usual Alice band. Her hair hung down on either side of her face, and the overall effect was so transformative as to nearly be a disguise. She was looking around the large foyer with frank curiosity—the desk, the staircase, the console table with its assorted collection of flashlights. "This is a beautiful house," she said. She pointed to a large frame hanging on the opposite wall. "I like that picture."

"Thank you. It's a Marc Chagall reproduction." Annie's taste, but there was no point in saying so. He kept it as a kind of amends, since he had exerted himself so strenuously against its prominent placement. He forced another smile until he could feel it becoming real. "Would you like some tea?"

In the kitchen, Keelan opened the pantry with a grim expression. Initially with reluctance, and then with wholehearted acquisitive panic, he had joined a recent minor stampede at the local Walmart while trying to buy some of the last remaining flats of canned goods in stock. It was galling to remember, especially in light of his public statements against giving in to fear. He had been casually stockpiling for a few weeks and hadn't expected to feel quite so invested. The whole thing was nonsensical given that the store was going to be restocked as usual with bulk food on Sunday. At least, that's what three employees in blue vests were trying to tell the panicked customers who were almost in tears at the prospect of leaving empty-handed. But his age and natural politesse meant that he had missed out on the good cans of stew, managing only one flat of Alpha-Getti and one flat of Zoodles—foods he vaguely remembered from Julia's childhood. She used to like them, of that he was certain. And it gave him some hope that they would end up laughing about this together: she would forgive him and they would weather this global calamity over bowls of Zoodles. He allowed the superstition in the idea with a kind of defiant guilt. He was an old man, after all. He was entitled to his private fantasies.

"Full cupboard," observed Edith, appearing at his elbow. "Have you been hoarding, too?" The question came out surprisingly judgment-free in tone. She seemed markedly more subdued than he remembered her from last semester.

"I suppose you could call it that," said Keelan. He made a note to do another local shopping run before driving into the city. He would show Julia how well he had prepared for all of them. "Hasn't everyone?"

Edith shrugged. "Everyone who can afford to, I guess? I saw some Oreos that were two-for-one and I got four packages." Her eyes were wry below her cap.

All of Keelan's provisions had been acquired with belated, if effective, haste. He was pleased that he'd never sold the Winnebago, and he'd been loading it with the bulk of his purchases. Rob Richards, an assistant professor with a love for camping, had made some sug-gestions at the end of a departmental meeting regarding camp stoves, fuel canisters, and hand-crank radios. Most of those present had laughed at the direness of the situation Rob evoked. Keelan himself had smiled as if humouring him, all the while taking detailed notes. Maybe they'd all been doing the same thing. This was at one of the last meetings, when they were making arrangements for offering distance-learning options after the suspension of classes on campus.

He took three orange pekoe teabags from the super-box of two hundred, and passed them back to Edith before filling the kettle. She plopped the teabags into the pot-bellied green stoneware, then sank into the closest kitchen chair. She drew her knees up to her chest, and from this small huddled pose she filled the time while the kettle boiled by asking him about his work. He obliged until a certain absent expression on her face made him wonder just how long he'd been talking. He switched tack abruptly.

"Ed, I never asked you about your summer course in New York."

"Oh, I told you about that?" She looked flustered. "Actually, I didn't go in the end. Just spent the summer in Boston with my parents." A high colour had come into her cheeks, and she changed the subject to some friends of hers who were talking about going to stay in the country.

"It's not a bad idea," said Keelan. "Isolation is a good strategy for avoiding disease. If not for preserving the fabric of society."

He found himself discussing some of the things he'd been considering in terms of worst-case scenarios: scarcity, police crackdowns, rioting, buying a gun. Even though he was the very person, the so-called expert, warning the public against this type of thinking. He was sure Edith would find his confession of hypocrisy provocative and shocking.

Edith did not look shocked. "Milk and sugar?"

"What? Oh, I'm sorry." He blinked, trying to switch gears. He followed her gaze to the two cups full of strong, dark tea. When had he stopped drinking tea with milk? It struck him now as a bit uncivilized. "Creature of habit."

"Don't worry," she said. "I'll take care of it. Just point." She stood up, teacup in hand, already moving to the fridge with inquiring eyes.

"Yes, milk there. Sugar in the pantry."

She found the cutlery on the second try. The silverware jangled in its tray as she slammed the drawer shut with her hip. Then she stood at the fridge to pour in the milk, extracting and replacing the carton in one rushed motion as though its very appearance might be misconstrued as a reproach. Her spoon clinked as she swirled it in her cup and clattered as she dropped it in the sink.

There was a time when other people's sounds had oppressed him. When he and Annie were first married, they had lived in half of a cheap rented duplex in Baltimore, and he used to rage at the neighbours for their heavy footfalls, their guitar rock, their meandering late-night conversations about SCTV or the advisability of keeping large land lizards as household pets. He began to despise them. They were ignorant, they were inconsiderate, they were one evolutionary step away from swinging through the trees. He hated them, and he hated the thin segment of drywall that formed the almost fictional separation between their apartments. Keelan was working on his dissertation at the time, and any uncontrolled sounds would perforate his concentration as easily as a finger in a soap bubble.

Now, the sounds of Edith in his kitchen brought him a vague comfort. He had underestimated the silence of the house without Julia, though she had been, in her own way, as quiet as he was.

"I saw you on TV last night." With a hot cup of tea in her hands, Edith was curious and content, more like the young woman he remembered from last semester. "Do you think it's true? Are we all done for unless we cooperate?"

"Yes," he said, and she flinched. He wondered if she was also feeling the strain of trying to remain normal. "Well, who can say? But I hope you haven't suffered any unfortunate after-effects of the whole ARAMIS Girl thing."

Edith froze, then slowly placed her cup on the table. "What ARAMIS Girl thing?" He was taken aback by the blankness of her expression.

"All the terrible things that have been happening to people like you . . ." Keelan hoped he wasn't making some sort of racist blunder while trying to express sympathy. "The hate crimes, I mean. It was abominable to release that photo."

"Oh." She shook her head as if to dismiss any notion of concern on her own account. "I'm fine. But . . . do you think the ARAMIS Girl ought to have come forward?"

"Well, I imagine it would be extraordinarily difficult at this point," he said. "Still, it *would* seem to be her responsibility. It's possible these hate crimes would be reined in if she were to make herself known. Though it's equally appalling what has happened to her reputation. We've utterly failed her as a society. But I assume the poor girl is dead by now."

Edith nodded. She crossed her skinny arms and hugged them to her chest.

"Is there something else bothering you, my dear?"

She blinked, and a tear rolled down her cheek. "Just, I was following the posts on my friend's website, and then he stopped updating it. I'm worried he's sick. Or worse."

"That's concerning. Have you tried writing to him?"

Edith nodded again. "I'll give it another try." She stood up, arching her back in a deep stretch that sent her black shirt slipping down off one slim shoulder. "I hope you have enough to keep you busy." She pushed in her chair. "I'm going back to Boston for a while, but I can still order books for you online."

"Sure, sure," he said, following her to the door. "Actually, I'm getting ready to leave soon, too. I'm going to go get my daughter and her family from New York. The city doesn't seem safe anymore."

"Oh," said Edith. "I can vouch for that. I mean, I've heard." A dark look passed over her face. Then she cocked her head slightly. "I didn't know you had a daughter."

"She was angry at me for a long time," said Keelan, surprising himself as the words came out. "Maybe she still is."

Edith stopped in the doorway. "Oh. Why?" When Keelan only shook his head, a defence against the sudden, terrifying conviction that he might begin weeping, she added, "Just . . . are you sure she'll want to leave with you?"

He was relieved to return to practicalities. "No." He ran a hand over his beard where it left his chin. "But maybe she'll humour me."

"Maybe." Edith pulled her cap down lower on her forehead. "I used to be mad at my parents for not understanding me." She stepped outside after a brief glance up and down the deserted street. "They still don't get it, but they try to be accommodating." She gave him a quick wave before turning to leave. "Good luck, Professor."

"Thank you, Ed." He closed the door, reflecting upon her words and wondering if he could have been more accommodating to Julia—agreed to go to the family counselling session when she had asked the first time. But it had all seemed so unnecessary, so *Dory*. He'd resented her. After all, he and Julia had had no issues until Dory arrived on the scene. *Ergo*, Dory was the problem, not him. Moreover, everything he'd apparently done wrong had been so long ago.

He'd recounted his supposed misdeeds to the therapist when he'd finally been dragged along. In his own memory, those years were good ones, filled with productivity—since his books, the best ones, the ones that had made his reputation, were written then. Yes, they were speculative, those early titles—*Ethics for End Times* and *The Survivalist's Code*—but they were also bestsellers compared to any average philosophy textbook. And bound to get a bump with the current crisis and this spate of interviews.

It was true that he didn't remember much about Julia from her teenage years. There were her friends, whom he didn't much care for. There was the dreadful tuba she began playing and practising with an unfortunate regularity. But her grades never faltered. She never pierced anything on her face. Unlike her peers, she was capable of uttering a sentence without the constant interjection of the word *like*. According to every measure he was capable of assessing, he had been a good parent.

In hindsight, the real trouble began the evening of her high school graduation. Julia had come into his office, tiptoeing around the stacks of paper on the floor until she reached the clearing near his desk. She was worrying the little fringe on the bottom of her jacket as she stammered, with eyes lowered, through what she had to say. Her secret. Then she looked up at him, and her gaze was like an ignition setting off a bomb in the bottom of his heart.

Something reverberated, deep in the pit of his Ukrainian-peasant stomach or maybe his Irish-barrel chest, and all he remembered saying—his sin of sins—was "Oh dear. Are you sure you want to be doing that?"

And what was so wrong with a little dismay? It was a different time back then, and the path he had seen for her was strenuous and obscure, littered with obstructions thrown up by prejudice. She had stood there, tremulous and determined and heartbreakingly brave, and as he listened to her and the aftershocks of the bomb began to rattle him, he was shot through with fear. He could see that her way in life would be harder.

"No parent wants that for a child," he said aloud now. It was an echo of what he'd said in the first place, when Julia had revolted, pleaded, insisted, and ultimately stood firm in the wake of her revelation. His crime had been nothing more than that. Maybe it was the unclear referent that had caused the problem. *That.* A hard life was all he had meant.

"Bullshit," is what Dory had said, years later, in therapy. "Clichéd bullshit."

And Julia recalled, in the same session, that he had seemed embarrassed and disgusted when she'd come out to him.

"You couldn't look at me, Dad," she said, and her tone was just as bitter, as ravaged, as Dory's. And apparently it was this way of his, this nervousness she'd taken for repulsion, which had hurt her even more than the thoughtless words that had come out of his mouth.

She wasn't wrong about the discomfort, though he'd had no idea it had been so transparent. But there was no way he could confess the source of his unease.

"Admit it," Dory had said, rounding on him with the air of one who thought she had turned the corner in a debate. "We disgust you."

"No," said Keelan. He would insist upon this until the end of time. For the shame was his, not Julia's. He was not repulsed by lesbians. It was the opposite. Quite the opposite, though his only evidence was a lifetime of harmless daydreams, and the videos stored even now on his computer.

Annie knew his secret, and if she had still been alive, Keelan was sure that she would have laughed off any misplaced guilt or worry of his in that regard. They'd shared their fantasies, though it had taken almost ten years of marriage to get to that point. Theirs was a more prudish generation, no question. But these little places in the mind were so intimate, so fragile. And it was hardly priggish—only decent— to keep them from one's children.

But it was also possible that even if Julia and Dory knew the truth, it would furnish no defence. They could deem his fondness for lesbians as nothing more than fetishization, and he wondered if they would be right. If he couldn't reliably probe the bias of his own thoughts, all he had was a feeling of innocence. That and the freedom of his own actions.

Keelan wandered over to the desk and took up his pen.

In some ways, my dear, I've been waiting for the world to change. Not just because of my books, since I never expected events to vindicate me within my lifetime, but because I need the world to be more or less than we all suspected. I need surprise. The history of knowledge is built on leaps and reversals, and more than anything I have wanted to live through enough change to feel as though I am witnessing history. That is the consolation to the grand majority of us who can never feel as though we are a part of making it.

I'm proud of you for always standing up to me. And I'm happy you're becoming a mother. And I'm grateful that history is on our side this time.

Keelan made his final arrangements with the silent speed of someone who has stopped worrying. The garage, when he unlocked it, felt silent and strange and somehow immune to everything that had been going on. He threw a bag of snacks in the front seat of the car and swung a suitcase into the back, still unpacked from his last conference in Denver. He found a map in the glove compartment, and he thought, again, about a gun, the government, a sick baby coughing. The way out of town was empty, but where it joined up to the main highway, the road was jammed.

ARAMIS Girl Located in Boston

Nov. 17, 2020

BREAKING NEWS—The so-called ARAMIS Girl has been located in critical condition in an ARAMIS ward in Boston, Massachusetts.

The 21-year-old Asian-American woman was identified to hospital staff as ARAMIS Girl by her parents upon admission on November 16. However, they denied reports that she was a super-spreader of the virus, claiming that she only developed symptoms the day before she was admitted to hospital.

Though the patient has not yet been independently verified as the restaurant server who was present at the first infection cluster in New York City, anonymous sources within the hospital have confirmed she matches the physical description of the unknown third woman in the infamous ARAMIS Girl photograph released by Dr. Keisha Delille of Methodist Morningside Hospital on September 2.

ELLIOT

—

NOVEMBER 2020

Elliot's first call of the day was a welfare check on East 147th Street. A pair of sisters in California hadn't heard from their mother in a few days and she wasn't answering the phone. He mounted the steps of the red-brick building and visited the super, who occupied a glass-fronted office just inside the entryway. She was ensconced behind a wraparound desk and appeared to be playing computer solitaire. A typed sign on her door said KNOCK FOR EMERGENCY.

Elliot pushed it open without knocking. "Hello, ma'am. I noticed the outside lock is broken."

The super turned away from the game on her screen and shrugged. Elliot could see her noting his uniform. "Doesn't seem to make much difference," she said, with what seemed like an effort at politeness. "I used to buzz in everyone who rang, anyway." She rolled back a few inches in her desk chair. "People aren't really missing the human touch these days."

Elliot showed her his badge. "We received a call about apartment 4A. Can I have the key?"

She produced it from a drawer and prodded it across the desk to him, using a piece of plastic tubing she seemed to keep for this purpose. She wouldn't meet his eyes. He wondered if she suspected what might be awaiting him on the fourth floor.

Elliot mounted the stairs without passing any other tenants. It was not so different from his own building: seemingly rent-controlled, and unrenovated since the 1970s.

He began to smell the slightly sweet, putrid odour as he was unlocking the door, and he braced himself for a dash inside. Protocol required a hazmat team, but only once he had eyes on the deceased and could call it in.

The delicate duty of death notification was passed along to officers in California, but Elliot waited at the precinct for the call he knew would come from the sisters, for the details they both needed and dreaded to hear.

At home later that evening, he discarded his mask and gloves, showered and changed, then turned on the television and tried to erase from his mind what he had seen in the apartment, as well as the raw guilt and grief of the woman's daughters. He had listened as they told him about their mother, a retired math teacher who was planning to move out to the West Coast.

"She loved the city," the older daughter had told him. "Broadway, galleries. Even her crazy neighbours. If it wasn't for ARAMIS, she might never have agreed to leave."

"She'd already bought her ticket," said the younger one. Her voice sounded hoarse. "Nine more days and she would have been with us. Just nine days."

Elliot had said, "I'm sure she knew how much you loved her." But he thought about the time between phone calls and emails, the space between messages so much larger than the space between two people in the same room. Communication technology lashed people together, but there was no substitute for being there.

When a commercial came on, Elliot muted the TV and read a new email from Sarah: *Hi Ell. Owen has been looking at the forecasts and says the warm fall is a good thing for lowering transmission rates. A small mercy, I guess.*

The note went on, but reading it left him more depressed than before. For all the writing Sarah did for her job, her particular voice—caring, teasing, yet determinedly sincere—was often hard to discern in her brief emails, and Noah was only present via the occasional photo. And Elliot suspected he was doing an even worse job with his own messages. But there was no way around it. Sarah had explained that the boat's satellite phone couldn't handle Skype, and they were rationing their minutes for internet access and weather forecasts.

The daily emails at least assured him their boat was still afloat, but Elliot had a hard time mustering enthusiasm for his side of the correspondence. It sometimes felt more like a duty to discharge than a lifeline to the person in the world who understood him best. He hoped he would learn to adjust.

He jumped when he heard a knock at his door. It was late and he wasn't expecting anyone. Elliot got to his feet silently. He'd added an old-fashioned barricade: a quick job, with brackets and a sturdy piece of plywood. He didn't have much worth stealing, but he'd seen enough on the job to know how little that mattered. Just last week, Johnny's place on the first floor had been robbed by someone who was probably disappointed to have found only a thirty-year-old television and an array of collapsible walkers, which they had nevertheless stolen. Johnny had been beside himself until Elliot had installed a barricade for him, too. With each passing day, the ARAMIS crisis created more tension between those with resources and those without.

There were people who prowled at night, in defiance of the curfew—scavengers poking through the trash looking for still-edible food, supplies, things to sell. A risky proposition, given the amount of contaminated items being jettisoned according to ARAMIS protocol.

But the creepers were solitary and non-violent, so the police ignored them. They were the least of their problems. Meanwhile, the tourism industry had collapsed, and a segment of unscrupulous hotel owners were advertising rooms as affordable refuges from infected neighbours, but without offering any additional protection against the contamination risks that came with living in close quarters: shared door handles, elevators, stairwells, ventilation systems.

The peephole revealed a man at the door, an older gentleman with a long white beard, wearing a crumpled tweed suit beneath an open camel overcoat. The beard was cartoonish, but also highly distinctive. No matter where or when, Elliot would always recognize him: Keelan Gibbs, his mother's old rival.

He opened the door. "Hello, Professor Gibbs. What are you doing here? It's nearly curfew."

"Elliot." Keelan squinted at him. It had been a long time since they'd seen each other. "I've been looking for my daughter," he said. "I thought I knew where she lived, but I guess she moved without telling me."

"And you thought I might know?"

"You used to be married to my daughter's wife, yes?"

Elliot waited for the usual pain to come and was pleased when it didn't arrive. He'd almost forgotten the connection between Julia and Keelan. At one point it had angered him that Dory had taken up with someone linked to his family in a tangential way, as though it were not enough to disrupt a man's life by divorcing him—she had to remain in it, ever after, as a permanent reminder of his failure.

"I'm sorry, Professor Gibbs, but I don't have Dory's address," he said. "I've sort of made a point of not knowing it, since the divorce." He knew he could always reach out via Sarah if necessary.

"I see." The old man seemed to sag. The professor had a rolling suitcase and was leaning his weight on its fully extended handle. Elliot wondered how far he had walked. "Then I'm out of ideas. How absolutely absurd. It took me a week to get everything ready. I even turned around once when I was already on the highway! I thought I needed more supplies, in case things took a turn. And now I'm finally here and I have to head right back to Lansdowne."

"Why don't you come in, Professor?" He held the door open.

Keelan stepped inside, staring as Elliot secured the latch, the deadbolt, and finally barred them inside with the piece of wood. "I got your address from Information."

Elliot was surprised that the professor would remember so much about him, including that he lived in the city.

"It's funny what you remember," said Keelan, as though he had read his thoughts. "When I went to Julia's place and she wasn't there, I started to feel like I was in a bad dream. Then I went to a hotel and tried to be very methodical about it." He scanned the apartment in an idle way as he twitched the handle of his suitcase. Elliot saw it through Keelan's eyes and felt a moment's self-consciousness about its bachelor barrenness: couch, table, desk, bed—everything unadorned and visible from the door. "Of course, I checked for an address for her and for Dory, but there's nothing listed. Then I went to Dory's publishing house, but it was closed. And I couldn't for the life of me remember Julia's company, if she ever had one. I think she works from home." Keelan sighed and pulled at his beard. "I spent so long getting everything in order only to forget the most important thing of all."

"Would you like to sit down?" said Elliot. He led them a few paces further inside. "Did you try calling her?"

"Yes, of course." The professor sat down heavily on Elliot's couch. "No answer. But Dory hates me. Maybe she's telling Julia not to pick up."

That sounded harsh even for his ex, but Elliot preferred not to weigh in. He went to the kitchen and poured a glass of water for the professor.

"Thanks," said Keelan. His hand shook as he accepted it. "I don't mean to make Dory the villain in this."

"Don't worry," said Elliot. "Dory's not exactly my favourite person."

"Mine either," said Keelan, glancing up quickly. "Don't repeat that."

"To who?" said Elliot. He sat down in his desk chair and wheeled it over to face the professor. "Seriously, Dory and I don't talk."

The professor drained the glass of water and set it down on the coffee table. "There seems to be a lot of that going around."

"I saw Julia a couple of months ago," said Elliot. "She came to see me."

"She's okay?"

"She was then." Since Julia's visit, Elliot had thought back to their earlier encounters, as children and teenagers thrown together every so often at their parents' departmental gatherings. At nine or ten, watching a movie in someone's basement as the adults mingled upstairs, Julia had covered her eyes during a scary part and fallen asleep that way, a slip of elbows and knees in the couch corner. Another year: hanging out in Elliot's backyard during a summer barbeque, they'd counted fireflies after the sun went down. That time, Julia had been a goth with dyed jet black hair and black lipstick, and Elliot's mother had quizzed her about nihilism and French existentialism and the ideological basis for her extreme style. Julia had said that, contrary to the usual reports, her choices were all meaningless. He remembered laughing at his mother's expression of surprise.

"And she's pregnant?"

Elliot raised an eyebrow, wondering why the older man sounded so unsure. "Not anymore. She would have already had the baby. I think she said she was due in mid-October."

Keelan blinked. Beads of water clung here and there to his beard. "So where are they?"

"I don't know," said Elliot. "But I can email her." He looked at Keelan. "Did you try that already?" If Julia was truly choosing to ignore her father, Elliot didn't want to be the one engineering an unwanted reunion.

"No, I didn't bring my computer." Keelan seemed upset that Elliot could not simply point him in their direction. "There was one at the hotel, but my password notebook is at home and nobody there could help me."

"Don't worry," said Elliot. He rolled back to the computer and typed a short message. *Hi Julia. Your dad is with me and wants to see you. Can you tell me your address? Thanks, Elliot.* It sounded so ordinary, so civil, after Julia's cryptic last messages to him. "Okay, sent. Now we wait."

"More waiting," said Keelan. Then he yawned without bothering to cover his mouth. "I thought I'd be with my daughter by now."

The traffic sounds had quieted, and Elliot checked the time. "It's after curfew, Professor. But you can stay here. The couch is a pullout."

"Is my car going to be okay on the street?"

"Should be." Elliot wondered why Keelan had bothered to bring his suitcase up if he had come by car. Unless he had foreseen their whole exchange, right down to the invitation. Maybe the old man really was a genius.

"So you and Dory don't get along either," said Keelan. He slid his arms out of his overcoat and unbuttoned his suit jacket. "She's not an easy woman."

Elliot shrugged. "It's never fun to get dumped. That's all."

"You're a diplomatic young man." With a grunt of effort, Keelan bent over to untie his shoelaces, then placed them underneath the side table. "Did you see me on television?"

"I did," said Elliot. "But I don't watch much news besides the headlines."

"I don't blame you. All the commentary—it's intolerable stuff, really." Keelan shook his head, but Elliot thought there might be a smile behind the beard. "They've been having me on as an expert. *Ethics for End Times*, you know. *The Survivalist's Code*."

Elliot remembered Gretchen complaining about the books when they were first published. "Sensational," she'd said, and it had not been a compliment.

"I think it's smart to consider how people might actually behave in a disaster," said Elliot. "There's no reason to think we'll just helplessly stand by while terrible things are happening all around us."

"You've read them?"

He hadn't really, only skimmed parts, but the professor sounded so pleased that Elliot nodded.

Keelan used the bathroom while Elliot pulled out the couch and made it up with a clean set of sheets. As soon as it was ready, the older man sank down onto it fully clothed and pulled the covers up to his chin.

"Goodnight, Professor." Elliot turned out the overhead light and began tugging down the blinds.

Keelan rolled over onto his side. "Do you think they miss us?"

Elliot thought it an odd question. The wrong question. After all, Julia and Dory had chosen to sideline them. Or maybe he and Keelan had not made enough of an effort to remain in their lives. Perhaps they were all at fault. But the professor seemed to be waiting for his answer.

"Probably," said Elliot. But all he could think was, *Why should they?*

In the morning, Elliot came to with tensed muscles and an unsettling awareness of someone moving about in his apartment. He jolted awake and threw off the sheets.

"Professor Gibbs?" he said, switching on the light. The older man was stumbling around the room, grappling at every piece of furniture in his path. "Keelan?"

The professor's eyes were confused and feverish. "Do I know you? What is this place?"

"It's my apartment. I'm Elliot. You know my parents." This was met with only a blink. "Frank Bailey and Gretchen Howe, from the department. From Lansdowne."

The professor opened and closed his mouth, then screwed up his face and shook his head. "My mind has been very strange this trip, very scattered. The city . . ."

Elliot backed away as Keelan began babbling, realizing with a sinking horror that neither of them had been wearing personal protective equipment the night before. Elliot usually relied on a stash he kept in a gym bag in his car. Now he rummaged in the closet until he found the last package of Shillelagh Precaution Kits Sarah had given him. He put on a set, cursing himself for not doing it as soon as the man arrived. It had been so long since anyone had visited him at home that Elliot had forgotten the very basics of the new normal.

Keelan was now wide-eyed, panicking. He jerked his head from the floor to the ceiling and back again, and from corner to corner of the room, as if looking for a problem, the source of his concern.

"What's happening to me?" he said, in a faint, pleading voice. The older man's vulnerability was almost more jarring than his dishevelled appearance. Keelan was famous at the university for the fastidiousness of his three-piece suits and his immaculate beard. Now his dress shirt, half-unbuttoned, was streaked dark with sweat, and his frown lines were deep and pronounced, like fissures in the earth. His light blue eyes were glazed and uncomprehending.

Elliot knew there was no point in calling the health line or waiting for a screening unit. There were a few early ARAMIS symptoms that were becoming well-known via the media: paleness, excessive sweating, disorientation, glassy eyes. Keelan seemed to be exhibiting all of them as he gripped the kitchen counter.

Elliot eased him into a chair and gently put a face mask on him. But the flimsy nitrile gloves would not go on. Though weakened, Keelan was still an outsize figure: tall, with a core built like a marble plinth designed to hold his colossal chest and head. His hands were huge. Though the gloves would probably stretch to fit, the task required delicate manipulation, and Keelan was mumbling and swiping the air in front of him with his fingers as if to brush something away from the sides of his face. Elliot dug around at the bottom of his dresser until he found a gift Sarah had picked up for him: gigantic hand-sewn mittens she'd purchased directly from an artisan but which were far too large and ostentatious for him to ever wear. He eased the sealskin mitts onto the professor's hands like flippers.

"We have to take you to the hospital," said Elliot. He shouldered his knapsack and extracted a set of car keys from the pocket of Keelan's camel coat. Though the professor was still sweating, Elliot knew the fever would progress to chills soon enough, so he wrangled him into the coat even though it meant starting over with the mitts. Keelan moaned in protest but could do nothing to stop him.

Somehow they got downstairs, with Elliot holding Keelan's arm over his shoulders and looping his own arm around the professor's waist. On the street, cabs hissed by in the rain. Elliot had a momentary urge to hail one—it would be the fastest way to get to the hospital—but even if one agreed to take them, it would be too risky for the driver.

"Where's your car?" he asked. Elliot had parked his own car eight blocks away, in a spot where he wouldn't need to move it. Keelan was silent and blotchy, his mouth puckered, just concentrating on breathing.

Between a bus stop and two loading zones, there was nothing parked along the block, so Elliot moved them slowly towards the corner, their clothes soddening with each step. A crowd was gathered on the sidewalk, and he could hear raised voices. These days, any group of people seen together in public was a startling sight.

"What the hell?" muttered Elliot. In spite of himself, he felt drawn to the throng. He remembered watching Keelan on television, saying, "There is a natural urge for human beings to congregate, even when it is obviously contrary to their best interests. That's when the state should step in."

"Police!" shouted Elliot, and a few individuals hurried along on their way. But even a thinned group was an obstacle. Elliot was strong but already feeling hobbled from supporting Keelan's weight for so long.

"This man has ARAMIS," he shouted. "Let us through."

Most scattered immediately. With the crowd gone, Elliot could see an unconscious woman lying on the ground and a teenaged girl crouched down beside her. The girl was shivering in a T-shirt, her drenched hair dripping down her back as she held a sweater to the side of the woman's head. The woman must have slipped on the wet curb. Her eyes were closed and blood trickled from her head into a pinkish puddle that was draining into the gutter. The girl, who was not wearing a face mask, had a tense, fixed jaw and was audibly mouth-breathing. Elliot was reluctant to get too close.

"I called 911," she said, almost defensively. "They're on their way." She nodded down to the sweater in her hands, presumably the one she had been wearing. "They told me to press something on the wound."

Elliot thought it was a bad sign that they'd already hung up on her. "That's good," he said. "You're doing a great job." He could see the girl's face relax.

Another middle-aged woman was next to her. Maybe she had been there the whole time. "Don't worry," she said. "I'll stay with them." As Elliot nodded and moved away, he glimpsed her removing her jacket and giving it to the girl.

Once they'd crossed the street, Elliot heaved Keelan over an empty metal newspaper box, then jogged up and down the street pressing the car keys. An old Volvo responded and, flooded with a short-lived relief, he fetched Keelan and helped him into the back seat, with little assistance from the man himself.

Elliot drove to the hospital at a pace he tried to keep steady, one eye on Keelan's prone figure in the rear-view mirror while trying to remember what Keisha had told him about the point allocation system. If there was a shortage of ventilators, the professor wouldn't cut it. He was widowed, his only daughter was grown, and he was definitely over sixty-five, maybe even over seventy. At the moment, his eyes wavered in and out of lucidity, but by tomorrow they would be blank and unseeing, radiating a depersonalized pain.

Elliot had often imagined—unwillingly at first, at the start of his quarantine, and then in a kind of self-flagellating way when he knew he would survive—what had happened to his friends in their final days and hours. But after what he had witnessed during his posting at the hospital, he no longer needed to imagine it: patients wheeled into the isolation ward, their livid faces half obscured by medical equipment, unmoving but still wet with tears. He had heard a rumour that a handful of people had died in the waiting room, too sick or afraid to come to the hospital until it was too late.

Soon the old man would be unable to move. The progression of the virus and the onset of symptoms had a broader spectrum than most people believed, and the inflammatory pain had not been widely reported. Certain patients reported only weakness, while others described muscles that burned like they were on fire, with intense pain triggered by even the slightest movement. During his time at Methodist Morningside, from the other side of the isolation ward doors, Elliot had heard screaming from ARAMIS patients whose lungs had not yet weakened.

It was no stretch to picture Keelan succumbing in a matter of days to the virus that had already claimed so many. Maybe even in a matter of hours.

The thought that came to Elliot's mind was: *What does the virus get out of it?* It thrived, he supposed. It got stronger. It survived.

At the intake desk, Keelan leaned on Elliot as he inquired about admittance. Elliot knew plenty of staff members in Emergency from his shifts there, but in a stroke of bad luck he didn't recognize anyone on duty. The receptionist insisted he fill out an admittance form, then instinctively retreated back into her cubicle as she pointed towards the ARAMIS waiting area, set off to the side of the main room.

Elliot helped Keelan into a seat in the corner. Out of the rain and under the bright fluorescent lights of the hospital, the professor seemed to have regained a certain awareness. "I need to get Julia," he said. "Take her home." He closed his eyes and rested his head against the wall. "Letters in my coat."

Elliot patted his arm. "Okay, sir. You're in good hands here."

"Don't go," said Keelan, bolting upright. "Take the letters." He gripped the plastic seat with the oversize mittens as though afraid of sliding off. "I was going to come before. I should have come before. But now I have everything ready."

Elliot unzipped his knapsack for his stash of spare evidence bags. With his gloved hands he opened Keelan's camel coat and, in an inner breast pocket, found an unsealed envelope stuffed with pages of handwritten letter. He placed it in one of the bags.

"They need to leave," said Keelan. "Both of them. Promise."

"I'll get them to come see you. I promise," said Elliot. He waved to a nurse who had come out to scan the room.

"No." The professor shook his head. "No, no. It's too late. Bring them home. Make them go today."

"Okay, I will. I'll bring them home."

The promise extracted, Keelan sank back into himself.

From Elliot's time posted in Emergency, he knew the waiting room was not where things were supposed to happen. It was a place of suspension, a hiatus between problem and solution. It was the vestibule of life's interminable emptiness, where the lesson to be learned was serenity, lest you throw yourself on the mercy of outdated issues of *Time* or *In Touch Weekly*. Eventually, the nurse read off an inaudible name and a man and woman got to their feet, and the room—packed to capacity with every possible census demographic—returned to its previous state of expectant disquiet. The world was there in the ER, the city in all its infinite colours and accents and emotional frequencies, and this time Elliot was no longer set apart by his uniform. He was one of them, vying for a limited set of resources. He could almost hear his father's Hobbesian voice in his head, warning him of "a war of all against all." But the inwardness and pitifulness of most of those present made the very idea seem absurd. If his mother were there, she would probably have deplored the marketization of the medical industry and bemoaned the devaluation of the caring professions. He wondered what Keelan would have made of the situation if he weren't deteriorating so rapidly.

From his years on the force, Elliot knew everyone reacted differently to tragedy, but what he'd seen in the past few weeks made him uneasy about how unpredictably people might behave. The fear that had slunk in during his solo patrols was now lodged in his throat like a lump he could neither swallow nor ignore.

Keelan batted Elliot's side with a giant mitt, in a gesture of entreaty that caused him obvious pain. He was a fish drowning onshore, waiting for someone to show him mercy. The professor's gasping wheeze was only slightly less horrific than his visible anxiety. His eyes rolled around with a wild helplessness.

The nurse returned and, meeting Elliot's gaze, gave a minute shake of the head that was both acknowledgement and dismissal, a signal of *not yet*. Elliot tried to make his own breathing shallow, to avoid inhaling whatever ARAMIS was coming off the older man. He began to sense the urgency of contacting somebody. He had no number for Julia, no number for Dory. Shifting slightly, he managed to slide his phone out of his back pocket and dialled his mother, who answered after the second ring and responded with her typical efficiency.

"I'll see what I can do. Somebody must have Julia's number." Gretchen's voice thickened as though she was getting choked up. "It's a good thing you're doing, honey."

"Thanks, Mom." Elliot hung up, feeling a momentary reprieve from disaster. Then the professor lunged forward in a coughing fit and, when it passed, remained half-supported against Elliot's chest. Elliot had no idea how long they spent like that. His legs began to fall asleep. The ceiling-mounted televisions conferred a dissonant sense of normality carrying on, urgency dribbling away.

On the news was a story about the Taser-related deaths of three civilians following the Police Commissioner's authorization of the use of force against people violating quarantine. The familiar photo of ARAMIS Girl flashed on the screen just as Keelan moaned, his whole body quivering. Elliot struggled to his feet but only made it up into a semi-crouch that radiated pain through his leg muscles.

"We need help here!" he shouted. But the rest of the room was unresponsive, already a casualty of the fear that ARAMIS was spreading like a secondary infection. The other people who had been glancing over, their attention drawn by the professor's rattling breaths, were now averting their eyes. But in any case, they were too far away to see his face, the heavy brow cresting with spasms. Elliot found he could not look away, though the sight was distressing. Keelan's eyes had returned to their former glassiness.

Elliot sat down heavily and Keelan lolled across his lap, as though no longer moving under his own power. His head rested on Elliot's thighs, his long beard fanning out like a skirt around the borders of his mask.

"Hang on, Professor," said Elliot, tears smarting his eyes. The virus that held the professor in its grip was implacable, nature at its most terrible. Elliot had never felt less prepared to deal with an emergency that was right in front of him. He thought of Julia, far away and unaware of what was unfolding. All the sad, failing efforts of human beings who would never, ever get it right, whether they were trying or not. Everyone, no matter who they were or what they intended, left pain in their wake. There was enough hurt in the world to burn it down ten times over. It was delusional to think any individual could make a difference.

Keelan opened his mouth, but only a strained, scraping hiss emerged. And then he was gone and Elliot was shouting again, asking for help though he knew it was already too late.

October 17, 2020

Emma, my dear granddaughter,

As an Aslet, I'm sure you know that what some people believe to be inevitable is just that—a belief. Reality is very different. With sufficient funds, anything can be accomplished.

On that note, I have good news: you and Stuart have been pre-approved for Haven Archipelago! Haven is one of the oldest and most exclusive survival projects, and those of us who have been long-term investors enjoy certain privileges—such as extending invitations to family if space remains available. Though the current catastrophe has taken the world by surprise, many of us have been preparing for this sort of calamity for a long time.

I wrote to your parents, but they intend to "weather this storm" without me. Securing an invitation for your sister's family could be trickier. I hear she married an Arab, though a wealthy one. Please encourage her to be in touch with me to discuss further.

Also, given your profile, I realize you and Stuart might be fielding invitations from other communities. Would you mind sharing the details? Haven is fantastic, but one always wonders if one is actually getting the best as promised—and paid for.

It's a shame this can't reach you any faster from our secure location, but we've had it on good authority that the old-fashioned kind of mail is ultimately harder to trace.

We haven't had much of a relationship, I know, but let's make up for lost time. I'd like to meet my newest great-grandchild.
    Walt

P.S. Just to clarify, you and Stuart will still be responsible for all fees, etc. Hope to hear from you. *W.*

EMMA

—

NOVEMBER 2020

Emma can't be sure if the barista loves or hates her. She thinks she would be fine with either—it's just that she can't tell, so it remains a ragged edge on the fabric of her day. A morning irritant, a blind spot. Another small failure.

"It's my first time out with the baby," she says. Her voice is rough and croaky.

The barista has a narrow face, with shockingly crooked teeth, and he gives her a tentative smile—or is it a smirk? Either his features are too odd and inscrutable or she is still too unsuited for the weirdness of fame. He isn't wearing a face mask and Emma wonders if he has removed it for her sake, in some misguided attempt at connection. She is among the fraction of the population who ignore the official munic- ipal infection precautions: face masks, curfew, no large gatherings. Most people don't go outside when they don't need to, let alone with a baby. But Emma isn't afraid. She has already been through it all.

He produces her latte with its perfect crema pattern that is now- adays so common that no one even comments on it anymore. Emma remembers when she used to compliment the baristas on their pat- terns (their latte art? wasn't it called that?) at this very coffee shop. How quickly everything changes. How fast luxuries become com- monplace. Her own life has taken wing into proportions her old self would scarcely recognize. This is partially why she comes to this same coffee shop with its adoring or hateful baristas, its sameness, its physical solidity—to remind her of who she was/is and will be/will be/will be.

She keeps her eyes on her coffee as she carries it to the closest table and sits down, one hand on the back of the baby carrier strapped to her chest. The baby is asleep, so she feels alone. Emma is not afraid, as some new mothers are, of a baby who never sleeps. She thinks, on the contrary, it would be companionable. She has already been awake for hours and hours—for days and days, really—thinking about this coffee or something like it. Something to get her through to the next day, and the next.

There is almost no one here. ARAMIS has been ravaging Austin, although it is possible the worst is over. But the authorities won't roll back the restrictions until the morgues are emptied, the dead buried. The mayor made that mistake before, lifting the state of emergency prematurely, which led to a new spike in infections. A grieving mothers' group burnt his figure in effigy, and he gave a tearful apology on television. He tried to resign, but the city council wouldn't let him. MAYOR MUST STAY AND FACE THE MUSIC, MOTHERS SAY. Across the café, a young man in a face mask and a Dove Suite T-shirt gives her a small wave, and by long instinct her mouth twists up into a momentary smile until, just then, the baby stirs. She looks down at her, relieved for an excuse to turn away. The baby is still sleeping, only restless. Emma tugs at the muslin blanket covering her daughter's face. It is too porous to function as a mask, but it should keep people from pointing fingers. You almost never see children outside anymore, let alone babies.

The baby makes a small cry then. Pressing a hand to the table, Emma gets to her feet but feels the ground tilting, the floor turning to quicksand. A head rush. She closes her eyes, but when she opens them again the room is still swaying, as though the whole café has pushed off to sea on the swollen waters of the Colorado River. She drops back into her chair, back into her childhood *mal de débarquement*, when the earth itself became hostile, churning, anything other than a safe place to land.

It's only fatigue. It will pass—it is already passing. But Emma is afraid of becoming someone she doesn't recognize. So maybe it is better to remain so unsure, so unsettled, so full of the feeling of never arriving, never being comfortable, never having a home except with Stu. Stu is home.

If she is always a little bit adrift, then at least she will still be herself.

At home, the apartment is ablaze with morning light. They have three sides of the building, a full half-floor of the tallest property in Austin. The east wall of windows has been fitted with automatic curtains for which the button still needs to be repaired. Emma remembers Stu jabbing at it one morning, pre-coffee, hair askew, the hoarseness of sleep still in his voice.

"Add it to the list," he said.

The list was real and ongoing, and it worked. A spiral notebook comprising pages and pages of tasks and goals, great and small.

> ~~Choose a lead single.~~
> ~~Have a baby.~~
> ~~Find a nanny.~~
> ~~Change the light bulb in the guest linen closet.~~

The list is now sitting on the corner of the dining room table, a rustic affair in hickory with chairs for fourteen. Emma has not touched it in weeks.

Like the dazzlingly bright apartment, the baby is ablaze, too; it hurts to look at her. They'd decided on her name together before she was born: Blaze Aslet-Jenkins.

Stu balked when she first suggested it—he said Blaze was a name for a stripper, or a horse. But that objection became technical, as they both liked it, *loved* it even, in spite of their better judgment. It had come to Emma in her third trimester, in a dream from which she had woken up happy. It was precisely because she was not the kind of person to traffic in dream revelations that the name had come to seem important.

Blaze is a gorgeous, gleaming baby with large, watchful eyes, and everyone who has ever seen her says she looks like Stu. But then, of course they would say that.

Their apartment is a haven that she and Stu have taken pains to make their own. The old posters from their first apartment have been framed and restored to hide the tack holes and crumpled corners. A beautiful commissioned collage of gig flyers from their first college shows is hanging in the front hallway. Besides the studio with its own mixing booth, there is a home theatre with surround sound and reclining leather couches, and a gleaming deluxe chef's kitchen because it is basically impossible to buy a new condo without one.

The large living room—with its flat-screen television that is now always on and its giant grey L-shaped couch and its panoramic view of the Hill Country—has fulfilled the destiny of its name and become the room where they do most of their living. She deposits the baby in the bassinet by the couch and empties her pockets onto the coffee table. Her cellphone is flashing with a message.

"Call me, Em," says Ben's voice when she hits Play. "I can't keep talking to your voicemail. We really, really, really want to see you." Emma deletes the message along with several others she knows she won't bother answering. She unmutes the TV when a news anchor reports that ARAMIS Girl has been found in a hospital in Boston.

"Aha," says Emma, her pulse quickening. She had imagined ARAMIS Girl holed up in a basement apartment somewhere, ducking reporters like another plague and guarding her privacy before it could be stripped away by force. Stu never thought she would be found alive. The baby makes a small, almost inquisitive gurgle when Emma mutes the television and opens her laptop to a screen full of unopened emails. She considers deleting them, but decides instead to leave them there, unread. She shuts the laptop with one finger.

The baby is happy in her bassinet. Emma has made a place for herself on the couch alongside her. In spite of the broken curtain button and the excess of light, she cannot make herself go into the bedroom. But whether or not the baby is sleeping is immaterial. The baby is doing well. And the album is still doing well, too. After the concert disaster, there had been rumours their label might drop the band, but nothing came of it. Stu didn't seem to care either way. He seemed to want to be punished for what had happened in Vancouver. He'd disappeared for a while into his own grief, and Emma, felled by her own suffering and by her anxiety over the impending birth, had left him to it. And now, in spite of all of Emma's failures, or maybe even because of them, everything with the music is going well.

The letter has been lying on the rug under the coffee table since she flayed it open last week with a butter knife. Forwarded from the record label, the creased envelope arrived with the smeared ink of multiple redirection notices. She'd picked it up again once or twice to reread the invitation from her grandfather to a millionaires' bunker, paired with his comparison shopper's probing questions. Initially, she had crumpled the letter, then smoothed it to show to Domenica, before returning it to its envelope, handling it as one might an artifact in a museum, with a cool curiosity and an eye to the historical record. She felt tainted even though she knew blood was perhaps not so different from water, after all.

Across the room, sunlight glints off the open lid of the grand piano, a furnishing recommended by the designer even before she learned they were musicians. Steinway, ebony black, high gloss. Another luxury-deemed-necessity for an oversized space. Emma gets up and circles it as she does every so often, remembering the day it arrived and the detailed measurements taken by the piano movers to ensure it would be neither warped by the sun nor chilled by a draft, and how she and Stu had rolled it back and forth by inches for nearly an hour to find the precise angle for maximum visual impact upon entering the room. The fallboard is open, but the keys are dust-free. She touches one, stopping just short of the pressure needed to strike the hammer. Everywhere she looks, things are bright and pristine.

The apartment is clean because Susannah comes once a week to clean it. Emma is an atheist but prays on a daily basis for the health of Susannah and Susannah's family. Except for fresh, perfect lattes, Emma has everything she could need at her fingertips. She ordered groceries and toiletries on the internet even before ARAMIS, in order to avoid running into fans with a box of tampons in her hands. Now her lettuce, oranges, toilet paper, tampons, and diapers are brought to her door by delivery men who accept her generous tips with discreet, gloved fingers. In their eyes, visible above the face masks, she sees alarm and distrust, but this is the kind of thing that no longer unnerves her. In other buildings, she has heard, the delivery men simply knock and leave the boxes at the door. This is the usual practice and the one recommended by health authorities. But here in this extravagant building there is a hope of greater reward, and so she does not disappoint. Hope springs eternal.

The thing about the sickness when it came was its relentlessness. It didn't stop for a googling, a rundown of symptoms. There was barely time to get over your surprise—your totally irrational surprise that it could be happening to you. There was no time at all to feel the sudden wrenching fear, or for the flicker of hope that you might be wrong. No, it was like getting walloped with a hammer, and before the clanging in your head could subside, you were beside yourself: one moment of seeing it happen, the last moment where you were really there, and then you were gone into the pain and mostly into the fever. It was a blessing you didn't know what was happening—not really. There was never that recognition of hopelessness. Although, what would be worse? Knowing you're going to die, or not knowing? They both strike Emma as horrible.

If the baby died, she thinks she would want to die, too.

Blaze has been fed and burped but is still fussing. Emma remembers there is an unopened package of pacifiers in the baby's room. She hesitates for a minute—pacifiers are disputed territory in a war in which she hasn't yet bothered to take sides. But Stu would tell her to do whatever feels right. She picks up the baby and makes her way down the back hallway. Between the decorated but still-unused nursery and the bedroom they expected to be occupied by a nanny, she pauses in front of the framed family photo she always used to bring on tour. She squints at Harold, standing a bit apart, still sunburned under his large hat. He might already have been broke by then, and lying about it to everyone. Fathers are different now. They are allowed to love, to communicate, to be soft. Blaze would be as comfortable in Stu's arms as in her own. Her own father had always kept her at arm's length.

The phone rings—the loud jangling of the landline with extensions in the kitchen, the bedroom, and the control room of their home recording studio. She makes a note to unplug all of them. Stu poked fun at her when she had them installed: "More retro chic for the retro babe? What's next, a fax machine?" But she'd liked the idea of a phone that didn't move, like an anchor keeping her in place, even just for a few minutes. Then Stu had laughed when she ended up buying the cordless for the living room a few weeks later.

Now the baby is squirming in her arms. Emma can't open the pacifiers without a pair of scissors. Impossible plastic packaging. The phone is still ringing. The virtual voicemail service once offered by their telephone provider seems to have ended without warning. She keeps meaning to check whether they are still being charged. Another thing for the list.

‹‹‹|||›››

The last thing they crossed off the list together was hanging a mobile of hot-air balloons from the ceiling of the nursery when she was eight months pregnant. Made in France, the mobile featured real woven basketry and hand-dyed cloth stretched over delicate wiring. They'd both agreed they didn't want any plastic crap or cartoon tie-in stuff in the room for their baby-on-the-way.

Emma had signed for the package and ripped open the box, then waited in the control room of the studio while Stu finished working on a new song. Music was the only thing that seemed to take him out of the funk he'd fallen into after the concert. He kept saying he wished he had a time machine, to take it back. As though it really was all their fault. He even said it to a Canadian reporter who called.

But the plunge into songwriting brought him little peace outside of the studio.

"The mobile came," she said, pressing the intercom button when he stopped to retune his E string.

He finally looked up with a distracted smile, still half bobbing his head in time with the chords he'd been strumming. "What?"

"The mobile for the nursery. I want to hang it, but I'm nervous about climbing the ladder."

"Okay, five minutes. I want to get this done first."

Emma sighed, her legs twitching with impatience. "That'll take forever. *This* will only take five minutes."

Stu gave her a momentary grin through the glass. "Cool your jets, toots," he said, before returning his attention to the fretboard and whatever melody was in the process of making itself known.

Emma waited six minutes, but Stu remained bent over his guitar, oblivious to her glare. She was cranky and peevish. She hated relying on someone else. It was infantilizing, just at the moment when she was supposed to be learning how to take responsibility for someone else.

She stalked to the hall closet and dragged out the ladder. She was making a racket, but Stu wouldn't be able to hear anyway.

Tucking a hammer into one pocket of her maternity jeans and some nails into the other, she took a tentative step onto the ladder, already feeling unsteady. The pregnancy had shifted her centre of gravity. She had to step sideways to accommodate her belly. Then she heard a sudden noise at the doorway and almost slipped, grabbing on to the wall to steady herself.

It was Stu. He was shaking his head, a gritted set to his jaw, but his eyes were full of concern.

"When I realized you were gone," he said, moving to ease her down off the ladder, "I figured you were doing something stupid like this." He cupped his palm to her face.

Whenever they made up after a fight, Stu always fingered the curve of her cheek, as if tracing the path of an imaginary tear, before kissing her on the chin and then her lips. It was a ritual that began after their first real fight. She'd found herself resenting the gesture because it reminded her of how bitterly she'd cried then—not over whatever trivial thing they'd argued about, but for how the fight itself had shattered her silly notion of perfect happiness. But for Stu she knew it meant something else: the depth of her forgiveness and an ability to believe in a love that was bigger—a love that staked and meant and worked towards something more. So she let him do it. She had come to realize that a gesture, like a phrase, like a song, could mean different things to different people. What mattered was the exchange itself: the link, however tenuous, stretching out between one soul and another.

Another thing for the list: she wants to create rituals for Blaze with intention. She wants to create them with purpose and design before time passes and they end up mourning something else that has slipped away—the songs they sing, the games they play, even the food they eat. This is what people remember about their childhoods. But Emma is so tired, so very tired, and she sings whatever comes to mind. For games, she can think of Peekaboo and "This Little Piggy" and nothing else. She eats any old thing, usually raw. For now, Blaze is tiny, so it doesn't matter; but soon, sooner than Emma can imagine, it will all matter. Blaze will begin storing memories, and maybe this hodgepodge of a life will become the thing they wish they could get back to, the time when things were simpler, when they didn't even know how good they had it. There is no telling what the future might hold. This, too, is what keeps Emma awake. At four in the morning, she opens the computer and types into the search bar: *How long can a*

human being stay awake without dying? The answer, it turns out, is still unknown. Sleepless, TV-bleary, half-incoherent, she wonders if she is somehow at the forefront of research. Maybe there is a purpose to surviving all these empty, torturous hours spent treading back and forth across the living room.

She imagines one day looking back at this time and longing for a bright, silent apartment and a sleeping baby. A coffee shop where someone waves at her. Hours and hours of effortless, delirious wakefulness. She wants to cling to every moment before it passes. Before she is carried off into the unknown future. She wants to hold on almost as much as she hates that unreachable feeling, that restlessness of soul.

It's a childish impulse. Children hate change for change's sake. And yet at some point, Blaze will look back on everything from her childhood and hate that she can't get back to it all. The world is cruel, Emma thinks, to make children happy by default.

Just then, Blaze makes a cry Emma has never heard before—it sounds like a question. As if Blaze can sense the sleepless circularity of her mother's thoughts. Emma stops pacing the room and sits down; she doesn't trust her own balance at these times.

"Sorry, baby," she says, adjusting her hold. Blaze leans back her head ever so slightly to look at her.

In some ways she'd like to share their baby with the whole world, but she doesn't know how. There are a few old friends whom Emma misses, but she can't imagine actually getting together with them. With her bandmates, everything is still too fraught. It is only with her sister that all frankness has persevered. With everyone else, intimacy has been like a patio door sliding shut in increments, so slowly she couldn't track it, or even take notice. She was so busy. Too preoccupied. It was her own fault. After every album, the door was a little more closed. But as it shut on her old friends, any number of potential new friends presented themselves, ushered in by fame and fortune. But where could you start with people like that? Who would believe or understand her life, its ordinariness? There was no possibility of complaint. And she is afraid of the internet. Of rumours. Things getting out. So it is to Dom, and Dom alone, that she confides.

◂◦||▏||◦▸

A few weeks before her due date, she'd called Dom in the middle of the night in Abu Dhabi.

"I'm not sure I want to go through with this," she said. Stu was out at a show and Emma felt alone and huge and singularly burdened.

"It's a little late," said Dom, who'd picked up on the first ring.

"I'm serious," said Emma. "I might be okay with everything changing, but I'm not ready to start living for someone else. I still want to live for me."

"You will. You'll get a nanny. You'll take the time you need. You'll stop feeling so bad once you realize that you're going to feel bad no matter what you do."

"That's your pep talk?"

"That's my pep talk."

Now Dom says, "You should talk to the boys. They need you."

"Mmmm," says Emma. "I can't."

Dom and Emma have been on the phone for seven hours. The bill must be in the thousands. When her sister answered, Emma said, "If you hang up, I'll die." She'd meant it as a joke, but her voice broke and Dom is now taking her at her word. Emma carries the cordless from room to room. Dom's breathing, husky and impatient, is more familiar to her than her own. The impatience is lifelong, not specific, and is audible only to Emma, who hears it in her sister's quick, restive inhalations. Dom has always taken things in quickly, only to let them spool out at leisure in long, elaborate dramas. Like with Ahmad, her husband, whom she married after knowing for only ten months and to whom she is still married, though the convolutions of their union could fill a trilogy. Whereas Emma has moved forward in short spurts and small, spinning increments.

"I hate that we can't turn on the same channel," says Emma, "and watch the same thing the way we used to before you moved."

"Why don't you tell me what's on?"

"The news, as usual." Emma scans the closed captioning. "They're playing that same old clip of the professor they've had on since Owen Grant went to sea."

"The one who looks like a wizard? I've seen him. What's he saying?"

"The usual. We'd better be careful or the human race is done for."

"Better safe than sorry," says Domenica. "That used to be Mum's motto, more or less."

Emma murmurs an acknowledgement. Her mother's fears overshadowed so much of their voyage: storms, pirates, Y2K. And yet she'd kept them moving forward in spite of all the unknowns.

"Do you remember those stories I used to tell you on the boat at night?" says Dom. "Those nights I was so sick?"

"Yes. Stories about home," says Emma. A home that stayed in one place, that endured. It seemed impossible at the time, and it turned out it was. "Our old house that I couldn't remember." But she could still picture all the rooms as Dom had described them on those stormy nights. "It's hard to imagine why Mum and Dad ever wanted to leave."

"Is it? There are a lot of different ways to be happy." Domenica recently took her daughters away with her to London, but returned home after only six weeks. She'd said she needed the space to choose her own life again. Or at least to try.

"I didn't mean they shouldn't have done it." Emma imagines strapping Blaze to her chest in her carrier and venturing further than the coffee shop. The idea is frightening, even destabilizing, but there is a pull there, too.

"Never mind. What do you think about now," Dom asks, "when you can't sleep?"

"Nothing," says Emma. "Anything." *Anything other than what happened*, she thinks but doesn't say. "Nothing or anything or Blaze."

Dom's daughters, Aliya and Leila, can be heard occasionally in the background as the nanny gets them their dinner and herds them through their nighttime rituals. She tells them to put their pyjamas on, to brush their teeth, to not complain. Talking and giggling, the girls' voices are indistinguishable to Emma.

"Your girls are closer than we were," she says. "Closer in age, I mean."

Dom ignores this. "You're not the only one who feels alone, Em," she says.

"I know," says Emma, her voice catching. "It's the human condition."

"No, I mean, pick up the phone once in a while. And not just to call me."

Emma makes no answer. She stops her restless pacing through the static rooms of the apartment and returns to the couch. The baby is calm and watchful from her bassinet. The mid-morning light floods the room. Emma holds the phone to her ear and stretches out her legs, which have begun to cramp. There is a flat purple throw cushion wedged underneath her right shoulder blade, probably exactly under her Dove Suite tattoo, which she keeps forgetting is there, like a ghost clinging to her back.

Eventually, she sleeps.

⸪||⸫

Nights are harder because that was when it started. The phone rang in the middle of the night. It was the sister of the nanny they'd interviewed and hired before the baby was born. The sister said Bernadette was in the hospital with ARAMIS.

"I don't know how much time y'all spent together last week. But before she got real bad she asked me to call. Wasn't sure how you'd be doing with the baby about to come and all."

Emma had thanked her and hung up the phone. She felt the need to pee even though she'd already gotten out of bed twice. She was thirty-six weeks pregnant.

"Bernadette has it," she said to Stu, who'd clicked on the light. He looked ashen.

"That's not good," he said.

The darkness wakes her around nine. In the darkness she doesn't sleep but feels free, as though she might be anywhere. Staying in one place doesn't feel as good as she once thought it would. Not anymore.

Imagine not being in a band. Imagine a regular job. Imagine being a barista. But people do that for the money. It would be stupid to take a job just to feel normal. To have something else to think about.

Stu would say it *is* a job. Your job. A job you like. Just think about it that way.

And it's not like the job was easy. Not even close. So much online gossip and jealous rumours. And worst of all was the blowback from the benefit concert in Canada. One of the features published on Stu last month by a snarky online rag was subtitled *Instant karma?*

Blaze cries and Emma sits up. Cradling her, she goes to look for her laptop.

A day after the phone call, Emma came down with a fever. The thermometer gave a tinny beep to announce its reading, and Stu said, "A hundred and four." A hundred and four was bad.

Emma had her hands on her belly. She couldn't think of anything to say besides *I'm sorry*, so she didn't say it.

"I can't tell," said Stu, "if my legs are shaking out of fear, or if I'm sick, too."

It was after midnight when they agreed Emma should go to the hospital. She was starting to cough and was too dizzy to even sit up. But Stu said he felt too shaky to drive, so he called them an ambulance.

In triage, they were both admitted to the hospital as presenting with ARAMIS. Emma saw a nurse fastening Stu's hospital bracelet to his arm before her eyes fluttered closed. She was on a gurney being followed by several medical residents who were checking online databases for case histories of ARAMIS in women with full-term pregnancies.

Her lung capacity was already reduced from the pregnancy, so she was ventilated, pumped with antivirals and antibiotics. Then a week and a half went by, her only memory a series of strange dreams. Blaze was delivered by C-section and isolated in quarantine for two days before Emma regained consciousness. The baby's blood tested positive for antibodies to the virus.

In another room in the same ward, it might have been the same for Stu—the fever, the weakness, the coma, the dreams—except that his body weakened irrevocably and both lungs were compromised and failed within four days of his being admitted. Eventually, the ventilator was removed and assigned to another patient with a better prognosis. Emma wasn't there when it happened. She doesn't know if he was afraid. She never got to say goodbye.

᎐ᖗ|||ᖘ᎐

Via the grainy video feed, Ben and Jesse look like they could use some sleep. They almost look old. Or not old, just nearly middle-aged. Old compared to the kids coming up. The little prodigies on YouTube. Just a few months ago, Ben had shown her and Stu a clip of a five-year-old singing "Nessun Dorma." He was superb.

"Why do we even bother?" Stu had joked. "Let the next generation take over already." Ben had laughed and said he was already selling his drum kit on Craigslist.

These boys, as she calls them. These men. Ben in his faded U2 shirt, half a week's stubble sprouted unevenly over his neck and chin. Jesse's usually perfect hair lying flat and dark with grease, the hollows around his eyes nearly purple. Whether they're her family or her colleagues or both, Emma knows, seeing them, that they're hurting, too.

She can tell from the Lone Star flag and the Dixie Chicks poster that Ben and Jesse are together at Jesse's place. They all live in Texas now, most of the year, but Jesse is the only one of them who can call it his home state.

"Don't shut us out, Em," says Ben.

"I'm not," she says. Seeing their anxious faces, she feels a sudden responsibility for making everyone feel better. "How's your Canadian girlfriend? The long-distance thing going okay?" Ben had started dating Emma's Vancouver tattoo artist after the benefit concert.

"Marisol's good. She's pretty funny, actually. We Skype a lot."

Jesse cuts in. "So the next album, Em. We need to decide what we're doing."

"Do we?"

"There are all those tracks we've already recorded. Hell, some of them are even mixed."

Jesse means all the extra songs that didn't quite make the cut for the fourth album, the one they released before ARAMIS. Not all that long ago, though it feels like an eternity now.

"They'll keep," she says.

"Maybe. But right now we have momentum."

Emma leaves that alone. The band is her and Stu's band, really. They were never in charge, technically—just actually, factually. Artistically, acoustically. They started it and generated the material, even if they all share the credit. With Stu gone, it should be *her* band. Her songs. But here they are, crowding her.

Jesse pulls a scrap of paper out of his back pocket and begins reading out a list of posthumous albums he thinks could be relevant to the process.

Emma cuts him off before he gets past *From a Basement on the Hill*. "We already have a way of doing this, guys," she says.

"Not without Stu, we don't."

She falls silent.

Ben says, "It's just . . ." She knows he can read the anger on her face. "We need to do something, don't we? I can't stand this sitting around. I need to think about something else."

She nods. "I get that," she says. "I do."

"Yeah," says Jesse. "That's it." His mouth twitches.

And Emma realizes he's afraid. Afraid she's going to take Stu's legacy for herself and move on without them.

At the service, her parents seemed almost embarrassed by the weight of their grief. Faye stared at the ground, and Harold clutched the program like a ticket to some faraway place where things weren't falling apart. They looked shocked and scared, like most of the attendees. If it could happen to Stu, it could happen to anyone. Emma had gotten word that Gertie Coleman, the folk singer whose career Stu had helped resurrect, had died, too. The same week. As the priest read a passage from Isaiah, Faye fiddled with a tennis bracelet while Harold kept an arm around her. Solid, protective. It had comforted Emma to see them. Dom was in the U.A.E., unable to fly in due to border quarantines. And presumably their grandfather had already sought shelter in his secure location, along with all the other wealthy people who had paid to be there, though Emma didn't know that then.

Afterwards, Ben had pulled her aside and said, "Do you want to head back with your parents?"

She'd said, "No, I want to go home." Her home. And it was true, but at the same time Emma didn't want to be alone with the baby in that huge, soundproof, concrete high-rise. She was still afraid. Of the sickness, of her daughter. Of living without Stu.

If she screamed, she wanted somebody to know.

After midnight, she calls Domenica. Blaze is in her bassinet, sleeping her restless baby sleep. Emma could watch her all night long.

"I want you to come here," says Dom. This has been an ongoing refrain since Stu's death. Emma knows her sister will never be able to get over the fact that they asked to visit her in Abu Dhabi and she turned them down. Though Domenica can wear guilt as lightly as anyone she knows, for which Emma is grateful, too. She and Stu could probably have travelled anywhere they wanted, pregnancy notwithstanding, and they didn't. The only person she can really blame is herself.

"Not now," says Emma. "But we will." She imagines Blaze growing older, sitting up, playing with her cousins. Something comes to her as she pictures it, like a small seed of hope blowing in.

"I'm going to hold you to that." There is a smile in her sister's voice. "You've always been the brave one, Em."

"I can't be," she says. "Not anymore."

"But don't you see?" says Dom. "Being brave means you keep going, even when you know how bad things can really get."

Emma stands in front of the large dark windows, peering out onto her city that has endured so much suffering. She holds the receiver to her ear, so she can listen to her sister breathing. "Dom," she says, "will you tell me a story?"

Her sister begins speaking quietly and without hesitation, spinning a tale of princesses and magic, adversity and fate. She is well practised in delivering stories made to order, with the requisite kind of happy ending.

There are lights on everywhere; Emma is not the only one awake. If she stands here long enough, morning will come.

The next day, she leaves a message on Ben's voicemail.

"I think you're right," she says. "This is how we keep him with us." That isn't what Jesse talked about, not really, but it's what Emma needs. She can't think of another way to stay alive.

Blaze is strapped to her chest as she gathers up her notebook and a few odd scraps of paper where she's jotted things down. The home recording studio is the way Stu left it. There are picks scattered on the floor and his blue Coronado is on the guitar stand. Emma's Korg is in the opposite corner. She unplugs the telephone in the control room and steps into the soundproof booth with her daughter, a melody already at work inside her heart.

Hey guys. Sorry for the lack of posting but things have been a bit hectic. We've been overrun at the refuge with ARAMIS pets—animals rescued from dead or sick owners who can no longer care for them. We've had so many come in we had to start turning them away, although I ended up bringing a few home. That's really why I've been MIA. It's a long story, but let's just say it's causing some ongoing problems with my landlord. I know some of my friends keep tabs on me here and I'm sorry for worrying anyone.

Anyway, I know there's a lot going on, but don't lose faith in keeping up with your practice. The universal language is more important than ever right now. I've made a little cheat sheet that could come in handy.

Peace, Jer

Useful Esperanto Phrases for the ARAMIS Crisis

Hello. Nice to meet you. *Saluton. Mi ĝojas renkonti vin.*

My name is _____. *Mia nomo estas _____.*

Are you hungry? *Ĉu vi malsatas?*

Are you thirsty? *Ĉu vi soifas?*

Can I help you? *Ĉu mi povas helpi vin?*

I have food enough to share. *Mi havas sufiĉan manĝaĵon por dividi.*

I know where we can find some clean water. *Mi scias, kie ni povas trovi iom da pura akvo.*

There is shelter not far from here. *Estas rifuĝo ne malproksime de ĉi tie.*

Let us walk together after dark. *Ni iru kune post mallumo.*

The ARAMIS Girl Speaks

Xiaolan Fraser
Guest Writer

For as long as I can remember, I've felt invisible. And at other times, I've felt too visible for all the wrong reasons—for the shape of my body, the colour of my skin. But like so many of us, I grew up obsessed by celebrity. I wanted to be the girl who stood out, who drew everyone's eyes, the one everyone recognized as special. I wanted to be seen, to be somebody.

Needless to say, I've been cured of that desire.

Yes, I was working as a server at cipolla when Zhihuan Tsiang—the man identified by the World Health Organization as the real index patient—ate there on July 31, but I didn't get sick. I only became aware of the public health advisory after I left New York City to go back to Lansdowne, where I was attending college. At that point, I self-quarantined myself for the recommended three weeks. I never developed any symptoms. And this was weeks after Mr. Tsiang ate at the restaurant and infected some of the other patrons and staff.

Later, I did get sick. Very sick. But only after I contracted the virus in Massachusetts in November.

I was not irresponsible, just unlucky. My actions were not criminal. By the time the insane manhunt caught the attention of people who suspected I might be ARAMIS Girl, I was already in intensive care. My parents were at my bedside, or as close to it as the doctors would let them get. I am grateful to the doctors and nurses at Boston Memorial who helped to keep me alive in spite of all the haters camped out in front of the hospital with signs saying I deserved to go to hell.

I do regret not coming forward sooner. I was scared of the death threats already circulating online and by what was happening to other Asian Americans across the country. I wish I'd recognized earlier that I might have been able to make a difference, but at a certain point I truly did not know whether coming forward would have made everything better or worse. Maybe I was being a coward.

For everyone online saying they hope I die of ARAMIS, I hope you never have to learn what it's like to wake up to find out the entire world hates you. At least my experience has taught me one thing: I'd rather be unknown than infamous.

ELLIOT

———

DECEMBER 2020

Elliot was listening to his parents argue, except they would have called it a conversation. Gretchen was hunched over her coffee at one end of the kitchen counter, while Frank fiddled with some oatmeal on the stove. Elliot had his laptop open and was trying to keep out of it by avoiding eye contact.

"It's just a matter of time before someone infects us," said Frank. His striped bathrobe sagged open to reveal a white undershirt and flannel pyjama bottoms. "Or before looters break down our door."

"Civil society hasn't quite disintegrated yet," said Gretchen. Her voice was shaky but still sardonic. "Just because we're afraid doesn't mean we should walk out on our lives."

"Elliot did," said Frank.

Elliot winced but kept his gaze fixed on his screen. After Keelan died, he'd called his parents from the hospital and driven to Lansdowne that same day. Some reflex of retreat had kicked in even before he'd taken the time to question why he was on the highway to Massachusetts. There was, of course, the practical yet not insurmountable problem of his contaminated apartment, but mainly what he'd felt on the road was an overpowering urge to get out of the city itself. After instructing his parents on a few precautions to do with segregating bathrooms and dishware, he quarantined himself in his childhood bedroom for three weeks, taking comfort in the plates of food that appeared at his door and in the sounds of home carrying on downstairs, feeling halfway between an inmate and an invalid. All things considered, he'd felt cocooned rather than confined during his second isolation. And when the twenty-one days had fully counted down, he'd capitulated to his mother's uncharacteristically emotional plea and called his supervisor to request one week's vacation. Through all the mayhem, his captain remembered Elliot had been exposed at the very first infection site. "Enjoy your family," he'd said. "This isn't the time to be losing our best men."

Gretchen sniffed, and Elliot glanced up to check whether it was a sound of derision, disagreement, or impending tears. These days he couldn't always be sure.

"That's not the same thing at all, Frank. Ell was just here for his quarantine," she said. No weeping, only dissent. "He has to get back to work in . . . how long now, honey?"

Maybe she had noticed the growing shadows under his eyes or the way he continued to avoid discussing his return to New York, but she asked him this same question every day. Elliot had yet to confess it out loud, but his reluctance to go back to the city increased with every passing hour. Now he wondered if his mother had implanted the doubt in the first place and was nourishing it faithfully with her own fears, as though coaxing it to grow. Before answering, he scrutinized her for some such agenda, but she only looked curious, guileless, perhaps forgetful.

"Three days," said Elliot finally.

"So we still have a little time," said Gretchen. "Three days. Unless of course . . ."

"Unless what, Mom?" The only reason to repeat the number was to hammer home the urgency of some sort of decision on his part. It was as though they were each waiting for the other to say it first. "Unless I decide not to go back?"

His mother only cocked an eyebrow. "Unless you've been thinking that you'd rather be with your family at a time like this. Otherwise, we can just wait until you go."

Elliot said nothing, not wanting to admit just how far he had come around to her point of view.

"Sarah didn't wait," said Frank, oblivious to the silent standoff. "She left months ago. Quite rightly, in my opinion."

"Yes, but that's New York City, dear." Gretchen tilted her head in the way that meant she was waiting for the other person to catch up. "This is Lansdowne."

"You say that, but just wait until Candace from up the street is smashing in our door because she hears we have the last jar of peanut butter in Massachusetts."

"Don't be absurd," said Gretchen, her voice flat. "We don't have any peanut butter."

Since coming out of quarantine, Elliot had found himself watching his parents with an eye to their growing frailty and inimitable quirks. His father was a bit thinner, his mother more slumped. They remained the moral and intellectual beacons that had dominated his childhood, but here and there the signal was interrupted by ambivalence and bickering. It didn't help that the memories of Keelan dying in his arms were still so fresh—the oily sheen of his sweat, the grotesquely purpling skin, the guttural rasp of each hard-fought breath. And, worst of all, the faltering awareness that had seemed to return at the end to his pale blue eyes: a silent, anguished plea to be saved from drowning on dry land. The images came unbidden to Elliot during second helpings of Frank's brisket, while watching British murder mysteries with Gretchen, and in the middle of the night, no matter whether he was sleepless or dreaming. His parents were basically the same age as Keelan. How long would they be able to carry on without him? And what if his sudden concern only masked a more palpable dread of seeing his beloved city brought low?

He clicked through a few news stories online, including one headlined *ARAMIS: THE REVENGE OF SMALL-TOWN AMERICA?* Apparently, pundits all over the country were calling for a return to a simpler way of life, as infections in major cities kept doubling and tripling, especially among children. Hospitals full of comatose kids, and yet somehow the best idea on the table was to flee to the boonies. But even in Lansdowne, Elliot had driven past shuttered businesses and empty schoolyards. He found it unsettling, the way the media seemed determined to turn every issue into something divisive, group against group.

"It's just a matter of time," said Frank, turning on the fan as a spot of something on the burner began to smoke. "People are starting to get sick here. We've already lost Keelan."

There was a tremor in Gretchen's chin. "I heard Rachel's in the hospital, too. A neighbour is taking care of her little boy, and they won't let him visit in case he catches it." She added some milk to her cup. "It's possible that we can do more good where we are." Then she locked eyes with Elliot. "What do you think? Are we terrible people if we pick up and leave?"

Things were truly dire if his mother was deigning to ask his advice. "It's not for me to say," Elliot said as he glanced down at his phone, buzzing with a text from Jake, a rookie on his squad. *Hit the panic button. Can't buy a fake LV on Canal for love or money today.* They'd joked that when the last hawker abandoned Canal Street, it was time to get out. He erased the text and turned off his phone.

"If you ask me," said Frank, "the sooner we leave, the better. Like tomorrow."

How quickly a place of retreat could become yet another risk to flee, Elliot thought. The last three and a half weeks in Lansdowne had been a physical relief, a gradual melting-away of the months of stress carried in his back and shoulders. Before he'd left, the city had started to smell, as though every day were garbage day. All the municipal services were understaffed. The snow and cold had come on like a mercy to stifle the pervading smell of rot that reeked like an admission of guilt from the core of North American capitalism. Then there was all the usual violence and exploitation that never seemed to go away, even during an unfolding global tragedy. He'd heard of fake antivirals being sold on street corners and opportunistic thieves ransacking the homes of those who had fled. The cumulative effect was like a sped-up eon of erosion on his crumbling faith in humanity. These days, when Frank used an example from the news to illustrate the brutality of man against man, Elliot could scarcely muster the energy to disagree with him.

"Now that you mention it," Gretchen said, taking a sip of her coffee, "Keelan's daughter approached me at the supermarket yesterday. She said she'd like to join us at the cabin if we decide to go."

Elliot lowered his laptop screen. So Julia and Dory had come to Lansdowne, after all. He hadn't heard a word from them since he emailed Julia about her father. He'd explained where he'd parked his car then mailed her the keys so she could drive her family out of the city, as per her father's wishes.

"She brought up the cabin?" Frank turned off the burner and tipped the porridge into a bowl. "That's very forward."

"She said they have a Winnebago full of supplies Keelan had been stockpiling. They're just looking for somewhere to go."

"They have a house on wheels. They could go anywhere."

"Not really, Frank." She gave him a sharp look. "There are travel advisories, blocked roads. And she has a newborn baby."

"Oh, I know, I know." His father waved a hand as he rummaged in a drawer for another spoon. "But babies are very portable, from what I've heard."

"Humph." His mother looked over in his direction. "Elliot? What do you say?"

His elbow jumped on the table, narrowly missing his coffee cup. His reflexes had been on high alert for so long that they were starting to revolt. The other night, when the wind tipped over a metal garbage can, he'd made it halfway to the bedroom door, gun in hand, before waking and remembering that, for the moment at least, he was safe.

"What does it have to do with me?"

"Weren't you paying attention? It's Keelan's daughter. Julia. She wants to bring her family to the cabin. That includes Dory."

Elliot felt his lips go numb. "I'm surprised you're bothering to consult me. You love Dory."

"Yes," said Gretchen, looking as if she was forcing herself to repress a sigh. "But you're our son. Didn't you once tell me that entitled you to preferential treatment?"

"I—I didn't think you were listening."

"Well, I was. So?"

"Do what you want," he said. "I'm over it."

"Good. I will." His mother was never one for reading between the lines if she knew she wouldn't like what she'd find there.

Elliot refreshed his inbox to see if there was a new email from Sarah, but he had no unread messages. He tuned out his parents as he scrolled down to check the date of her last communication. Sometimes he worried he was developing the same anxiety she'd battled for years. If she didn't write every twenty-four hours or so, he found himself imagining their boat capsizing in a rogue wave. He knew from Sarah this was called "catastrophizing." Worse, he was beginning to realize how easily concern could transform into paralysis—every course of action was potentially fraught with moral and mortal perils, waiting only for an anxious mind to bring them to light.

Before long, his parents were finishing breakfast and Gretchen was arguing they had a responsibility to take in as many people as they could. "If we can't trust the state to do it, we have to take care of each other," she said.

"Well, it's the lifeboat dilemma, dear," replied Frank. "How many can our poor cabin support?"

"It has more beds than we need, as you know perfectly well. And the food will be plenty, by the sounds of what they're bringing. We'll have to do our share, too."

"Indeed, we will," said Frank. "From each according to her abilities. To each according to his needs."

Gretchen tapped her fingers on the counter. "Doesn't that sound like fun, Elliot?"

"More than you know, Mom."

She got up and began sorting the mail, which they had let amass in great slippery piles of bills, flyers, food delivery menus.

"Here's one for you, Elliot," she said, holding out a white envelope. "Did you think to have your mail forwarded? That's clever of you. I was going to mention it."

He reached out to take it from her. "I didn't, actually."

"Maybe someone from back in the day then? An old friend from school."

Elliot turned the envelope over in his hands. It looked official, not personal. The logo on the return address—*Genosys Family Resources*—seemed familiar. "I haven't lived here in over fifteen years."

The phone rang, and his father answered it.

"It's Julia," said Frank, covering the receiver. "What should I tell her?"

Gretchen turned to Elliot. "It's up to you," she said. "But we leave tomorrow."

Elliot stood on the doorstep of Keelan's home, listening to the muted peal of the doorbell echoing inside the old Queen Anne house and looking at his own car parked in the driveway. He'd driven Keelan's Volvo straight from the hospital to a high-tech car wash, where he'd used his police discount for an electrostatically charged aerosol decontamination of the vehicle. It had occurred to him on his drive out to Lansdowne that, in spite of the expensive cleaning, the car seemed unchanged besides a faint smell of disinfectant. The very business of living required a certain amount of trust.

Dory flung open the door. She was wearing a striped dress with a red belt, and her eyes behind her glasses were liquid green and staring at the sight of him. Her face, even half-covered by a mask, was comforting in a visceral way that caught him off guard. He'd told his mother he wanted to meet with Dory before deciding whether or not to invite her to the cabin. Now he wondered if he'd made a mistake.

"Elliot." It was almost a whisper. "You're here." Then she was peering past him down the deserted street. "Is your mom with you?" she said, seeming flustered.

"Just me," he said, standing well back from her even though he too was wearing his personal protective gear.

"I'm sorry Julia cornered her like that," said Dory. She stood aside to let him in then locked the door. "We thought the bereaved daughter might make a better ask than the maligned ex-wife."

"I haven't maligned you."

"Well, that's something. Why don't we sit down?" Dory motioned for Elliot to follow, then strode across the foyer and down the hall in a pair of high-heeled shoes.

"How many times do I have to tell you?" called a voice from upstairs that he recognized as Julia's. "It took my mother years to convince my dad to refinish the floors. She would die if she saw you doing that."

"Your mother's already dead," Dory shouted up in response. Elliot had a sudden memory of one of their first dates, when Dory had cackled at an off-colour joke about puppy mills.

He followed her into the living room to a set of plump flowered sofas. She sat on one, and he sat across from her on the other. Between them on the rug lay a few stuffed animals and other baby toys.

"So you're a mom now," he said, after a pause. "By a sperm donor . . . ?"

"How else? A close personal relationship with Zeus?" Dory pushed a lock of her dark bob behind her ear. "It's someone we know, someone who works for me." She waved her hand. "He signed everything. It's all in order."

"Isn't that unethical? If he's your employee, I mean?"

She shrugged. "Probably." A laugh escaped from them both and, as their eyes met in amusement, it was as though no time had passed. How had he forgotten that it was her very wickedness he had loved? She crossed one leg over the other. "But I wasn't about to order it off the internet. Kyle is smart, good-looking. Gay. It's all good."

"If you say so." Elliot shifted slightly on the couch. "I hope you've been careful about this place."

"We paid for a fumigation before coming. And a cleaning service." Dory smoothed the nap of her dress across her knees. "Even though the hospital told Julia they think Keelan probably caught the virus in New York. But how would they know?"

The topic seemed to make her antsy. She stood up and went into the kitchen, her footsteps clacking against the tiles. He watched as she pulled open a cupboard and stared inside. Even in three-inch stilettos, she had to crane her neck to see the top shelf.

"Pop-Tarts or a granola bar?" she offered.

"I guess Keelan didn't do much cooking."

Dory shook her head. "Didn't seem to." She ripped open a package and slid out a Pop-Tart. "Julia told me we have you to thank for getting us here." She reached up a hand to remove her mask. "I admit I'm still a little fuzzy on the details."

Elliot nodded. "I'm just the messenger, really. I made a promise to Keelan."

Knowing it was hospital protocol to destroy the personal effects of ARAMIS patients, he'd snuck Keelan's letters to Julia out in his knapsack. Since it wasn't safe to put them in the mail, he'd sent her digital images of each page. "Did Julia get the photos of his letters? She never wrote back to my email."

Dory took a bite of the pastry then pulled a face. "Julia has been pretty messed up over everything," she said, wandering back to the living room. "Especially the letters. Talk about a guilt trip from beyond the grave." She chewed slowly then swallowed. "Obviously, I know that wasn't your intention. Or Keelan's. But somehow even his apology has screwed things up for us."

Elliot looked away towards an end table and picked up a framed photograph of a pale woman with long dark hair. She had a winsome but vague smile, as though the photographer had captured her in a moment of distraction. Julia's mother, probably. "Grief can make people behave badly," he said.

Dory toed a rubber giraffe on the rug. "All these years I told her she didn't owe him anything." The toy squeaked as its neck bent in two, then again as Dory released it and the head bounced free. "When people let you down, you have to cut them loose."

"Thanks a lot."

"God, Elliot. When will you learn that not everything is about you?" Before he had a chance to respond, Dory strode to the bottom of the stairs. "Jules," she called. "Come down here already and say hi to your predecessor. It's the least you could do after stealing me away from him."

Elliot felt his face getting hot. He didn't look at Dory but he could almost hear her grinning. She loved to put people on the spot.

Dory sat back down. "So let me give you the lowdown. Julia is Mama and I'm Mommy, and Mama has an elaborate chart for feeding and sleeping that is clearly at odds with reality."

Julia came downstairs, frowning at a handheld video baby monitor. "I heard that."

"Look who's here," said Dory.

Julia moved closer. She was vaguely hippie-ish in a cotton printed top and stretchy gaucho pants. "It's been a long time," she said. Her eyes moved over him without meeting his gaze. "I don't even know what to say. I guess I should start with thank you. For everything you did for my father, and us."

Elliot stood up. "Of course," he said, confused. It seemed Julia didn't want her wife to know she had paid him a visit. "Congratulations on the baby. I'm really happy for you both."

"Thanks," said Julia, with a bit more warmth. He noticed her eyes were listless and bloodshot.

"Is the baby asleep?" he asked. "Should we be quiet?"

Julia glanced down at the monitor then back at Dory. "Still awake."

"There's not much point in tiptoeing around her," said Dory. "This baby seems determined never to sleep."

"That doesn't mean you need to be louder than usual," said Julia. "You've got to quit it with those shoes."

Elliot thought by now Julia would have realized there was no point in fighting with Dory, because Dory actually enjoyed it. It had been the worst part of their marriage, and Elliot had felt wounded by every harsh word that came out of his own mouth.

But Dory sidestepped the accusation. "Do you want to see her?" she asked him. "She's awake, anyway."

"Sure."

"She's probably gone to sleep now that nobody's looking," said Dory, the sound of her shoes dulling at last on the carpet as she led the way upstairs. "Maybe she just wanted some privacy."

Julia sounded sour as she trailed behind her wife. "Have you noticed that all of your childrearing suggestions involve some degree of neglect?" To Elliot, over her shoulder, she said, "Dory keeps hoping that doing nothing will turn out to be the elusive parenting secret everyone else has somehow overlooked."

He again felt the edge of animosity between them and was surprised that it worried him. He fumbled to change the subject as they reached the landing. "What's your daughter's name?" he asked.

"Shhh," murmured Dory, pushing open a door at the top of the stairs. "Look."

Elliot crowded into the doorway with both women to gaze down at the crib. The baby was finally asleep, her limbs splayed like a starfish. She looked perfect, like the chubby babies in diaper commercials, and her perfection seemed at odds with the kind of world into which she'd been born. Her tiny chest was rising and falling, her head stretched back to reveal bits of lint stuck in the folds of flesh around her neck. Then Dory reached out to clasp Julia's hand, and Julia closed her eyes and leaned into her wife. The gesture seemed alien to the Dory he'd been married to, and, inexplicably, it soothed him. He felt a wave of love for the child, around whom three practical and prickly adults were standing by helplessly, peaceably. For the first time in months, something relaxed inside him.

"Why don't you follow us up to the cabin tomorrow?" said Elliot. His voice was a whisper. "There's plenty of room."

᙮᙮᙮

At the cabin, Elliot inspected the mousetraps as the others unpacked.

"Exactly how long do you think we're all going to be staying out here?" asked Gretchen, eyes boggling at the supplies from Keelan's Winnebago.

Dory shrugged and passed her another bag. Frank said, "Until classes are reinstated? Longer?"

"Hmm," said Gretchen. She began stacking tins inside the upper cabinets.

"And if somebody comes here trying to rob us of this bounty," added Frank, "well, Elliot has a gun."

"Nonsense," said Gretchen. "Don't be a fantasist."

"Elliot has what?" said Julia from the couch, where she was nursing the baby; otherwise, Elliot had a feeling she might have shouted.

"Don't worry," he told her. "It's locked in the car."

Gretchen carried on as though neither of them had spoken. "We'll share what we have, of course. And we'll figure out how they can help us in return." She settled down next to Julia and the baby. "It's a bit exhilarating, to be honest. A test case in cooperation."

His father sighed from the opposite couch. "It's naive to assume these random, desperate strangers will have anything to offer."

Dory spoke up. "It isn't naive to assume people will do the right thing. People are surprisingly principled."

"Until they get a taste of power," said Gretchen. "Then they'll throw anyone under the bus to keep it."

"Another debate for another day, my dear," said Frank.

As the conversation continued around him, Elliot began emptying his rucksack: a few clothes from his parents' house, his laptop, a paperback thriller with an envelope stuffed in it as a bookmark. Julia went to heat up some soup in the kitchen and Dory took her place on the couch. He noticed the two of them didn't seem to be speaking to each other except when it came to the baby. Then he listened to his mother and his ex fall back into their old rapport as though it had never ended, which perhaps it never had.

"We're happy you're here," said Gretchen. She held out her hands for the baby and cradled her with a sigh of satisfaction.

"Have you seen the latest numbers?" asked Dory in a low voice. "The infection rate among children is terrifying. We know five families with kids in the ICU."

"That's horrible," said his mother. "You must have been beside yourselves about the baby."

Dory nodded. "Eventually, they hope the overall rate is going to plateau and drop off, maybe in a month or two if they can contain it."

"Thank God you got out," said Gretchen. "I wonder if Keelan really did know something we didn't about the likelihood of a crisis." She ran one finger softly along the baby's cheek. "I read those books of his when they came out, but of course a book can never capture all of one's thoughts on a subject."

Elliot noticed that his mother seemed to have an anxiety around other people's knowledge. It was probably what had helped her stay ahead in her career—her endless curiosity.

"His books are all about cooperation and responsibility," said Frank, keeping his voice low in deference to Julia's presence in the next room, "but it's worth pointing out he didn't hesitate to acquire more than his fair share of supplies. Panic makes people do terrible things—even people who should know better. It'll soon be every man for himself out there."

"*Man* being the operative word," said Gretchen, wrinkling her nose, and Frank groaned. "All jokes aside, it's an appallingly dark view of human nature. You'll notice nobody else is agreeing with you."

"Only because you've scared them off, my dear." Frank's smile was gallant. "But Elliot works in law enforcement for a reason. I'm sure he can attest to the presence of an antisocial element."

Gretchen and the others turned to look at Elliot where he lingered on the rug, surrounded by the contents of his rucksack.

"There are always people who will take what they can get," he said.

His mother gave him a close look just as the baby started fussing. "You'd be better off quitting and staying here to help your family. I know you're not satisfied as a cog in a violent, corrupt system, Ell." She continued scrutinizing him even when he glared back. "I can tell it's getting to you. There's no need to stand by some previous decision now that you know better."

"Wow, good to finally know what you really think, Mom." He had to raise his voice to be heard over the baby's thin cries.

"I'll take her," said Dory, carrying the baby to the bedroom. Even with the door closed, they could hear her singing as she changed the baby's diaper.

"Hard to believe we all start out in life so defenceless," said Frank.

Gretchen sat back and put her feet up on the coffee table. "Yes, how *do* all these wailing bundles of need get taken care of in such a cruel, cold world?"

"Struggle for existence!" Frank chortled. "Are you trying to pass off biology as altruism?"

Elliot settled down in the armchair with his book. He pulled out the envelope he'd tucked into it and finally ripped it open.

Re: Donor 154-095-91066

Dear Mr. Howe,

We are writing to you regarding your sperm donations between October and December 2001 as part of the Glendowns Fertility Research Project. Subjects who participated in certain medical trials at our facilities consented to unlimited use of donated sperm and were compensated accordingly. However, you may be unaware that many families were able to have children thanks to your generous donations.

As you may know, attitudes surrounding the anonymity of donors have evolved in recent years, and the rise of social networks has facilitated contact between donor offspring all over the world. Attached, please find correspondence from the Donor Offspring Registry, with whom we are cooperating according to legislation currently before Congress.

Sincerely,
Genosys Family Resources

Dear Donor 154-095-91066,

Hello! Let me begin by thanking you for your generosity and telling you about our non-profit organization, which began as a website created by a mother whose son wanted to find his biological father.

Our mandate is to help donor children connect with blood relatives for the purposes of satisfying lifelong curiosities, sharing medical information, and to prevent future consanguinity. Children resulting from donor sperm can, upon reaching the age of 18, make use of our site to connect with donor fathers and potential half-siblings who have previously consented to contact. We also liaise with donation clinics to release donor names according to applicable state laws.

To date, 46 individuals resulting from your donations have connected with one another via the registry. We are holding correspondence from some of them in trust for you.

We are proud to have united many donor children with their donors and biological siblings. You will find a number of their stories on our website, and by registering as a donor on our site and releasing your name you can connect with the many amazing individuals you have helped bring into the world. This could be the first step on an incredible journey of discovery for you and your extended genetic network.

Sincerely,

Erin Elmwood
Liaison Officer
Donor Offspring Registry
www.donoroffspring.org

"Oh Jesus!" Elliot said. The torn envelope fluttered to the floor as the conversation between his parents stopped abruptly. "Christ."

"Elliot," said Gretchen, sounding rattled by his tone. "What is it?"

He held out the two pages for his mother to read. She scanned them quickly.

"Good lord," she said.

Elliot laced up his boots and went outside. Even after the door slammed behind him, he could hear his father and mother talking in loud voices, the baby crying, Julia and Dory coming out of the bedroom—all of them no doubt examining the preposterous letter and questioning his patently absurd life. He went around the side of the house out of earshot, past the low eaves covering a large woodpile and an idling axe that popped with red. He took out his rage on the logs, chopping the dry rounds into splits and kindling for the stove.

In between swings, he saw Dory approaching, donning her winter coat.

"Not in the mood," he called out. "Not to mention I have an axe."

"I just want to say it sucks. Especially if you didn't know."

"Guess I should have read the fine print." He couldn't remember now, what he had or hadn't read. It was infuriating to think that his own life could be a mystery, even when he'd already lived it. He split a final log, preparing himself for a diatribe about the secret he'd kept from her during their marriage. "I'm an idiot, basically."

"Yes," said Dory. The hood of her coat was flipped up and her voice seemed to come from the trees. There was a strange edge to it. "But I'm sure you meant well."

Elliot shivered. "Actually, I don't know if I did." He recalled being angry at his parents in the generic way he always was back then, for their constant well-meaning pressure to follow in their footsteps—though it would be another three years before he finally quit school. And he had been mad at Keisha, too, for being so upset about the breakup that had immediately preceded him signing up to donate. He'd been interested in the money, sure, but he couldn't swear there hadn't been some defiance there, in joining the trial. He'd felt guilty afterwards, but then, he'd felt guilty beforehand, too. As long as he could remember, he'd had a keen awareness of just how flawed a person he really was.

He paced over to a spot where he could make a pristine boot mark in the snow. Around the corner, there was a precipitous drop to the frozen lake. All was white and grey as far as he could see.

When he returned, Dory said, "I'm sorry your mom is still giving you a hard time about your job. I know it bugs you." Her face grew sombre. "But I'm surprised to see you here. Isn't there more than enough work for you guys right now?"

"Plenty, yeah." So many police officers had contracted ARAMIS in the line of duty that the union was talking of a strike. And last week the rookie had texted him about seeing a group of officers signing out tear gas canisters and automatic rifles from the armoury, a process that no longer seemed to require the same chain of approval as before.

Plus, the mayor was making noise about cracking down on precincts with the most curfew violations—coincidentally the poorest neighbourhoods, with the worst infection rates. "A bad time to take a vacation, I guess. But I wanted to spend some time with my parents." Elliot looked at the snow, littered with scabs of bark and splintered wood chips.

"Things are getting worse out there, aren't they?" said Dory.

Elliot hadn't spoken to anyone about the city he'd left behind, but Dory had always been good at getting to the heart of things. "To be honest, I'm terrified of becoming part of the problem," he said, and she nodded as though she understood. He resented that it was so easy to talk to someone who wasn't even in his life anymore. "I'm thinking of quitting the force." It was the first time he had said it out loud. "I'm ready for a change."

Dory seemed shocked into a momentary silence. Her eyes roved over his face as though looking for something she might have missed. "Well. Change can be good," she said finally, though she sounded dubious. Then she added, "But you've been avoiding me. Since you told us we could come."

He didn't think he'd tried to steer clear of her, though they certainly hadn't had any in-depth conversations. "Maybe a little. But so have you." He replaced the axe where he'd found it.

"Did you notice Julia freezing me out?"

He'd forgotten her habit of tuning him into other people's problems as a way to help him forget about his own. "Give it time."

As he bent to the task of arranging the split logs in the woodpile, Dory kicked the snow at her feet. "I don't know why I can't let it go," she said. "All those things Julia told me about how Keelan treated her when she was growing up. I think partly we fell in love with the stories we told each other about the sad girls we used to be. How badly our parents misunderstood us and our terrible childhoods." She hunched against the cold, leaning back against the cabin. "But Julia wants to be finished with our childhoods. Especially now, with the baby and everything. She wants to be healed and to move on."

Elliot had no idea if his ex-wife really felt as lost as she sounded. "Would that be so bad?" he asked.

She shrugged. "Maybe not. But I don't think leaving the past behind is all that easy. Do you?"

"No." He risked another glance at her, and he saw that behind the glasses her eyes were wide and glassy. He blinked, surprised. He wondered how long he could be in her presence before he would be forced to reassess everything he'd ever told himself about their marriage and its end. He thought he'd mastered moving on, but only insofar as it meant not looking back. "And what do *you* want?" he asked.

Dory unfolded her arms and gave him a simple smile. "I want you to forgive me."

Elliot had known plenty of couples who'd separated over the years. Yet most had clashed bitterly in the lead-up, or drifted apart in obvious and irrevocable ways. For him, their divorce had come out of the blue. "You know, I never stopped loving you. And that made it hard."

Dory didn't seem as taken aback as he'd expected her to be. "For me, too." Her gaze was serious and not unsympathetic.

He said, "I felt a fool."

She nodded. "I'm sorry I hurt you." She reached out as though to touch him, then thrust her hands into her pockets instead. "You know, you'll be an amazing dad."

"Thanks for the vote of confidence."

Dory frowned, as though uncertain if he was serious, and without thinking, he flashed her a reassuring grin—part of the wordless vocabulary of their former marriage. He remembered what Sarah had once said to him about how people's lives could never truly be disentangled once they'd come together. He'd found the idea stagnant at best and horrifying at worst, but for the first time, as Dory smiled back at him, he saw the comfort in it.

When Elliot and Dory returned to the cabin with armfuls of firewood, Gretchen got up and walked out. Elliot occupied himself with stacking the wood against the wall, bracing himself for a parental onslaught about his donations. But his mother came back with a case of beer. "I can't believe I forgot this on the first load." She placed it heavily on the coffee table. "And some whisky," she said, pulling a bottle of Laphroaig out of her shoulder bag.

"Thank god," said Elliot, reaching for it.

"It's a hell of a thing," said Gretchen. "I suppose I ought to be scandalized, but I actually feel a strange kind of pride. Forty-six grandchildren!" She returned to her spot on the couch. "And Noah, of course."

"In another time and place," said Frank, "you'd be hailed as a matriarch." He held out his hand for the whisky, poured some for everyone, then raised his glass and clinked it to Gretchen's.

"You know, there's not enough blood there, between fathers and children," said Gretchen. She watched as Dory and Julia carried their drowsy baby into a bedroom, along with a portable crib. "Men—all the men I know—are unbound."

"What do you mean?" said Frank. Elliot said nothing. He already knew that whatever his mother was going to say would annoy him.

"Just look at our own kids," she said, proving him right. "Elliot scattering his seed far and wide, with no involvement whatsoever with those children, and Sarah, binding herself forever, all alone, to a child almost entirely of her own making."

"I think our kids are special cases."

"Maybe." Gretchen leaned her head on her hand, then turned her attention to her son. "So what are you going to do, honey?"

Elliot thought he saw something tender in her eyes, an unusual openness that didn't assume she already had the right answer. Somehow he was sure she knew he'd decided not to return to the city: that she was feeling grateful, maternal, even indulgent. He got up from the table and returned to the armchair.

"Let's not talk about it right now, okay?"

His parents nodded.

Dory came back into the living room. "Has it sunk in yet?"

Elliot could tell she wanted to tell a joke but was somehow restraining herself. He refrained from answering but grabbed the bottle and took another slug. From the bedroom, he could hear the hushed melody of a lullaby winding down.

Gretchen said, "He doesn't want to talk right now."

Julia returned after putting the baby to sleep. "I wonder what my father would think of us all being here."

"He'd probably try to take credit for it," said Gretchen, smiling. "Claim it was all his idea."

"Poor old Dad." Elliot saw that there were tears on Julia's face.

"I wish he were here," said Gretchen, and Frank agreed. The rest of them began exchanging stories about Keelan in low voices, sparing a glance in Elliot's direction every once in a while. But he was happy to be out of the conversation.

He took one shot then another, then cracked open and chugged beer after beer until his panic began to subside. The cabin seemed to breathe with him, responsive and alive, as the wind whistled in and out of hairline cracks in the walls. He sensed his parents' need and the history he shared with Dory and Julia—and beyond that, whatever connection lay between him and the forty-odd donor children spread all over the world. He noticed his eyes closing.

"You should go to bed, Ell," said his mother. He was aware of her hand on his arm, tugging him up. Then her arms were on him in an embrace, as his father patted his back. He felt a strange dislocation in time, as though he were a child again. He let her lead him to the bedroom he used to share with his sister, where he collapsed into his bunk.

A baby was crying in his dream, and when he awoke, it was still crying—but quickly shushed. Elliot sat up, disoriented until he remembered his ex-wife and her new wife and child were in the other room. He had an aching bladder and a spinning headache after the whisky and four beers. He had an urge to piss and throw up, and also to speak to Sarah. He needed to tell her about the letters. Using his phone as a flashlight, he tiptoed past his parents, asleep in the main room, to creep outside and take a leak in the bushes. The cool air was refreshing.

Afterwards, Elliot leaned against the front door of the cabin and withdrew the letters from his pocket. Even crumpled, they remained shocking. Then he checked his email. Sarah still hadn't written. He started typing to her on his phone, snapping photos of the letters and attaching them to the message.

Sarah,

See attached. I commit myself to your infinite wisdom. What do I do?

In this case, cause and effect seem too thin on the ground to be able to make sense of anything. Do you know what I mean? Trying to connect that time in my life to anything as important as forty-six human beings and their families seems impossible. I feel stupid and guilty and cheated. And embarrassed.

Do I register on the website?? Won't they be disappointed?

I still want to have kids, but I was going to wait until I was a better person.

Elliot

He held his phone up in the air, checking his signal, making sure the message was sent.

He knew what Keisha would tell him to do. He had two unanswered texts from her: *Results are in* and *Aren't you curious???* He was eager to tell Sarah about his possible immunity, but he didn't want to alarm her—or inadvertently encourage her or Noah to take even the smallest unnecessary risk.

Thinking now along protective lines, he moved across the clearing to his family's parked car and reached into the glove compartment to extract his service weapon. He regretted bringing the gun into the philosophical debate that would probably carry on over the next few days. He hadn't even checked with his parents to see if they knew of anyone else up at the lake. Stalking a wide perimeter around the side of the cabin, he began circling the property. From the lake to the upper slope with the outhouse and back towards the other side. With the gun in his hand, his body was taut and ready and tingling with anticipation in the unknowable dark. When he heard a sudden noise in the underbrush, he stopped and fired into the air. The gunshot reverberated through his body and blared across the lake. He forced himself to exhale, his breath ragged. All was still, the snow undisturbed apart from his own footsteps. Then he stood there, taking in the tranquility of the forest at night. But the darkness turned out to be full of noises: branches snapping, animals rustling, ice creaking and groaning in the lakebed. Night birds called out in counterpoint. And the more he listened, the more he heard. For once, he felt small and untethered. The most faltering and uncertain creature of them all.

When he got back to the cabin, Julia was waiting for him outside with an electric lantern. She had a parka thrown on over her pyjamas.

"What are you doing up?" he asked.

"I heard a gunshot," she said dryly. "I have a baby in there."

Elliot could feel himself flushing. "Did I wake anyone else?" He peered in the nearest window, but all was dim and undisturbed. He quickly returned to the car and replaced the weapon, hoping to move past his overwhelming feeling of ridiculousness.

"I'm sorry," he said, coming back. "I'm still messed up over this whole 'sudden paternity' thing."

Julia gave him a flinty look, her face pale and haloed in faux fur. "Oh well. I'm sure the kids will understand. You were *going through* something."

"Yeah." He was disconcerted by the change in her, the hardness in her voice. When she'd dropped by his apartment, she'd been earnest but ironic, as ready to plead her case as to laugh at herself. "So why didn't you tell Dory you came to see me? You've put me into a bit of an awkward position."

"She wouldn't have liked me meddling," said Julia. "She doesn't like having to accept help."

"Don't I know it." He almost smiled, but he was annoyed that there was not even the pretext of an apology. "I don't care for lying, though."

"What's a white lie to a white knight?" Julia blew on her hands then shoved them into the pockets of her parka. "I know you have some kind of saviour complex. That's why we're all here, isn't it? You're always trying so hard to prove you're one of the good guys. Saving us, trying to save my dad." Her breath cooled into clouds. "But you haven't really forgiven anyone."

"What's to forgive?" he asked, but his reply was mechanical. "People change. Marriages end."

"But you still think it's my fault." The porch creaked as Julia stepped towards him, glaring at a point somewhere to the left of his forehead. She was all jagged edges, as though battered by the events of the past few months.

Elliot was still drunk and riled up, but he felt an affinity for her, in the transparency of her grief manifesting as misplaced anger. "I don't," he said, darting his head to catch her gaze and hold it. Somehow, in saying so, he felt it become true. "It wasn't your fault. Maybe it was just easier to pretend like it was."

"That's nice of you to say." She pulled her coat down as far as it would go before sitting down on the cold stoop. Up close, she looked worn out, her skin dry and dull. "And what you said before, you were right. Words do matter. But not as much as actions."

"Right." Elliot recalled their last conversation and everything he'd said about marriage. "Vows are just words. Dory needed to be with the right person. I can see that now."

Julia shook her head as though he was missing the point. When she spoke, her voice was fierce and intense. "No, I'm saying I'll never forget what you did for my father." Then she tightened her shoulders, folding in on herself. "Sorry." She rubbed her chin against the collar of her jacket.

Elliot felt ill at ease with her gratitude, since his final hours with Keelan still registered as a failure. "I wish I'd managed to get in touch with you sooner. I don't know if it helps, but with a one-month-old at home, they wouldn't have let you in the ward. Or at least strongly counselled against it."

Julia gave no sign of having heard him. Elliot tried to banish the memory of Keelan lying prone in his lap. Part of him longed to tell her of that terrible day in the hospital, to share and disarm the images so they were no longer his to bear alone.

"Your father was at peace," Elliot said instead. "He wasn't in any pain at the end." There was so little else to offer besides this compassionate omission.

A puff of condensation from her nostrils: a silent snort.

"Your dad loved you so much," he went on. "And he knew you loved him, too."

Julia stretched out her legs as she wept silently, her flannel pyjama bottoms sagging onto the steps. "I'm just . . . tired." She wiped her face with the sleeve of her jacket. "It's a scary time to have a kid. Even if we survive, it's hard to see where we go from here. Nothing is going to be the way it was before. Us against them. Neighbour against neighbour. You know what I mean?"

"Every generation thinks the world is going to hell. That's not new." Elliot remembered one of his parents saying that even the ancient Romans thought as much.

"Everything is falling away," Julia continued, flicking a hand around in a jerky, truncated wave. "The insects, the animals, the forests, the ozone. If it isn't ARAMIS that ends this freak-show evolutionary lottery, it'll be something else. We don't know how to talk to one another, and we can't listen." She swallowed. "It's hard to see the point of doing anything besides what's right in front of you."

It was discomfiting to listen to her voice his worst fears with the same hopelessness he had been trying to suppress for weeks. He heard the self-protectiveness in it, the terror of failing, and the overwhelming grief for all of humanity's missteps. Elliot paced back over to the turning circle and the car. He could see that the keys were inside.

"Hey, what are you doing?" said Julia, as he got into the driver's seat. When he glanced over at her, she seemed taken aback. "Don't leave. I was joking. Or at least, I was just . . . talking."

"I know," said Elliot. "But I *am* leaving. Going back to the city," he said. The relief was sobering. He could feel his head clearing, the path of duty laid bare and beckoning. He thought, too, of all those children he had helped bring into the world, the dozens of unknown ties he had yet to explore. "Society is still worth protecting, don't you think? Maybe now more than ever."

She stood up, looking fretful. "Are you sure? Why not wait until morning? I really hope it's not because of me."

"It's not because of you. Less traffic now." And less pressure from his parents. "Bye, Julia. Tell them for me?"

She nodded, then hopped off the porch and approached him with quick, hurried steps. He saw the shock of cold on her face as her feet in their flimsy slippers hit the snow. Then her arms were around him in a swift, tight hug. When she pulled back, her smile was small and tired, but real. "Good luck. And stay safe."

As he slowly negotiated the rutted, icy road, Elliot felt renewed by their conversation. He was starting to believe there were second chances in life to make things right. There were a million chances, really, given how connected everyone was these days. With a million chances, he might finally be able to do the right thing.

Dove Suite Snags Song of the Year

"Song for the End of the World" by indie-rock quartet Dove Suite has topped Trillis's annual "Year in Music Insights" list as the most streamed song in America.

Though only released at the end of November, the single has surpassed even the summer's biggest hits. "If you'd asked me if it was possible for a single to come out at the end of the year and dominate in this way, I would have said no," says Gregory Fischer, who helped compile the list for the streaming service. "But this has been an unusual year for music and for Dove Suite in particular. All the drama surrounding the band probably increased public interest."

Husband-and-wife bandleaders Stuart Jenkins and Emma Aslet both contracted ARAMIS in late October, during the final weeks of Aslet's pregnancy. Aslet and the child survived, but Jenkins passed away from respiratory failure. The couple also spearheaded the "To America With Love" ARAMIS fundraising concert in Vancouver on September 26, which became notorious for proliferating the virus within Canada as well as for a stampede that claimed the lives of eight concertgoers and injured 58 others.

"Everyone knows that this is someone who has suffered greatly," says Fischer of Aslet. "We look to art to show us how we can survive the pain of this world. And right now there are a lot of people in pain, a lot of people who have lost loved ones. This song has become a kind of anthem for them."

The song has also been wildly popular on conventional radio, where it debuted at number one and has been holding steady ever since. Dean Lefferts of Sound City Records predicts it could become the "Hallelujah" of the ARAMIS age. "It has that bittersweet quality." Though the new Dove

Suite offering has not yet spawned as many interpretations as Leonard
Cohen's famous song, a YouTube search for the title reveals more than 150
different cover versions, by well-established and unknown artists alike.
Neela Sim, founder of the Dove Suite fansite LightningHearts.com, reported
in a recent blog post that "Song for the End of the World" is frequently
being performed at memorials and funerals across the country. The post
included photos sent in by ARAMIS survivors who were inspired to get
tattoos featuring the song's lyrics.

The band released a statement in response to the Trillis announcement.
"Music has always been a way for people to come together, and that has
never seemed more important than it does right now. If we've learned
anything over the past year, it's that sometimes a voice in the darkness can
reach out and save you from feeling alone."

The catchy single is also the 18th most streamed track globally.

SARAH
AND OWEN

Sarah popped below to the navigation station to check the charts as they prepared to leave Bimini and cross to the Berry Islands. As she calculated their route to Chub Cay, she listened for Noah, who was still singing to himself in his cabin.

They had set sail out of Cape May, New Jersey, with no fanfare and only Elliot to see them off. Sarah had stowed their three bags—packed and repacked many times over several days—while Noah bounded around the yacht, exultant over his new kingdom. Though she'd put on a brave face, she felt dangerously untethered as they motored away from her brother and everything safe and familiar. Not at all the intrepid joy of her teen sailing days, nor the sure purpose she'd felt when she decided to quit school and move to Bolivia—she could still recall the crescendo of pleasure from her scalp to her fingertips as the plane lifted off. Back then, she had willingly put herself in the hands of fate. If the plane went down, nobody would blame her for all she had failed to do in life: complete her master's degree, establish a dazzling career in some field or other. Find a boyfriend of any consequence. Guilt had already swept her off course like some inexorable riptide, like the current that had nearly drowned Jericho. Nothing she had undertaken since that terrible night in the river had seemed to matter quite as much, even as each new decision felt fraught with hidden and ever-multiplying consequences. Living Tree had promised forgiveness, community, and freedom from the unknown. For a while, that liberty had made her ecstatic, buoyant. High on life. Though she also remembered the eventual flipside of that unfettered feeling: the loneliness that crept in once her certainty had soured.

"There's a breeze out of the east." Owen was peering over her shoulder at the charts. The day-long sail across the Gulf Stream had boosted his confidence, even as the northerly winds and swift, relentless current had tested all of Sarah's rusty navigation skills. "Shall we try to sail the whole way? Go where the wind takes us?"

She tried to return the smile, but her face felt tight. "We should at least motor out of the anchorage. And we need to leave soon to make it there before low tide."

"I can take the wheel if you like. I think Noah is awake."

Sarah nodded. "Sure." He bounded back up on deck.

The first few days on the boat with Owen had been strange, as their relationship, established mainly over the phone, became embodied. She felt hounded by the mere bulk of him, though he moved around her with such circumspection that she knew he must be going out of his way not to crowd her. And it was no wonder: she could sense the barbed energy she was putting out. She tried to curb her anxiety by plotting and replotting their route, but it spiked no matter which way her thoughts tended—ARAMIS, Noah, Elliot, her latent sailing skills she prayed would return. Not to mention the sheer bodily strain of living in close quarters with a near stranger. But the more their minds were bent towards their journey, the easier they were with each other.

She had steered them 987 nautical miles down the Intracoastal Waterway from Norfolk, Virginia, all the way to the Florida Keys. Mostly they were motoring by day and mooring at night—by far the safest option as they were a stone's throw from dozens of other boats, all cruising the sheltered route down to Miami. The Ditch, as it was known—a mix of canals, rivers, bays, and inlets—was a crash course in navigation. They were protected from ocean swells, but they needed to pay close attention to buoys and the depth sounder. Running aground was the peril of the Ditch, and *Buona Fortuna* had a full keel and a five-foot draft. Shallow water put Sarah on edge, and she'd longed to be out in the ocean right up until they'd faced the choppy nine-hour passage across the Gulf Stream to Bimini, in the Bahamas. Next, as weather allowed, they would cross to the Berry Islands, then to Nassau, to Rose Island, and finally to the Exumas for the rest of the winter. She wished they were there already.

As she stowed the charts, she remembered a saying about the journey being more important than the destination—a commonplace already too indulgent for the circumstances. She had a child and a man in her charge, and nothing mattered more than getting them all where they needed to go.

Sarah kept an eye out as Owen guided the yacht from the slip and set them on a steady course for the crossing. It was a perfect day, with favourable winds. After breakfast, she sat across from Noah at the table in the salon, watching as he copied a row of Gs, capital and lower case. A little before noon, Owen returned below.

"What shall we have for lunch?" The writer beat out a rhythm on his belly and Noah giggled.

"Hmm." She pretended to deliberate. "Soup?" Soup was their usual meal, the default.

Owen laughed and Noah joined in as he always did, despite not getting the joke. Owen went to the galley and Sarah stayed at the table, progressing with her son through the alphabet, until she felt fingers lightly brushing her upper arm, a gauzy touch that was almost sensuous. She turned to see Owen bearing a large mug of soup that he put into her open hands.

"Captain," he said. He reached out and smoothed her son's blond cap of hair, then ran his fingers through his own silvering locks, a reflexive preening. "All hands on deck when you're done eating. The water is as clear as a window. I've already counted thirty-four starfish as big as dinner plates."

"I want to see!" cried Noah.

"Come on then."

It was when he was with Noah that Sarah took the most interest in Owen, as the boy seemed to bring out a touch of whimsy in the writer. After they'd safely motored into Chub Cay that night, Owen announced he had a surprise for them both. He disappeared into his cabin, then returned with something behind his back.

"I've been expanding my artistic horizons." He held up a large rectangle of white Bristol board decorated with thick black lines outlining a star and two border stripes. "We'll fly it to signal our quarantine." He glanced up at her, anticipating her objection. "I know about the Yellow Jack, but that flag means you're quarantining with someone sick aboard. And the yellow Quebec flag is a request for authorities to board and give your vessel the all-clear. But so far there's nothing to signal that we're a healthy boat choosing to keep a safe distance from others."

The flag was cleanly done, with straight lines and even proportions. "When did you design this?"

"Bit by bit over the last few days in Bimini." Owen showed Noah the colours for each section and smiled at Sarah as the boy began filling them in with a jagged scribble.

Later, Owen perfected Noah's scrawl with calm, close circles: yellow field, blue star, red stripes. When the flag was finished, he slipped it into a large plastic sleeve he seemed to have brought for the purpose and, stringing it onto the rigging, ran it up the flagpole. Then he blogged about its creation and meaning. He was hoping it would take off among the other cruisers.

••||||••

There was never quite enough space for privacy, a fact that pleased Owen but seemed to grate on Sarah. He found himself confiding his every thought to his shipmate, whether it was how work was going on his new manuscript or what he'd learned scrolling through the NextExtinction.com message board that day. The lost intimacy of his marriage, restored. And for the first time in his life, he had nothing to hide.

She'd laughed at him when he showed her photos sent in by fans who had likewise taken to the sea, flying the flag he'd designed. "You're like a proud papa." Her laughter was a relief, a boon. It also felt like progress, evidence he had helped. He was sure she laughed more than she used to.

The only time he kept his own counsel was when he logged into his email to check if Rachel had written back, though he told himself not to expect it and she never did. But since Wi-Fi coverage was spotty in the Bahamas, they hadn't done more than cursory satellite email checks and uploading blog posts since Key West. For that reason, they'd planned a stop in the capital, which was regarded by many cruisers as overly crowded but a necessary evil for restocking supplies and buying replacement parts.

In Nassau, they dropped anchor and flew the flag. When they were close enough to shore, Owen booted up the computer and searched for a network.

"We've got a good signal here. We're connected."

Sarah nodded, a quick jut of her chin. She made no move to get up, and Owen knew why. After a few weeks with no real updates, logging on to the internet was an exercise in dread, of all the bad news they feared to learn.

"I'll do it," he said, taking a seat. He clicked through to his email, but there was nothing from Rachel. He checked the latest WHO outbreak reports against their planned route, but their itinerary remained clear. Then he did a quick scan through the *New York Times* and *The Guardian*.

"The Secretary of State is sick, hospitalized. Egypt declared a state of emergency. The mayor of Omaha died and so did a Fox News anchor. And the singer from Dove Suite . . . quite a few weeks ago now, actually."

"Let me read it," she said. She touched Noah on the shoulder. "Go play with your cars, sweets. I'll call you when it's time to Skype with Uncle Elliot." The boy ran off, and Owen gave way at the desk. Sarah clicked through in silence, and he watched as she skimmed two or three news stories before opening her email. There were tears on her cheeks.

"I knew Stu Jenkins at school," she said. "Did you ever meet him there?" Owen's mind was blank, but he furrowed his brow as if dredging his memory. "We lost touch, but he was kind."

So Owen downloaded the new Dove Suite single, and they listened to it as they continued catching up with the state of things on land. Power outages were creating disturbances up and down the East Coast, likely another casualty of understaffing due to sick workers. A friend of Sarah's had forwarded her a cellphone video of a scuffle outside of a Home Depot offering a sale on backup generators.

"It's not just that we're safe from the virus," said Sarah, watching the grainy footage that juddered like a low-budget horror movie.

"We're protected from joining in the panic. Do you know what I mean? If we're not there, we won't be tested. We can't get it wrong."

Later that night, he mixed them drinks after Noah was asleep. Whisky and soda for him, rum and coke for her. She took it from him with a blooming grin, and for once their silence felt easy, as though whatever remained of their niceties had been wrung out over the last few passages. She reached up to remove the clip she used to keep her long red hair out of the winches. Owen considered that she was a woman of great beauty, without the hardness of one used to wielding it: pale skin, thick wavy hair, a Pre-Raphaelite painting in jeans and a faded shirt. But her awareness of her loveliness was like an open wound, a target on her back. Rachel had worn her beauty carelessly, as if it hadn't mattered. Sarah dragged hers around as though uncertain of its value and wary of the kind of attention it might bring to her. Owen noted that the urgency of the fortune teller's injunction had faded the further he got from home. But surely by going away he had done his part? At sea, he could only sin so much.

"How many times have you flown over this ocean?" he asked.

"A few." She listed them: family sabbatical vacation, class trip, a vague back-and-forth to and from South America.

"How many times have you swum in it?" He stripped off his shirt and reached to turn on the underwater lights, sneaking a glance at whether she was gawking. She was not.

"I'll get my bathing suit," she said, slipping off the bench. She came back wrapped in a towel that she only removed a moment before clambering down the boarding ladder and splashing in.

And so, through trial and error, he learned that Sarah would not relent towards him in that way, and though at first this seemed to him to be a simple misunderstanding, a primal error that he attempted with increasing urgency and diminishing dignity to remedy, once he accepted the fact of her rejection, he relaxed. He found that he wanted to please her, soothe her, keep her happy. They fell into a routine of meals and watches, boat maintenance, and playing with Noah. Once they'd dropped anchor, they were a jurisdiction unto themselves, far enough away from any schedule besides the tides, the sun, the stars. Sometimes they ate spaghetti or ravioli out of the same can on the deck at night, passing it back and forth, the pasta sauce cold and thick and sweet, its oil glistening in the moonlight. Perhaps, Owen mused, keeping things platonic was akin to keeping things Platonic; he wondered if he'd entered a higher plane. The clean and totally novel feeling of a life free of lies.

Noah was a constant source of wonder. Living far from his Midwest nieces and nephews, Owen had little occasion to spend time with children. He'd dreaded and avoided them, and later he'd resented them as contributing to the downfall of his marriage. And he'd written about them, at first in a fit of creative anger, and later with a deliberate minimalism, avoiding opportunities for a misstep that would reveal his nearly total ignorance. But the little people he'd sketched in his novel were nothing like the solemn and curious child with whom he now found himself. He was often taken aback by the boy's easy affection, which he was sure he'd done nothing to earn. While Sarah sailed them to Rose Island, he spent time showing the boy pictures of the marine life swimming in the depths of the water below: pancake batfish, white-spotted catshark. Their names made Noah giggle and he loved to repeat them.

Their second day moored on the banks of Rose Island, Noah rushed on deck full of excitement.

"Mommy! Come and see! I found a secret."

Sarah got up, followed him down below. A few minutes later she came back smiling. "Do you want to go and see?" Owen lowered his book only slightly. For the boy, every new locker or cabinet was an undiscovered country. But Sarah said, "Go. You'll like it."

Owen followed the boy to his berth in the bow of the boat.

"You have to lay down," said Noah. "And look kind of sideways with the light on. I never saw it before when it was dark."

Owen lay his head down on the pillow, turned this way and that until he saw it—a little pencil drawing of a bicycle, made out of joined-up stars, sketched onto the wood panelling.

He touched his fingers to the grain. "It's magical."

Sarah tried to describe the isolation of their journey when she wrote to her brother. *Now I understand why you were crawling up the walls when you were in quarantine. And I'm not even here alone.* She hadn't realized how much it had mattered to her: the affable friction of other lives bumping up against her own. A trio of girls laughing at a café, exchanging recipes and dark confidences with the same easy freedom. A baby fussing in a stroller with tears like jewels on her apple cheeks. A clump of teenagers talking too loudly at the back of a bus after school, so wrapped up in their own dramas they didn't notice the glares and smiles of the other passengers. She had always taken comfort in these small glimpses of the lives lived all around her, balancing her worries and fears against the collective anguish of nine million souls grappling with their own private woes. It was a way to keep perspective, to prevent her misgivings from ballooning out of control. But at sea, her concern for Elliot found no natural limits. She had emailed her parents, begging them to convince him to join them in Lansdowne. Then, once he'd left the city, Sarah felt better for a while, until her parents reported the rumoured arrival of ARAMIS in town.

Later, her mind was drawn back to the trust fund she'd helped Owen set up for his ex's son, and how the boy and his mother might be faring. But when she asked about Rachel, Owen only shook his head.

"No word." It was like a light behind his eyes being blown out.

Luckily, there was a respite from thought in action, something Elliot had discussed with her more than once. Sarah cooked, she swam, she played, she taught. Very occasionally, she wrote. Often it would be Owen reminding her that something was due to Shillelagh. She was grateful for the days when they moved between anchorages and the sailing required nearly all her focus.

Living as humbly as they were, she liked to imagine that the privilege she'd always shied away from had finally sloughed off like a second skin, even though she knew—sequestered offshore on a yacht in the tropics—that it was never more in effect than at that very moment. But she had always been attracted to the simple life. At Living Tree, it had been paired with hard labour, renunciation, and guilt—heaping scads of it, before breakfast and after dinner via sharing circle. ("Shaming circle, more like," Elliot had said when he'd heard about it.) Over time, Sarah came to realize that she was not the only one who had joined the commune out of a sincere desire to atone for some past wrong. There were former addicts, people who had cheated on spouses, and those who had fallen out with a close relative who died before a rift could be mended. They were encouraged to remind one another of why they'd come, and to comment on each other's progress on the journey to purification. The struggle in the river with Jericho was often referred to by the leaders when Sarah was called upon to share. She could see the others scrutinizing her, sure they were wondering why anyone would try to kill themselves over her—what could possibly be special about her. But on the boat, the minimalism of their life only pared away the extraneous concerns, the paltry vision of herself reflected in the eyes of others. She felt as free as the dolphins that sometimes trailed in their wake, living lightly on the planet. The past no longer lashed her to its unlived possibilities, and the unknown future had ceased to paralyze her. She faced the wind and the weather as they came. Inside, she felt stronger, surer, more herself than she had ever been.

They'd been anchored off of Rose Island a week when Owen came on deck looking so dazed that Sarah was sure something terrible had happened on land, some cataclysmic upset related to ARAMIS, and her fear for Elliot and for her parents seized her with a full-body panic.

"What's happened?" she said, almost screaming even though Owen had not yet said a word. "What? What?"

Noah was next to her, strapped into his harness. Tuning into her fear, he began whimpering.

"Rachel's dead," said Owen.

The most natural thing to do was to put her arms around him, so she did, even though it was at odds with the boundaries she had taken such pains to establish. But as she reached out, he sank to his knees on the deck, so she joined him there, as did Noah, and her son hugged Owen's back while he leaned his head on her shoulder and wept.

When Owen finally raised his head, Noah came around to inspect the writer's face. He dabbed at it with his shirt sleeve for what felt like forever. "All better," he declared. Then he returned to the cockpit where he'd been playing with figurines.

"I betrayed her, over and over," said Owen, when the boy was occupied. "I cheated on her. I lied. I thought that because she was the only woman I loved, it didn't really matter."

Sarah's mouth felt dry. "As in, what she didn't know wouldn't hurt her?" It was like a sharp cramp, remembering how easily, how thoughtlessly, she could have been one of those women.

"She'll never forgive me now," said Owen. He could barely get the words out.

His honesty was ugly, even if it came as a bit of a relief: there was something real behind the facade. "So this is about you," said Sarah. She didn't feel like relenting just yet. "Whatever story you've told about yourself."

"No." He paused. "At least, I hope not. But what will happen to the boy now?"

She knew from Owen that Rachel had no other family. "She should have been on this boat," said Sarah. "Not me."

Owen drew his hands across his cheeks and stood up. "I wouldn't even have made it out of the harbour without you. You're the closest thing to an angel I've got." And for a moment Sarah felt a warm flush of comfort. Then a pang of worry that it would be wrong to start trusting him.

But together it was their job to create and convey the selfless wisdom and generosity of his online persona—a complete fiction except insofar as the profile seemed occasionally to inspire Owen with thoughts of living up to it. After the news came about Rachel, they threw themselves into the blogging they'd been neglecting, and Sarah found she had faith in the Owen Grant she had helped create. She thought he did exist somewhere, if not exactly within Owen himself. The fact that people believed in him did make him real, in a certain sense. And their confidence in his ability to protect them also gave Owen something to hang on to in the aftermath of Rachel's death, during which he seemed to fluctuate between anguish and a kind of giddy heedlessness, as though the worst had already happened and there was nothing else to fear.

◆ılılıı◆

For Owen, the days took on a kind of suspended reality, reinforced by the crystalline beauty stretching out in every direction. The islands seemed like a strange place to feel sad. Their third day in the Exumas, Sarah slipped and fell on her way to retrieve a thermometer. She snapped at him for leaving water on the companionway. And since a harsh word on their calm boat felt like a profanity, he rose and followed her to the forward cabin, where Noah lay in his bunk, feverish but uncomplaining.

She answered his unspoken question. "There's no cough or dizziness." She spoke at a normal volume, but Noah gave no sign of hearing her. His eyes were closed, his face screwed up with pain. "It isn't presenting like ARAMIS, but he's definitely sick."

"It can't be the virus. We haven't interacted with anyone for days. Well, the customs official, I suppose, but we were careful."

"What about the bonefish we caught?" said Sarah. "Or the shearwater that landed on deck? Maybe they were carrying it."

Owen made a non-committal sound and retreated to the computer station. He checked the message boards and sent out a few queries over the radio. He learned that the local hospital had reported several possible cases of the virus, though the facility wasn't equipped to carry out definitive diagnostic tests. Between the static and the silences, he was unnerved by the sound of Sarah crying in Noah's cabin. But for once in his life, a woman was weeping and it was not his fault. He was almost grateful, yet his relief was monstrous.

Owen considered their first-aid supplies. For all the contingencies he'd prepared for, he somehow hadn't considered this one: that the little boy might catch the very virus they were trying to outrun. The sun was going down, so Owen reefed the mainsail and checked the tides. He prepped the cockpit for an anchor watch, then returned to the boy's cabin, where Sarah did not even seem to register his presence, crouched as she was over Noah, whose face was flushed. Owen withdrew before she could notice him. He wanted a moment alone.

Returning to the computer, he considered the original plan. Three months sequestered in the Bahamas to wait out the pandemic. If the virus hadn't abated by then, they would choose another remote anchorage with a generous tourist visa. It was ludicrous to sail a thousand miles only to expose themselves to infection at the first sign of any illness, yet surely the hospital at Georgetown would be better equipped than they were to treat someone with ARAMIS. But every interaction with the outside world was a source of risk. Feeling muddled, Owen's head buzzed like an out-of-range radio, with unwelcome thoughts intruding upon his resolve at every frequency. He imagined Rachel dying alone in Lansdowne, her boy kept away for his own protection.

When he went to the galley to make a cup of instant coffee, he saw Sarah shooting him worried glances as she prepared some broth for Noah, as though fearful of what he might be deciding not to do.

"There are a couple of suspected cases at the big hospital in Nassau," he said. "They've halted admissions and are trying to treat offsite to avoid an outbreak."

"Oh," said Sarah.

He was prepared to describe the treatment plan he'd come up with: the acetaminophen, the cold compresses, the isolation. Watch and wait aboard *Buona Fortuna*. It made sense, unless of course the virus progressed rapidly to Noah's lungs. He blinked, and in that same moment the boy's clammy face came back to him, his glazed eyes a silent appeal to Owen's better self.

"So we'll take him to the small hospital here." As soon as the words left his mouth, his racing thoughts came to a halt.

Sarah fairly sagged with relief.

"Thank God."

They went ashore, Sarah thought, like penitents. Like people who thought they didn't need the world but had barely lasted a minute without it. She felt like praying and wished she had some faith to turn to. In the absence of one, she was amazed at how natural her desire to abase herself, to make promises in exchange for a reprieve from tragedy. If she could get hold of a goat, she would surely burn one if it meant saving her child. If Noah got sick, she would cease to exist. She, who was built out of failure, could not survive that one.

This was the pitch of her mad thoughts as she clutched her son to her breast and Owen rowed them ashore in the dinghy. He disembarked first and held Noah while she clambered out. But when she turned to take back her son, Owen pushed on ahead, still carrying him in his arms. She had tried to ask in a look if he knew what he was doing, the choice he was making, but it was possible her eyes betrayed only her terror. Or he was too rushed to consider the alternatives. Owen was already halfway across the beach, calling out to people to ask where he could get a taxi.

The cabbie eyed them in the rear-view mirror and was driving as quickly as Sarah could wish, speeding either out of concern for Noah or to be rid of them as soon as possible. He delivered them to the hospital, a long, low pink building that still looked new. There was a small patrol of armed men outside, though they were not in uniform, and Sarah couldn't tell if they were police or volunteer militia. She thought the men seemed wary, but the sight of Noah appeared to soften them. Or at least, besides a few exchanged glances, they made no move to stop them from coming in.

◄||||►

They were triaged into a makeshift waiting area for suspected cases of ARAMIS. Owen knew that the major cruise lines visiting the Bahamas were not yet enforcing medical screenings in the manner of airports. It was even possible his own journey had encouraged a few non-sailors to take to sea on luxury liners. A cruise ship from Miami could easily bring asymptomatic passengers who could sicken en route, and though the Exumas were off the beaten path, they were far from unreachable.

In the waiting room were three other people, groaning and sweaty, who seemed like they might have it. Between them, Owen thought, the sickness was almost surely there. And yet he was overcome by a strange calm. When he realized he'd forgotten his protective gear on the boat, he'd experienced a fleeting panic, followed by a profound sense that they had surrendered themselves to fate. But having arrived at a moment of clarity in deciding to head to shore, he was not so easily going to give it up. It was the call of absolute duty that he had answered, and the fact that he had heard it, that he had done the right thing, seemed almost blessed. Owen had spent his life being pensive and equivocal, but there was peace in certainty, in giving in to an impulse beyond reason.

Sarah was rocking Noah slightly. The boy's silence was unnerving. She leaned over to whisper to Owen, "I'm sorry." She was eyeing the other patients just as he was, but she looked anguished. He patted her arm.

Through the windows of the examining room, Owen cast an eye out for their boat, but they were too far up the shore. *Buona Fortuna* had been a fixture in Elizabeth Harbour for a few days now. He imagined the gossip on the beach, the islanders discussing them as American ARAMIS refugees. And though the yacht was no more than a blip on the water, he wondered if some considered it a blemish on the perfect landscape, or worse, a harbinger of scores to come.

Owen found the hospital staff reserved but gracious, which, he thought, was how people had to act when someone came to them hat in hand, or child in arms, to confess that they were wrong, that it was hubris to think they could survive on their own. Owen himself felt almost cleansed by the admission. What *Buona Fortuna* represented out there on the water was inhuman and unsustainable.

The doctors and nurses who examined Noah were clad in full protective gear, more even than the intake staff at the hospitals in New York, but what they had in disposable garb, they lacked in high-tech equipment. There were no samples taken, no special tests run. They were given some acetaminophen, and when Noah's fever responded to the medication within a few hours, they were sent home.

"Come back if it spikes again."

They returned to the boat. Owen wondered if Sarah was feeling as he was: more aware with every passing moment of how exposed they'd become, to so little purpose. The ride back in the dinghy was silent apart from the rumble of the motor. Sarah was holding Noah now. Her son's head rested on her chest as it had on Owen's, and he remembered the weight of the boy as he'd carried him into the hospital: how heavy and yet how surprisingly manageable.

A few hours later, Noah threw up and started feeling better. His temperature declined further, returning to normal. Owen sniffed the tin of butter they'd slathered on yesterday's toast. Its contents smelled rancid.

"Food poisoning," he said, swallowing.

"He has a sensitive stomach." Sarah sounded queasy, too. "I should have mentioned."

"We did the right thing," said Owen. He stared back at the shore, the distance they'd crossed in the dinghy. "No regrets, no matter what."

He felt bound to her, to them. United in their undertaking.

That night, while Noah slept, Sarah knew she ought to rest but couldn't make her eyes close. Surprised to find a Wi-Fi signal when she opened the laptop, she checked her email and found a message from her brother with the extraordinary news that he had fathered forty-six children. She got up and went to tell Owen. It was the kind of revelation that required discussion, exchange, and mindless, audible repetition until the words could arrange themselves into some kind of sense.

"Owen?"

She expected to find him on deck, but all was dark above save the glow of their anchor light. She returned below and opened the door to his cabin. He was standing oddly, holding an upper rail.

"You'll never believe this," she said. "Here's a teaser: how many sperm donations does it take to make forty-six babies?"

"Swimming," said Owen, and she looked at him quizzically. He sank down onto the side of his berth. "My head."

Sarah radioed the Coast Guard.

"Remain on your vessel." The receiver crackled. "We'll shoot if you try to come ashore."

Sarah thought she must have misheard. "Are you going to come and help us?"

"If you come ashore, we will shoot."

She blinked. Another nearby boat radioed. "There's an outbreak at the new local hospital. They're blaming you for it."

"But there were already people with ARAMIS at the hospital. That's how he caught it. The virus is already here."

"All the island hospitals are on lockdown from tourists now."

She watched the lights on land and wondered what they would

do if she rowed him ashore anyway. Would they really fire on them? She stared at the charts, wondering where they could go.

"I'll sail us someplace else," she said aloud. "Somewhere people will help us." But how to navigate and sail and tend to Owen and still look after Noah and keep him safe? It was an impossible proposition.

"What's wrong?" said a small voice. Noah. Reflexively, Sarah looked down at her shoes. When she'd made Owen comfortable in his cabin earlier, she'd covered her face, hands, and clothes, but not her shoes. She had no idea if she needed to or not.

"Stay at the other end of the boat!" she shouted. Noah scuttled back, his eyes fearful and chastened above the mask. "Go to bed," she added. "Bring a book. Wait for me until I come and get you." Then, more gently, "Owen's not feeling well. He needs me to take care of him."

Sarah figured out how to lock the hatch to Owen's cabin from the outside. Noah was frantic when he discovered it wouldn't open and called out to him.

"Don't worry." Owen's voice was faint behind the door. "I like it closed."

Later that night, Sarah sat with her son, a cold sweat surging over her skin, as she quizzed him about how to use the radio and the flags to summon help. She got light-headed just imagining how quickly she could succumb to the virus, the terror that would leave him with. So she spoke to him in a near-constant stream of instructions and repetitions, as though the words were an incantation that could keep the worst at bay.

She didn't know how to tell Owen that they were being refused by the hospitals, but he asked her very few questions. The times he was lucid, he spoke urgently, though the virus had reduced his voice to a rasp.

"You've got to get me off this boat. Dump me in the ocean."

"Can't," she said. Not *wouldn't*.

She slept in a crunch of nerves and knotted muscles, and woke with bleeding cuts in her palms where she'd dug into them with her fingernails. "Noah," she shouted.

"I'm here, Mommy. I'm safe." His voice across the hull bringing her back to life.

She rose, bandaged her hands, donned her gloves. Everything depended on her not faltering, never missing a trick. They had acetaminophen and ibuprofen, bandages and disinfectant. Tourniquets, even a scalpel. She gave Owen fluids and pain relievers, everything she could look up online and administer from their supplies on board.

She took her own temperature morning and evening for five days, but it stayed steady even as delirium took her shipmate. Owen mumbled apologies that seemed meant for the world at large. The terrible sound of his laboured breathing was both a horror and a relief. When he asked for, or about, Rachel, Sarah said, "It's okay," which gave him no peace; then, "She's okay," which was better, and finally, "She's coming," which seemed to loosen the fluid around his lungs just long enough to allow a deep, shuddering breath. He slept after that. Sarah checked on Noah, whom she was alternately bribing and threatening to stay in his berth. Years' worth of birthday and holiday and just-because gifts glutted his cabin, keeping his tiny fingers occupied. His mind distracted.

Owen stopped breathing three days before Christmas, at dawn. She locked the door to his cabin, then sat down on the other side. Burying her head in her knees, she tried to muffle her howls.

She went above deck and sat with the sunrise and a thermos of tea. Afterwards, before Noah awoke, she emailed Elliot and asked him to tell Dory about Owen. The Shillelagh office was closed, but Dory would be able to locate the writer's next of kin. She wrote a blog post for Owen and updated his Twitter feed, a bizarre exercise that gave her a deranged spark of hope as she finished typing. She lowered his homemade flag and hoisted the yellow one. She radioed the nearest marine authority, and a U.S. liaison to the Coast Guard sent notice that they would be boarding for health screening once the quarantine expired.

"We can also assist with instructions for a burial at sea."

For days, the world had shrunk to the size of their vessel, but minutely it began to expand again, as though with the short, tight breaths of fresh sea air that Sarah gulped above deck. She felt paper-thin, one-dimensional, strained even by this effort to inhale, exhale, persist. But she kept moving forward mechanically, knowing that she couldn't afford to do anything else. Their plan was set; it was already in motion. She plotted the course to the nearest anchorage that would take less than half a day's sail. She couldn't bear to stay where they were any longer, even if she was comforted by the sight of the other boats, and the strength of the Wi-Fi signals being beamed out, she guessed, from Georgetown.

In Owen's inbox, there was a message forwarded from Rachel Levinson's attorneys, sent several days earlier. She clicked on it and began reading. The masts of distant boats seemed to recede towards the shore as she read the note, while *Buona Fortuna* rocked in the swells as though in time with the Earth's beating pulse. Outside, the sunlight blazed the ocean into a mirror.

Noah came up behind her, a bounce in his step, already wearing his mask and gloves without prompting. He watched her with his solemn stare, hair mussed from sleep into a tangled, golden halo. He was a human animal, a living miracle, a normal yet extraordinary boy. She realized she only feared death because it would mean leaving her son entirely on his own. And the thought of Noah being alone, of any child being alone, once again summoned a shivery clamminess beneath her clothes, acid flares of warning from her clenched stomach. Swallowing, she prayed the words she had drilled into Noah would bring him to safety if the worst happened, that some impression of her love would endure in his memory. She closed the computer.

"What are you doing, Mommy?" he asked as she pivoted from the laptop to the chart table.

She pulled out the ship's log and glanced back over the record of their journey, all the dates and times, the waypoints and wind speeds, every nautical mile that had brought them with great effort and expense to exactly where they were. "We're going to turn around," said Sarah.

Owen,

I never intended to stay silent for so long. Only for as long as all the time you took from me. Or so I planned, in my blacker moods. But I may not have the time. I'm in the hospital with an elevated temperature that I fear is getting worse. My neighbour is sick with ARAMIS, and just last week I was over there for coffee.

The worst isn't that you betrayed me. Or even that I thought I knew you but didn't. (Though it's true, that hurts.) The worst was the initiation into a new kind of life, one with intimate knowledge of how easily we can betray one another. And ourselves.

Yet that glimpse of chaos was what gave me the courage to have Henry. If everything is unknown, then doubt is a reasonable response. Sometimes waiting for certainty means you'll be waiting forever.

There are so many things I've wanted to tell you since he was born. Parenthood is a maelstrom: intense, unseemly. It cracks you open. I hope something does that for you, Owen.

And the trust was a generous idea. Though I did laugh out loud when I heard that's what you were giving us. Trust. I know the irony won't be lost on you.

But more than the trust, Henry needs a family should anything happen to me. Somehow I know, by asking, that you will make sure of this. So, perhaps not all certainty is gone, after all. Maybe not all is lost between us.

When we loved, we were our best. We were infinite.

Rachel

ELLIOT

——

DECEMBER 2020

On his way back to the city, Elliot tried to think of forty-six names. *John, Jane, Rebecca, Jason, Patrick, Lisa.* A wet snow began to fall, perfect crystals plummeting into slush. *Donovan, Gabriel, Sabrina, Martin, Amber, Corey.* He tried to keep up a rhythm in time with the wipers. *Francis,* swish, *Nick,* swish, *Allie,* swish, swish, swish. It was impossible to think of so many names, let alone forty-six real people behind them. The scale of the thing was preposterous. Then his thoughts returned to the roll call of everyone he had lost to ARAMIS: *Bryce* and *Keelan. Jejo, Cam, Lucas, Declan, Teresa, Paloma, Felix.* Another incomprehensible list.

There was a slowdown around a car being towed, and Elliot peered in the windows of the cars merging into the next lane. His children could be as old as eighteen. They could be driving. They could be anywhere, anyone.

He turned on the radio as he approached the Triborough Bridge. The Dove Suite single followed by some boppy holiday earworm by a recent televised-contest winner. (The song: intolerably catchy. The teenaged singer: old enough to be his son?) At the tollbooth, a middle-aged Bridge and Tunnel Authority officer asked him to roll down the window. Then he slid open the wicket and pointed a temperature gun at Elliot's neck.

"Normal. All clear."

"Good idea, that," said Elliot, nodding at the thermometer. Such instruments would have been handy screening tools at the hospitals, shelters, and the quarantine cordons he'd been stationed at. "Just hope it's not too late."

"Things aren't as bad as you think, man." The window slid closed.

Elliot drove down East 39th Street. Coloured lights were strung up everywhere: in front of the deli with no name, the entrance to the parkade, and the pizzeria with the ninety-nine-cent slice. Never mind the power outages. Some things were more important than prudence. Elliot could sense his mood lifting. He should have known better. How quickly he'd forgotten a fundamental truth: the closer you got to the heart of a calamity, the more resilience there was to be found.

He swung into a parking spot a few blocks from home as flakes began to fall. Slush on the ground whitening as he walked. Steam rising out of the sewer grates. A dusting of snow on the ledges and fire hydrants. A few pieces of windblown detritus skittering across the asphalt from one gutter to another. There were no bodies in the street, no smashed windows. No wrongdoers at all; only wayward litter flouting the city's ordinances. A crushed packet of jaywalking Junior Mints. A jaywalking disposable razor. All the people he passed were traipsing where they needed to go, carrying groceries or backpacks or, in one case, a bright pink Hello Kitty umbrella. Scarves and mitts and hats combined with other protective gear in a way that looked almost normal, weather-appropriate. Everyone was carrying on, living their lives with a persistence that was at once extraordinary and completely typical. Elliot felt like an animal returned to its natural habitat, with an animal's surer sense of rhythm and purpose. Relief flooded his limbs and he wanted to take off in a sprint, a doggy lap of joy. He was where he needed to be, his certainty born out of a hope he'd thought extinguished.

Elliot was so relieved that when his phone rang, he actually answered it.

"I'm a grown woman," said Keisha in a dry voice, "and I realized I don't have to wait for *you* to call *me*."

"Very funny," he said. He stopped walking. He was glad that he hadn't checked the caller ID and that, whatever her news, it was coming to him this way, outside of any normal decision-making process. The knowledge, just like the result, was out of his hands. "What's the prognosis?"

"I wouldn't go so far as to say you're immune. Resistant, though. Antibodies are present. It's extremely promising from a research point of view."

"So I'm a medical marvel."

"It's a breakthrough, anyway. Some other researchers have discussed testing for resistance among hospital staff who haven't become ill, but those tests are still underway." Keisha's voice was buoyant. "You're the first real subject on the books, though there are also a few labs across the country doing DNA tests on people with multiple exposures, trying to pinpoint a common genetic marker."

Elliot used his foot to kick the snow off a fire hydrant. "You're trying to find more marvellous people?"

"Yes. It's possible there was a similar outbreak, thousands of years ago." The connection crackled. "In tandem with the vaccine, we're looking to develop a genetic test for susceptibility. You know, manage prevention and medical resource allocation, blah blah." Elliot could tell by the descent into slang that Keisha's excitement was practically at frenzy level. "Next I'd like to test the DNA of your immediate family, too. Parents, sister. Okay?"

"I'll talk to them."

"Great. And in the meantime, don't drop out of touch like that again."

"I was with my parents in Lansdowne." He was ashamed saying this, thinking of her working in the hospital. "But I just got back to the city."

"Perfect. Come by the lab. I'm here now."

At the hospital, there were no officers that he could see, only a new contingent of garbed personnel in white vests marked VOLUNTEER telling people where to go. In spite of himself, his eyes were drawn to the sign overhead pointing the way to Emergency, where Keelan had died while Elliot sat by helplessly and watched. His own breathing went shallow as it had that day, not only to avoid contagion, but as if in taking in less oxygen himself there would have been more for the professor's struggling lungs. With an effort, Elliot forced himself to breathe deeply. He didn't have to go back there today. The woman who directed him up to Keisha's lab was friendly, energetic. Her name-tag said ROSA. The bright lights gave her an incandescent glow, rather than the green, deadish cast they imparted to his own skin. He asked her how things were going.

"Better now. Best week since I started." She stopped to direct someone else then turned back to him. "Still over capacity, but things have slowed down. They say infections are on the decline."

He opted for the stairs, realizing he'd come to fear the city more from a distance, in the hypothetical, than he ever had up close. He'd listened to his parents, watched too much of the news, let his own exhaustion and paranoia do their worst. But in spite of this realization, he found his pace lagging as he mounted the steps. What had happened in the ARAMIS ward was not mere rumour or catastrophizing, but death itself: ravenous, indiscriminate, dehumanizing. Without mercy. He ought to be running in the other direction instead of returning to the place where he had witnessed more blood, rage, and blind grief than at any crime scene. But once his feet brought him to the right doors and he pushed his way through, he found that the ward, too, was not as he had left it. There were more of the white-vest volunteers; many were sitting and talking with people in the waiting area. At the nursing station, he asked for Keisha.

"She's doing rounds on another floor, but she'll be up soon." The nurse pointed him towards a smaller waiting room. Inside, there was a young woman sitting alone. Narrow shoulders, glossy black hair curtaining her cheeks. Dressed all in black, right down to her face mask, she sat rigidly at the end of the row of chairs. She was wholly given over to waiting: no phone, no magazine. A defiant chin, wary eyes, small graceful hands folded in her lap. He recognized first the familiar, overwhelming urge to impress her.

"I think I know you," he said.

"You and the rest of the planet," she said, tucking her hair behind her ears. Her forehead was pinched, eyes shadowed. The slightly diminished face of the ARAMIS survivor. "Sorry, I don't do selfies."

"No, from the restaurant," said Elliot, as the recollection turned and clicked. *This* was ARAMIS Girl.

Surprise softened her brow. "You're the cop."

"You remember me." It was his turn to be surprised.

The young woman didn't sound quite as friendly. "I assumed you were dead."

"Not yet," he said. "I'm Elliot."

"Xiaolan." Then, inexplicably, "But you can call me Ed."

Outside in the hallway, there was a passing clatter of rolling carts and raised voices. Elliot flinched, and reached for conversation to cover it. "So where were you all that time? You must have known people were looking for you."

From the way Ed's face darkened, he knew it was the wrong question. "More like stalking me. And I wasn't even sick then." She almost spat it out. "Not till way later. It was all a fabrication, a media sideshow."

"You decided to come forward, though."

"No. That was my parents." Her voice was flat. "They're so privileged they still believe that the truth will set you free."

"You don't agree?" He kept his comment light, put a smile into it. "I've found it to be fairly freeing of late."

She wasn't impressed. "I guess authority makes sense to them because it's always been on their side." Her brow furrowed a little more.

"Parents have an unfortunate habit of being opinionated, don't they?" he said. Then quickly added, "Mine certainly are." He wanted to commiserate, not condescend, but he worried he'd left room for doubt. There might be fifteen years between them, maybe more.

Her chin jutted up and then down, appraising. At last she seemed to take his efforts for what they were, a sincere attempt to put her at ease. "I woke up from a coma, and the life that used to be mine was gone." She crossed her arms, hugging her chest. "After that, I basically had to own it since it's the only one I have."

Elliot could hear the defensiveness in her words, sensing the kind of restless energy that sought out opposition. If it wasn't a law of physics, it ought to be: pain required an outlet. He knew it both from the streets and from his colleagues.

"That sounds like a terrible thing to have gone through." He meant it.

Ed exhaled, shrugging. "There are worse things, I imagine." The gaze she returned to him was suggestive, perhaps questioning what exactly he had seen in the line of duty. When he didn't say anything, she pushed her hair back again, touching two fingers to her face mask where her lips were hidden. "So why are you here?"

"More tests." He wasn't sure exactly what Keisha had in mind. "Apparently, I'm resistant."

"Dr. Delille thinks I might be resistant, too. Since I didn't get sick immediately after that night at the restaurant."

"But you caught it later." Elliot remembered Keisha saying resistant wasn't the same as immune, but he couldn't sidestep his dismay. "Don't all survivors test positive for antibodies of the virus?" It was a hopeful fact that the media had seized upon.

"That's why Dr. Delille thinks it could be interesting." All animus had gone out of her voice, leaving only a gentle intimacy to the way she pronounced Keisha's name. "They have my hospital intake sample from Boston that she can compare to the samples we take today."

"Ah."

"That's the new global research policy," said Keisha, coming into the room. "If an ARAMIS patient survives, the hospital is supposed to keep their sample for testing." Her head tilted towards him in a friendly nod. "Elliot, you got here faster than I thought."

Ed stood up. "Dr. Delille."

Keisha looked at Ed for a long moment. "I'm glad you came." She went to the young woman and, extending her gloved hands, took Ed's in her own in a sterile version of a once-normal greeting, now so scarce as to seem strange.

Elliot watched, a bit bewildered. He wondered if Ed knew that Keisha was the one who had released the photo and unintentionally created ARAMIS Girl in the first place.

As if reading his mind, Ed said, "Dr. Delille wrote to me and invited me here." When Keisha let go of her hands, she retrieved a shoulder bag that had been stowed under her chair. "I don't blame her for what happened."

Keisha said, "We're making the best of it."

Elliot nodded. He didn't need to understand everything.

"Any questions before we get started?" asked Keisha.

Ed raised a hand, but when they turned to her, she stayed silent. Finally, she blurted out, "I'm sorry for not coming forward sooner. People got hurt because of me. Maybe even sick."

Keisha shook her head and with a slow, deliberate movement cupped a hand on the young woman's shoulder. Like Elliot, she seemed to realize that Ed was as skittish as something hunted. "You did your best with the information you had once you had it." Her voice was gentle. "There are a lot of people who used ARAMIS Girl as an excuse for the bad things they wanted to do anyway."

The talk between the two women flowed on as they walked into Keisha's office, and as Elliot lingered at the threshold he heard Keisha say something about sequencing their DNA. Ed was attentive, earnest, helpful. Keisha, through whatever pangs of her own conscience, had made things right there.

Keisha. Baffling to realize he'd first met her when she was around Ed's age. They'd been boyfriend and girlfriend, nearly inseparable for a few months, which until recently seemed even more incomprehensible than the confounding progression of bodies through time—that once he had been just twenty years old, and before that eleven, and before that, five, but now he was not. His life had always made sense moving forward, but for a long time he thought looking back would be a runner's mistake, the skewed over-the-shoulder glance that would set him stumbling off pace. But now he felt he understood that not all change was failure. The past couldn't always be dragged into the present, but it was never really over, not while there was someone to remember it. And people did not belong to one another in the particular, only in the general. They were always being called upon in different ways and to other people. They were being called into the future.

He watched Keisha roll out a desk chair as Ed took a seat nearby. The last time he'd visited Keisha, he'd thought the key to the future might be right there in that laboratory. Before the drug trial mishap—*mishap*, what a word—he'd imagined witnessing some discovery that would change the course of history. Something in the blood, the chemicals, the test tube. Something that could be seen under a microscope and put to use. But he saw now that what would save them was already there, turning like a windmill in their hearts, in every attempt to repair, cooperate, persevere. Communicate. Connect.

"Elliot," said Keisha, calling him out of his reverie. "Are we going to do this?"

"Yes," said Ed.

Elliot paused for just a moment before he stepped forward into the laboratory and everything that was about to come next. "Let's try," he said.

When you're at the mercy of the wind, you begin to understand sacrifice. The contract of Agamemnon: what you would give up in order to get the thing you really need. Except in this case it would be a fleet of ships, the outcome of a whole war that we'd cast aside, for the life of one little boy.

Sometimes a certain kind of man requires a certain set of circumstances to learn some fundamental truths. I think I finally understand that all we really have is each other.

There are signs of life. Splashes of fish. The slosh of mammals in the water—dolphins, whales. The sound of their breathing when they swim close to the boat.

Calm water is best for a burial at sea, but we are hoping for rain. We are praying for a squall. If it rains, if it pours, there might be a measure of relief.

Instead, we look to the stars. From the deck, there's a constellation that looks like a bicycle. Two faulty tires connected by a brighter frame. And with a squint and a tilt, the lesser stars coalesce into spokes and wheels of light, a pattern that emerges and fades back into the infinite.

Excerpt from "A Song for the End of the World"
Lyrics by Dove Suite

Word is this one is the last,
The very last great extinction
My only thought is at least . . .
at least we have that distinction

And what is the time of arrival?

The truth is before you came
I was getting ready to leave
So this is just another love song
For all the love songs
Still unwritten
For all the lovers
Still to grieve

ACKNOWLEDGEMENTS

Thank you to the Canada Council for the Arts for financial support during the writing of this manuscript.

Thank you to my agent, Martha Webb, for her perception and encouragement, and to everyone at CookeMcDermid.

Thank you to my editor, Anita Chong, for her vision, sensitivity, and precision. This novel owes a great deal to her.

Thank you to Jared Bland, Lisa Jager, and everyone at McClelland & Stewart who brought their insight and expertise to this book, as well as to Gemma Wain and Erin Kern.

Sections of this novel have been around for a long time and I am grateful to the few people who read them and offered suggestions. Thank you to Linda Besner, for reading an early draft and providing helpful feedback one chilly night on the patio of Casa del Popolo. Thank you to *dANDelion Magazine*, where a version of Edith's chapter first appeared as the short story "No Word for It." Thank you also to everyone who ever expressed a willingness to read part of this manuscript, even if it never came to pass.

I am grateful for writing pals across all genres and disciplines. Writing is an utterly humbling endeavour at every turn, but thankfully it is one where you never stop learning. For ongoing friendship and support, writerly and otherwise, thanks especially to Jonathan Ball, Linda Besner, Diane Dechief, Mylissa Falkner, Kat Kitching, Leigh Kotsilidis, Erin Laing, Jessica Lim, Vivienne Macy, Ian McGillis,

Maya Toussaint, Kathleen Winter, and Alice Zorn. Thank you to the knitting club, and to Dina Cindrić and the Monday Night Choir. Thank you to my community in Montreal. Thank you to all my dear friends and correspondents, near and far, past and present. I don't know what I would do without you.

Thank you to Garderie Fairmount and Paquebot Mont-Royal.

Thank you to McGill University, especially to members of the Department of Philosophy, the Department of Microbiology and Immunology, and the Yan P. Lin Centre for the Study of Freedom and Global Orders in the Ancient and Modern Worlds. All errors are my own.

I am grateful to Rebecca Solnit's *A Paradise Built in Hell*, which provided me with strong evidence to support my instincts about disasters. I learned about the notion of "elite panic" from her remarkable book.

Thank you to all the book clubs, libraries, literary festivals, producers, booksellers, and professors who have extended invitations over the years and have offered the opportunity to connect with readers and other writers. I am immensely grateful.

Profound love and thanks to my family, especially to my mother Joan Ainsworth, Pat and Norman Webster, and Vivienne and Larkin Webster. Much love and gratitude to all my Ainsworth and Webster family.

Wondrous thanks to Derek Webster. Words are everything, but sometimes they're not enough.

AN INTERVIEW WITH
SALEEMA NAWAZ

This interview with author Saleema Nawaz was conducted on March 18, 2020. One week earlier, on March 11, the World Health Organization announced that the outbreak of COVID-19 could be characterized as a pandemic, and on March 13, the United States declared a national emergency, following similar announcements throughout Asia and Europe. Subsequently, several Canadian provinces also declared a state of emergency.

What inspired you to write this novel? What were some of the key questions you wanted to explore?

The idea began with characters I'd created for a few short stories I'd written and a plan I developed for bringing them together against the backdrop of a crisis that would test them in different ways.

Some of the thematic questions surfaced over the course of writing and editing the manuscript: What do we owe to ourselves and to one another—and does that change if the other person is a family member, a friend, or a stranger? How much do intentions matter if it is our actions in the world that have real effects on other people? And does a crisis bring out the worst in people, or the best?

Another practical issue I was exploring was what it would be like to live at a time when normal life was shifting to accommodate the new realities of an emerging pandemic. When would we start to let go of our regular routines, and how soon would a new normal take over? What would that feel like?

What kind of research did you do for the book, and what was the process of doing that research like? Were there any specific real-life epidemics that you used as models for the ARAMIS pandemic in your book?

I had the initial idea for the novel in late 2012, and I researched, wrote, and revised the manuscript between 2013 and 2019. I knew I had a certain amount of creative flexibility with a made-up illness, but I wanted ARAMIS, my fictional virus, to serve not only my own dramatic purposes, but also to conform to how diseases behave in reality and, ideally, to remain consistent throughout the book.

So I spent a lot of time on sites like PubMed and The Lancet, reading epidemiology papers and learning about agent-based modelling (computer simulations that can help us understand and predict complex human interactions, such as the spread of an infectious disease), generation time, and the basic reproductive number, as well as non-pharmaceutical intervention (NPI) methods like quarantine and contact tracing.

I read estimates of the disease burden on the U.S. of an avian flu pandemic, with and without different types of intervention strategies. I studied the CDC guidelines around community mitigation and read the emergency preparedness plans of many different cities in North America. I also read papers on the ethical and legal considerations of preparing for pandemics, given the limited supply of medical resources.

In particular, I spent time considering the kind of epidemic curve that could fit the five-month timeline I'd established and still remain plausible with the kind of social-distancing measures that have been put in place in different locations over the course of the novel.

To that end, I also studied the history of the Spanish Flu of 1918–1920, including disease modelling based on reported deaths in Europe as well as the city-by-city responses and outcomes across the United States. I read about genetic resistance to HIV and malaria, and ongoing research into genetic resistance to other diseases, such as Hepatitis C. I also read a lot about SARS, especially after I decided that the virus in the book would be a novel coronavirus, and I studied the public health literature that came out in the wake of that crisis. As outbreaks such as Ebola and MERS-CoV emerged over the long period I was writing the novel, I followed them closely to pick up examples of containment strategies, media coverage, and overall global response.

There has been a long tradition of plague narratives in film and literature. How do you see your novel fitting into this tradition? How do you think it stands out?

One idea I wanted to explore from the beginning was how the stories we tell can influence our behaviour in the real world, for better or for worse. It seemed to me that some of the disaster tropes of Hollywood and dystopian fiction could compound unrest in a population already being primed for fear by the 24-hour news cycle and by politicians stoking divisiveness.

Pandemics are a time of great upheaval and uncertainty, and we often turn to stories for guidance when the world frightens us. But most of the pandemic narratives we have are far from comforting! With my novel, I wasn't consciously thinking about writing into or against the tradition so much as exploring that legacy.

Some readers have said that the novel is actually an optimistic take on disaster, and I think that may be true. I consciously tried to ground it in reality, so it isn't a novel of extremes. It is scaled to the personal, to this particular group of characters and the choices that they face.

How would you respond to the fact that your novel has been called prescient for its depiction of how a pandemic would affect our lives?

There's a reason that we have always had and will continue to have plague narratives—it is an age-old challenge for our species that is not going away. Epidemiologists have long warned us that it was just a matter of time before the world would face the challenge of another serious pandemic, so in that sense, the novel isn't especially prescient.

If the depictions of life during a pandemic seem accurate, it may be a reflection of the substantial research I carried out while writing and editing the book. But as events continue to unfold, I have no expectations that reality will hew all that closely to events in the novel. Truth is usually stranger than fiction, and it certainly feels very strange at the current moment.

How has writing this book influenced how you feel about the spectre of global pandemics and how we as a society might respond to them?

I think it is important for people to trust the science and for that information to be widely available. We need greater transparency, clear communication, and increased trust in public health authorities and among global partners. International cooperation is key. We may need to isolate at home, but it is not a time for isolationism. We need to come together in solidarity.

As a society, we are more connected than ever, which has serious implications for current and future pandemics. But that interconnectedness also suggests myriad ways in which we can face challenges and support one another, whether that ends up being neighbour to neighbour or country to country.

Your novel situates the ARAMIS outbreak alongside some of the major challenges of our times, including climate change and economic inequality. What was the thinking behind this?

Every crisis has a way of exacerbating existing problems, and some of us are more vulnerable than others to any kind of upheaval or instability. I think it's difficult to write a novel grounded in reality that doesn't at least acknowledge those challenges.

One of the book's main characters is a novelist who has to deal with the unexpected blurring of fact and fiction after his pandemic novel begins to have eerie similarities to the epidemic that strikes in your novel. What has that experience been like for you, knowing that your novel will be coming out into a world where COVID-19 exists?

A book's release always feels a little bit surreal, as characters and stories that were once just figments of your imagination go out into the world, where you hope they will take on a life of their own in the minds of readers. But with a real pandemic going on, it does feel uncanny to find myself living through some of the same situations that I'd imagined for my characters and facing similar dilemmas.

I know, however, that I am not alone in finding the current moment odd and unsettling—most of us probably feel this way. The seriousness of our current reality makes it much easier to keep the normal uneasiness about a book's release in perspective. That is the secret and surprising bonus of living through a time of disaster: it can strip away extraneous concerns and help you focus on what is truly important.

What do you hope readers will take away from reading your novel?

I don't like to be prescriptive when it comes to readers, but I do hope that these characters can become real for a little while and that the book, like any novel, might provide a moment of respite, insight, or hope.

SALEEMA NAWAZ is the bestselling author of the novels *Songs for the End of the World* and *Bone and Bread*, winner of the Quebec Writers' Federation Paragraphe Hugh MacLennan Prize for Fiction and a finalist for the 2016 Canada Reads competition. She is also the author of the short story collection *Mother Superior*, and a winner of the Writers' Trust of Canada / McClelland & Stewart Journey Prize. Born and raised in Ottawa, she currently lives in Montreal.